FEARLESS

JENNIFER JENKINS

Month9Books

FEARLESS by Jennifer Jenkins
All rights reserved. Published in the United States of America by Month9Books, LLC.
No part of this book may be used or reproduced in any manner whatsoever without written permission of the publisher, except in the case of brief quotations embodied in critical articles and reviews.

Trade Paperback ISBN: 978-1-946700-26-1
EPub ISBN: 978-1-946700-24-7
Mobipocket ISBN: 978-1-946700-25-4

Published by Month9Books, LLC.
Cover design by Danielle Doolittle
Series and title design by Victoria Faye
Cover Copyright © 2017 Month9Books

Month9Books

For Mom and Dad--
Who taught me to live without fear.

FEARLESS

Chapter One

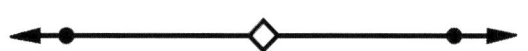

Twenty-three days.

Tomorrow, twenty-two.

The day after, twenty-one.

Gryphon shut his eyes to force away the unwelcome thought and placed his uninjured hand on his knee, doubling over while pulling air through his lungs. He did this less because he needed the air and more to reassure his body that it wasn't suffocating. Zo had led their eclectic company through a narrow slot canyon. The vertical mountain peaks dividing this remote camp from the rest of the region made access to the Allied Camp impossible. Zo claimed the slot canyon was the only way in and out of the Allied Camp, unless you wanted to loop around and approach it from the south. Gryphon might have admired the strategic location if his heart rate wasn't still beating in double-time.

Twenty-three short days. Every minute speeding by like fine sand between wide-spread fingers. Too fast. Too far beyond his control.

Her gentle hand rubbed small circles on his back as she whispered a blessing. The aftereffects of the claustrophobia caused his head to pound, but even with the high-pitched ringing in his ears, Zo's voice brought him comfort. It wasn't long before all dizziness left him.

"You going to make it, soldier?" asked Zo. Her smile reached her eyes, making them more clear and beautiful than ever. He'd give anything to see her smile like that every day, from now until fate took her from this world.

But he only had twenty-three days. And though he and Zo had spent the better part of a week together finishing their journey to the Allied Camp, no amount of pretending everything was fine could make him forget the promise he'd made to his best friend, Ajax.

The first time Ajax begged Gryphon to turn himself over to Chief Barnabas, Gryphon had refused. Gryphon had only just gotten Zo back and was already making plans to spend the rest of his life with her. He'd asked if he could claim her as his and by the grace of the stars, she'd said yes.

He didn't understand the traditions and customs of her people enough to make such a claim. But she'd said yes, and on that very night, as they fell asleep in each other's arms, Ajax had appeared.

Chief Barnabas, Gryphon's former leader, had banished Ajax and the rest of his mess brothers from the Ram Clan because of Gryphon's flagrant betrayal. Ajax had knelt at his feet on the soggy forest floor and wept, begging Gryphon to turn himself over to Barnabas for execution in only four weeks' time

As ashamed as Gryphon was to admit it, he had been willing to sacrifice his brothers' lives to be with Zo. He'd already abandoned his dreams for advancement within the Ram Clan for that one chance. But when Ajax's begging had turned desperate, pleading for not just his own livelihood, but also the welfare of his wife and newborn son, Gryphon couldn't refuse his friend. Couldn't allow his own desires for a life with Zo to trump the welfare of so many.

When Gryphon finally agreed to turn himself over to Barnabas, he learned that the Ram Clan, including the Nameless slaves, was leaving the Gate once and for all. The fabled Great Move was under way.

The Ram wouldn't survive another season inside the Gate. Depleted soil and minimal game had been their plight for decades, forcing them to rely on plundering the other clans for food. The legendary grain stores of the Raven had been the Ram's last hope, but when those were destroyed by fire—the work of Gryphon's own hand—it left the Ram with no other option. The Ram would have to migrate south.

And in twenty-three short days, Gryphon would meet his people where the rivers Iiná and Totoom converged, just outside the entrance to the Valley of Wolves.

Gryphon took hold of Zo's hand that had been rubbing his back. He brought it to his lips and kissed it before pressing her palm to his cheek.

Serenity. The peaceful feeling emanated from her hand. Another healing blessing.

It seeped from her fingertips, healing all of the dark and broken places inside him. It also seemed to numb the lingering pain of his arm—an injury sustained when he had used his forearm to block a killing blow from his ex-unit commander.

Had Zo always been so powerful? The gift of healing was very rare and usually passed down the maternal line. Healers, with their potions and herbs, worked miracles on dying men, alleviating their suffering and speeding the healing process. While fighting the Clanless, Zo had tapped into a new kind of healing power. A power she promised to explain to Gryphon once she was ready—whatever that meant.

Joshua stood in line with a small band of Kodiak a few yards away. The redheaded boy bounced on the balls of his feet as he looked down past the flowered, sloping meadow into the valley below. The sun illuminated their left sides while casting harsh shadows on their right as they looked down at their futures.

Not my future. Zo's and Joshua's future.

Zo tugged Gryphon's hand and led them to stand with the rest of their company. A different kind of panic inched throughout Gryphon's body as he surveyed the land before him. Judging by the hundreds of tents and fires burning across the small valley, there had to be over a thousand men camped inside the refuge of the mountain. All his life, Gryphon had been taught that no army of men could defeat the Ram. And to his knowledge, no two clans could. But this ... He surveyed the lands and swallowed. This was something Ram officials had not expected.

And it frightened him.

Zo walked a few paces ahead of the group. As she moved, the lines of her body danced in graceful waves. "What's wrong?" she asked, looking back when he didn't follow.

Gryphon struggled to find words.

Retracing her steps, Zo walked back to meet him. A chill shot up Gryphon's arm as Zo placed her hands around the bend of his elbow. She looked up at him expecting a response, but he couldn't remember the question.

"Still sick from the slot canyon?" Her head tilted to the side with the question.

Gryphon regained his senses and gestured to the massive throng below. "I didn't realize there were so many."

Her fingers slid down his arm to grasp his hand. "I know you're worried about your people, Gryph. We'll figure something out."

Worried about his people? Yes, but more worried about Zo. About Joshua and Tess and leaving them all to fulfill a deadly promise.

Worried about saying goodbye.

Before Gryphon had a chance to respond, two-dozen men bearing spears and drawn bows descended upon them from behind. They wore armor of boiled leather and carried rudimentary round shields, similar to the Ram, though inferior in make. Joshua pulled out his knife and Ikatou, their Kodiak companion, shouted an order that had all of his men pressing their backs to one another. Gryphon joined their ranks and yanked Zo into the middle of their protective circle.

"Let me through!" she ordered.

To Gryphon's great annoyance, Ikatou made room for Zo to step outside the circle and address their attackers. She looked as calm as the sea, her piercing blue eyes surveying every man without fear.

It did not matter to Gryphon that these were Zo's people. He didn't want spears aimed in her direction.

"I bear the mark of the Allies." She raised her hands to show they were empty and pulled the tie of her cape loose. The heavy wool fabric cascaded to the ground. Gryphon didn't appreciate the stunned expressions of the soldiers, the way their eyes ran the length of her body.

Zo pulled her collar down over her shoulder just enough to expose the crescent moon tattooed on her back—the mark of the Allies.

The leader of the small group nodded in Gryphon's direction. "Who are they?"

"These men are Kodiak refugees whose families have been taken as Nameless slaves by the Ram." She hesitated for a moment then gestured to Gryphon and Joshua. "This is Striker Gryphon and his apprentice, Joshua, both sons of the Ram."

Gryphon closed his eyes and cursed. Was she trying to get them killed?

Spears rattled against metal and wooden armor as murmurs passed over the rank of Allies. The leader said, "They are not welcome here, Wolf, as you well know."

Gryphon noticed Zo's hands lock into fists. Her words darkened to flat command. "These men have risked everything to save me and my sister. Escort us to Commander Laden and let him be their judge." The leader stared at her for a long moment then turned to his men. "Take their weapons and do as she says. The commander will want to question them either way."

Gryphon released a long breath and made eye contact with Joshua, nodding the "all clear." Joshua handed over his knife. The soldiers approached Gryphon with more caution, flinching as he unsheathed his short sword with his unbandaged hand before he took it by the blade and offered them the hilt. He kept his dagger concealed at his back. If they wanted it, they'd have to come and find it.

"Let's move," the leader called.

Fools, Gryphon thought. He'd never let an enemy enter his home without searching him for weapons. And no matter how much he tried to look past their differences—for Zo's sake—these men, this entire camp, was the enemy.

At the base of the wooded foothills, the soldiers led them in a careful straight line in-between rows of young maize. Each plant stood only six inches high, but the soil looked rich and provided a slight spring beneath his step. There was no doubt this would be a good, healthy crop. His hungry clan would literally kill for this ground.

Beyond the fields, the group wove around tents filled with men who stood gawking at Zo and her strange new companions as they passed. Their frank stares faltered when they saw Gryphon. He thought of his dagger, ready to carve out a few eyes if necessity demanded.

As far as he could tell, there were no women in the camp. Many men looked a lot like Gabe, with his square jaw and light eyes and hair. Some, like Zo, had darker features—the brownish black hair common inside Ram's Gate. Overall, from what he could tell, the Wolves' skin was fairer than the Ram, less olive and more peach in hue.

Wolves. In all his life, he'd only ever seen a handful of the Ram's sworn enemy, but today he strode through their camp, surrounded. The towering buttes protecting the valley seemed to bend over him on all sides, minimizing the already narrow strip of land. Old hatred as sharp as the long swords Wolves loved tore through his consciousness. What was he doing here?

This was a mistake.

Near the center of the camp they came to a tent twice as wide as it was tall. A bright blue banner flew from a spire at the top. Two guards were stationed outside in full armor with spears in hand and swords belted at their waists.

"State your business," the shorter guard ordered.

Zo leaned in to whisper into Gryphon's ear. "You and Joshua keep to the back of the group." She didn't give Gryphon a chance to protest before working her way to the front. When the guards at the tent spotted her, their eyes widened in recognition.

"Tell him I'm back," she said softly. "Tell him I survived."

Chapter Two

The flaps of the large tent opened and Zo led the Kodiak, Gryphon, and Joshua inside.

Low-burning oil lanterns cut through the darkness, casting fierce shadows along the planes of Commander Laden's face. It had only been a few months, but Zo noticed an obvious change in her friend and commander. Gray hair invaded his dark sideburns and hairline while heavy shadows lingered beneath his deep brown eyes. Despite his evident exhaustion, his jaw still cut a firm line and his shoulders were piled with taut muscle.

His most notable feature—a jagged scar running from his brow, down his notched and repeatedly broken nose, to his chin—was still as prominent as ever. Though the men in camp would never admit it, Zo knew it intimidated them. Laden appeared to be a beast of a man, but Zo knew a different side of him, and no matter his scarring, she had no trouble seeing the handsome man of his youth beneath the frightening lines.

He leaned over his pine desk, his body propped up by his fists, giving orders to a man wearing animal teeth strung in a necklace.

"If you and the other lieutenants can't fix the problem, I will." The Commander leaned toward the man and growled, "And believe me, no one wants that."

The soldier offered a curt nod and marched out of the tent while Commander Laden bent over to pick up a document on his desk. At their approach, he inhaled a long-suffering breath, and reluctantly pulled his gaze from the paper before him.

The document fluttered to the desk, forgotten. "Zo?" He blinked. "Dear girl," he whispered under his breath, his intelligent eyes searching her face as though he were trying to solve a riddle.

He crossed the distance between them and pulled her into a familiar hug, planting a fatherly kiss on the top of her head. "Stone gave me your letter. When Tess arrived to find you weren't here … let's just say the poor girl has had a rough few days."

Zo could only imagine. She'd lied to her eight-year-old sister when they last parted, telling Tess she was going on ahead with a group of scouts when really she'd offered herself up in a trade to the leader of the Clanless. She hadn't wanted to betray her sister's trust, but there hadn't been another viable option. Tess was like the wind. She went wherever she pleased, no matter the threat of punishment and without thought of the danger involved. This was evident when she secretly followed Zo across the wilderness to infiltrate Ram's Gate as a spy a few months ago.

"How are the Nameless refugees?" asked Zo, smiling sadly at the thought of her sister's distress.

Laden grumbled and released her from his embrace. "Hungry." He sighed. "When I finally allowed you to take on the mission inside Ram's Gate, I prayed for your survival. I never expected you to bring two hundred Nameless back to camp with you. Our resources are dwindling. And unless Chief Naat and the rest of the Raven Clan arrive with provisions, we will have a lean few months until first crop."

Zo scoffed. "Since when has the leader of the Allied Clans refused able-bodied refugees? Of all the people in the region, Ram slaves have more right than anyone to fight." She knew Laden didn't really resent the Nameless, but she still couldn't help rising to their defense. "You can train them, Commander. Just like you have the rest."

"Speaking of guests." He gestured to the other men in the tent. Zo had nearly forgotten they weren't alone. "Now would be a great time to explain the presence of these men."

"These are the Kodiak who helped me escape the Clanless."

The Kodiak, with their shaved heads, full beards, and large bodies seemed to fill the whole tent. Ikatou stepped forward and offered the Commander a clipped bow. "I am Ikatou Apirana Turupa, son of the claw and the tooth."

Laden returned the bow. "Welcome, Ikatou. What brings you to my camp?"

"We left our clan to retrieve our family members taken as Nameless slaves a few months ago in a Ram raid." Ikatou glanced over at Zo. "We banded with the Clanless leader, Boar, when he promised us access into Ram's Gate. After he traded the Nameless safe passage over the mountain for Zo, she convinced us of his treachery."

Laden frowned. "You seem to be a man of shifting allegiance. I'm not sure what you want from me, Bear, but I can promise you that no man is welcome in my camp unless he agrees to fight for our cause."

Ikatou's ears reddened. "Our allegiance is to our families." He ground out the words and his hands flexed. His posture poised to throw his fist into Laden's face. "We have no love for you or your camp. But we share the same enemy and will fight for you so long as you help us get our families back."

Laden crossed his arms in front of his chest, regarding Ikatou with quiet authority. "One thing I will say for your people, you certainly don't mince words." He put out his hand, and after only a brief pause, Ikatou closed the handshake. "You are welcome here, Kodiak. We will do our best to help your families, but I can make you no promises."

Ikatou met eyes with Zo then turned his attention back to Laden. It was only a short glance, but its message seemed to sear the partially healed cuts on the backs of Zo's hands. The cuts were meant to remind her of her promise to help Ikatou and his men free their families. They'd killed the Clanless leader, Boar, when he'd broken his promise, and she had no doubt they would carry out the terms of her blood oath if she failed them too.

She hadn't told Gryphon about the pact she'd made with the passionate Kodiak leader, just as she hadn't bothered to explain the frightening new depths of her healing abilities. She and Gryphon had endured so much, a part of her wanted to forget about the future. To close her eyes, like a child playing hide-and-seek, and hope her problems couldn't see her if she refused to see them.

So many secrets.

They agitated and festered like an untreated wound. Zo hated keeping anything from Gryphon. She would tell him about her blood oath soon enough—once they had some time to enjoy one another's company without talk of wars and her destructive new abilities.

"You are welcome here," Laden said to the Kodiak, snapping Zo's attention back to the present. "My guard will show you where the few Kodiak Allies make their camp. You'll be given rations, work, and time on our training fields."

"And we will discuss how the Allies plan to help our families at first light tomorrow," the Kodiak stated with a firm nod.

Zo held her breath. The Kodiak's demand crossed a line and Laden wasn't known to tolerate such disrespect. He surprised Zo by taking one of her hands and absently tracing her fresh scars with his thumb. He didn't take his eyes off the Kodiak as he dipped his chin. "Until tomorrow."

Laden gestured for one of his guards to lead Ikatou and the others from the tent, leaving Gryphon and Joshua to stand alone, their hands clasped in an "at ease" position behind their backs.

Laden must not have seen them over the massive forms of the

Kodiak. One look at Gryphon and all confidence melted from the Commander's face.

"Who … " He checked his tone, reining in his initial shock until his voice took on an almost deadly quality. "Who are you?" He walked over to Gryphon and looked him square in the eyes. They were perfectly matched in height.

Gryphon didn't flinch under the commander's scrutiny—a fact that said a great deal about Gryphon's character. Not many withstood the intimidating inspection of Commander Laden.

"You are the Ram Tess and the Raven twins spoke of?" He walked a complete circle around Gryphon and Joshua, studying, calculating. "They say you saved Zo and Tess at Ram's Gate."

"And you are the coward who sent her there." Gryphon stared at the back wall of the tent, flexing and unflexing his fists.

Commander Laden reluctantly peeled his gaze from Gryphon and looked to Zo. "Whatever threat this man has given you, you need not fear it, Zo. I can protect you from him and his clan now that you are outside the Gate. So tell me truthfully, can these Ram be trusted? Were you followed? Is your arrival a part of some plot to learn our location?"

Zo knew it would take some convincing for Laden and the Allies to trust Gryphon and Joshua; still she couldn't help but feel defensive.

"They are the reason Tess and I are alive. They have left their home and abandoned their Clan to bring us here. I trust them more than any living person on this earth." Saying the words out loud confirmed the truth to her very soul. She looked down to her fidgeting hands and focused on not letting tears breech the barriers of her eyes.

"This boy and his little pup," Laden stabbed a finger in their direction, "have been trained their entire lives to believe that you are nothing more than an animal. They are a poison. A plague. No matter what lies this boy has fed you, he is our enemy."

"You're wrong," said Zo. "I've been inside the walls of Ram's

Gate. I've seen the hatred you speak of, but Gryphon is different."

"Gryphon?" Laden rearranged the papers on his desk, seemingly needing to give his hands an occupation. "A very *Ram* sounding name, isn't it?" He ran a rough hand through his dark hair.

"We were careful coming here," Zo added, doing her best to ease his agitation. "No one followed us."

Laden's mouth formed a thin line as he surveyed Gryphon and Joshua. "I will need some time to consider all our options."

Zo noticed Gryphon's face turning various shades of red. His arms shook with rage. "What's wrong?" she mouthed.

Before Zo thought to stand in his way, Gryphon exploded from his position next to Joshua and in one impossibly quick motion, grabbed the commander by the neck with one hand. "How could you send her to the Gate?" he shouted. "How could you do that to her?"

Four guards converged on Gryphon, wrestling to free their leader. Joshua loyally jumped in to help his mentor.

Spittle flew from Gryphon's mouth and he yelled even louder. "You had to know what they'd do to her!"

The guards finally wrestled Gryphon off Laden and held him face down on the ground, wrenching his injured arms behind his back. Joshua was forced to the ground next to him. Neither continued to fight.

Zo's heart hammered. She looked from Gryphon to Joshua to Commander Laden and back to Gryphon. What was he thinking? It was hard enough to convince the commander to trust them without openly attacking him in his own tent.

But since when had Gryphon governed his actions with regard to his own safety? His sudden boldness affected her so deeply that she found herself completely and utterly lost for words.

As the guards lifted him to his feet, Zo rushed over and placed a hand on Gryphon's chest. With that one desperate action, she hoped to convey all her voice failed to. *I'll take care of everything ... and ... thank you.*

The guards yanked them away, leaving Zo with her hand stretched to where Gryphon's warmth had been.

Commander Laden cleared his throat and massaged the side of his neck. "If nothing else, the boy has some nerve." A genuine smile spread across his face.

"He's just angry. You can't hold him prisoner. Please, release him."

Laden nodded, the weight of his command brought him back to the point. He spoke calmly. "I will do what is right for the Allies. His fate is uncertain, but his service to you will not go unaccounted for."

"But, sir!"

"Enough." Commander Laden's voice boomed throughout the tent.

Zo's mouth clamped shut. Her nostrils flared as she narrowed her eyes at him.

Laden waved for her to sit at his desk. "Do you trust me, Zo?"

Zo glared at him for a prolonged breath. Laden's liquid dark eyes showed so much more uncertainty and warmth than his posture ever betrayed. Finally, unable to stand it any longer, she relented with an affirmative nod.

Laden lowered himself into the seat in front of her. "Then know that I will do everything I can for the lad, so long as he's willing to help us." He leaned forward. "Now, I want to hear the whole story. Everything that happened from the moment you stepped foot inside the Gate."

Zo told him everything. About her slavery to the Ram, her work as a healer, Gryphon sparing Gabe's life, and how they all parted ways after leaving the Gate. Her time with Boar and Ikatou, and the little she knew about Gryphon's time with the Raven.

He swore under his breath then sat staring at the wall of his tent. A minute passed. Then two. Zo knew better than to interrupt his thoughts so she clamped her hands in her lap and waited, thinking how nice it would be to hug Tess.

"Simmika!" Laden called, startling Zo from her thoughts.

One of Laden's guards threw back the tent flap as he entered, then bowed.

"I need a new scouting team. Send a Wolf detachment this time. Have them monitor all movement at the Gate. I want to know how many mess units enter and exit. Have them report back in three weeks. No later."

"Sorin!" Laden yelled.

Another man appeared, wearing a string of black feathers around his neck. "Alert Captain Eton. Tell him to send his 200 warriors to escort the Raven who are expected to arrive on the south shore. They may need our assistance."

The man called Sorin smiled. "We'll have a difficult time limiting them to only 200, sir. All of the Raven will want to reunite with their families."

"Two hundred, Sorin. Not one man more."

The dark-skinned Raven nodded. "Yes, sir."

"Yates!" A portly man appeared. He was the only man Zo had seen not carrying any sort of weapon. "Send for Millie to attend to Zo. Assemble my lieutenants to gather in the meeting tent in one hour. Also," he paused, as though considering, "have the Pack leaders arrange some entertainment for the men. I think this camp could do with a bit of music and it's time for our newest recruits to receive a proper Wolf welcome."

The man nodded and scurried out of the tent to fulfill his orders.

When only he and Zo were left in the tent, Commander Laden settled back into his chair, rested his elbows on the desk, and rubbed his face. Zo could only imagine the stress that came with being responsible for so many. After a moment, he looked back up to Zo with a weak smile. "I'm proud of you." His voice was heavy. "As much as I hate to concede anything to a Ram, that boy was right to be angry with me."

"I was going whether you sanctioned the mission or not."

He nodded. "Now that I know you're safe, I honestly can't say that I regret sending you. You achieved far more than I could have ever dreamed. Hard decisions can yield the greatest results. I just want you to know that … I'm sorry. For everything. Especially what you and your sister had to endure within the Gate."

Zo wouldn't gain anything from arguing. It had been her decision. She'd begged for months and months to be allowed to go. Of anyone in camp, a healer had the most chance of being admitted into Ram's Gate. Her nearly black hair and above average height was so uncommon in Wolves that she could almost pass for a Kodiak. Besides, she'd had a score to settle on behalf of her parents … a hatred that wouldn't be pacified. "I'm glad to be back, sir."

An older woman wearing an apron, her white hair pulled back in a kerchief, entered the tent. "Ah, Millie. Please take Zo to the women's tent, where she can see her sister and rest until dinner."

The woman curtsied and led her from the tent, but before Zo ducked under the tent flap she paused and looked back at Laden, the closest person she had to a guardian in the world. "I care for him, Commander. Please, show him an ounce of the mercy he has shown me."

Chapter Three

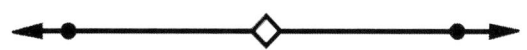

Gryphon and Joshua sat on the ground with their hands chained to their feet. The rusted metal of the handcuffs made Gryphon wonder how many men over the years had shared his fate by these chains. The air smelled of venison stew, making his mouth water. The tent glowed amber in the afternoon sun, trapping the heat within.

Joshua stared at the closed tent flaps as if trying to make out the number of soldiers standing guard outside. "How many are there?" he asked, worried.

"If they're thorough, four. If they're scared, six," said Gryphon.

"Can we take them?"

Gryphon snorted. If his hands were free he might have ruffled the kid's red hair. "Not while we're bound."

Joshua shivered, despite the warmth of the tent. "My nose itches," he complained. "And I gulped down the last of my waterskin when we came through the canyon. I could *really* use a private moment, if you know what I mean."

Gryphon's stomach groaned with hunger. "We'll be fine. Zo won't let them keep us here. Not for long."

He could only hope she had that kind of sway with Commander Laden.

"What if Zo can't convince them to let us go?"

Gryphon felt himself sigh. "I'm sorry, kid." He hadn't thought of Joshua when he attacked the commander. It wasn't like him not to weigh every outcome of a decision before acting.

"For what? You did the right thing," he said, shrugging—a difficult task considering the situation.

"I lost my composure."

"You were angry," said Joshua.

"I allowed my anger to control my actions." He always lost control when it came to Zo. "Hear me now. Just because you feel the urge to act doesn't always mean you should. It's called self-control, and losing it can get you killed fast." He waited a moment then said, "I was wrong to attack the commander."

But it hadn't felt wrong. If anything, closing his fist around that man's neck had felt like justice. If Laden hadn't sent Zo to Ram's Gate, Gryphon would still have a home, a clan, a place where he belonged. Most importantly, he wouldn't be walking to his death in less than a month.

But then, he also wouldn't have met Zo.

That one sobering thought halted all rage.

The tent flaps whipped open and, to Gryphon's surprise, Commander Laden stepped inside. A handful of guards followed, but Laden waved them away. "I will speak to them alone. Give me the keys and leave us."

A guard made to protest, but one pointed look from Laden silenced him. The guard handed over the keys, bowed, and walked away. Laden was not a man to question. Absolute authority.

Joshua chuckled under his breath. "I counted six."

Commander Laden stood before them, his dark eyes piercing and determined. He walked a slow circle around Gryphon and Joshua, his hands clasped behind his back. "You, son, are not very bright."

Gryphon ground his teeth.

"You, a Ram, waltz into this camp under the skirt of a woman and assault the commander of the Allies within minutes of arriving." Laden came full circle and stopped before Gryphon with a penetrating gaze. "Inside Ram's Gate, the Seer would have contrived a slow death for a man with your nerve."

Gryphon wasn't surprised to hear the Seer's reputation extended beyond the walls of Ram's Gate. The beady-eyed woman was known for her creative punishments. Being Chief Barnabas's right hand, she had authority to exact any pain she wished upon either Ram or Nameless. Gryphon could only imagine the loathing the Seer had for him—the rogue who escaped her "justice."

Laden said, "You are either a fool or you have no regard for your life. Which is it?"

Gryphon bolstered as much dignity as he could from his current position on the floor. He didn't respond, but stared at Laden unafraid.

To Gryphon's surprise, the commander dropped to his knees and unlocked the manacles binding his wrists. He moved to do the same for Joshua. Gryphon jumped to his feet and squared his shoulders. "Why?" he asked. He didn't want any favors from Laden.

"It's complicated," said Laden. He rubbed the side of his face as he spoke. "I never planned to send a spy into the Gate. Too dangerous, with almost no chance for success. Zo is like a daughter to me. She approached me a year ago, blind with revenge. She was determined, and you know once she is determined no one can sway her. She promised she had nothing to live for if she couldn't serve the Allies. After months of pestering, I relented.

"I did everything in my power to help her. Coached her in customs and the social structure of the Ram. I hoped her abilities as a healer would save her from the cruelties of life inside, but there was one problem … "

Gryphon spat out the words. "She was too pretty." Heat crawled up his neck and into his face. "You must have known what would become of her." His voice rose. "That some officer would claim her. Maybe that's what you hoped for. Officers have information."

Gryphon's chest heaved as he struggled to regain his calm. He could not afford to attack this man again. For Joshua's sake.

Laden waited for Gryphon to finish before he addressed him. His voice sounded heavy, a low song rent with fatigue. "Have you ever led a group of men, Gryphon?"

Gryphon flinched. "No, sir."

"Then you have no idea what it feels like to carry the weight of men's lives on your shoulders." He sighed. "The men who fight for me have families, wives and children who depend on them. I am accountable to them. As much as I have grown to care for Zo, as much as I consider her my own daughter, I am not in a position to relinquish a chance to damage my enemy. That's what war is, a constant string of hard decisions loaded with painful risks."

Gryphon found himself nodding and stopped. He would not sympathize with this man! Besides, why would Laden feel the need to justify himself to his enemy? "That doesn't explain why you're letting us free. I might have killed you."

Joshua cleared his throat, obviously bothered that Gryphon was pressing the issue. But Gryphon was too curious; he needed to know.

"Killing you would be a poor reward for all of Zo's work inside the Gate." Laden firmly gripped his shoulder. "And I'm familiar enough with your training to know if you wanted to kill me earlier, you easily could have."

Laden turned to leave but called over his shoulder. "Clean up. I want you and the boy in my tent for dinner within the hour to discuss my conditions."

"Conditions?"

"The terms you must agree to if you want to save your sorry necks."

Gryphon stood, staring at the dusty tent flaps long after the commander left.

"What just happened?" Joshua asked, rubbing his wrists.

Gryphon scratched the back of his head. "I honestly have no idea."

Chapter Four

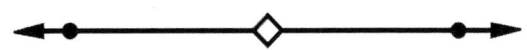

The women's tent was small, located close to the command station, and situated directly across from the Healer's Tent. This was mostly due to the fact that all three Allied healers were female. Aside from Zo and Tess, the only other woman allowed to live fulltime in the Allied Camp was Millie, an older healer Laden had commissioned to take care of Tess and Zo for the last five years.

Zo heard Tess's laughter even before she opened the flaps of the familiar tent.

"Again! Again!" she cried.

Zo ducked into the small room, took in the amber glow of the walls, the familiar row of bedrolls tucked into the tight quarters, and two figures hunched over a down pillow covered in white feathers. The stranger across from Tess wiggled her slim brows, plucked a stray feather from Tess's hair, cupped it in her hands, and blew to create a high melody that she would have mistaken for a bird were it not for the contrary evidence before her.

Tess laughed again, throwing her body back onto her bedroll. When she turned her head enough to spot Zo, she sat up with feathers poking out of her braided hair and stared.

Tess's bottom lip sucked under. Her eyes welled up with tears. She climbed to her feet, the colorful custom skirts of the Wolf Clan dancing around her in the process, and said, "Zo?" Never had one word wrenched at Zo's heart with so much agonizing pain.

"I'm here, bug." She held out her hands but Tess didn't run to her. Instead, her sister pushed aside a few tears and stomped right past Zo's outstretched arms with quivering chin held high, refusing to speak or make further eye contact. When the tent flap closed behind Tess, Zo couldn't help but stare at the fabric so thoroughly separating them.

"She's glad you're back, child. She just doesn't know how to show it yet," said Millie as the old woman poured hot water from a kettle into a wooden bathing tub already half-filled with water.

Zo understood Tess's anger. Even at eight, the girl didn't appreciate any kind of coddling, especially not the kind that included lying to spare her feelings. Zo thought to go after her, but knew the wisdom of Millie's advice. She'd give Tess time to simmer a bit.

From her pocket Millie withdrew a few sprigs of lavender and a lump of pumice soap and added them to the steaming water. It didn't take long for the calming scent to fill the tent.

The tub was a work commissioned by Laden when they first came into the valley. Caring for two young girls in a military camp required some special arranging. While everyone else in camp bathed in the river, Millie, Zo, and Tess bathed in the circular tub in the privacy of their tent.

"I have to tell the cook to expect more for the Commander's dinner. Raca can help you clean up." She set out a drying linen and a bundle of Zo's old clothing on the only table in the room. "You'll feel better after you clean that stinky layer of filth off your body." Millie's tired smile did little to reassure Zo as she left without even introducing her to the stranger in the room.

"She really is a darling girl."

Zo turned around to meet Tess's former companion. "I'm happy to see you again, Wolf."

Blinking at the dark-haired woman, Zo asked, "Raca, is that really you?"

Zo barely recognized the young woman she'd met while traveling to the Allies only a few weeks earlier. On the road, the Raven girl had done well to hide the majority of her beauty. But here, safe among the Allies, Raca didn't bother concealing her hip-length hair and womanly figure. Dark charcoal outlined her eyes and the afternoon sun shining through the walls of the tent turned her skin the color of slightly burnt honey.

"I wasn't expecting to see you here," said Zo as she accepted the Raven girl's hand. "The last time I saw you, you were on your way to the Nest."

"When Gryphon explained the flight of our clan, we had no other option but to return to the Allied Camp and wait for our kinsman to join us. My twin brother is very excited that his wife and small children survived the journey well. And it was our duty to see that our little brother, along with the other flock of warriors who stayed behind to slow the Ram pursuit, reached the Allies safely."

Raca explained that she and her twin brother, Talon, had been commissioned to visit the Allies as ambassadors. They hadn't confessed as much to Zo when they first met merely because it wasn't safe to advertise their high rank among strangers in the wilderness.

"I'm surprised Gryphon didn't tell me."

Raca laughed. "I suppose he had more pleasant things to consider with you at his side."

Zo blushed. "If you call our fight with his old mess unit 'pleasant' then I suppose you're right."

"Well, I can help you if you wish." Raca gestured toward the water, casting a sideways glance at the tent flaps.

"I think I can manage," said Zo. "But thank you."

Raca nodded. "Then I'll leave you to it." She ducked out of the tent in something of a nervous rush and left Zo, for a second time, to stare at the flaps in mild confusion.

After a long soak, Zo scrubbed the filth from her body and hair. The lavender soothed away a building headache, but Zo still couldn't bring herself to fully relax. How could she, knowing Gryphon and Joshua were in Laden's custody and Tess wasn't speaking to her? She leaned back, rested her head on the back of the wooden tub, and raised her hands above the water to examine the raised cuts marring her skin.

The words she'd spoken before Ikatou's giant bear claw ripped through her skin resonated within the currents of her mind. *"I willingly tie my life and blood to the task of freeing the Nameless … I swear to do all that was promised in my own blood … "*

The Kodiak were famous for their oaths and promises. They would die before breaking their word, and expected no less from others. What was worse, she didn't even understand exactly what her promise entailed. In her mind, it meant taking them to Commander Laden, and making sure the Allies agreed to help. But freeing the Nameless was more complicated then rushing the Gate with a few thousand men. No force had ever breeched the walls of Ram's Gate, and the few that had met the Ram in battle paid sorely for their bravery.

Laden had been preparing his army for years, and the chances of him being willing to act right now—just because Zo had a few cuts on her hands—weren't high. As much as she knew Laden cared for her and honored the memory of her parents, his first objective was to look after his cause. He wouldn't put one life before so many. Not even hers.

"Gracious, child. Were you planning to spend the night in that water?" cried Millie as she hurried into the tent. The light outside had dimmed with the setting sun and Zo realized she was shivering in the tepid water.

"The officers will be waiting on you!" She held up a blanket for Zo to use to towel off and helped her into a traditional Wolf dress, complete with a colorfully embroidered skirt and white blouse. Zo pulled tight the laces of a soft leather jerkin while Millie battled her long hair into a complicated web of braids befitting a girl of her age and standing.

"Where's Tess?" Zo asked.

"The child took her meal with the little Ram demon. The one with hair as red as hell itself."

"They released him? Did they release Gryphon as well?" Zo glanced longingly at the flaps of the tent. She still hadn't recovered from the weeks spent thinking he'd been killed. Every moment away from him now made her anxious. Somehow, with Gryphon alive and in her life, even the thought of her blood oath was less frightening.

"The Ram soldier is still under guard, but he's out of his bindings." Millie tugged on a strand of Zo's hair to secure another braid. "For now," she added under her breath. "As for that boy, Tess follows him around like a pup. I'd chastise her for it but the boy has been kind to her, and I prefer her laughter to the sulking she's been doing for the past week."

Millie tied off a final braid and said, "Now, let me look at you." The old woman tucked a few stray black and silver strands of hair behind her ear and stepped back to appraise Zo.

And then frowned.

"What?" Zo's shoulders slumped.

"You've lost so much weight. I need to take in your clothing."

The laces of her jerkin were tightened as much as the bodice would allow, but Zo barely felt the pull of the leather around her torso. She pressed her fingertips into her face, wondering if her cheekbones stuck out as much as her ribs. "Next time I'm a Ram slave, I'll be sure to ask for seconds." She tried to offer a smile, but the effort pained her.

"Never mind, child. You're still every bit as beautiful as your mother. The men will have a hard time concentrating on anything Commander Laden has to say with you in the room." Then more quietly, she added, "There's been a hum around the camp with your arrival among the men. Some are young and strong lads who would do a fine job of taking care of you and Tess."

"Not interested," Zo said, and she grabbed her cloak from the floor and pulled it around her shoulders. She thanked Millie and walked out into the cool spring night.

"Zo!" Millie called after her.

Zo turned and hugged the sides of her cloak closer to her body.

"I know you care for this Ram ... but I wish you wouldn't." She sighed. "Please be careful, child. He's not to be trusted."

Zo's jaw locked, but she managed a terse nod just the same. "Thank you for your concern, Millie. It's nice to be home."

Millie snorted. "This isn't home, child. This is a military camp."

Zo shrugged. "It's the only home I have, Millie."

Chapter Five

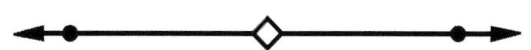

With the help of a bath, a shave, and a fresh shirt, Gryphon walked with head held high through the Allied Camp. The four Wolf soldiers assigned to escort him to the meeting tent carried themselves well enough. Their silent march and clipped commands proved them disciplined.

And Gryphon would've loved to throw a fist into any of their faces.

Old hatred dies hard. Loathing for these Wolves seemed a part of his genetic makeup—something he was born to do. Too many stories told around campfires in Gryphon's childhood centered on the greed of the Wolves—all untrustworthy traders and farmers who professed a high moral code but didn't know the meaning of honor. Even Zo's longtime friend, Gabe, had lied to her and Gryphon so they would each believe the other dead. All because he'd wanted her for himself.

These Wolves ... they weren't to be trusted. Laden least of all.

Gryphon shook his head, seething over Gabe's betrayal as he walked among the people he'd vowed to hate—to kill on sight— when he was a member of the Ram Clan. Regardless of the flaws of his own people, he didn't think he could ever trust another Wolf, beyond Zo and Tess, again.

From what he could tell, the meeting tent was the largest of the whole camp and located in the direct center of the narrow valley. Guards wielding long swords stood as sentries around the tent. With hands rested on the pommels of their long swords, their eyes tracked Gryphon's every movement.

Gryphon walked into the dim structure and waited for his vision to adjust. Four torches carved with elaborate designs burned at each corner of a long table in the center of the tent. Commander Laden sat at the head of a diverse group of men—some feathered, some furred—and rested his clasped hands on the table, looking on as the other men shouted over one another.

"I say we just kill the Ram and be done with it," said one man. "I volunteer as executioner," said another, gaining him several laughs, a few growls, and unanimous table thumps.

Laden was the first to notice Gryphon and his entourage of guards. He pressed his hands flat to the table and pushed back his chair with the back of his knees as he stood. The rest of the men seated at the table turned their heads and all discussion died.

"Your chair, Ram." Laden gestured to the empty chair at his left.

The soldiers surrounding Gryphon fanned out in front of the tent entrance, leaving Gryphon to walk with the room's unwavering attention focused in his direction. The detailing of the chair and elaborate, long table surprised Gryphon. He took his seat, back erect, using the heavy moment to assess the men seated around the table.

He was, by far, the youngest of the company. But his age was not his only disadvantage. Seeing these men … taking in their lined faces, their scarred hands and calculating expressions, Gryphon could almost sense their power of mind and leadership. He knew how to fight. He knew strategy and war. But these were leaders of men. No matter their animosity toward Gryphon or the inferiority of their clans, they had his begrudging respect. Just like Laden.

"While we wait for Zo to join us for dinner, I want my lieutenants to understand how you came to join us tonight," said Laden. He looked out to address the men seated at the table. His posture changed, his voice hardened. "I want them to know the whole story so they can form a just opinion of you and your intentions, and plot our course of action."

Had Gryphon not learned to govern his emotions, he might have laughed out loud. Did Laden honestly believe these men would ever see him as anything other than a Ram?

"I've come to your camp as a friend to Zo, the healer," said Gryphon. "Nothing more."

"Not good enough." Laden shook his head. "Start from the beginning. From the first day you met Zo, and don't spare a single detail." He leaned forward and added, "Your life depends on their mercy."

Gryphon's fingers found the carved grooves on the side of the wooden table. He let his fingertips slide along the intricate lines. They served as a necessary distraction as he cleared his throat and said, "I am a son of the Ram." He looked directly into the eyes of the men seated at the table. "I love my clan." He took a few fortifying breaths to muster courage. "A child born into any culture knows nothing other than what he has been shown. I never truly appreciated the faults of my clan until I met Zo. Since that time, I've been forced to reconcile myself to a different understanding of what is right and what is wrong."

Laden nodded his encouragement for Gryphon to continue.

"The first day I met Zo she saved the life of my apprentice, Joshua." Gryphon launched into the details of Zo's work as a healer, of learning her true identity, of capturing Gabe and sparing his life in the prizefight. He spoke of the complications with his best friend Ajax, his need to protect Tess, Zo, and Gabe from his own people, Stone and the Nameless rebellion, and the confusing help he received from the Historian.

"My clan seeks power and is proud, but they are motivated by their hunger and depleted resources." He paused to consider his next words. In the end, honor outweighed his better judgment. "You should know that, although I am banished from my clan and my shield is lost, I still love my people."

Gryphon rested his hands in his lap, knowing he probably shouldn't have added that last part, but he wanted these men to see him for what he was.

"Then why are you here?" one man at the far end of the table said. He wore a thick, dark beard and his metal-studded arm guards rested heavily on the table. "You admit you are loyal to your clan. You must be smart enough to know that we can't let you live when your allegiance lies with our enemy."

Gryphon's faced heated as he stared down the table at the older man. "I'm here to deliver Zo and provide Joshua, my apprentice, a home. If it costs me my life, then so be it." He didn't intend to stand, but the conviction of his words demanded it. "But I will say this much," he swung his head back to Laden and pointed a finger in the leader's direction. "Fighting will not solve this conflict. All your army will accomplish is getting a lot of people killed. None of you can understand the strength of the Ram. Not really. Not until you've devoted your entire lives to training in the *Agoge*. So long as Barnabas is chief, the Ram will never be reasoned with." He panted, feeling a tad foolish he'd let his temper run unchecked.

"Sit," said Laden.

Gryphon lowered himself back into his seat and ground his teeth.

"What I don't understand is why you let Gabe fight on the day of his execution." A calm man—clearly Raven, judging from his smaller build and darker complexion—leaned back in his chair and folded his thin arms across his chest as he studied Gryphon in a calculating sort of way. "Why risk letting him live? Surely you knew you would be killed if the wrong people discovered your deception."

Suddenly, Gryphon was back inside Ram's Gate on that prizefight platform, looking down at the crowded square where hundreds of Ram and Nameless waited for him to decide how Gabe should die. It had been Gryphon's right to determine the Wolf's path to death since he had captured him. Zo had sat with Gate Master Leon near the stage. It was her pained expression that sealed Gryphon's decision to let Gabe fight. It was her fearful cry that inspired the suicidal plan to fake Gabe's death.

Did she know how much power she wielded? From that moment forward, every decision he'd made bowed to two masters: his conscience and Zo's happiness.

Gryphon glanced down the table at the Raven. He cleared his throat and said, "I'd never met a more worthy opponent then Gabe. He didn't deserve to die."

"But the consequences—"

"Were nothing compared to the pull of my conscience," Gryphon cut in.

Laden sat back, running his hand over the coarse salt and pepper stubble of his chin, a smirk lifting one corner of his mouth, disrupting the scarred lines in his face. The heads of every man seated at the table eventually turned in his direction. Laden's gravity of presence told Gryphon that, no matter the views of the council, their leader's opinions carried the greatest weight.

The tent flap opened. The four guards jumped aside, one foolish enough to offer a slight bow to the newcomer. The poor soldier's cheeks turned red when he realized his mistake.

Zo's clean and decidedly feminine appearance made Gryphon's eyes widen. She wore a modest, traditional-looking dress, but it showcased the velvet skin of her collarbone and neck while clinging to the graceful bends and curves of her body. He envied the material and wished he could see her alone, without having to share her charms with the room of gruff men. How could he ever force himself to leave her when the time came to fulfill his promise to Ajax?

Only twenty-three days ...

"It appears Gryphon's *conscience* has arrived," said the Raven who'd questioned him earlier.

"Please join us, Zo." Laden gestured to the chair at the foot of the long table: a position of honor. One of the guards lunged toward the chair and pulled it out for her to sit. She thanked him, and Gryphon wanted to punch himself for being jealous.

When Zo sat, Laden gave the order to have food brought in. Trays of boiled potatoes, carrots, and turnips, along with steamed greens and hot bread, were placed on the table for the men and Zo to serve themselves. The crowning dish was a large mutton roast, glazed and golden and served from a spit, carried by one man from person to person and carved and served by another.

Zo's mouth watered at the sight of the dish. Lamb was a favorite among Wolves, especially during spring and fall festivals. But sheep were sacred to the Ram, and she gently shook her head, refusing the dish out of respect for Gryphon.

Across the table, Gryphon hadn't touched any of his food. He held his hands in his lap and politely refused the lamb as well. Gryphon looked up, noted her empty plate, and offered her a slight nod of gratitude.

He looked so handsome and clean. After spending the last few hours apart, she longed to take his hand and go for a walk in the foothills surrounding the camp. To spend time together without the threat of Clanless and Ram on their heels. To hear his deep laughter—a laugh she'd rarely heard since he'd asked her to be his in the meadow on the night after their escape from his mess unit.

What would it be like to just live a contented, peaceful life with the person you loved? She let her thoughts travel a little further down that road than she ought—thinking of her and Gryphon spending nights by a warm fire, of him carving a block of wood into some animal form or another while he hummed one of the many melodies he favored.

But he hadn't mentioned anything about his request to claim her. And she'd been too shy to ask him to elaborate. In Wolf custom, a man had to gain the permission of the girl's father or guardian before he could court her. She couldn't imagine Laden granting such a thing.

Besides that, Gryphon had been different ever since that night. She'd hoped it was only the looming thought of entering the Allied Camp that had kept him quiet. Even now, when she smiled at him across the table, he seemed to hold something back. Did he regret his hasty offer?

Laden set down his fork and wiped his mouth on a napkin. "I suppose all that remains to be discussed is the future. I assume you know I can't let you leave."

Gryphon didn't seem at all surprised by this news.

"You admit you are loyal to your clan, so you can't fight for the Allies." It wasn't a question. Laden knew better than to assume Gryphon would willingly raise his sword against his brothers. "And you cannot leave, or else we run the risk of you revealing the location of our camp." He idly stroked the shadow of a beard at his jaw line. "What am I to do with you?"

"If I swore an oath not to reveal your location?"

"Not good enough," said Laden. He thought for a minute then softly tapped the table. "And since we don't keep prisoners, I see only two options: either remain here and earn your keep by training my men, or we kill you."

Zo choked on a half-swallowed bite of potato as the men at the table all murmured disgruntled opinions.

When Zo found her voice, she rasped, "You can't do that!"

"You would trust me to train your men?" Gryphon raised a brow.

"Should I?" Commander Laden countered. Several men around the table fidgeted in their chairs.

"I'm a Ram. I doubt they would accept me."

"You are Ram and know the strengths and weaknesses of your clan. Who better to train them for combat *against* the Ram?"

Zo wanted to reach out to Gryphon. To urge him not to commit to anything on her account. He'd sacrificed enough for her. She'd help him leave the Allies if that's what he really wanted. No more favors.

"And Joshua?" Gryphon asked. "What will become of him?"

Laden didn't hesitate. "As payment for your service to Zo and Tess, the boy will always have a home and place with the Allies, so long as he keeps our laws." Laden leaned forward. "But you haven't answered my question, lad. Can I trust you?"

"This is madness," the wiry Raven muttered into his mug before taking a long drink. "He'll sabotage the camp. Kill us in our beds."

Gryphon turned toward Zo, uncertainty etched across his face. Did he hope to find the answer to the Commander's question written in her eyes? Laden might not be asking him to fight against his people, but training others to fight the Ram wasn't really all that different. She didn't know what she'd expected, but not this. Not from Laden.

"Don't do this for me," she blurted. "You've done so much … I can't bear the thought of you sacrificing more."

He smiled at that, as though something she said was amusing or perhaps ironic. He drew a deep breath and then said, "You have no chance of victory against my people, Laden. But I will train your men so long as it earns Joshua a permanent place among the Allies."

Laden stuck out a hand and Gryphon accepted it in a firm shake. Then Laden addressed the council. "The Ram and his apprentice are under my protection. If any man harms them while they are my guests I will drag them to the top of that mountain," he pointed northeast, in the direction of the giant mountain range dividing them from the Ram, "and tie them to a tree to await their death."

Laden met eyes with the two Kodiak at the table. "Do we see each other?" he asked.

They both nodded and in mismatched harmony replied, "We see you."

To the two Ravens seated at the table, he kissed the tips of his fingers and touched his forehead. They did the same and said, "By the spirit of our ancestors, we will support you." And lastly, to the five Wolves, he stood and shook hands with each. Everyone in turn rumbled the same, "A promise," before taking his seat. Three different cultures, three different vows that, when boiled down, all meant the same thing: Gryphon and Joshua were safe.

The tension in Zo's body unwound.

When Laden reached the head of the table again, he dismissed the company with a charge to pass along his orders to their men. Laden's system of governing worked so that the information would be spread throughout the ranks of his loyal men within the hour.

Zo took Gryphon's hand and led him to the far corner of the tent, away from the exit and the ears of the leaving men. "Are you sure about this?" she exclaimed, before he had a chance to say anything. "I can talk to Laden. I can convince him to change his mind."

Gryphon shook his head. His wrist brushed her cheek as he ran his fingers down the length of one of her many braids. "So beautiful." Bending down, he placed a chaste kiss upon her forehead. "Until seeing you tonight, I had thought your disguise inside Ram's Gate almost laughable. It was so obvious how attractive you were." He smiled and kissed her cheek. "Now I can see it was actually a valiant effort."

Zo hadn't expected this reaction from him. It took her a moment to remember why she'd pulled him aside. Her hand went to her flaming cheek and she whispered, "Please don't do this for Laden on my account."

Gryphon straightened. "Laden's terms were reasonable. I never expected protection and shelter from the Allies without a price attached. Besides, it gives Joshua a chance at a decent future. At least until Laden decides to go to war against my cl—" His voice cut out and he closed his eyes. "I mean, the Ram."

Zo thought of the scars on her hands. "That day might be sooner than we think."

Gryphon nodded. "I agree."

When she noticed Laden approaching from the corner of her eye, Zo took a small step away from Gryphon, putting a little more space between them.

"You handled yourself well tonight, Ram," said Laden.

Gryphon offered Laden a clipped bow. "Thank you, sir."

"My trust isn't easily won. You will be under the protection of my guard, day and night, until I decide otherwise."

Gryphon, ever the soldier, did well to mask his annoyance, but Zo recognized the slight crease in his brow. The way his breath deepened and his nostrils subtly flared.

"That's not necessary," she blurted. "Gryphon isn't a threat. He wouldn't do anything to hurt Joshua and my people."

Laden turned a gentle eye on Zo. "You sound just like your trusting mother when you say such things." He raised his hand to her cheek and kissed the top of her head like he had a hundred times when she was a child. "I'm so relieved to have you home." To Gryphon he added, "My guard are waiting outside to escort you to your tent. You'll shadow me tomorrow before we put you to work."

When Gryphon didn't make a move to leave Zo's side, Commander Laden added, "You're excused."

Gryphon looked over at Zo and back to Laden, as though he might chance defying his first order.

"I'll find you tomorrow," Zo supplied. She wished she could hug him and reassure him that this new life would be a happy one as Gryphon stepped away from her side and toward the tent flaps.

"One last thing, Gryphon," said Laden.

"Sir?"

"I've given the order of your protection, but you'll still need to guard yourself. At this moment you are the most hated man in my camp."

"I understand, sir."

Four guards filed out behind Gryphon, leaving Zo and the Commander alone in the tent.

Without thinking, Zo blurted, "I want to share a tent with Joshua and Gryphon." The unplanned words surprised even her. Heat rushed to her cheeks and she struggled to meet Commander Laden's eyes. More softly, she added, "They are like my family. Joshua is like a brother to Tess and me. It might help him adjust."

When she finally caught Laden's disapproving glare, she took an involuntary step back. "To sleep together on a trek across the mountains is one thing. It's quite another to share a tent in an established camp. Until a man claims you properly and receives my blessing, you'll stay in the Women's Tent where you belong."

Zo might have argued if her throat wasn't clogged with shame. *He has claimed me,* she almost said.

... sort of.

"When were you planning to tell me about the blood oath?" Laden asked.

Zo covered her scars out of instinct. The change in topic left her sputtering, "I ... "

Laden held a hand out for her and led her back into the heart of the tent. He took two stone goblets from a cabinet near the table, along with an old-looking bottle of weak wine. They sat at the table and Laden poured. He handed her the glass and said, "Start talking."

The story of her bargain with Ikatou spilled over her lips like acid. She couldn't rid herself of them fast enough.

"Leave it to a Kodiak to rope a desperate person into a promise they don't have the power to keep."

Zo remembered less and less of her father every day, but it was times like these—when she really wanted the sympathy she usually

37

shied away from—that she missed him most. She imagined what it would be like to have someone put their arm around her and simply promise to make the problems go away.

Laden was amazing in so many ways, but he'd never been that type of a protector. He wouldn't swoop in and solve this for her. Not because he didn't care or didn't want to see her in pain, but because, as much as he loved her, he would always put his cause before any one person. Childish as it was, Zo wouldn't mind if, just once, he'd put her first.

"I don't have the power to fix this," she said. "But you do. Whether I like it or not, my fate is tied to the Nameless still imprisoned inside Ram's Gate. There has to be some way you can free them."

Laden didn't speak for several moments. His eyes glassed over, his thoughts drifting to a place beyond Zo's sight.

"Laden?" she finally asked, urging him back to present.

"I will not attack the walls of Ram's Gate. We can't breech their defenses—not until the majority of their forces are demolished—and we can't defeat them as we are. Your boy was right about that much. I need more support from the other clans."

"You're about to have the entire Raven Clan at your disposal. How much more could you possibly need?"

"I need the Kodiak. And I need time to train the new Raven and Kodiak who'll be joining us. He looked down his long nose at her with pity.

"He doesn't know anything about the oath yet, does he?"

Zo's brow furrowed.

"I'm talking about Gryphon." He clarified. "You're in love with him, yet you haven't told him?"

Zo pulled her hand out from under his. No matter how hard she tried to hide it, she knew her face revealed the truth.

"I don't blame you, child. I know how much you two have been through." His words were meant to comfort, but the worry plastered to his brow left Zo uneasy.

"But?" she asked. She had a feeling she didn't want to hear what he had to say.

"You care for this Ram. And I believe he's a good man at his core." Laden leaned forward, resting both elbows on the table. "But there's a mystery about him, Zo. Something he's not telling us."

Zo shook her head. "You don't know him like I do."

Laden threw up his hands. "You're right. I don't know him." He leaned in even closer to Zo. "But I know what motivates men. I can see things that others often miss." He sighed. "Just guard your heart. That's all."

Chapter Six

Gryphon woke before the sun. No horn calling men to report to the training fields. No walls blocking the loud wind as it shook the tent and howled on its way. No hike up the familiar mountain peak to burn off the palpable anxiety assaulting his body. Only the sound of two boys arguing.

"How can you possibly expect to save Gryphon's life?" asked Joshua. "I mean, doesn't that sound a bit arrogant to you?"

A calm, steady voice countered in methodic speech. "How does the feather protect the mighty eagle?"

"Well," Joshua seemed to consider for a moment. "It doesn't."

Gryphon opened his eyes to find Sani, the Raven chief's son, who claimed to owe Gryphon his life, arguing with his apprentice. "The feather gives him flight."

Joshua stared at Sani, his eyes ready to roll in impatience. "So you're saying, you're going to help him ... fly?"

Sani, ever patient in an almost condescending way, sighed audibly. "I'm *saying* sometimes small things can make a big difference."

Gryphon chose that time to stretch in his bedroll and sit up. "It's a little early, isn't it, boys?"

Sani and Joshua both had the decency to look ashamed. "Good to see you again, little chief," said Gryphon to Sani.

Sani folded his arms across his chest. The skin of his forehead crinkled around the braided leather band he wore. "You intentionally left our Flock in the wilderness. I am your '*Atiin*. You must allow me to fulfill my purpose."

Gryphon lay back onto his bedroll, his head already pounding. "I don't want an '*Atiin*, boy."

"And yet fate has deemed one necessary." Sani rolled out his bedroll, placing himself directly in front of the tent flaps.

Before Gryphon could ask him what he was doing, Joshua pulled a fresh shirt over his head and pulled on his boots, saying, "Does he *always* talk like this? It's worse than lessons." He joined Sani by the tent flaps, as though they had somewhere to go.

"What's the hurry?" Gryphon raised a brow at his apprentice.

"Chores." Joshua shrugged, as though Gryphon should expect nothing less. "Sani and I are assigned to help the ironworkers sharpen blades, and then both Tess and I have to take a shift in the fields," said Joshua. "And once I'm done, Tess is taking the three of us hiking to a lookout point to watch for the Raven. Tess said, before she left for Ram's Gate, she had a fort up on the ridge with a view of the whole camp."

Gryphon's jaw hung open. "Who gave you orders? When will you train?" Gryphon had never imagined Joshua doing farm work. Inside Ram's Gate, his only job was to grow his strength and skill so that one day he could join a mess and become a Ram warrior. It was the only way to gain full citizenship within his clan.

Gryphon had never agreed with his clan's practice of keeping slaves, but he'd also never considered life without someone who tended the crops and performed other menial tasks.

"Are there others your age here?" He tried to remember seeing any another children or youth in the camp, but couldn't.

Joshua shrugged. "Not unless you count a few Nameless refugees and Sani." Both boys were only thirteen years old, but they couldn't be more different. Where Joshua was vivacious and carefree, Sani was somber and responsible; Joshua tall and gangly and Sani more compact and coordinated. Opposites in every way.

"Sani trains alongside his brother and sister," said Joshua. "Laden doesn't let women and children join the Allies. They stay back with their families within their clans. That's why you don't see children running around."

Gryphon sat on the edge of his cot and laced up his boots, contemplating Joshua's information. Joshua and Sani went to leave the tent, but Gryphon called him back. "You and I are still training every night after dinner, do you understand? Sani, you can join us, if your father approves."

Joshua smiled. "Wouldn't miss it." He exited the tent at a run with Sani trotting behind.

How did the boy know where to find breakfast? How did he seem to know his way around the camp? They'd only arrived yesterday and already the kid seemed so happy and light. Perhaps the life of a Wolf farmer would suit him more than that of a Ram warrior.

He cringed at the thought, but also had to admit that it was better to have the boy surrounded by Wolves and farms than bloodshed.

He'd try to diminish his lingering prejudices surrounding the Wolf way for Joshua's sake. If nothing else, at least Gryphon knew he was doing right by the boy. That there was hope for happiness in his future.

As for Gryphon, he'd never felt more homeless, even in the wilderness. He lay back in his bedroll and watched the flapping ceiling of the tent, pondering his decision not to tell Laden about the Ram leaving the Gate and moving against the Wolves. His first reaction was to think of his brothers. Till now every betrayal he'd committed was done out of necessity for Zo or Joshua. No one was supposed to be punished for his actions except for him alone.

Telling Commander Laden about the Ram moving out against the Wolves was entirely different. If the Allies had time to join the main forces defending the Wolves, then the Ram would suffer enormous casualties. With numbers stacked so heavily in the Allies' favor, they might even have a chance at victory.

But would that be so terrible? His conscience pricked him. At least it would mean Zo, Tess, and Joshua were safe. It would mean freedom for the enslaved Nameless.

Could he condemn his own people?

Gryphon growled and rolled out of bed to dress as he considered the alternative. The price for his silence would be the lives of women and children who lived unaware of the coming Ram forces in the Valley of Wolves. Zo's people would be completely destroyed without the help of the Allies. The Ram would not spare even the most helpless babe. And after the blood dried, new homes would be built upon the ash of their bones.

Gryphon curled his fists into his hair until his scalp burned. These were Zo's people. He'd warned the Raven without hesitation. How could he justify not warning the Wolves?

Because I hate them.

And why was he given this responsibility? Why should one word from him manipulate the destiny of so many?

"This way, Ram." A light-haired guard poked his head through the tent. He had the same look as Gabe and for that reason alone, Gryphon decided not to trust him. He followed him to Commander Laden's tent. When he ducked inside, Laden was giving orders to a pair of soldiers. Millie, the older woman he'd briefly met the day before, gestured for him to sit at one end of Laden's desk. She set a plate of fried eggs and bread before him.

"Thank you." He turned to face the woman and asked, "Could you tell me how to find Zo?"

The old woman left without meeting his eye and arrived a moment later with a mug and kettle. As she poured a fragrant tea, her hands shook so violently that she spilled.

She's afraid of me.

It was possible the Ram reputation was enough to frighten anyone from an outside clan. But it was also possible her fear came from personal experience. That thought made Gryphon shift uncomfortably in his seat.

"Thank you," he said again, picking up a fork. He hesitated before bringing the food to his lips. "It is ... safe, isn't it?" he asked.

The older woman forgot her fear long enough to scowl at him, ramming her hand onto her hip. "About as safe as having a Ram in my camp."

Her camp? Gryphon held her gaze while he slowly spooned eggs into his mouth and chewed. New seasonings he'd never tasted filled his mouth. He quickly took a second bite, and around a mouthful, said, "It's good. Thank you."

Millie's lips formed a thin line and she walked away, grumbling about Ram devils and feeding the enemy.

"You just won your first ally," said Laden.

Gryphon hadn't realized he and the Commander were alone. "She hates me. I frighten her."

Laden nodded his agreement. "It will take them time to learn to trust you."

Gryphon didn't bother pointing out that he didn't plan to stay long.

Twenty-two days.

Only long enough to get Joshua settled and find a way to say goodbye to the people he cared for most.

"Wolves, you'll find, are more tolerant than the Ram. It's fortunate for you they value forgiveness and justice. Though they might hate you and all you represent, they will weigh the help you've given Zo and Tess in their judgments. Just as I have."

Gryphon doubted it. "I don't need them to like me."

Laden snorted into his mug. "Yes, you do."

At that, Gryphon looked up. "How so?"

Laden sighed. "The Allies are not a Clan, Gryphon. We are an army that exists to serve one purpose: to bring down the Ram. No one in this camp plans to stay here forever. Most spend the winter months back home with their families. They come here to train and prepare for a fight, but they are Kodiak, Raven, and Wolf first, and Allies second."

Gryphon nodded his understanding.

"When this fight is over, the Allies will dissolve. People will go back to their lives with their own clans, customs, and traditions."

"I still don't know what this has to do with people approving of me."

Laden scoffed. "You have no clan, Gryphon. The Ram will not have you back after your betrayal. Where will you go? Who will become your people then? How will you provide for a wife? Trust me. A man without a banner is no man at all."

Gryphon took a long drink of tea, doing his best to pretend that Laden's words hadn't affected him.

"If these people don't grow to trust you, you'll never be welcomed *anywhere* after this conflict has passed."

So long as Joshua was accepted, being welcomed by the Wolves or any other clan wasn't Gryphon's concern. He wouldn't live long enough for it to matter.

"Among the Wolves, I am Zo's *fastnandi*—her guardian. By their law, you would need my permission to marry."

Tea sprayed from Gryphon's lips. "How can you ... we have not discussed ... we're not—"

Laden waved away Gryphon's sputtering. "Zo's father was my best friend. He'd roll over in his grave if he knew his daughter was in love with a Ram. And don't give me that face. I know you love her too, boy. Unless you're a spy, you wouldn't be here if you didn't."

"I do love her. I don't pretend to deny it." *I just can't act on it. Not anymore.*

"She's of age now, and I already have men lining up for the chance to win the girl's heart. But if I know Zo, she won't entertain any offer but yours. An offer you'll never make, so long as I withhold my blessing."

Gryphon didn't care that none of this mattered. He wanted to jump over the table, wrap his hands around the man's neck, and finish what he started yesterday.

"And just in case you're thinking of running off with the girl, you should know that if Zo eloped with you she would not be welcomed back. Your children wouldn't be considered legitimate Wolves. They'd have no pack to claim them and no family sword passed down to them at birth."

Gryphon's head reeled with the implication. He and Zo. Children. Future. These were things he hadn't allowed himself to even dream.

"My point is, if Zo is determined to have you, and you are determined to have her, and by some miracle, I relented and offered my blessing, life would be easier for her and your potential children if you were accepted among her clan."

Gryphon found himself struggling for air and Laden rewarded his panic with giant laughter. He wiped the tears from his eyes and said, "Listen. As much as I don't want you here, as much as I'd love to string you up like the lying Ram you are, for Zo's sake, I'm going to try and help you not break her heart. The girl has survived more than most. She deserves happiness, even though right now she has a twisted sense of what that looks like." He leaned forward, resting one elbow on the table and pointing his fork at Gryphon. "Just know that if you hurt her, I'll make it my personal mission to ruin your life. Is that clear?"

Gryphon nodded.

"Good." Laden stabbed at his eggs and added, "Then just stay by my side today. Let the Allies see us together. Smile every now and then. Show them they can trust you."

They pushed back from the table, and Gryphon followed the

Commander out of the tent. As usual, four guards fell in line behind them. Maybe, for Zo's sake, Gryphon could try not to hate everyone in this camp. Try to smile. Try to pretend like his presence among these people wasn't its own special kind of torture. They were giving Joshua a home, after all.

Laden led Gryphon through the camp. Gryphon soon learned the large, narrow valley was divided into different sections, giving the Kodiak, Raven, and Wolves their own areas filled with tents, supplies, ironworkers, tanners, weavers, and more. Laden explained that of all the Allies, nearly eighty percent were Wolves—many of whom had trained with him off and on for several years. The Raven made up fifteen percent now, but that figure would swell greatly once the whole Raven Clan arrived.

"Why so few Kodiak?" asked Gryphon. "Don't their caves lie just east of here?" They approached a large practice field bordering the outer rim of the camp where hundreds of men, young and old, sparred with wooden practice swords.

"Chief Murtog's wife was killed in a Ram raid over a year ago. He has retreated to his Caves. Several Kodiak joined us after they lost their families, but many follow their chief's example and keep to their homeland, like an animal licking its wounds.

"Before Zo left for the Gate, I toyed with the idea of sending her to entice the chieftain. I knew his clan needed allies, and I need his warriors for my army. They're strong, though a bit wild. With the proper training and discipline they might be our greatest weapons against the Ram."

"Perhaps Ikatou can convince him," Gryphon mused.

"My thoughts exactly. But he'll need help." Laden didn't elaborate, but Gryphon didn't doubt the leader already had plans for enlisting the Kodiak chieftain.

A young man jogged through the training fields and met Commander Laden with a quick bow. "I'm sorry, sir. Trouble at your tent. The Kodiak, Ikatou, is demanding to speak with you."

Laden rolled his eyes. "There's no patience in a Bear." To Gryphon, he added, "Watch them train. Notice the different technique a long sword requires. It is the Wolves' preferred weapon. The reach is longer, but you must be faster with your hands to get the extra length around. An expert Wolf swordsman can defeat a Ram with a short sword because of the superior weapon, but most Wolves are not experts and a long sword does little against a Ram phalanx of shields."

"Spears," said Gryphon, eyeing the men on the practice field. "It's your only hope of breaking a phalanx."

Laden stared at him, blinking back his surprise. He probably hadn't expected Gryphon to offer such information … and Gryphon hadn't planned to be so forthcoming.

"We have plenty of spears. What we don't have are enough leaders who know how to fight with them against the Ram."

"Sir," said the young messenger. "The Kodiak?"

Laden growled. "Take a look around, Gryphon. I'll see you in my tent for dinner this evening to discuss your first assignment."

Gryphon stared after Commander Laden as he stormed away with the messenger and the four guards who'd been following them. They must have been Laden's private guard.

Hadn't Laden only last night vowed that he didn't trust him to walk the camp alone? He must have forgotten to have his guard remain behind.

Gryphon wasn't about to remind him of his rather careless mistake.

He let his gaze settle over the training field. Multiple sparring matches were taking place in the open area. Tall grass lay matted from the traffic of boots, providing a soft cushion under Gryphon's feet as he meandered along the perimeter.

He considered leaving the field to find Zo or Joshua, but found himself caught up in the clank of wooden swords and the buzz of training. He missed his old workout regimen—the burn of muscle and the thrill of exertion, the mental battle of pushing himself just a little beyond what he'd previously thought possible. Standing on this training field was the closest he'd been to feeling at home since leaving the Ram.

There was so much he didn't understand about the world. But he knew war. He knew this.

The few Kodiak present were difficult to miss, not only due to their sheer size, but also because of their poor handling of the blade. Ravens too struggled with the weapon. While their movements were stiff and fast, the Kodiak put too much force behind each jab and thrust of the sword. Around them, Wolves carried out complicated movements with true technique. For some Wolf warriors, the sword was an extension of their arm, just like a claw to a beast. They made the work appear effortless.

Gryphon let his mind wander as he moved closer to observe a more advanced pair of fighters. *Breakfast in Commander Laden's tent. Now dinner?*

Did Laden intend to have him at his side through every meal? It seemed strange that the Commander of such an enormous alliance would bother devoting so much time to Gryphon. Did he show Gryphon favor out of respect for Zo? More likely, he distrusted having a Ram in his camp and wanted to keep a close watch on him.

It wasn't fair to judge Laden after watching his forces train for an afternoon, but Gryphon couldn't understand why Laden had them all training with swords when he could be playing to the strengths of each clan. If he were plotting to overthrow the Ram, he would use the Raven's bow and the Kodiak's strength as well as the Wolf's agility against his people. More than anything else, they would need to learn how to break down the phalanx. That could only be done by sheer force.

"You're a brave man."

Gryphon startled and turned around to find three Wolf soldiers about his age flanked by four others. They each carried a wooden practice sword in their hands and a menacing grin on their lips.

"The Commander should have slit your throat the minute you entered Camp," said the taller Wolf in the center of the pack.

Fighting around the practice field diminished and a reluctant crowd gathered. Something in the air shifted. The same something that always stirred and swelled inside Gryphon's stomach every time he sensed an enemy near.

He eyed the men forming a loose circle around him and scowled. If a fight broke out, no one would win. He was careful to keep his stance casual, his expression neutral.

"What? Not going to defend yourself, little lamb?" The tall Wolf reached out and struck Gryphon across the cheek with the back of his hand. The force of the blow made his head snap to the side. Young men around the circle hissed and jeered. A few clapped each other on the shoulders, clearly enjoying the chance to see a Ram whipped. Blood pooled inside Gryphon's mouth, but he didn't bother so much as balling a fist.

Pushing old hatred aside, Gryphon tried to calm his rage by imagining the humiliation many of these Wolves must have felt at the hand of the Ram. He'd give them this small win for Zo's and Joshua's sakes. He had nothing to prove.

The Wolf stepped even closer to Gryphon, his stance too open and his fists too low to properly protect his face. Gryphon fought the urge to roll his eyes at the untrained fool. How easy it would have been to knock the man on his rear and bloody him in the process.

The Wolf's fist reared back to strike him again. Gryphon saw the attack coming long before he swung. The feet and hips always betray the fist. He'd learned to anticipate such attacks during his daily hand-to-hand trainings with Ajax. Rather than take another blow to the face, Gryphon ducked out of the way—a subtle move that required him only to lean a few inches to the side while keeping his feet planted.

A few of the men in the circle laughed as the miss sent the Wolf off balance.

"I will not fight you," said Gryphon. This ignorant Wolf would not force him to lose his composure. During his short stay with the Allies, he'd gain nothing from creating more enemies.

"Suit yourself." The Wolf took one step back and then charged Gryphon, wrapping his arms about his middle and propelling himself forward with all the aggression of a bull. Instinct won out and Gryphon, in one swift twist, launched his attacker into the arms of the men around the circle, knocking several off their feet.

Gryphon stood panting, looking around for another challenger.

"Take him out," someone called, and a flood of men charged at once. Gryphon threw the first two down but was tackled from behind by a third and landed with the weight of several others on top of him. He laced his fingers behind his head, using his arms to protect his face. Fists landed against his stomach and ribs. He retreated into that mental place he knew so well as a child when he was given his yearly beatings. A place where pain and anger couldn't reach him. Yet with every fist that connected with his body another layer of self-control crumbled. Old hatred, the kind ingrained in him from birth, roared to life, vicious in its demand for vengeance.

"Stop!" someone's muted call joined the chorus of shouting. But the fists didn't stop flying and the animal inside Gryphon clawed at his resolve not to fight back.

But a man could only take so much.

"Enough!" Gryphon bellowed. He kneed the man closest to him in the head, and bent an arm behind another man's back until a satisfying pop sounded along with the man's cries. Somehow, Gryphon gained his feet and cried out, enraged as he attacked every bit of flesh within reach with savage brutality.

Someone brandished a knife, and Gryphon turned and swept his legs out from under him, stomping on the man's wrist until he dropped the blade.

Large arms clamped down around Gryphon's torso, pinning his own to his sides before he could reach for the knife. He elbowed the man holding him in the stomach and turned to break his nose when he recognized the familiar face of Stone, the leader of the Nameless rebellion.

Other soldiers were there as well, pulling the Wolves away and helping the few wounded to their feet.

Gryphon had been so enraged with battle fever he hadn't noticed the fighting stop around him. His chest pumped in double-time as he surveyed the damage. Already one of his eyes was swelling shut and his bloodied hand braced an aching rib at his side.

One of Laden's lieutenants shouted orders that sounded muffled to Gryphon's ears.

"What the hell do you think you're doing?" Stone said, clapping him irreverently on a tender shoulder. "The last thing these men need is another reason to hate you."

"Good to see you, too," said Gryphon. "How's Eva?" Losing his balance, he dropped to one knee as the adrenalin drained from his body.

He heard the wind of a sword arcing through the air before the back of his head exploded with fresh pain. A numbing cold rushed from the point of impact as he fell to the ground, and darkness invaded his vision.

Chapter Seven

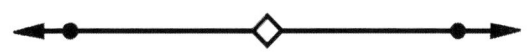

Zo sat with Ikatou and Commander Laden in the meeting tent. She winced as the Kodiak shouted his frustration.

"We cannot wait any longer. My children are behind that wall. My wife! My little girls!" He snatched Zo's hand up from the table and waved it in Commander Laden's face. The pressure of his grip made Zo wince, but she hung her head and allowed him to play puppet master. "I've been promised help. If you will not help me, I will take the blood owed me by oath!"

Laden shot to his feet, his chair flying behind him. He pounded his fist on the table, the power of his strike sending an echoing *boom* to every corner of the tent. He'd once told Zo the only way to reason with a Kodiak was through shouting and dramatics. He slipped into the role like a natural. "Your terms with the girl do not demand immediate action. I will not lead my men to be slaughtered because of your Kodiak impatience!"

The Kodiak's face and neck turned crimson as he glared at Commander Laden. "Will you, or will you not help me, Commander?" he said each word with determined precision.

Zo looked between the men, knowing whatever Commander Laden said next would determine her fate.

Laden sat back into his chair and rested his forehead against steepled fingers. "I will help you, but first you must help yourself."

"What do you mean?" Ikatou's brow sprouted rows of lined skepticism.

"I need to you lead a team to the Caves and convince Chief Murtog to join us."

Ikatou scoffed. "We left because he wouldn't move against the Ram in the first place. When his wife was killed in the raid that took my family, he stopped fighting. Stopped caring about anything. Those who stay only do so because of their promise to support and defend their chief."

"Are you and the others who left the Cave considered traitors and oath breakers?" asked Laden.

Ikatou stared at him for a long moment, apparently shocked by the question. Laden made it his business to understand the customs of all of the clans. It was one of the reasons he'd managed to form the Allied Army.

"We should be called oath breakers," Ikatou finally said. "The chief is too overcome with grief to issue the order, but my people see us as such, just the same." He cleared his throat. "The shame is … heavy."

Laden walked over to the Ikatou and said, "Convince your chief to join us at the Allied Camp. If you can get him to come here, I will formulate a plan to free the Nameless."

Ikatou shook his head. "It will not be easy."

"It is the last hope of your clan, my friend. Murtog has a soft spot for feminine charm. I suggest you take Zo and Raca with you on your journey."

"Me?" said Zo. "I just got here. Tess and Joshua need me."

"Exactly," said Laden. "And this is how you can help them the most right now."

As ashamed as she was to admit it, Tess and Joshua weren't the first people to come to mind. The idea of leaving Gryphon, after they'd finally been reunited, made her physically ill. The trek to the Kodiak Caves was only a few days' journey, but it didn't lessen her anxiety over the separation.

She opened her mouth to protest further but was interrupted by one of Laden's guards entering the tent. "Sir, a fight on the training fields. The Ram."

Laden cursed and stepped toward the tent flaps. He turned back to Ikatou saying, "You will leave in two days' time."

Zo ran out of the tent after Laden and into the blinding sun. She gathered her cumbersome skirt into a fist and sprinted toward the training fields. What was Laden thinking, having Gryphon spend his first day out among the Allies without protection? A string of insults tailored for Laden built on the tip of her tongue as she ran through camp, dodging tents and fire rings, to get to the training fields.

She literally ran into Eva as she raced onto the trampled practice field.

"He's not here," said Eva. The Ram woman's hand traveled to her stomach as if to soothe her and Stone's unborn child.

"Where is he?" Zo panted.

"Stone took Gryphon to the Healer's Tent," said Eva. Her hair was cropped short around her head, accentuating her pronounced Ram nose. "I was just coming to find you." Zo hadn't seen Eva since leaving the Nameless in the wilderness. They'd escaped the Gate together. Survived the wilderness together. And though Zo didn't particularly like the Ram woman, they shared the complication of falling in love with the enemy.

Laden arrived at the field, greeted by two of his lieutenants. His handsome face distorted with fury. She took off in the direction of the Healer's Tent, leaving the sound of Commander Laden's clipped orders in her wake. The Commander ruled the Allies with absolute authority. Whoever broke his order would be punished without question.

The Healer's Tent stood larger than most to accommodate three rows of beds. Zo rushed into the patched buckskin and wool structure to find Gryphon lying in the farthest bed from the flaps, in the back corner. He wasn't alone. Three other men lay in beds on the opposite side of the tent, near the flaps.

Stone stood as a sentinel at Gryphon's feet with thick arms folded across his chest. The large Nameless leader answered Zo's questions before she even asked.

"He was attacked. Did his best not to fight back, but eventually lashed out." He nodded in the direction of the other men in the tent. One sat on a bed hugging his elbow to his chest, sweat beading on his brow. Millie was bandaging another's chest while a third lay unconscious.

"I'm fine," said Gryphon from behind Stone. "You're making it sound worse than it was."

Stone stepped aside and Gryphon offered Zo a painful smile. His left eye was swollen shut and bruises were already peeking out from the sleeves of his shirt.

"They beat him soundly," said Stone. "Don't let him tell you otherwise. He passed out for a solid five minutes after a coward took a wooden broadsword to the back of his head."

Zo didn't waste a moment. She lunged for her kit and removed the knife she kept hidden in a sheath on her thigh. "I can take things from here, Stone. Thank you."

Stone nodded and ducked his head as he stepped out of the tent.

Gryphon eyed the knife in Zo's hand. "You planning to finish the job your clansmen started?" He smiled weakly.

"Not funny," said Zo. She took hold of the bottom of his shirt and cut a vertical strip in the front. After setting the knife down, she took hold of the fabric on both sides of the cut and tore the shirt open, leaving Gryphon's chest bare.

He blinked with his one good eye. "Most women would wait until we were alone, but I can see you want to waste no time." His attempt at a wink was as pathetic as it was endearing.

Zo wasn't in the mood to hear his efforts at lightening the situation. "Lie down," she ordered, pushing him back onto the waist-high bed so she could better examine his injuries.

"Just a few hard hits. Nothing I can't survive."

Zo shook her head and walked her fingers around his muscled chest and ribcage. At any other time, the sight of Gryphon without his shirt would have burned her cheeks, but he was hurt, and in a way, it was her fault.

Every few inches her fingers touched a spot on his skin that made Gryphon release a sharp exhale and ball his fists. Upon further examination of each rib, he actually cried out in pain.

"Those bloody cowards," said Zo. She reached for her kit and found Tess at her side. Tess handed Zo her favorite concoction of oils and herbs without a word. Zo nodded her thanks and applied the medicine before placing her hand over each broken rib and offering a blessing.

Her hands warmed as the familiar words—words handed down from her own mother—passed her lips. The pull of the energy stirred in her stomach and swelled up through her chest, down her arms, and out through her hands. She took his pain and willed the body to heal, pushing her own energy into him to speed the healing process. The healing energy never used to travel through her with such speed and power.

When she and Gryphon were attacked by Gryphon's old mess captain, and Zo was faced with the likelihood of losing Gryphon forever, she'd somehow managed to tap into a new pool of energy, something that she'd never known existed within her. When she drew from the pool, it *felt* different from the healing her mother had taught her, powerful in its depth and frightening in its ability to drain her own energy.

"You're shaking." Gryphon reached out and placed a hand on her cheek.

Zo caught her breath, savoring Gryphon's gentle touch, before she placed her fingers over the swollen tissue around his eye. Heat flowed through her hand as she channeled her love for him. She pressed her free hand onto the bed for balance and let the remainder of her energy flow into him.

When she dropped her hand, her fingers were so cold she could hardly bend them. But the swelling around his eye had vanished, and even the dark bruise that had formed was replaced by healthy pink tissue.

He watched her in stunned silence, all attempts at humor lost in the intensity of the moment. Taking hold of her hand, he pulled it to his lips and kissed each finger.

Zo leaned her head against his shoulder, sharing some of the warmth she'd just given him. Did he feel her love during the healing? She certainly had. It blinded and consumed her, and left her heart sputtering and gasping for renewal.

"Tess?" She lacked the breath necessary to speak louder than a whisper. "Will you … "

Her little sister nodded. "I'll tend to his bruises."

Millie walked over and frowned at Zo. She'd somehow found herself sharing Gryphon's narrow healing bed, resting in the wing of his protection, half asleep. She hadn't remembered burrowing into his side. Her eyes fluttered open and shut. She was barely able to stay awake as a strange and distant pain grew in her stomach. A contracting pain that made her shudder along with the cold.

"What manner of healing was that?" the old woman asked Tess, her voice muted and distant.

Zo's position shifted as Gryphon inched off the bed and slid his arms beneath her knees and back. He lifted her as though she were a child. She tried to protest against his exertions, but knew his ribs were strong and whole. She had felt them shift and mend under her hands during the healing. *Somehow.*

Gryphon carried her into the adjoining Women's Tent and laid her down in her own bed. She let her fingers slide the length of his firm chest, let her eyes flutter open and linger on his handsome face as he leaned over her semi-unconscious form to kiss her forehead and then her lips.

"I love you, too," he whispered in her ear. The warmth of his breath against her skin carried her into a dream-filled sleep where fiery pain lanced her abdomen and spread through her veins, radiating to every corner of her body.

Millie's distant question tumbled through her semi-conscious mind.

"What manner of healing is this?"

Trapped in her pain, Zo had to wonder if the concern in Millie's voice was actually foreboding. This new level of healing—whatever it was—hurt.

Gryphon stared down at Zo, tears invading his vision. He brushed them away—one thought plaguing him, staining the beauty of the moment.

How will I ever leave her?

Twenty-two days remained before the scheduled meeting. Twenty-two. How would he explain his decision to Zo in a way she might understand? It was one thing to torment himself, but after feeling Zo's healing hands upon his body, upon his face, he understood, like never before, just how much his absence would distress her.

She loved him. There was no room to question her feelings when the velvety warmth of her love and compassion ran through his very veins. With her touch, the fierce pains of his body had faded to almost nothing—replaced with achingly sweet light.

He pulled the blanket bunched at the bottom of her bedroll up around her shoulders before small hands tugged him away from Zo's sleeping form.

"Let her rest. You still have bruises I need to mend," said Tess.

Millie frowned over Tess's shoulder but didn't say anything to contradict Tess.

Gryphon walked back into the Healer's Tent in something of a daze. Tess worked on him in silence, except when she murmured her quiet blessings. The flow of the child's healing touch was like a babbling brook compared to Zo's fast-paced current of power.

When she finished her work and began clearing away supplies from Zo's kit, Gryphon asked, "Is everything all right, Tess?"

Tess's tiny lips pursed and she looked away.

Gryphon sat up from his bed and frowned. "Are you mad at me?" The girl had hardly spoken a word to him since he arrived yesterday.

Slamming the medical kit on a table filled with other supplies and bandages, Tess blurted, "Why do people always have to leave me?"

Gryphon blinked. "Excuse me?"

Tess sighed. "I'm tired of being left behind. My parents. Zo. One day Joshua will leave to go fight some war. Gabe left us under the tree and you will leave me too."

"How do you know?" Gryphon asked, his throat dry.

"Because that's what people do. I *hate* Zo."

"No you don't."

Tess perched her hands on her narrow hips. "I want to hate her. It would be easier. She *lied* to me, Gryph."

"She was just protecting you."

Tess sighed, her anger waning. "Sometimes I think protecting means lying."

Gryphon tugged at Tess's arm and pulled her to sit in his lap. "Sometimes we have to leave to protect those we love." He thought of his best friend Ajax, his wife Sara, and their newborn child. Then he considered the lives of the other brothers in his mess. The shame and dishonor that would befall their families if their Ram citizenship wasn't restored. Gryphon had no choice but to leave, for their sakes.

But I'm a liar, too.

Tess sat lost in thought for a long while before she finally nodded to herself and said, "I think if you really loved someone, you wouldn't leave them behind. When you leave, you choose something else instead of them. It isn't fair."

She swatted a tear from her cheek, her bitter tone contradicting her innocence. "One day I will be the only one left, because everyone will choose someone—or something—instead of me."

She sprang from his arms and ran from the tent.

Chapter Eight

Zo and Raca sat with a group of Nameless women assigned to
help in the Healer's Tent.

Not *Nameless,* but *Freemen.*

She mentally chided herself for forgetting the distinction. They
all gathered around as she showed them how to treat a number of
basic wounds. Laden had asked her and Millie to teach them so they
might be useful if the Allies ever confronted the Ram in battle.

Since women were not permitted to fight, those not training to
assist healers were assigned to work in the new Freeman district of
the massive camp, tending fires and grinding bushels of raw grains
into flour for bread. Another group dug the remainder of last year's
crop of potatoes, carrots, turnips, and onions from the ground for
stews. There was wool to be woven and clothes to sew, men to train
and rules to establish for the newest members of the Allied Camp.

Because many of the Freemen had lived most of their lives
as Ram slaves, Stone, their leader, didn't take to the idea of them
merging into the other clans. Zo learned that upon the Freemen's
arrival, Stone was appointed chief of the Freemen and helped his

people find their own identity apart from the Allies.

"Have you seen him today?" Raca asked Zo once the women were all busy cutting bandages from sun-bleached wool.

Zo looked up from her work and frowned. "Who?"

"Gryphon." Raca chewed on her bottom lip. "I hear he was badly beaten in the training field yesterday."

Zo studied Raca from the corner of her eye. She knew the Raven chief's daughter had formed a friendship with Gryphon while they were travel companions on the journey to the Allies, but the concern in her voice made her suspicious. "I worked on him yesterday. I understand, beyond some sore muscles, he's doing fine."

Zo, on the other hand, ached all over. Gryphon's healing had fatigued her more than usual, and when she woke in the morning, pain lanced throughout her body, especially her stomach area. She'd changed her clothes with the speed of an old woman and, before pulling a clean shift over her head, noticed strange, deep bruising around her ribs.

Gryphon hadn't come to see her yet today. Laden probably had him busy with assignments. She doubted he even knew that she would be leaving for the Caves in the morning.

"I worry about him," Raca continued. "My brother tells me Laden demoted two of his lieutenants, and that he publicly punished the Wolves who joined the attack against him. If the Wolves disliked Gryphon before, they hate him now."

The horn signaling midmeal echoed in the distance. Most of the Allies ate with their own clans, but Zo, Joshua, Tess, and the few emissaries to Commander Laden shared the Meeting Tent at mealtime.

"Laden doesn't tolerate any form of dissention in his camp," said Zo. "He's always been strict of character, even when I was a little girl."

Raca's eyes grew wide. "You've known him for a long time then?"

"Almost as long as I can remember. He and my parents were close."

Zo stood on tiptoe, hoping to spot Gryphon in the crowd of men.

"Some disagree with Laden's punishments," Raca whispered at Zo's side. "Because the attack was made against a Ram, they don't feel like the Wolves should have been punished so harshly."

"Zo!" Joshua's pitch-changing voice reached her through the crowded buzz of chatter from the men whom, she recognized now, were not headed toward their camps for midmeal, but instead to the southern portion of camp.

Zo saw the boy's red hair pass through the crowd before materializing in front of her. Out of habit and instinct, Zo pulled the boy into a hurried embrace. Spending the past months constantly worried about the people she loved forced such behavior.

"The Raven Clan. They're here!" Joshua returned Zo's quick embrace.

Raca squealed. "Finally!" She raced off in the direction of the rest of the camp while Joshua took Tess by the waist and hoisted her onto his shoulders. She giggled in delight as he and Zo raced after Raca to witness the arrival of the Raven Clan.

Joshua, being the impatient tick he was, led Zo and Tess in a wide arc around the crowd that had gathered, forcing them to climb into the foothills on the side of the narrow valley. It seemed almost every man, woman, and child of the Allies wanted to witness the approach of the Raven.

Zo's emotions warred between elation and nerves. Gabe, her childhood friend, would be leading the Raven to the Allies. The last time she'd seen him he'd kissed her, not disguising his hope that they could be together when they reunited. As a couple. But the kiss had accompanied a lie as black and horrible as Zo could possibly imagine.

Gabe had told Zo that Gryphon was dead—that he'd been killed by a Ram spear when he tried to escape his captors. She wanted to believe that the falsehood had been an accident—that maybe he'd been mistaken. But he'd lied to Gryphon, as well.

No matter how much Gabe professed to care about her, how could he lie when he knew it would cause her so much pain? What kind of a person did something so terrible?

Zo tripped over a loose rock and landed hard on her hands to break the fall. The impact jarred her already sore muscles. Brushing bits of rock and burs from her palms, she climbed to her feet and held her aching ribcage as she looked out over the little valley. From their spot on the hillside, it was hard not to admire the giant mountains framing the camp on all sides and the two small streams that funneled into the pond on the southeast end.

Laden couldn't have chosen a more secluded, beautiful place to build his army. There was plenty of wood for lumber and plenty of water, and the natural protection of the mountains formed a perfect place for the Allies to grow in power and influence. The Allies camped in the north end of the valley, leaving acres and acres of land open for the Raven to establish a home as well as grow crops to support their people.

Zo remembered the first time she'd entered the secluded camp. Barely twelve years old, she'd looked out over the valley with the small group of supporters Laden had gathered, wondering how they would survive with only a few bags of seed and a few months of provisions. She and Tess were recent orphans, and Laden, her parents' closest friend, had taken them under his protection.

He'd been kind to them both. Tess was only three years old when Laden took them on. No matter how many stories Zo told Tess about their beautiful mother and warrior father, Tess struggled to remember ever having parents aside from Millie and Laden.

"I see them!" Tess cried out, pointing down the valley at the only trail that led through the southern canyon.

From their high vantage point, the column of Raven walking toward them looked like a giant dark snake winding its way into the valley.

"So many," Joshua exclaimed in wonder.

Somewhere near the head of that group would be Gabe.

"Let's hurry." Tess, who still sat perched on Joshua's boney shoulders tapped at the boy's head as though he were a mule in need of directing.

Joshua laughed. "You better hang on!" He took off down the mountain gripping Tess's ankles. Her screams of delight harmonized with his pretend battle cry. Zo followed behind, shaking her head at the unlikely pair. A Ram and a Wolf, both raised to be enemies. They, more than anyone else, were proof that hate wasn't born in the blood. It was cultivated by societies who feared that which they did not understand … that which was different.

Zo took a fortifying breath and walked down the mountain after them, wincing with every step.

Gryphon stood beside Commander Laden at the front of a wall of Allies. He searched the distant faces of the Raven refugees as they traveled the final steps of their weary journey to a new home. Though they were still more than a hundred yards away, their defeated posture resonated with Gryphon.

These were people who knew great sorrow—the kind of grief that only comes from losing your home. Such loss went deeper than physical pain. It was as though a portion of your soul—the piece that defined you—was missing, and without it, you had no idea how to be whole again.

Gryphon lived that pain daily, and seeing these Raven so displaced made him remember his own grief. His own sorrow at not belonging.

His own displacement felt especially real today. He'd walked the training field with aching muscles, making quiet suggestions to men trying to throw spears at long targets. Most took his instruction well, but few dared look at him as he spoke. Whether they feared him or despised him, it didn't really matter.

Twenty-one days, he reminded himself. Soon he would leave this horrible place.

A place that could never be his home.

From the corner of his eye, he caught a glimpse of Joshua with Tess seated on his shoulders on the fringe of the group. Zo was with them. She appeared to say something that Tess didn't appreciate because the little girl folded her arms in anger while Zo walked along the front line of the group in his direction.

Gryphon's gaze jumped between Zo and the hundreds of men who gawked at her. Torn between wanting to rip out their eyes and the desire not to miss a single moment watching the way she moved in her traditional Wolf dress, Gryphon opted for the latter. No sense in making more enemies when there was a good chance one of these unworthy swine would someday win Zo's heart, build her a home with four walls, and protect her with their poorly mastered sword.

As the Raven came even closer, thoughts of Gabe came to mind. Even though Gryphon hated him on multiple levels, there wasn't another man in Gryphon's acquaintance who could protect Zo and Tess the way Gabe could.

"Gryphon." Zo reached out her hand to him as she came to stand at his side, so close their shoulders touched. She released his hand in exchange for hugging his arm. She gripped his bicep with one hand and his forearm with the other while her cheek pressed against his shoulder.

Gryphon's eyes pinched closed. His free hand covered hers. How could such a soft, trusting touch be painful? Would she want to hold him if she knew the truth of his promise to Ajax?

"You're tense," she said. Then she hesitated before adding, "Thinking of Gabe?" She turned to face him. "You remember your promise, don't you? You said you wouldn't kill him."

A smile cracked Gryphon's attempt at composure. "I remember."

Given the nature of Gryphon's fate, holding a grudge against Gabe—as awful as the lie of Zo's death had been—seemed petty. Zo was alive and he might need Gabe to help keep it that way should something happen to Commander Laden.

Chief Naataain raised a clenched fist, and the lines of Raven warriors halted. Countless feathers hung around the chief's neck, and heavy wrinkles lined his face, distinct even from twenty yards.

Commander Laden stepped out to meet the chief and as they spoke, Gryphon noticed a blond head a few rows back.

Zo stood on tiptoe, scanning the crowd of Raven with thin lines wrinkling her forehead. From her lower vantage point, she hadn't seen Gabe yet.

"Don't worry," said Gryphon. "Gabe is only a few rows back. He's safe."

Zo scowled and pushed Gryphon's arm away. "Maybe for now. Just wait until I'm done with him."

Without bothering to wait for the two leaders to finish their discussion, Zo stomped toward the crowd of Raven. Both Chief Naat and Laden stopped talking and watched her in puzzled wonder as she passed them.

"Gabe!" she called, when she reached the wall of warriors.

The crowd parted, and Gabe walked toward her with his signature half-smile peeking through the weeks of blond beard on his face. His sword hung from a sheath at his hip and a bow was strapped to his back. Even Gryphon had to admit the man cut an impressive figure.

He jogged toward Zo, and with little effort scooped her into his arms in a complete spin. Zo rested her ear to his chest and returned the embrace as her skirt danced around her ankles.

Gryphon hadn't realized he'd drawn his dagger until the familiar curve of the hilt cut into his hand from squeezing it too tightly.

When Gabe set Zo back down on her feet, she drew back her fist and threw it into Gabe's face. Gryphon, along with the rest of the Allies and Raven witnessing the display, gasped in unison, then in laughter as Zo hissed words impossible to hear.

When she finished her rant, she spun on her heel and crossed the divide separating the two groups with head held high. She offered Laden and Chief Naat a firm nod, communicating an *as you were,* and stepped back in line with Gryphon and the Allies.

"Sorry," she mumbled to him, taking back his arm as though nothing had happened. "That couldn't wait another minute."

Gryphon smiled and stared across the valley, locking eyes with Gabe. Visible even from this distance, the skin on Gabe's left cheek had turned an angry red. His stance mimicked that of the sword strapped to his side—hard and unbending.

Though he knew Gabe had already been brought low, Gryphon lifted his arm to rest behind Zo's back, his hand cupping her narrow waist. Staking his claim.

He had a feeling his blow cut deeper than Zo's.

Chapter Nine

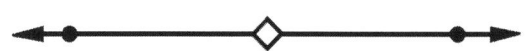

Laden stood before the crowd and cast his hands out wide. "In one week's time, the Allies will host our first ever *Ostara* in honor of our new guests, the Freeman and the Raven. At dawn, two companies will leave this valley to invite both the Kodiak chief and the Wolf alpha to join us for the festivities. This Wolf tradition will mark the uniting of our clans as well as the wedding of the Freeman leader, Stone, and his soon-to-be bride."

Zo squirmed next to Gryphon. She still hadn't told him that she would be included in the company heading to the Kodiak Caves. She massaged the hand that struck Gabe—a painful reminder that she shouldn't have been as happy as she was to see him safely home.

The crowd disbanded. Raven warriors rushed to meet their families. Commander Laden called for Gryphon to accompany him back to his tent. With a sigh, he turned to Zo and said, "Do you feel like he's trying to keep us apart?"

Laden certainly had kept Gryphon busy since their arrival.

"Find me after?" she asked.

He must have noticed her throbbing hand, because he plucked it from her side and raised it to his lips. "Count on it."

As Zo watched Gryphon's and Laden's retreating forms, the buzz of laughter and conversations around her fizzled. Heads turned in her direction. Heat warmed her back—the temperature difference subtle, but noticeable—as someone came up behind her, invading her personal space.

Zo closed her eyes, knowing and dreading the source.

"Go away, Gabe."

"Please. We need to talk." Gabe rested his hand on her lower back and guided her through the crowd. Zo might have fought him, but she didn't have the energy or inclination to make another scene.

"I don't know what to tell you," he said, walking at her side. "I'm sorry."

Zo pushed past him as they wove through a sea of curious onlookers. So many of these men knew her and Gabe to be the best of friends. Over the last few years she'd heard rumors of Gabe's intention to propose marriage one day, but she and Gabe had never so much as kissed before a couple of weeks ago, and even that hadn't been her idea.

Gabe was a friend. A brother. She couldn't deny her physical attraction to him, but she'd never cared for him in a romantic way. He'd surprised her with news of Gryphon's death, and she was in shock when he met her unsuspecting lips with his.

"Sorry isn't good enough, Gabe. Not for this."

Gabe jumped over a black and barren fire pit to keep pace with Zo. When he landed, he snatched up her hands before she could yank them away. "Zo, when I left Gryphon I truly believed there was no way he'd survive. I didn't want you to agonize over the long and painful question of his survival. I lied because I believed it would be the truth, even if it was an eventual truth."

Zo stopped struggling against Gabe's hold on her. "But why lie to Gryphon?"

At the mention of Gryphon's name, he threw his hands into the air. "Listen, I panicked. I care for you, Zo. We'd just survived the Gate, and I thought we'd finally be together. Then I saw the way you worried over Gryphon. I felt you leaving me for him. I couldn't stand it."

They'd been friends since traveling to this small valley together as children—had played together, laughed together. He'd been the big brother she and Tess had needed. In a way, not loving him felt like its own brand of betrayal, making his ugly lie seem small by comparison. "Gabe." She took a step toward him, hesitant and uncertain. "I have always loved you and will always love you. But—"

"Don't," he said. "I can't hear the rest."

"But, my love for you is like the love I have for Tess. Constant. Familial."

He stood erect, not meeting her gaze as he stared over her head. His nostrils flared and his face crumpled into a pained expression. "Just tell me. Can you forgive me?" he asked.

The simple question made Zo's throat thick with emotion. "Can you forgive me?" she asked, leaving off the painful words: *for not loving you in return …*

Gabe pulled her to him with such speed, Zo didn't have a moment to brace herself for the contact of Gabe's body pressed against hers. He squeezed her with Kodiak force, compressing the air from her lungs and sending sharp pain through her ribs and sore muscles. Then he cupped her face in his hands and spoke with gentle ferocity. "I will always be here for you, Zo."

But how could he keep such a promise? And how could she accept it? No matter how much she wanted a safety net in life, she refused to use Gabe as an alternative to Gryphon.

He deserved better.

Gabe backed a step away. Then another. Finally, after one last, long look, he turned and walked into Commander Laden's tent, likely to give a report of his travels since leaving the Camp.

Zo hugged her arms to her tender stomach, still shaken by their conversation. She replayed every word and relived every touch in her mind. She didn't know how long she stared at the tent—maybe two minutes, maybe an hour—before a large hand—a different hand—pressed against her lower back.

She startled, but instantly relaxed when a glance from the corner of her eye confirmed it was Gryphon.

"You all right?" His deep, rolling cadence—the accent of the enemy—was like being swathed in a warm blanket.

"Gryphon."

His dark hair fell into his warm brown eyes. He looked between her and the tent. "What do you need?" Four words. So simple, yet so precisely encompassing why she'd grown to love him. Gryphon, the selfless Ram, who saw a world in need. Gryphon, willing to right every problem around him.

Zo bit her lip and took his hand in hers. "I think I could use some time away from camp."

Gryphon nodded, but glanced over his shoulder at the four guards Laden had tailing him. "Any chance you pups want to give us a few minutes?"

Zo tugged on Gryphon's hand and pushed onto her tiptoes to whisper in his ear. "You shouldn't bait them. They're here to protect you."

A muted, cynical laugh rolled from Gryphon's chest. "A nice sentiment, Zo. But they're here to protect the camp."

Zo frowned. "We're going for a walk," she said over Gryphon's shoulder, daring the guards to defy her. "I'll see Gryphon back to his tent in an hour or so." She paused, sensing an argument from them. "You don't want to make an enemy of the camp healer, soldiers. Not before a war."

Zo tugged on Gryphon's arm, pulling him in the opposite direction.

"No way that works," Gryphon muttered under his breath.

"Just don't look back," said Zo. "I'm practically Laden's daughter, and I've risked my life for the cause. They'll back off." She honestly doubted it; Laden didn't stand for any level of insubordination. Still, she hoped to scare them enough into keeping watch from a distance.

At this point, she'd take any time she could get with Gryphon.

Gryphon and Zo passed the northern training fields and walked through the rows of maize and wheat to the foothills at the north of the valley. They headed toward the slot canyon where they had entered the camp, taking a trail to the west until it met the sheer mountainside.

"The view up here is amazing!" Zo stretched her arms out wide, ignoring the pain in her ribs, and peered back in the direction they had come. There was no sign of Gryphon's guards. The thought made her smug and more than a little surprised. She drew in a large breath of mountain air and absorbed the red glow of the dying sun as it cast its final rays across the valley. "Especially at dusk, when campfires light up the valley and the stars come out."

When Gryphon didn't respond, she turned around and asked, "Are you all right?"

He stood silent, his expression tense and somehow primal.

"Gryphon, I—"

Zo's question turned into a light scream when Gryphon, the Ram, charged her. He wrapped his arms around her legs and hoisted her over his shoulder.

Zo's laughter turned into a gasp of pain with the jarring motion.

He stopped, skidding over loose rock and dirt, at the sound of her cry. "What's wrong?" He gently lowered her to the ground, scanning her face for the source of her pain.

Zo waved away his concern. "It's nothing. Just a little sore." Her hand went to her ribs out of habit.

Gryphon frowned. "Sore from what?"

Zo shrugged. "I'm not sure. I just woke up with it hurting."

"Have you seen Millie about it?"

Zo rolled her eyes. "I'm perfectly capable of taking care of myself, Striker."

Gryphon raised an eyebrow. "May I ... " he cleared his throat in obvious discomfort. "May I see?"

Zo's mouth went completely dry. Her pulse quickened, and before she could even evaluate her answer, she caught herself nodding, swept up in the uncertainty of his open gaze.

Zo slowly tugged at the laces of her jerkin, not fully untying them, but loosening them just enough to lift the blouse underneath to expose her stomach and lower ribs. For all they'd endured together, she shouldn't have been so nervous. So ... shy.

Gryphon hissed as he reached out and brushed his fingertips along the line of her lowest ribs. The bruising was a dark purple and spanned the length of Gryphon's hand. Zo closed her eyes to fully appreciate the sensation of his careful touch. When his hand fell away, his features turned hard and ... deadly. Like a Ram.

"Who did this to you?"

"What? No one."

Gryphon clasped her hand and led her over to a large, flat boulder where they could sit down. "Please, Zo." He looked away, chest heaving, breathing heavily through his nose. Anger rolled off of him, so tangible she doubted she even needed her heightened abilities to sense it. "You don't just wake up with something like that. Please ... tell me who did this. I need to know."

"No one hurt me," she said. "I really did just wake up—"

"No!" Gryphon stood up and took five steps away from her before wheeling back, an accusing finger pointed at the campfires in the valley below. "I don't know what this *filth* does to their women, but I won't sit by and let it happen."

"You're really going to lecture Wolves on the proper treatment of others?" Zo snapped.

"I swear on my life, Zo. I'll kill the man." He looked down at her, fury and fire battling for dominance in his handsome and frightening face. "Was it Laden?"

At that Zo actually laughed. "Gryphon, please." She stood and walked over to him, reaching her hands up to his shoulders, pushing a bit of serenity into him as her fingers melted down his arms and finally clasped his hands. "I swear to you that I am no one's victim.

This is just a random fluke. An anomaly. Who knows? I might have fallen while sleepwalking."

Some of the tension in Gryphon's stance relaxed. He lowered his forehead to rest against hers. "I'm sorry." He sighed. "I just don't trust these people, Zo." He stepped back and took her by the shoulders. "I need to know that you're safe with them."

"These are my people, Gryphon."

Doubt crossed his expression. "But they aren't mine." Dropping to his knees in front of her, Gryphon took her hips with his large hands. Zo swallowed, hypnotized by his strength as well as his careful touch. She let her fingers weave into his dark hair as he rested his forehead against her stomach.

"You know, I never properly thanked you for the healing yesterday," his voice was muffled. "When I peeked into your tent this morning before joining Laden on the training field, you were still asleep. I wanted to let you rest."

Zo dropped to her knees to join him on the ground. His arm snaked around her back, supporting, embracing, protecting. He traced the outline of her jaw with his rough fingertips and Zo managed a weak, "It was … a pleasure." She shuddered as his hand moved to her neck and then slid off her shoulder, down her back.

Unable to resist any longer, Zo grabbed his shirtfront and pulled him to her. His lips met hers in a beautiful collision of desire but quickly melted into something softer. Her hands fell away from his shirt to rest on his broad shoulders as her lips moved against his in a gentle, natural rhythm. Cupping the side of her neck, Gryphon communicated his tender, selfless adoration.

Giving, instead of taking.

Loving, instead of demanding love.

His lips slid along her cheek and neck. Zo tilted her head back while basking in his touch. The sky had darkened enough so the stars stood out against the blackish-blue expanse.

A shiver rippled over her skin as he nibbled on her ear. "Can I just keep you here, Zo?" He spoke between kisses. "Can we never leave this spot?"

A stab of guilt struck her. She still hadn't told him she had to leave in the morning. "Gryphon." With all her self-control, she leaned away to look into the endless depths of his brown eyes. "I ... haven't been completely honest with you."

Gryphon froze, bracing himself. "What do you mean?"

Zo hesitated, hating to kill the moment but unable to bear the thought of deceiving him further about her promise to Ikatou and the Kodiak. "I'm leaving."

Gryphon searched her face. "No, you're not." His eyes darkened, daring her to contradict him.

She swallowed. "I'm going with Ikatou to the Kodiak Caves in the morning. The trip should only last a week or so. Laden wants us to convince Murtog to come and take part in the *Ostara*. He hopes to persuade the chief and the rest of his men to join our cause."

"What is this *Ostara* everyone keeps mentioning?" he said, flatly.

Gryphon, a Ram, wouldn't be familiar with the customs of her people. "It's an old tradition. Wolves hold them every spring to celebrate the equinox, trade goods, and discuss any threats to the region. This *Ostara* would be different because Laden hopes to have all three clans—Wolf, Raven, and Kodiak—present."

"But why does Laden need *you* to convince Murtog to come? Why not send someone else?"

Zo sighed. "He thinks Murtog will find the invitation less threatening coming from Raca and me."

Scoffing, Gryphon said, "Murtog needs a new bride. Laden's using you as a lure. You and Raca both." He rubbed the back of his neck. "You've done enough for that man. He can't expect you to go back out into the wilderness on another dangerous journey."

"I've made promises," said Zo.

"To hell with your promises!"

Zo flinched at Gryphon's tone even though she knew she wasn't the object of his anger. From the first time she'd met him inside Ram's Gate, he'd always seemed so levelheaded. So in control. But since coming to the Allied Camp, he'd been more volatile, as though even the tiniest disturbance could put him over the edge.

It had to be the stress of staying in a camp surrounded by men he'd been taught to see as the enemy.

He shook his head. "I'm sorry. I just feel this … need to protect the time we have together." He kissed her forehead again. "Please." He kissed the tip of her nose. "Tell Laden to send someone else."

"Gryphon." She slid her arms around his neck and rested her head on his shoulder. "You speak of time like it's fleeting. We will have lots of time together. As much time as you want."

She inwardly cursed herself for sounding so needy. She didn't want to be the type of girl to beg or hint at the future. When Gryphon had asked if he could call her his, she hadn't thought to have him clarify what that meant, exactly. Had Gryphon been a Wolf, she would have assumed they were officially courting, which was a step that almost always led to marriage. But nothing about Gryphon and Zo was usual.

"If there is one thing my life as a Ram soldier has taught me, it's that you can never trust time. We could have days. We could have years. One can never know. And with this war on the brink of boiling over, there is a real chance that—"

Zo pressed her hand to cover his mouth. "Shhhh. I can't even bear hearing it."

Gryphon took hold of her wrist and gently pulled her hand away. His lips were pressed into a firm line, his chin wrinkled and tense. The muscles in his neck flexed, as though some internal war waged within him. He finally managed, "Please, just stay. Commander Laden will understand."

She held up the backs of her hands, showing him the jagged cuts she'd refused to explain when he'd abducted her from Ikatou's camp. The wounds had only recently closed, leaving uneven pink lines to serve as a reminder of her blood oath. "I'm not going for Commander Laden."

Chapter Ten

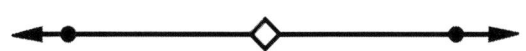

Gryphon wanted to throw a boulder into the mountainside—
enough rage boiled within him that he probably could.

"I could kill Ikatou! How could he force you into that agreement?
How could he take advantage knowing you had no other option?"
Gryphon walked away from Zo, staring out over the dark valley
dotted with campfires. He only had twenty-one days before he had
to meet Ajax and offer Barnabas his head. The thought of Ikatou
robbing seven of those precious days that might have been spent with
Zo drove him to the brink of madness.

Had he known about Zo's promise to help Ikatou free the
Nameless before Ajax had knelt in the mud at his feet, no amount
of begging would have swayed him to agree to help his friend. Not
when Zo needed him to help fulfill this ridiculous task.

The Great Move was underway. Barnabas would be leading not
just his warriors, but women, children, and even the Nameless from
the Gate in a mass exodus south to relocate in the Valley of Wolves.
If there was ever a time to free the Nameless, it was now.

The problem was, Gryphon hadn't told Laden or Zo about the

Great Move. He hadn't wanted to give Laden that much of an upper hand against his people, and he hadn't wanted to break Zo's heart by admitting how he'd obtained that information. If Zo knew they only had a few short weeks left together, she'd be livid.

He didn't want to ruin what time they had.

"You can't blame Ikatou," said Zo, coming to stand beside him. "You and I both know the lengths a person is willing to go to protect family." She reached out to take his hand.

Did she consider him her family? If things were different, he would have done whatever it took to convince Laden to offer his blessing. He would have learned the proper customs of her clan. She deserved the very best life had to offer.

He shook his head. So many would haves and should haves.

Zo must have misinterpreted his silence. "Ikatou has four daughters, Gryph." Her hands slid up his arm to grip him above and below the elbow. "Can you imagine having your little girl stolen from you to become another man's slave?"

Gryphon closed his eyes in shame for his clan and people. And then, he allowed his imagination to travel in a thin stream of thought to one of the many would haves of his future.

He imagined Zo sitting on an outcropping of stone with the sun shining down on her tanned skin as she sang a silky-sweet tune. A little girl, with her mother's wild hair, stomping in and out of the stream at Zo's feet. A boy a few years older, picking up a small stone from the bank and throwing it into the water, too grown-up for the games his little sister played. The boy's almond eyes the same sharp blue as Zo's. And even though he wouldn't admit it, the boy clearly loved being near his mother.

Then he imagined someone swooping in and taking all of that away.

"Gryphon? Are you all right?"

He looked down into Zo's piercing eyes. *By stars and shield, she is beautiful.*

"Gryphon?" Zo asked again, concern lining her face. "It's only a two-day journey to the Kodiak. I will be back before you even have the chance to miss me."

He picked up her scarred hands and kissed each one in turn. "Impossible."

Just as impossible as Zo's chance of helping Ikatou free his family and the other Nameless.

Unless ...

The Great Move and the distraction of his execution.

Telling Laden would be the ultimate betrayal of his people ...

Gryphon closed his eyes and prayed for forgiveness.

His decision was made.

Gryphon left Zo at the flaps of her tent, his lips still tingling from their kisses, his heart pounding like a hammer on an anvil. He stormed through the camp, giving no heed to the muted conversations and blatant stares of soldiers sitting around crackling fires. He assumed his four guards were waiting for him outside his tent, but he wasn't ready to head back just yet.

The Kodiak faction was situated on the eastern rim of the camp. When giving his tour of the valley, Laden had explained that the Bears struggled to sleep under an open sky and so near the other clans. On this side of the narrow valley, the solid rock mountainside leaned over the earth just enough to provide shade and shelter from the rain and wind. It was a prime location for anyone, but Laden had given it to the Kodiak as a peace offering in hopes that, should the Kodiak chief leave his caves and join them, he would be flattered by the gesture.

Only a few fires burned on this side of camp. The flames

illuminated the angular faces of the men named for their size and temperament. He spotted Ikatou sitting with the group of men who had traveled with them to the Allied Camp only a few days ago.

Ikatou must have sensed him coming. He looked up from the fire, squinting into the night. Slowly gaining his feet, Ikatou stepped away from his comrades and walked toward Gryphon.

"What brings you, Ram?"

Gryphon didn't so much as hesitate as he strode toward Ikatou, slamming his fist into the bear's face. "You bastard."

At least ten men jumped to their feet and charged, but Ikatou's growl made them pause. "Go back to your fires." He worked his jaw, as if to test that it still worked. Then he eyed Gryphon and scowled. "She finally told you, eh?"

Chest pumping, adrenaline racing, Gryphon knew he was outnumbered, and that if Ikatou hadn't stopped them, those men could have easily ripped his limbs off. He'd always been trained not to attack in anger, and he certainly couldn't afford to lose his temper again.

And yet, his tightly wound body didn't agree.

He dropped his shoulder and launched himself at Ikatou, arms out wide, ready to tackle the bear to the ground. Ikatou anticipated the second attack and jammed his knee up into Gryphon's chin, dropping him to the ground.

Laughter and jeers filled the Kodiak camp as Gryphon lay facedown on the ground, his vision swimming. Ikatou grabbed a fistful of Gryphon's hair and yanked his head back, using his knee to pin Gryphon to the ground.

Gryphon breathed through the pain, fighting back a gasp, and managed, "How could you drag an innocent girl into this mess? She would have helped you without a blood oath."

Ikatou put more pressure on his spine and Gryphon arched his back in pain. "If you're done making a fool of yourself, let's take a walk and I'll tell you."

Humbled, Gryphon grunted and Ikatou released him. His jaw throbbed where Ikatou had kneed him, but luckily it had missed his nose. He'd broken it so many times, he didn't know if it could take another hit.

Ikatou led them away from the other Kodiak. It didn't take long to find privacy in this corner of the valley.

"I risked my life and the lives of my men to save Zo in the wilderness. But for some of them, saving Zo from Boar meant destroying the only hope we had of getting into Ram's Gate to find our families. The blood oath was necessary."

"But now that you are here, and you know Laden is willing to help, why don't you release her from it?"

Ikatou shook his head. "It doesn't work that way."

"Why not?"

"I'm not the only Kodiak protected under the blood oath. Besides," he took a few steps before adding, "it's clear that Laden loves the girl." He gestured to Gryphon, "So do you—the only Ram fighting for our cause. You both would do anything to see her safe and guarded. As long as Laden knows her life is attached to the Nameless, my family has an actual shot at survival and freedom."

Anger in its purest form threatened to overtake Gryphon again, until he considered Zo's words from earlier: *Can you imagine having your little girl stolen from you to become another man's slave?* Gryphon thought back to his daydream of Zo by the stream. Of the little ones surrounding her. Closing his eyes, he let his tight fists relax and tried to calm his beating heart. "Promise me you will protect her while she is away."

Ikatou folded his arms across his chest and surveyed Gryphon with a critical eye. "We Kodiak take those words quite seriously. By now, I'm sure you know that."

"Exactly why I asked."

"Will she become your wife, Ram? Do you love her as family?"

Gryphon went completely still. "That is not your business, Bear."

83

"Until my family is safe from the clutches of your miserable clan, the girl is my business." He leaned in. "Answer the question … please." The *please* was clearly an afterthought.

"If our maker sees fit to spare my life to see the end of this war, and if Zo is willing, she will become my family, my w-wife by law." He swallowed, pushing past the pain of their coming separation, of the ugly promise he'd made to Ajax.

My wife.

As a Ram, he grew up assuming he wouldn't marry until turning thirty years old. Only twenty now, he'd have a full decade to put it off.

My wife.

Two words that carried so much weight. Such responsibility. Such sacred promise. Gryphon took a half step closer to Ikatou, shooting all the challenge he could into his gaze. "I answered your question, now you answer mine. Will you promise to protect her?"

Ikatou met his gaze and understanding passed between them. He pulled a dagger from his belt and dragged the blade across his palm. "I swear by blood and by bone to protect Zo with my life."

Gryphon blinked at Ikatou's blood-dripping hand for a half-second before accepting the moist handshake. He looked the Kodiak in the eye and said, "For what it's worth, I'm sorry about your family. I'll do what I can to help you see them again."

Ikatou nodded his thanks. "I believe you."

That night, Gryphon lay in his bed not bothering to try and shut his eyes, his mind devouring his predicament from every angle. He weighed the love of his clan against their war crimes and the enslavement of the Nameless. He weighed his love for Zo against his love for the brothers of his mess unit. They'd been banished because of him. Many were husbands and fathers whose families would be forced to live in shame if he didn't turn himself over to Barnabas. He knew all too well what it meant to grow up without a father while still carrying the weight of his shame. Dining on both insult and injury.

In the morning he'd only have twenty days before so many fates would be decided.

Joshua stirred beside him, his breathing deep and even. At least the boy was safe and happy. The Allied Camp suited him well. When Gryphon had returned from talking to Ikatou and rinsed his hand of the Bear's blood, Joshua had been waiting up for him along with Sani. The two made the most unlikely friends. Joshua hadn't wasted a minute retelling the events of the day. While Joshua had chattered on, Sani had patiently listened, nodding when occasion called for it, and sometimes offering one-word responses.

"And you know that Zo and Sani's sister are leaving in the morning, don't you?" Joshua had asked. "I volunteered to go with them, but Commander Laden said I had to stay."

Gryphon had ruffed the boy's hair and said, "I wish both of us could go, kid."

Instead of allowing himself to go mad with worry, he'd just keep his head down and use the following week to map out a plan to help Zo with her blood oath *and* help Ajax. Zo's return would be his deadline.

He rubbed the heels of his hands into his eyes and silently prayed for a solution. If only the Historian were still alive. He felt convinced she would have known what to do. This problem, no matter how much he wanted to fix it, was bigger than him.

But besides Zo, Joshua, and little Tess, he didn't know to whom he could turn for help. The obvious man to speak to about the matter was also one of the people he trusted least. But at this point, what other options did he have?

Fire! Fire! Fire!

Zo rolled to her side, pulling her favorite lamb's wool quilt up over her head to hide from the disturbance of another nightmare. But not even its familiar softness could dispel the fear of nights spent fighting the Clanless a few short weeks ago. Persistent as waves crashing against the shore. Burnt flesh suffocating the senses, balls of fire hurdling through the dark sky overhead and landing between mother and child. The panicked, helpless cries of fathers who didn't dare abandon their place at the perimeter of camp to rush back to their families. Never knowing how the next attack would come. Only that it *would* come.

"Fire!" Again, Zo shrank deeper into the thick folds of her bedroll.

Small but determined hands shoved against Zo's shoulder and hip. "Wake up! They need us!" Tess rarely showed fear, even inside the Gate when such weakness was more than justified. Hearing the tremor in her voice propelled Zo up and out of bed in one swift motion. Zo jammed her feet into her boots while threading her arms through the sleeves of an old tunic that used to belong to her father. The fabric reached her knees, but the simple shirt, combined with her mother's woven belt, always brought her a measure of comfort. A marriage of her parents displayed in one hasty outfit.

"Tell me," said Zo, as she quickly tied her hair into a rushed knot on the top of her head. If there really was a fire, the last thing she needed was for her wild hair to get in the way.

"A Wolf tent."

The dry buckskin lining would have easily fueled a fire. But Zo had never heard of someone being so careless.

"They're saying … they're saying … " but Tess was too breathless to finish. She grabbed Zo's hand and together they ran for the Healer's Tent.

"How many injured?" asked Zo. Outside, the darkness of the night was disturbed by a red and orange glow in the Wolf sector of camp. Shouts punctuated the pulsing, distant flame.

"Move!" a burly man yelled, as he and a group of men carried two makeshift gurneys toward the tent. Zo ducked into the Healer's Tent ahead of them to find Millie waiting with a hand to her chest and a face as white and ghostly as a three-day corpse.

"Careful!" Zo helped lower the first burn victim onto a bed. Millie and Tess helped with the second. "We need more water, and a fire."

"No fire!" one of the burned men cried between wails of agony. Moist skin blistered and bubbled along the entire left side of his body. The other man's burns weren't nearly as bad, covering mostly his hands, arms, and one side of his face.

Zo and Millie cut away cumbersome clothing and began pouring clean water over the wounds. Tess mixed powdered poppy and other herbs in a broth for the pain. The men drank with arched backs between gasps and sobs.

Zo channeled and challenged her new gift, pushing life and vitality into the damaged tissue where the burns were especially severe while purging possible infection—the real killer of any burn victim.

She cupped the swollen, red ear of the man on her table and whispered a healing blessing to draw away the heat and restore the flesh. For the first time since they'd come into the healing tent, Zo really looked into the young man's face. The sensation of déjà vu passed over her.

So many of the men in camp were familiar, but she had a sinking feeling she should know this man. "Weren't you just here?" Zo coughed into her palm, the smell of smoke on her breath, for some reason.

And then she remembered. These were the Wolves who'd attacked

Gryphon on the training field.

Suddenly, Commander Laden pushed away the flap of the tent and stormed into the infirmary. His face was smeared with ash and his eyes were swollen and bloodshot. Pointing a shaking finger at Zo, he said, "Report to my tent." His voice came out something of a growl.

Zo gestured down at her patients. "Now?"

He grimaced, casting a compassionate glance at the wounded. "As soon as you're able."

Chapter Eleven

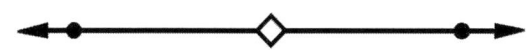

"You're telling me it was simple coincidence?" Laden paced. A single torch staked to the ground flickered at the center of the tent, casting dancing light on all surfaces within its meager reach and leaving the rest to the mystery of heavy shadow. "Do you know how many accidental fires we've had in five years of staying in this valley?"

Gryphon sat in the chair in front of Laden's desk, his hands resting casually in his lap.

"Not one." The Commander answered his own question, his voice calm, like the still moment before a mountain lion pounces.

"The tent of the men who attacked you catches fire. You are found conveniently without your guard." Laden counted Gryphon's strikes against his fingers. "You realize how bad this looks for you, I hope."

Gryphon had come back to his tent after his confrontation with Ikatou expecting to find the four guards waiting outside, but the entrance had been empty. He remembered vaguely wondering if they were out looking for him, but wasn't about to help them with their babysitting duties. Both Joshua and Sani had been fast asleep when he'd slipped inside. It had felt as though he had barely shut his eyes when shouts of fire punctuated the night.

"Where are my men?"

"If you're referring to my pathetic guard, I have no idea." Gryphon didn't want to explain that it had been Zo who had sent them on their way. He also didn't have any desire to explain that he'd spent most of the night alone with Zo up in the foothills.

The sound of muffled voices outside the tent preceded Zo's louder demand of, "I'm expected." She pushed open the tent flaps. "You wanted to see me?" She stumbled a bit upon seeing Gryphon, but quickly regained her composure and turned on Laden. "If you think he's responsible for the fire, you're wrong."

"His guard is missing," Laden said, narrowing his eyes. "He has motive."

"I sent away his guard tonight so we could be alone."

Laden's brows plummeted, turning his face angular. "You what?"

"I asked them to leave us, and they did. They knew he and I were together."

Gryphon held back a snort of laughter. Zo made it sound as though her bold threats had been nothing more than a gentle request.

Laden's nostrils flared. "You're telling me that you were with Gryphon tonight the entire time? That you escorted him to his tent before heading off to your own?"

A subtle pause. Barely more than a half second, but Laden, like any seasoned predator, could have easily seen the hesitation. "Yes," she said, matching his stare with one of her own, daring him to contradict her.

"And how can you be so certain he didn't leave after you left?"

Zo surprised Gryphon by turning and looking him directly in the eye. "Did you leave your tent tonight?"

"I did not." And Gryphon hadn't. He'd just gone to settle a score with Ikatou *before* making it there.

"There you have it!" said Zo.

"Dear girl," Laden said, frowning. "You forget this man was raised by our enemy. I don't doubt his loyalties to you, but it's foolish to assume they extend to the rest of us."

Very True, Gryphon mentally agreed.

Laden walked over to Gryphon and leaned back on his table, crossing his arms in front of his barrel chest as he examined his prisoner. "Strange." Laden frowned at Zo. "Did you, in your private time with this Ram, happen to punch him in the face?"

Were it not for Gryphon's interrogation training, he might have flinched at the Commander's observation. Instead, Gryphon spoke in a level tone. "This is nothing, sir." He thought to blame his swollen jaw on the rough handling of the Wolves when they'd dragged him out of the tent at Laden's summons, but he didn't dare. Laden was smart, and Gryphon had no doubt that he would question his men to corroborate Gryphon's claim. "Ikatou and I had a little chat about Zo's blood oath earlier." *Keep it vague. Hide the lie with truths.*

Zo blinked down at him. Her uncertain gaze made the hair on Gryphon's arms and legs stand on end. She would easily remember his jaw wasn't swollen when they were together earlier.

Please trust me, Zo.

Thankfully the Commander missed Zo's reaction. His attention was drawn by a tall soldier with a blond goatee and weathered lines pulling down the corners of his mouth. The soldier bowed.

"Report," said Laden.

"We can't find them, sir."

Laden watched him with arms folded across his broad chest. The harsh light and shadow of the torch distorted his usually handsome face, turning it gruesome and gaunt. "Explain yourself, Captain. This isn't a large valley."

"Our men have checked every tent, sir."

"And the guards at the northern pass?"

"Have nothing to report either, sir."

Laden's fist pounded against the table. "Not good enough!" He kneaded his fingers into his brow, as though taking a moment to collect his temper. "Send a Raven flock to the southern entrance. See if they find tracks."

The soldier bowed again. "Yes, sir." He turned to fulfill his order then paused before exiting the tent.

"What is it, Captain?"

The tired captain glanced over his shoulder, meeting Gryphon's eye with an unbridled scowl. "We think the Ram did something to them, sir."

Anger boiled inside Gryphon. But he didn't even have a chance to defend himself before Laden shouted, "If a lone, unarmed Ram took down four of my best guards in the middle of the night in the heart of my own camp without any witnesses, then ... " He took a breath and, pinching the bridge of his noise, said, "Send the flock. I want a report by noon tomorrow."

The captain bowed one final time and left the tent.

"I told them to wait for me at the tent," said Gryphon when they were alone again. He didn't want this to be considered Zo's fault. If these men had shirked their duty inside Ram's Gate they would have already been strung up and whipped for insubordination and leaving their post. "When we returned, they weren't there." Gryphon glanced at Zo, hoping she'd continue to go along with her original lie that they'd been together when they reached his tent.

She didn't appear pleased, and he hoped she'd listen to the full explanation of what had happened from the time he'd left her at her tent.

"If they weren't waiting like cowards at the tent," asked Laden, "then where are they?" Laden melted into his chair at the head of his large pine desk. "Unless we can find evidence to support you, I'll have no choice but to take action. I want to trust you, but as our enemy, no one will believe you without a witness. The Allies will demand blood."

"What kind of action?" asked Zo.

"A hand, at least."

Gryphon set his jaw, too dazed to process Zo's outraged protests. He had no desire to spend the last days of his life in horrible pain. But then Gryphon remembered that they were alone. No guards surrounding him. No bindings.

"You're bluffing," Gryphon blurted. "You want to scare me, but you don't really believe that I caused that fire." He paused. "You don't know what to do with me, do you?" A grin broke past the barrier of Gryphon's careful control. He knew it was reckless to goad the Commander, but couldn't help himself.

This man, so exact in his punishment of his own men when they defied his orders, paused in the face of justice. Even for a Ram. Gryphon respected him for it, in spite of himself.

A guard peeked his head through the flaps of the tent and said, "Chief Naat's son requests permission to speak to you." The guard glanced at Gryphon. His blond hair was pulled back into a tight knot on the top of his head, accentuating his forehead as his brows narrowed into an accusing V. "He says he has information about the Ram."

Zo reached out and placed a hand on Gryphon's shoulder. Her eyes closed. Her breath turned ragged.

Does she think I did this?

It shouldn't have felt like a betrayal, but it did.

Sani entered the tent with head held high, his posture strong despite his small frame.

Laden offered the Raven Prince a tight bow, but before he could do more, Sani spoke.

"I assumed you believe Gryphon to be the cause of this fire. I understand the victims were the same who attacked Gryphon the day after he arrived."

Laden only nodded. Perhaps he hadn't had the opportunity to converse with the intelligent kid yet. Sani always spoke with wisdom beyond his years.

"I've come to offer testimony that Gryphon arrived at our tent well before the fire started, and didn't leave until summoned by the guards."

If by summoned the boy meant ripped from the tent with bodily force, then he spoke truth.

"I know you and the Ram boy share a tent, but how can you be certain?"

"I sleep by the door and wake easily."

"I'm aware of the extent to which 'Atiin will go to protect those who've earned their devotion. Are you sure this isn't just a way to protect your charge?"

"I am absolutely certain Gryphon didn't commit this crime."

Laden excused Gryphon from the tent with a new set of guards assigned to follow his every move.

"I'll walk you back," Laden said to Zo when they were alone. It was a short walk to the Healer's Tent, but Zo appreciated the company.

"The boy could be lying. Like I said before, he has motivation," said Laden conversationally. "Raven take their role as 'Atiin very seriously. If Sani thought I might execute Gryphon—even if the Ram had started that fire and killed someone in the process—Sani would be honor-bound to intervene."

The commander clearly believed Gryphon didn't start the fire, which was good, but Zo felt a twinge of guilt for lying to the man she'd always respected. And she hadn't been the only one to lie tonight.

Seeing Gryphon's swollen jaw and tasting the apprehension in the air when he'd delivered the lie about getting in a fight with Ikatou *earlier* that day gave her pause.

Had he *only* lied about the timing of his fight with Ikatou? Or had something else happened after Gryphon left her at the tent?

Her feelings for Gryphon had been so sure, her confidence in his character so absolute. She wanted a life with this man. A future. But his crafty lie to Laden and his flawless mask of composure drudged up memories of Gryphon inside Ram's Gate—of the soldier trained to lie.

"Why don't you believe he started the fire?" Zo asked without thinking. The tremor in her voice was subtle, but she knew Laden hadn't missed it.

He stopped walking and stared into her face, scrutinizing every inch of her expression with a curious air. His studied gaze seemed to unlock her secrets, her every insecurity. The spell broke and he simply shrugged. "Ram don't take honor from covert acts of violence. They think it weak and cowardly. If he wanted to take his revenge on those men, he'd look them in the eye as he did it."

A cold chill rolled over her skin. "I'm going to check on the injured." She darted into the dark tent before Laden could say anything more. Inside, low-burning embers struggled to breathe warmth into the space. The light pulsed and died, casting ominous shadows across the sleeping forms of the injured men. Millie and Tess each slept on one of the spare beds—a common practice when an injured soldier required constant care.

Zo scratched the side of her face, where her skin felt tight and irritated. Gryphon a liar. Gryphon a Ram. Gryphon, not wholly who she thought him to be … It didn't feel true, but the logic was hard to dismiss.

But perhaps she was the better liar. After all, she had lied to herself, convincing herself that Gryphon's caring for her was the same as abandoning everything he'd been raised to become.

"What happened to your face?" Millie hovered over Zo, holding a kettle in one hand and new muslin dressing in the other. Zo blinked away the effects of a scattered and restless sleep and, in a daze, reached up to brush the hot skin around her ear.

The skin was smooth, but tender and slightly swollen. "I … I don't know."

The old woman seemed to forget how to move or speak. Her eyes glazed over and some of the color drained from her usually rosy cheeks.

"What's wrong?" Zo asked, sitting up and taking Millie by the arm. "What is it?"

Zo took the hot kettle from Millie and walked over to hang it on the hook by the fire. She should have been hurrying to pack for her trip to the Kodiak, but Millie's reaction frightened her. She forced the old woman to sit and ignored a slight pain in her ribs as she crouched before her. "You're scaring me," said Zo.

Millie's lips moved but generated no sound. When she finally did manage to speak, her voice came out in something of a choked whisper.

"You're broken, child." A tear leaked out of the corner of her eye. "You're broken."

Zo shook her head. "You're not making any sense."

"The barrier is breeched. The floodgates." She hiccupped. "They're open."

"Millie?"

The woman's worried eyes snapped into focus. "Where did you think the magic came from, child?"

"Are we talking about healing?"

"Healing, whether by body alone or with the help of a healer, is a magic as old as time. And just like anything else, it demands payment." She reached over and ran her fingers along the wooden legs of the bed. "Everyone—healer or no—is born with the magic to burn away impurities and heal the wounds of the body. A scratch on the arm. A broken bone. Mankind doesn't require a healer to mend themselves. That magic lives within all of us."

She raised a withered finger. "A healer just helps it along. Without the fuel of a healer's magic, the flame can flicker and die if the wound is too great. As healers, we are an accelerant to that flame. We grow the fire and keep it burning until the body is whole and well again."

Zo nodded. "We are the payment." She'd learned all of this ages ago.

"Wrong. Our love is the payment. But the order of life demands balance in all things."

"I don't understand."

Millie sat for a moment, chewing on the inside of her lip. "Imagine a reservoir of water. We, as healers, can fuel healing fire with our love, but we must be able to keep the fire from consuming us. Once we are finished healing, our fire is doused by the water we've stored in our reservoir.

"The creator made us so that our healing magic cannot exceed the level of our reservoir. Once that 'water' is used to douse the healing flame, it needs time to build again. If not, the fire of healing would grow beyond our ability to douse the flame when the healing is finished."

"And you think I've opened some sort of floodgate?" Zo shook her head, still not understanding.

Millie began to mutter to herself again, her face pale, her eyes wide with worry. "A healing that wasn't meant to be. A flame so hot the slow waters couldn't quench. The gates open. The reservoir broken. The water no longer gathering … "

Was it possible that her experience healing Joshua had caused this? She'd didn't see how. Even though she'd felt broken in the week following the boy's healing, she couldn't deny the power that now felt so close to her—a current that ran under the surface of her skin. She almost told the older healer as much but the words died in her throat when Millie spoke first.

"The healing flame burns away the bad. A healer's reserve of water dammed no more. Can't access the flood to douse the magic. A reservoir of saving energy reduced only to a mere stream." She reached out and ran a shaking finger down the side of Zo's face. "A stream that can only carry the problem elsewhere."

Chapter Twelve

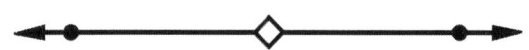

"Won't you at least come and see us off?" Zo asked Tess while adjusting the strap of her pack. Another trip. Miles and miles with provisions strapped to Zo's back and rocks biting into the soles of her well-worn boots. The sour prospect mixed with the idea of leaving her loved ones yet again. Even though the trip was meant to only last a week, Zo didn't know if she'd ever be comfortable apart from them again.

Tess wrinkled her nose at Zo, but didn't offer any kind of response as her little hands helped Millie hang herbs on a line outside the Healer's Tent.

Zo persisted. "Joshua will be there. And I hear the Raven have a special way of sending their people off. It might be interesting."

Tess bent down to grab another bundle of herbs to hand to Millie, dutifully ignoring Zo.

"Don't worry about us, Zo," said Millie, her voice the model of forced lightness. "Young Tess and I have big plans to sew you both new dresses for the *Ostara* the Commander has planned." Usually the old woman would have made some type of joke about Zo's failure in the art of sewing unless it involved stitching men, but after their confusing talk about floods and fires, Millie simply averted her eyes and swallowed.

"I'll miss you," said Zo. "And I'll only be gone a week or so ... " She waited for her sister to say something, anything. Even outright anger would be better than silence.

Finally, Zo sighed. "Be sure to study with Millie while I'm gone, and look out for Joshua and Gryphon." She turned to leave, but couldn't bring herself to walk away. Closing her eyes, Zo whispered, "I love you, bug. I'm sorry for everything. As soon as this war is over, I promise never to leave again."

Glancing over her shoulder, Zo noticed Tess's hands hovering idle over the basket of herbs. The little girl's shoulders seemed to shake, but that could have been Zo's imagination. She waited another few moments, hoping her sister might turn around and send her off with a proper hug and goodbye.

But she didn't.

With a reassuring nod from Millie, Zo hitched her pack higher onto her shoulders and headed toward Laden's tent, where the others had planned to meet directly following morning meal. She'd been able to abandon her traditional Wolf clothing for buckskin trousers and a simple tunic with a leather belt tied around her waist. A small sheath hung from her belt, housing her dagger. Another hidden sheath was strapped to her calf.

Eva, the Ram woman who'd followed Stone to the Allied Camp, had taught Zo how to properly wield and even throw the small blades while traveling through the wilderness. Zo managed well enough until the time came to actually kill an animal or harm a human being. It went against her healer-blood to destroy what she'd dedicated her life to preserving.

"Zo?"

Zo jumped a foot in the air and might have fallen were it not for the strong set of hands that found her waist.

"I'm sorry." Gryphon's touch carried its own kind of power—relieving tensions, offering support. "I was just looking for you."

"What is that?" she asked, pointing to the black painted teardrops under his eyes.

He sighed and threw up his hands in surrender. "Joshua and Sani have finally found something they agree upon."

Zo ran her finger along the dried paint. The skin there was soft, unlike his constantly stubbled cheeks and hardened muscular build. Being close to him, touching him, breathing his air—it wasn't so different from the sedatives she sometimes gave her patients. "And what is that, exactly?"

Gryphon played with the ends of Zo's hair as he spoke. "They're both determined to make my life difficult."

Zo couldn't help but think of the previous night and the fire. She frowned. "I think you do that just fine on your own."

"Sani tells me the black tears are a way of showing sadness when the Raven send warriors off. Instead of showing their weakness by crying real tears, they paint them on their faces." Gryphon snorted. "Sani probably thought he was doing me a favor, but I'm sure Joshua just wanted to play a prank while I slept. I don't think I like Sani and Joshua spending time together. They bring out the worst in each other."

Zo imagined the two boys who were raised to hate one another, tiptoeing into Gryphon's tent with a pot of paint.

Zo looked around. "Where is your new guard?"

Gryphon offered a lazy shrug. "They'll find me eventually."

"And have they found the missing guards from last night?"

Gryphon shrugged. "They probably deserted to avoid punishment for leaving their post."

For someone who had just faced the possibility of losing a hand, Gryphon didn't seem at all repentant. Didn't he want this to work out? Couldn't he even *try* to build trust with Laden and her people? Zo took a deep breath. "We need to talk."

"I'm sorry I lied last night," he blurted. "I didn't want Laden to catch you in your lie about leaving me at my tent. And I knew that if I told him I was out walking the camp on my own before the fire, he wouldn't have believed me."

She'd assumed as much, and she didn't want to hurt him by coming right out and accusing him of anything, but the coincidence of those men and the fire was too great to ignore.

"I didn't start it, Zo, if that's what you're wondering." His voice took on a harder edge. "As much as I can't stand being surrounded by Wolves every moment of every day, I would never compromise your and Joshua's situation."

He cupped her face. The intensity of his clear brown eyes seeped into her. "Trust me." A pause, and a softer, "Please."

Zo flinched as his fingers brushed the irritated skin that ran in a line from temple to jaw. Until then, she'd been able to hide the burn with her unbound hair.

Gryphon gently tucked her hair behind her ear and sucked in a sharp breath. "You're hurt. Who did this?" And then the lion was back, the gentleness of before replaced by the sleeping beast within.

"No one. I'm not really sure how it happened." Zo didn't understand Millie's explanation earlier, and she wasn't prepared to accept that she was broken as a healer.

"I believed you the first time, but this?" He turned away and began pacing. "Someone is trying to punish me. Your bruises. The fire last night. Now this burn ... " He stopped pacing, and the hurt that filled his expression—sadness and frustration magnified by the stained black tears painted on his face—was too much.

"You're protecting one of these animals," he snarled.

"These *animals* are my people, Gryphon, and you know me better than to believe that I would ever let someone hurt me and stay quiet."

They stared at each other, both seething, for several long moments before Raca found them. She wore buckskin pants, a vest, and a braided leather cord around her forehead. A lone black feather tied at the side of the cord was lost in the backdrop of her dark hair. "The company has gathered. Everyone's waiting on you." She looked between them and frowned. "Is everything all right?"

"Be right there," Zo managed, and Raca, after only a small hesitation, left them.

When they were alone again, Gryphon took Zo's hand and brought it to his lips. "I don't want to part like this." He kissed her hand again. "Please tell me what's going on."

Zo couldn't meet his eyes, but eventually the words just spilled over. "Millie says I'm broken." She chewed on her bottom lip, stalling to give her emotions time to settle. "She says that, somehow, the ailments of my patients are carrying over to me."

Gryphon frowned. "My ribs." He reached out and gently ran his hands over her bruised ribs. "Those men burned in the fire last night."

Zo nodded. "I didn't want to tell you because I'm still trying to hide from it myself." She looked up at him. "Who am I, if not a healer?"

Gryphon cupped the back of her neck and, before Zo had even a moment to prepare herself, bent down and touched his lips to hers. It was a tentative kiss. A brush and a peck. She tilted her head a fraction to one side and threaded her arms around his torso as he pressed his palms into her back, bringing her closer. The kiss deepened, its rhythm soft and deliciously sweet. Her heart fluttered when he abandoned her lips and moved along her jaw to her ear. "I *really* don't want you to go." His deep voice resonated strong and tender, sending a chill down her spine.

Zo squeezed him closer, tucking her chin and pressing her head into his chest so she could hear the steady rhythm of his beating heart. Doubt whispered in the recesses of her mind, lingering in the background of her thoughts. A pest that wouldn't fully be ignored. *He thinks my people are animals.*

Zo held fast to Gryphon's hand as they hiked up to the slot canyon at the northern end of the valley. Joshua and Sani followed behind, arguing about whether speed or strength was more important in hand-to-hand fighting, while Zo tried not to think about leaving.

They reached the high bench of the foothills and were met by the small company traveling to the Kodiak Caves consisting of Talon and Raca, as well as Ikatou and two of his Kodiak clansmen.

"Are you ready?" Ikatou asked Zo.

Gryphon's hand tightened around hers and she nodded. "Lead the way."

They hiked north until they reached the tall fissure in the canyon wall that marked the slot canyon. On either side of the gap, two columns of Ravens, clad in full warrior garb, waited. Each Raven had black tears painted on his face and a bow in hand. The warriors were all fixed on Raca and Talon, the future leaders of their clan. Brother and sister walked shoulder to shoulder through the tunnel of Raven. Ikatou and his two men followed single file, leaving Laden, Gryphon, Joshua, and Zo.

"I want to hear *everything* about the Kodiak Cave. I'm so jealous you get to see them," said Joshua. "Be safe."

He stepped in and hugged Zo, but she held onto him a moment longer and said, "Please watch out for—"

"Tess," Joshua finished. "I know. I always do." His lopsided, freckled smile turned Zo's heart to mush.

Laden stepped up next to offer her a warm hug. She inhaled his familiar scent. "Thank you for doing this, Zo. Remember, the goal is to get Murtog to join us for the *Ostara*. You will need to convince him to leave within the next four days to make it back in time."

Zo nodded.

"And Zo?" Laden cupped her cheek as though she were still a child. "Be safe, and watch that tongue of yours. The Kodiak can be … unpredictable."

When Laden had stepped away enough for Gryphon to come forward, Gryphon lifted his arms and Zo filled the space before the weight of his embrace folded around her. Zo laid her head on one of his broad shoulders. "I will miss you every moment you're away." He whispered so only she could hear, "Remember, you are far more important than Murtog or anyone else. Come back with or without the chief's agreement." He took the time to kiss the backs of each hand, where the blood oath scars had formed, then cupped his hand around the back of her neck and pressed his forehead to hers. "If you're not back in seven days, I'm coming after you."

"Gryphon!" Zo started, but he gently covered her mouth. "No arguments."

Tears pricked the corners of her eyes and she quickly batted them away. She pressed up onto her tiptoes to kiss his warm lips.

Laden, standing a few feet away, cleared his throat, and Zo forced her body to step away from Gryphon's. The final member of their travel party, she walked through the tunnel of Raven to join the others. Row by row, the Raven in the line turned to face her with military exactness. When she reached the slot canyon with the others, the heavily feathered Raven Chief stepped forward and said, "May the winds carry you and bring you safely h … home." He stumbled over the last word. A lance of pain shot across his face.

Thanks to the Ram, the Raven no longer had a home. They could never go back to their sacred Nest now that the Ram knew its location. Zo's heart ached for the man. For his whole clan.

The chief cupped his hands around his mouth and released a shrill *caw*. At the same moment, bow strings stretched back, loaded with the Raven's most deadly weapon. Arrows flew high in both directions in exquisite unison and landed in almost perfect lines a hundred yards away.

Zo looked back to find Gryphon staring, not at the impressive show of skill from the Raven but directly at her. So handsome and strong. So clearly concerned for her wellbeing.

She lifted a hand and waved, but then had no choice but to follow the line of travelers through the slot canyon, Gryphon disappearing from sight.

Chapter Thirteen

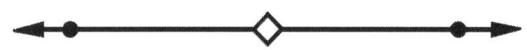

Laden clapped Gryphon on the shoulder. "Time for us to get to work, son. Staring at that rock wall won't bring her back any sooner."

Gryphon nodded and walked with Laden back down the foothills toward the camp. The first horn would sound soon, signaling training.

"It's taken some rearranging, but I finally have your first commission of men."

"How many?" Gryphon asked.

"Forty. All Wolves."

Fantastic.

"A few of my lieutenants and I will observe you for the next few days."

Gryphon scoffed. "If you don't trust me, why give me a band of men to train? Half of them will assume I started that fire last night."

"And the other half will think you killed your guard to do it," Laden conceded. "But you didn't start that fire, Gryphon. I think we both can agree that someone in this camp wanted it to look like you had." He walked beside him with fingers linked behind his back. "The

Wolves aren't as ignorant as you might think. I've been employing some old Ram training tactics with only the Wolves in the camp."

"What do you know of Ram training tactics?"

Laden ignored him. "Several of my officers are doing their best to teach proper technique, but no one has any actual fighting experience with this type of warfare." He paused for a few more steps then said, "To win this war, we have to defeat the Ram phalanx. And the only way to do that … "

Gryphon stopped walking. They'd reached the upper fields and a row of young maize divided their paths. "You can't be serious."

Laden nodded, his face a mask of solemnity.

"You want me to teach your men to fight as a phalanx?" Gryphon's jaw fell open. It was a type of warfare that demanded absolute trust, flawless execution, and an insane amount of discipline. It took a good phalanx years to learn to work well together—time the Allies certainly didn't have. "What you're asking is impossible. And even if they did learn the technique, there is no way they could match shields with the Ram."

"We've actually been training for some time now," Laden said, conversationally. "Instead of your typical twenty-men mess unit, we will have forty. A wall ten wide but four deep, instead of two." Laden went on to describe in detail some of the training they'd already undergone as they resumed their walk to the training field.

Gryphon still couldn't believe what he was hearing. "Four deep to counter the notorious drive and push of the Ram … " he mused out loud. Gryphon had to admit that if there was one advantage the Allies had over the Ram, it was their numbers. But still …

As they approached the training field where hundreds of men sparred, a growing sense of dread filled Gryphon's chest. "And my men? I doubt they'll be pleased to have a young Ram for a captain."

When the men on the training field spotted Laden, all sparring ceased. Laden's officers formed a clean line before a group of ragtag men of various ages and sizes.

They looked more like farmers than soldiers. Which, Gryphon had to admit, they probably were. Inside the Gate, Gryphon's only job had been to train and become a warrior. These men fought only when necessity demanded and they appeared weak for it.

Laden turned to face Gryphon, probably sensing his unease. "Relax, Striker. You'll do just fine. Ignore my officers. Ignore the rest of the training field. Just focus on your men."

Flexing his jaw, Gryphon spoke in a low voice so only Laden could hear, "These men hate me, sir. This isn't going to work."

Laden narrowed his eyes. "They must raise Ram softer than I believed. I thought a Striker wasn't afraid of anything."

Gryphon narrowed his eyes at Laden. He knew the Commander was goading him, but his pride got the better of him regardless.

"Four lines!" Gryphon ordered, staring the Commander down.

Smiling, Laden crossed his arms.

Gryphon left his side to walk among the forty, noting the shortcomings and strengths of each man with a single sweep of his gaze. Mostly he saw fear.

Fear of battle.

Fear of losing families.

Fear of him.

Good, thought Gryphon. Fear might keep them alive.

"We have little time to master this, so pay attention. The Ram have the power to demolish the Valley of Wolves and destroy your homes and everyone you love … " He paused. "Unless you are strong enough to stop them."

One of the men stepped forward. He had a little bit of a belly, but strong arms and fire in his eyes. His nose sat crooked on his face. His chin laced with determination and his fists balled at his sides. "Why should we trust you? Ram don't betray their own."

There was a collective sharp intake of breath.

Gryphon stopped in front of the man and frowned. He actually respected the man for saying aloud what everyone else must be thinking. "Trust me or don't. It makes no difference to me, Wolf. But know this," he raised his voice so his entire company and the onlookers nearby could hear him, "I am your best hope for defeating the Ram."

Gryphon didn't wait for a response. This wasn't the time for meaningless talk. There was work to be done.

When Gryphon had spoken with Laden earlier, the Commander had compared their fighting strategy to that of the Ram on every point. How many times had the Commander survived contact with the Ram over the years without meeting his own death? His knowledge of Ram fighting techniques and stratagem was eerily accurate. Laden had even rambled about secret training tactics—things Gryphon had been taught to guard with his very life—like they were common knowledge.

"Link," Gryphon called. The men weren't expecting the command. They scrambled together, assembling a shield hedge so every man carried his shield on his left, guarding the man to his left. They carried six-foot spears on their right. This too was another page ripped from Ram battle tactics.

Gryphon walked the perimeter of the phalanx, instructing men to tighten gaps that might welcome hungry spears. Overall, they were better than he'd expected. Not a huge compliment, given his limited confidence, but at least it was a start.

"Forward ten," he called.

The phalanx moved ten paces forward in a synchronized mass. Gryphon ran before the wall of shields, threading his sword through the more obvious gaps, and calling out orders to "Guard your man!" and "Stay together!"

When they halted, the line of shields slammed to the ground in a heavy thump.

"Birds," Gryphon ordered.

The back rows of shields wove together to form a roof over their heads to deflect an aerial assault.

Gryphon had seen enough. "Stand down," he shouted. Forty

men relaxed their shields and looked smugly to Gryphon.

"Where are you weakest?" Gryphon asked as he paced the front line of the phalanx.

"On the right side," one of the men called out.

Gryphon nodded. "Because you guard the man at your left and trust the man on your right to guard you. It leaves the last man on the right the most vulnerable."

Gryphon looked to the man at the far right of the phalanx. He was a monster of a man, with a tree-trunk neck resting on a mountain of body. A Wolf in a Kodiak body.

"How long has this group been together?" asked Gryphon.

"Nine months," came the answer.

Gryphon swallowed. He and his brothers of the mess had been family. Some, like Zander, had been part of that family for almost two decades. These Wolves didn't have a prayer.

"Are any of you family? Longtime friends?"

A few scattered raised hands dotted the forty. "Come forward," said Gryphon. Various clusters of men worked their way to the front of the group. Gryphon could see some family resemblances. Brothers. Fathers. Uncles. Sons.

The way this group had been arranged made sense in a lot of ways. Putting the best fighters at the front, with the back line pushing them forward. Giving the right flank a giant of a man. Logically speaking, that was the wisest setup.

But when was war ever logical?

"Are these your sons?" Gryphon asked a man with a full, graying beard.

The man nodded. "Yes, sir. Justin is twenty. Isaac is sixteen."

Gryphon arranged the sixteen-year-old boy to the left of his father and the twenty-year-old brother to the left of the sixteen-year-old. "Father protects youngest son. Youngest son protects the big brother he likely worships."

Gryphon went about rearranging the whole troop into four lines, placing the closet kin together. Then he conducted a series of drills to test each new line. Instead of putting the strongest in the front, he placed the best shields there to protect the rest. In each line, he assigned a leader at the center to call orders. Instead of captains, he placed fathers, men who were used to being listened to, in command.

Once every line was occupied with a series of tasks, Gryphon stepped back to observe his men. None of them knew that the Ram would be marching in only a few short weeks. Many lives would be lost. Too many. He'd have to think of some way to keep them alive, some way to help them learn the phalanx well enough to defend themselves so they might have a sporting chance.

It would be so much easier to give up. What difference did it really make to him what happened after he was gone? Men die. The strong overtake the weak. It was the most ancient order of life. He was just one man walking to his own death. How could he make any sort of difference? Why should he try?

Laden appeared behind one of the lines of men. He walked slowly, but not without purpose, to Gryphon's side. "I like what you've done. Clever, given our time constraints."

"Commander?"

"Yes, son."

"How do you know so much about the Ram?"

Commander Laden regarded him carefully, his lips pinched together on one side. The scar covering his face morphed into something dark and gruesome. "I learned the same way you did, Striker. One beating at a time."

On the second day of their journey, Zo, Raca, Talon, Ikatou, and his two Kodiak companions traveled a game trail east through the hilly terrain. Pine and fir trees grew amongst quaking aspen whose leaves shivered in the wind. The whistling of the leaves grew and died with every gust. Zo caught herself unconsciously scraping at the skin around her thumb until it was raw and bleeding as she constantly scanned their surroundings.

The area wasn't known as the Kodiak Hills simply because the clan made their home nearby. Giant brown bears roamed this region. Ikatou explained they were especially aggressive in the spring because they'd just come out of hibernation—some with new cubs to protect and feed.

Zo wasn't the only one wary of these hills. Both Talon and Raca walked with bow in hand and arrows loosely nocked. But their caution was contradicted by the three Kodiaks' lack of it. Ikatou and his men laughed and jeered at one another, growing louder and louder the farther east they traveled—much to Zo's annoyance.

As the sun began to set, Ikatou led them off the game trail up the side of the mountain to a small wooden hut that sat in the middle of a steep slope. Zo clutched plants and tree roots to help pull her up the mountainside. The weight of her pack threatened to pull her backwards, forcing Zo at some points to lean forward, her stomach nearly pressed against the slope.

By the time they reached an old wooden structure, Zo's breath came heavy and her heart threatened to jump from her chest.

"What is this place?" she panted. The cabin seemed to grow out from the side of the mountain, with only three of its four walls visible. The rundown structure boasted a door and only a few small windows. The wood was worn and some of the plaster between the logs deteriorating.

"Our resting place for the night," Ikatou panted, pulling open the door to the cabin with a grunt. He held it for Zo and Raca, and let the other men follow him inside. Four squares of soft light filtered through the high windows. They did little to dispel the heavy shadows of the bare room.

"Let's gather some wood and get a fire going."

Zo hadn't noticed the small stone fireplace built into one of the corners of the room until she knew to look for it. They dropped their packs and headed for the door. "Stay close to the cabin," Talon said to Raca and Zo. They both nodded and joined the others to collect wood and kindling for a fire.

It wasn't long before the five sat inside the cabin with warm cheeks and full bellies—thanks in part to the handiwork of Raca's bow and a pair of rabbits who'd crossed its path.

"Who would build a home in such a place?" Talon asked, as he threaded his hands behind his head and leaned back against his pack. The fire whizzed and popped as Zo studied the beautiful flames. She'd wondered the same thing and was glad Talon asked.

"Before the Ram desecrated our caves, men were stationed here to monitor this entrance into the Cave," said Ikatou. "I think my people are too lost and scattered, too demoralized mentally and too shamed by their defeat from the Ram, to bother guarding it."

Zo perked. "Did you just say this was an entrance?" She looked around the room again, uncertain.

Ikatou pulled back his bedroll and threaded his fingers into two holes in the ground. The floorboards groaned as he pulled up a large square of the floor to reveal a gaping black hole.

Zo, Raca, and Talon crawled over to get a better look into the dark abyss, but all that was visible were the top three rungs of a ladder.

"This is the entrance to the Cave?" Raca asked.

Ikatou laughed. "It's more of a back door. Chief Murtog's father found it by accident while hunting as a boy, close to Joshua's age. He fell down the shaft and broke both of his legs. Luckily he wasn't alone. It wasn't long after that they discovered the tunnel belonged to part of the great network of Kodiak Caves. The cabin was built as a marker and outpost for weary travelers, but this entrance is rarely used anymore."

"I don't understand. Why are you bringing us through the back door? We are ambassadors for the Raven and Wolves. Shouldn't we come through the main entrance?" asked Raca. She pulled her legs close to her chest and studied Ikatou with her calm, often unnerving demeanor. With the flickering light dancing on her brown skin and her hair brushed and hanging around her shoulders, she posed a striking figure.

Ikatou's companions grunted something to one another, and Ikatou shot them a dark look.

"What is it?" asked Talon, looking between the three Bears. "What aren't you telling us?"

Ikatou leaned over to place another log on the fire. Whatever secrets he kept, it was clear he wasn't ready to divulge them yet.

Zo reached out and placed a scarred hand on his forearm. The bear flinched under her touch, as though burned by the contact. "Tell us, Ikatou. You claim to value honesty. Tell us the truth."

Ikatou met her gaze and offered her a firm nod. "We are taking this entrance because we don't know if you will be welcomed in the Caves."

Talon and Raca exchanged a sharp glance. Zo guessed, given their travels together, they were quite adept at communicating without words.

Ikatou continued, "There are rumors that since Murtog's inaction after the raid, factions of Kodiak have taken to self-governing. We've been gone long enough that we don't know who is loyal to the chief and who is not."

Talon seemed to hold his composure by a thin thread. "Did you tell Laden of this?"

Ikatou slowly shook his head. "He would not have sent you if I had."

Nostrils flaring, Talon's voice bordered on shouting. It was the closest Zo had ever come to seeing a Raven lose his temper. "You expect us to follow you into that hole, when you have no idea whether or not we will be received or killed on sight?"

"Talon," Zo warned.

"An attack on either my sister or myself will be viewed by my clan as an act of war." He sat back and folded his arms. "We will not enter the cave under these circumstances."

Zo looked between the men, her thoughts running out of control. Laden said the Allies couldn't help Ikatou free his family unless Murtog was convinced to join the cause. And if Laden didn't help Ikatou, Zo's ridiculous blood oath would be broken.

Pinching the bridge of her nose, Zo said, "Let's just slow down for a minute. Tell us more about the cave. How many people will we see? Where exactly is Murtog?"

Ikatou explained that the caves were a network of tunnels with large caverns spread throughout. Murtog's den was located in the heart of the mountain. "I have no way of knowing who or what we will see. I haven't been inside the caves for almost two years. But I know I can get you to the chief."

Talon shook his head, arms still crossed. "Not good enough."

Ikatou's nostrils flared.

Zo had seen first-hand what happened when Kodiak lost their temper. If a fight broke out in this small cabin, no amount of peace talks would ever unite the Raven and Kodiak. There was just too much pride at stake, too many differences dividing them already, to withstand such a thing.

"I'll go down," Zo shouted. "My hair is darker than most Wolves. Even the Ram believed I was a Kodiak when I told them."

One of Ikatou's men snorted, not helping her case.

"If we go at night," said Zo, "we'll meet fewer people. Once we know the caves are safe and announce ourselves to Murtog's guard, we can come back and get Talon and Raca."

Ikatou nodded as he stared into the fire. "It could work," he finally said.

"Why do I feel like you're about to attach a 'but' to the end of that statement?" asked Zo.

Ikatou turned to Raca and Talon. "I realize my people are known for a lot of things, many of which might be considered negative in your mind. Where you value stealth, we prefer to meet a problem face on. Where you value a man's spirit, we value a man's might." He leaned forward. "But there is one thing I think our two clans have in common."

"What is that?" asked Talon.

"We honor the fearless."

Talon slowly rose to his feet, and by so doing caused everyone to follow. Zo braced herself, standing between the two men with hands partially outstretched.

"Are you calling me a coward?" Talon asked.

Ikatou, for once, seemed completely calm. He shook his head. "I know you're not a coward, Bird. That's exactly my point. But if you stay hidden in this cabin with the hope that the chieftain of the mighty Kodiak will waltz through his great halls to come to you, *he* will think you fearful. This is not a social call, Talon. You are asking him to stand with the Allies against our common enemy. This is a call to war. And it shouldn't be offered from a place of hiding."

Zo blinked, surprised by the conviction of Ikatou's words. She found herself nodding. This journey meant nothing if Murtog didn't agree to offer his support to the cause. They couldn't afford to have him think them weak.

Talon finally bowed his head. "For the sake of the cause, I'll join you. But we leave well before dawn, when more of your people are still asleep." He glanced over at Raca and Zo. "And the women stay here."

"No." Both Zo and Raca spoke at the same time and with the same fierce edge, leaving the four men in the company, Talon included, blinking back their surprise. "You listen to me, brother. We started this together. We will finish it together. Besides," she crossed her arms, "I have the better bow. If something does go wrong in there, you'll need me."

At that, Ikatou actually smiled. "For such a small person, you certainly speak with great conviction, little one."

"Never make the mistake of calling my sister small, Bear. Though her head might not come to the level of your chest, she is the largest person in this room," said Talon.

The group settled in for a few hours' sleep. Zo slept closest to the fire, with Raca lying next to her and Talon dividing the women from the Kodiak. He'd been kind to think of protecting Zo as well as his sister. Their relationship made her wish she'd had an older brother.

Beside her, Raca shifted onto her side, facing Zo. Her eyes fluttered open and met Zo's unintentional stare.

"Not tired?" the Raven girl asked.

Zo yawned her reply, "Too much on my mind."

Raca glanced over her shoulder at the snoring men, exhausted from two days of travel. She turned back to Zo and rested her head in her hand. "Want to talk about it?"

Zo shrugged. *Not really.*

"Is it about Gryphon?"

Zo's head snapped up, inspecting the Raven for any hint of emotion. She didn't like that Gryphon always seemed to be so close to Raca's thoughts. "I was thinking more about what a good brother Talon is to you."

The corners of Raca's mouth sank. She sighed and said, "Too good. His wife hates me right now."

"Why is that?"

Raca shuffled lower into her bedroll and stared up at the wooden rafters. "Because until I marry, I am my brother's responsibility. He and I have been traveling for weeks, visiting Laden and the Wolves, to find me a suitable spouse." She rolled her eyes. "I confess I haven't tried very hard. To be honest, I'm quite good at finding fault with men I'm supposed to consider marrying."

Zo scrunched her nose. At almost eighteen, Zo was approaching the age to consider such things, and Raca couldn't be that much older than her. "Why is that?"

Raca sighed. "It's foolish of me, I know, but I'd love not to have the pressure of marrying someone to benefit my clan. I'd love to … " Her voice trailed off, arm slung over her eyes, as if blocking out not just the light of the fire but the pressures of the world.

She rested like that for so long Zo thought she might have fallen asleep, but then Raca finished. "I'd love to marry someone for love, without outside motives." She rolled back over to Zo, her eyes now glistening. A tear leaked down her cheek. "When men see me they see only a position of influence. A game of political strategy. I want to be more than that. I'm just so tired of being invisible."

Chapter Fourteen

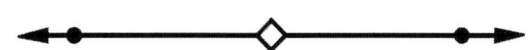

Laden was a traitor!

It was all Gryphon could think about as he trained his men the following day. Laden had actually lived and breathed the Ram way of life, then walked away to join, and eventually lead, the enemy.

Now that he knew the truth, Gryphon kicked himself for not seeing it sooner. Laden's coloring, his build—they were all common Ram traits. Even his face had the look of the Ram, though his heavy scarring had disguised the long nose and other telling features.

Of all people, Gryphon should have recognized him for what he was. He'd been a blind fool, but then so had the men of the camp. When a truth isn't expected, it is harder to see. He was almost positive the men of camp didn't know about Laden's Ram heritage.

If his suspicions were true—and he was almost positive they were—no one in camp knew Laden's secret. No one except Gryphon.

Why trust me?

At the end of a long day of training, the busy throng of soldiers bustled around the practice field. The sun had set, but Gryphon was a statue—a stubborn rock holding ground in a fast-moving river of people.

He and Commander Laden were the same. The revelation struck Gryphon like a boulder to the chest.

"Is everything all right?"

Gryphon looked up, surprised to meet the heavily hooded eyes of Commander Laden. Stubble cast an unruly salt-and-pepper blanket over the lower half of his face. He stood tall and proud, like any Ram warrior. But there was something different about him, an invisible burden Gryphon couldn't quite define. The mark of a man who understood pain.

"Walk with me," Laden commanded when Gryphon didn't respond.

The smell of roasting game and body odor wafted in the faint breeze as they weaved through the campfires. Men stood at attention as Commander Laden walked past with his hands clasped behind his back. If he noticed the gesture, it didn't show. Laden was the type of man who only looked forward.

Gryphon paused when they reached the Commander's tent, but Laden just kept walking. Jogging to catch up, Gryphon let the older Ram lead him out of the camp and into a thicket of young trees. The nighttime song of crickets filled the silence between them.

"How are your forty?" Laden asked conversationally, as he settled to the ground using a tree trunk for a backrest.

"Sloppy. Weak … " Gryphon ran a hand through his hair. "They don't stand a chance against a trained Ram mess unit."

Laden glanced up into the enormous sky. "Look at those stars, Gryphon." He sighed, never pulling his eyes from the heavens. "Makes a man feel his own insignificance."

Gryphon didn't look up. There was too much on his mind to think about stars. "Sir?"

Laden lifted a hand. "You want to know why I left. Don't you?"

This is what Gryphon liked most about the Commander: he seemed to know Gryphon's thoughts better than even he did at times. "Yes, sir. If you don't mind."

Laden rubbed his young beard, the coarse sound loud in the stillness of the night. "My wife had a difficult first pregnancy. She gave birth to a healthy baby boy. Every Ram father's dream." Laden smiled, but the expression slowly slipped off his face, like a raindrop weighing down a leaf.

"We didn't know there was another baby. The healers weren't in the room to help." Laden looked up at the night, but this time Gryphon could tell he wasn't really seeing the stars. "The cord was wrapped around her neck three times. My little girl couldn't get the air she needed because I lacked the skill to deliver her. I could tell that something was wrong after the first few weeks of her life. By the time she was six months old it was obvious she wouldn't pass another inspection." Ram children were constantly monitored to insure only the strongest children grew into adulthood.

He looked at Gryphon and frowned. "We named her Adelpha. She was beautiful."

"What became of her?" Gryphon gulped, thinking of Ajax's infant son.

"My wife's heart broke when she realized our daughter had suffered damage to her brain. She gave up. I think in her eyes, Adel had died already."

Laden crumpled a pinecone in his hand. "But Adel was our daughter. I refused to hand her over to Ram authorities. She wasn't perfect according to clan standards, but she was perfect to me."

Gryphon tried to imagine what it must have been like to know the society he'd served would kill his own child. He couldn't comprehend the pain. "So you took her away."

Laden cleared his throat. His hands shook as he wiped pinecone chips from his palms. "I left my wife and boy to save my little girl. I carried her out in a travel pack while leaving for an excursion with my mess. I gave her honeycomb so she wouldn't cry. A few of my brothers knew of my plans. They helped me conceal the child until I could sneak away. I went straight to the Wolves because I knew they had the best healers. I hoped they could do something for my little girl, even though I was a Ram."

"How did you two survive the journey?"

"We almost didn't. A pack of Wolves attacked us ten miles outside of their stronghold. I had Adel in a harness so I could easily carry her on my back while we traveled. I just had time to set her off the trail before they attacked." He pointed to the scars lining his face—the scars he'd hidden behind for years. "The Wolves brought me within an inch of death before they heard my daughter's cry. They took us to their healers. That is how I met Zo's mother."

Gryphon couldn't believe the irony. "Zo's mother saved your life."

"And you saved her daughter inside the Gate. A life for a life. The universe always manages to find balance."

"What ever became of Adel? Does she still live with the Wolves?"

Laden broke a thick stick over his knee. For the first time since Gryphon had known him, he looked wild and out of control. "She was killed in the same raid that killed Zo's parents five years ago. It seems Adel was destined to die by the hands of a Ram."

Gryphon was a statue again, even more so now, because he couldn't breathe. "I'm sorry," he managed.

"That's when I formed the Allies. I am a traitor. And proud to be one."

Gryphon didn't know how to respond to such an enormous admission. Words couldn't offer any balm to the pain of Laden's past, so Gryphon didn't speak. He just sat looking at the night sky with Laden, searching for answers that would not come.

"Wake up, Zo. It's time." Raca gently nudged Zo's shoulder.

Zo blinked the sleep from her eyes as she rolled over to attend to her bedroll and pack. Outside, the sky showed no sign of welcoming the day, and the chill air made her wish for another hour wrapped in her woolen blanket.

Ikatou pulled open the trapdoor in the floor and stepped aside to allow one of his brothers to climb down the ladder. As the bear disappeared into the darkness beyond, Ikatou gestured for the others to follow. When only he and Zo were left in the room he said, "You are the weakest member of the group. If you show bravery, the others will feed off your courage."

Zo nodded. She hadn't been too nervous until now. She placed a foot on the top rung of the ladder and accepted Ikatou's hand as she took the first steps into the darkness.

"More than anyone else, Murtog will see your blood oath as a sign of the Allies' commitment to the Kodiak. Whatever you do, don't cower in front of him. Though you are small, he must see you as a large, powerful person."

Zo nodded and, rung by rung, lowered herself into the black shaft of the Kodiak Caves. Above her, Ikatou mounted the ladder, pulling shut the trapdoor and snuffing out what little light the cabin had offered.

Never in Zo's life had she experienced such utter darkness. "Talon? Raca?" Zo whispered.

"You're almost at the bottom." Talon's voiced echoed all around her, taking on a ghoulish cadence. A hand touched her leg, another her arm, and finally her boots found purchase on the stone floor of the cave.

"It's cold down here." Her teeth chattered as she spoke.

Ikatou joined her at the bottom and the group huddled together around him. He pulled out a fist-sized stone that glowed warm yellow. I wondered if the natural properties of the stone made it glow or some other Kodiak mystery. The little light it offered was only enough to see the faces of those huddled around it.

Ikatou handed a bristled, knotted rope to the members of the company. Each knot in the rope formed a loop large enough to slip a hand through. He said, "It's dangerous to cast too much light around the caves, but there are places where the trail narrows and drops off on either side." He threaded his hand through one end of the rope and the rest followed his example. "From here on, no one talks. If we do this right, we should be able to get into the belly of the cave in about two hours."

Zo's spot on the rope put her second to last in the line, with a Kodiak behind her and Raca in front. Standing so far away from the glow of Ikatou's stone made seeing any part of the trail impossible. She clutched the rope around her wrist with one hand and held the other out to feel for jutting stone and winding cave walls. Occasionally the rope would tug from someone falling. Their muttered curses and gasps of surprise were fair warning that the way required extra caution.

Zo's outstretched hand connected with Raca's back, signaling the caravan had stopped. Whispers filled the cave and eventually Raca leaned toward her to pass along instructions.

"We're approaching the steam cavern. Ikatou said to lean against the rock at your left so we're ready if someone falls."

Zo swallowed hard, nodding even though she knew Raca couldn't see her. She passed the message on to the Kodiak behind her and doubled her grip on the rope as they descended deeper into the dark tunnel.

The faint smell of sulfur reached Zo's nose and the air grew wet and warm. Though she couldn't see the walls around her, she sensed the room widen into an area much larger than the tunnel they'd been traveling. She reached out to feel for the wall at her left and placed each footstep with care. Water dripped high above her head, echoing as it connected with stone to create a chorus of music that might have been soothing were it not for the slippery stone beneath her boots and the blind drop only inches away.

The deeper into the cavern they traveled, the more intense the heat. Water beaded down her back and ran from her brow into her eyes. The air turn so thick she could barely draw it through her lungs. Even if there were light, she doubted she'd be able to see anything through the thick steam surrounding them.

A sharp tug on the rope accompanied a ripple of gasps and one deep cry of surprise. Zo lurched forward, her nails raking stone to stop the rope from pulling her off the narrow ledge. The force of the weight dragged her wrist down and brought her to kneel on the trail.

"Please," came Raca's desperate cry. "Help us."

Raca, and she assumed Talon, hung off the side of the ledge. Their combined weight threatened to tear Zo's arm from its socket.

"Take her free hand!" the Kodiak behind Zo commanded.

Unable to see Raca, Zo reluctantly reached out into the darkness as the rope pulled and swayed with Raca and Talon's weight. Zo's fingertips brushed against a hand, but failed to grasp it.

The steam suffocated. Zo couldn't breathe.

"We have Talon," Ikatou whisper-yelled from somewhere ahead. "But we can't lift them both."

Behind her, the Kodiak growled, probably wishing she could trade him places.

"My hand! I can't hold on much longer," cried Raca.

Zo leaned even farther over the ledge, one hand batting the air around where Raca should have been.

And then, finally, their hands connected. "I've got her!" she gasped, choking on the thick air.

Huge arms wrapped around her waist. "Don't let go," the Kodiak whispered near her ear. Zo nodded, unable to speak, though she knew he couldn't see her. The Kodiak lifted both her and Raca into the air, supporting Zo as she clung to Raca.

The girl wiggled and kicked to find the ledge.

When Zo was high enough for her feet to find purchase on the ledge, she helped pull Raca until she collapsed on the ground at Zo's feet.

Both Talon and Raca whispered reassurances to one another between heavy breaths. Zo reached out and rested a hand on Raca's back as the girl stood.

"Forward," Ikatou's whisper filled the cavern, jumping off walls to reach them. In all of the commotion of the last few minutes, how much noise had they made? Would the sound travel far enough to wake the sleeping bears within the mountain?

Zo wiped the sweat from her forehead with the hand not bound to the rope and shuffled forward. Water droplets ricocheted off the floor of the steamy cavern. The vast room hung in eerie silence.

The path sloped downward. The trail widened and the air changed from moist warmth to cool again. In the almost total darkness, Zo found it difficult to tell how long they traveled. Minutes might have been hours. Her nerves were frayed, every step tedious.

Down, down, down they walked. Deep into the belly of the mountain. Zo shivered—extra cold thanks to the moisture that hung on her clothes and chilled her skin from the steam caves.

The rope rubbed the skin around her wrist raw. The tips of her fingers burned from fumbling against the sides of the cave, and she tried desperately not to think about the thousands of pounds of stone above them. When the trail finally leveled off, she thought she might cry with relief.

Faint blue-gray light filtered through what must have been a massive skylight high above the ground, set in the middle of a cavernous dome at least 300 yards in diameter. The blue light reflected off a steaming pond below, as though the Kodiak lived in the gutted cavity of a sleeping volcano.

Caught up in the wonder of her surroundings, Zo didn't notice the black line of shadows standing ten yards in front of them until a torch was lit.

Zo shielded her face from the light as her eyes adjusted.

Five bare-chested men stood apart from one another, their beefy arms hanging relaxed but ready at their sides. Black hair fell past their shoulders, tied back with twine. Their feet were bare but they wore swaths of brown fur on their calves and wrists.

The torchbearer came out to meet Ikatou. The two men stood practically nose-to-nose, evaluating without words.

Finally the torchbearer reached out an arm and cupped the back of Ikatou's neck. Their foreheads pressed together, noses nearly kissing. "You were wise to come through the cabin entrance, brother." The corner of his lip hitched up into a friendly, handsome smile.

Zo felt her body relax.

"Who are your guests?" The man's whisper filled the cavern. No wonder the Kodiak didn't approve of secrets; no conversation within these caves could be truly private with these acoustics.

The man approached Zo, Talon, and Raca with a frown. Zo knew their size alone was enough to label them anything but Kodiak.

"Wolf and Raven messengers for Murtog."

The man shook his head. "The chief will not be pleased."

"He needs to hear what we have to say."

The heavily hooded brows of the Kodiak furrowed. "He will hear nothing from you, Ikatou. You know this."

Ikatou nodded. "Please. Help us speak to him." He looked around the empty cavern. "Before the others awaken."

The man stood firm, unrelenting.

Ikatou marched over to Zo and raised the backs of her hands to the firelight. "This is important, Poi. For the sake of our people, I beg your help."

The torchbearer approached Zo and met her eye before taking her hand to examine the new scars. He looked up again at Zo, his gaze deepening into a question he must not have felt qualified to ask.

With a few quick hand gestures, his men fanned out to surround their small company. "I'll take you. But I cannot promise that he will see you."

Chapter Fifteen

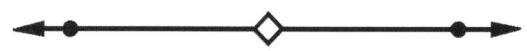

L aden cleared his throat and added. "I've told you my story, boy. Now you tell me yours."

"Sir?"

"I want to know what you've been keeping from me to preserve your loyalty to the Ram."

Gryphon's mouth hung open. "How … "

"How do I know?" Laden shrugged. "I've become quite good at reading people. Honorable men are especially easy to decipher. You have the decency to look ashamed every time I mention the future, which tells me you don't really plan to stay with us."

Gryphon cast his eyes to the ground. He'd considered telling Laden everything last night before the fire. It was the only way to protect Zo. But telling Laden now, after he'd already called his bluff, felt more like getting caught in a lie than coming forward with the truth. That small distinction mattered to him.

"What I can't understand is why you'd come all this way for Zo only to leave her." Laden paused, regarding him with his penetrating glare. "Were you even planning to tell her you were leaving?"

Gryphon's carefully guarded expression slipped. "You have no idea what you're talking about, old man." He turned to leave, more flustered than he cared to admit, when a heavy hand clamped down on his shoulder. "Don't be a fool, boy." Commander Laden seemed to choose each word with careful precision. "Don't break the poor girl's heart. She's already been to hell and back."

Gryphon closed his eyes and bit back a curse, but he didn't pull away.

"As much as you don't want to admit it, we are the same, son. More heart than prudence. The fact that you're standing here in my camp proves as much."

Gryphon turned around. "I'm not the one building an army to kill our people." Gryphon grimaced at his own duplicity. *I'm just training that army.*

Laden's mouth formed a thin white line. "Despite what you think, I will do everything in my power to protect the Ram from high casualties. I want to find a way to end this conflict without completely destroying them."

"Will you swear to that?" Gryphon asked.

"If I do, will you spill your secret?"

The blood oath. Zo's life in the balance.

Laden sighed. "You're a smart lad, Gryphon. Surely you can see the crimes of the Ram. Change must happen. Justice demands it."

Unable to disagree, yet hating himself for what he was about to say, Gryphon met Commander Laden's eye with steady appraisal. "What I'm about to tell you will make the Ram vulnerable."

Laden leaned in. "I'm listening."

"Your word," Gryphon insisted. "I need your word of honor that you will do your best to protect the innocent."

Laden sighed. "That fact that you even have to ask shows how little you know me." He stuck out his hand, shaking Gryphon's. "On my honor, I will preserve and protect the innocent Ram, including women, children, and others who do not wish to fight us."

A weight lifted from Gryphon, and he felt his body relax for the first time since entering the Allied Camp. No matter how far he strayed, he couldn't bring himself to completely abandon his clan—flawed as they were.

"What I tell you, I tell in the faith that you will use this information to help free Zo of this blood oath."

Laden arched a brow in interest.

"A few days before reaching your camp, one of my mess brothers visited me while Zo and the others slept." Gryphon went on to explain the favor Ajax asked and the promise made.

Fury etched hard lines across Laden's face, tightening his arms down to flexed fists.

"Ajax is the reason Zo is still alive," Gryphon explained. "If it weren't for my decision to leave, none of this would have happened. Getting Zo out of the Gate and coming here … it was the right thing to do. But I can't survive the guilt of knowing I've ruined the lives of my brothers. I can't sit by and do nothing. Not when I can fix things."

Gryphon wondered if Laden could see through his skin, deep into the recesses of his mind where all of his private thoughts were buried.

"You underestimate Barnabas's drive for power," said Laden. "Do you honestly believe your sacrifice will make everything go back to the way it was before? You think you can march up to the Gate and Barnabas will forget his anger toward the men of your mess?"

In the distance, Gryphon heard men laughing over their evening meal. It was odd to think people still laughed anymore.

"I'm not marching to the Gate." Gryphon took a deep, fortifying breath. What he said next would take him from being a deserter to a traitor. Men would die. Their fates would be sealed with only a few words from him.

"I agreed to meet Barnabas and his men where the rivers converge just north of the Valley of Wolves in exactly nineteen days."

Laden stood completely still, no doubt sifting through a hundred different scenarios at once. "Barnabas will come this far south?"

"Not just Barnabas … "

Then Laden, a man so sure of everything and everyone, staggered. "The Great Move." His eyes widened. "So soon?"

Gryphon nodded. "Barnabas is bringing everyone. Even the Nameless."

"Barnabas was always one for a show. He'll want his whole army to watch you die for defying him. The perfect form of *entertainment* for his men before they move on to the Valley to attack the Wolves." At that he looked up. "But this wouldn't be just another raid. This will be an invasion."

A cold chill shot up Gryphon's spine. He hated these Wolves and everything they represented. But invasion meant death. Children. Women. Elderly. None would be safe from Barnabas and the Ram spear. And this wouldn't be one lone pack. It would be an entire clan.

Laden walked forward, resting his hand on Gryphon's shoulder, meeting his eyes with fire. "We can't let the Ram reach the Valley of Wolves."

And just like that, Gryphon's anger and hatred melted, because this really wasn't about his prejudices. It was about the sanctity of life and the need to preserve it. He felt himself nodding, and agreed. "I know."

"There really is only one solution to this problem," said Laden. "The time has come for the Allies to leave our camp and march against the Ram. You need to meet Barnabas, as planned. We'll use the spectacle as a way to free the Nameless and any others seeking refuge from the Ram, the families of your mess brothers included."

Spectacle?

Gryphon blanched. He hadn't expected Laden to show such little regard for his life. But then again, this was the man who wittingly sent Zo into the Gate as a spy.

"Use my meeting to buy the Kodiak time to free their people

and the rest of the Nameless. When I leave, I need to know Zo's commitment to Ikatou and his men is fulfilled."

Laden, finally, had the decency to look ashamed. "That is a mighty sacrifice."

"Whether I die by the ax in a few weeks or from an arrow in a year, it makes no difference to me. Death will come. The only thing I can control is whether I am honorable in this life. I will not live with the guilt of knowing I could have done something to stop this war."

"Is that really what you want, Gryphon?"

"I want peace. Peace of mind and peace for the region. And if … if I had a chance at life, I'd want to share that peace with Zo. That is what I will fight for, Commander. That is my religion, clan, and purpose."

Shadows gathered beneath Commander Laden's weary eyes. With a reluctant nod, the commander thrust out his hand and waited for Gryphon to close the handshake. "I will do my part. I will send dispatch to alert the Wolves to prepare for invasion. All will be decided at the *Ostara* when the Wolf Alpha, Chief Naat, and—if Zo can work a miracle—Murtog join us."

Gryphon offered a short bow and turned to leave.

"Gryphon!" Laden called, causing Gryphon to freeze in place. He turned his head but not his body. "Yes, sir?"

"You are a good man."

Gryphon tried to swallow but his throat was too dry. He nodded and walked away, hoping his trust in the Commander wasn't misplaced.

They left the giant cavern and entered a wide tunnel filled with glowing stones, similar to the one Ikatou carried, embedded in the wall. The gleaming stones spiraled floor to ceiling in one giant coil that gave the illusion they were walking on air in a star-filled sky.

Though the lights were dim and the ground barely visible, Zo allowed herself to calm in the presence of such unexpected beauty. She turned to Ikatou and asked, "What are they?"

"Moonstones," he said, his voice barely carrying over the quiet echo of their footsteps. "A sacred stone reserved for royalty. This is the hall of stars, leading to the exalted one. The man in the sky is our maker and supreme leader, but his chief exacts his will."

Zo jogged a little to walk shoulder to shoulder with Ikatou. "Do you think of Murtog as a holy man?"

Ikatou choked on what might have been a shot of laughter. "No," he finally managed. "He is just a man. Flawed as the rest of us. But as our ruler, he has our oaths of fealty. It is the reason no one has ever tried to overthrow him. We would die before breaking such an oath."

"Even if he is a poor leader?" asked Zo.

With the faint light of the moonstones, Zo just made out his nod. It seemed to take all of his self-discipline to offer it. "Many are frustrated by Murtog's inaction to face the Ram. Some, like myself, have left to take matters into their own hands, but I still keep my oath of fealty to the chief. Without my word and honor, I am nothing, and neither is my family."

At the end of the hall they came to a large set of wooden doors where two guards stood as giant sentinels. The concentration of moonstones around the doors illuminated the guards clearly.

"What is this, Poi?" one of the sentinels asked as he scanned their company.

"Messengers from the Allied Camp," said Poi. "They come with word from Commander Laden with the voice of the Raven and Wolf."

"And the deserters?" the sentinel asked. Ikatou stepped forward, ready to rip the man's head from his neck.

"What of you, Bator? What man allows his family to be taken

without a fight?" Ikatou said each word with slow, careful intention. "Isn't that true desertion?"

Poi pushed his way between the two men just as the sentinel reared back to strike.

"Enough!" Poi said. "Now open these doors."

The guard crossed his arms. "You know the chief will not see them."

"Will you take the choice from him? Or have you joined the filth that would abandon their oaths to do as they please?" said Ikatou.

The guard glared at Ikatou, clearly despising the space between them. With a grunt he stepped aside, and Poi pulled the highly polished latch on the door. Hinges whined. Flickering torchlight danced along the floors and walls as Zo shuffled into the barren receiving room behind Ikatou, Talon, and Raca. She looked back to realize the others hadn't followed. Perhaps they didn't wish to see Murtog in his wrath at being disturbed. "This room leads to his private chamber. I'll announce you," said Poi. He approached the chief's bedchamber door like one might a wounded wild animal. As one of Murtog's guards, Zo assumed they'd have something of a relationship.

If Poi was worried …

"Sir?" Poi knocked. "You have company."

Nothing. Not a sound beyond the quiet murmur of the torches fastened to the walls.

Poi cleared his throat and straightened. Rolling back his shoulders, he didn't bother using a quiet tone. "Chief Murtog. May I enter?"

Again, no response.

Next to Zo, Raca adjusted her weight from foot to foot, humming with agitated energy.

Poi turned back to them, an apology fixed to his kind face. "You may have to wait here a bit. I don't recommend going back out there." He pointed to the door from which they'd just entered. "I'll have some food delivered in a few hours once the sun is up. In the meantime, I suggest you settle in."

"This is ridiculous!" said Raca. "We're just supposed to wait here and hope he comes out?"

Poi had the decency to frown as he dropped his gaze to the floor. "My apologies. But it is best. If he doesn't come out, I'd be happy to escort you back to the cabin at nightfall when I can guarantee your safety."

"Not a chance." Raca stomped over to the door of the chief's private quarters and yanked on the handle.

The entire room took a giant inhale of breath, but Zo was the only one to follow as she shoved her way into the room, pushing the door with so much force it banged against the opposite wall. "I am the daughter of Chief Naataain and the anointed princess of the Nest," Raca's raspy, melodic voice filled the room, bouncing off walls. Demanding to be heard. "I have traveled for several days to see you, and will be received with some degree of—"

Her words died on her tongue as she and Zo took in the scene.

The smell of sweat and stale food hit her like a punch to the face. A quick scan of the room showed weapons and hunting trophies lining the walls at crooked angles. A dressing bureau stood opposite the bed with doors open and clothing scattered on the floor. In the far corner, the low-burning embers of a fire cracked and whistled in a large fireplace tall enough for Zo to walk into without even ducking.

A man sat not on one of the grand, fur-trimmed chairs positioned before the fireplace, but on a three-legged stool. His large, rounded back faced them. An elaborate network of swirling ink rose and fell over contours of thick muscle across his back and shoulder. He's sat so completely still that Zo had to wonder if he was breathing.

The man stared into the fire with forearms resting on knees. Long corded hair was tied back by a strip of leather. Zo pressed against the stone wall, the *feeling* of the room so pungent she nearly buckled under its weight.

Pain. Loss. Misery. Regret. Sorrow. And most of all, *mourning.*

She'd never experienced such a visceral reaction to a person's emotions by simply standing in his presence.

Raca's features hardened and her fists balled as she stood in all her five-foot glory. A true warrior princess prepared to rip the head off of this man at her earliest opportunity.

"Leave me." With his back still to them, Zo had yet to see Murtog's face, but his deep, rumbling order left little room for discussion.

"I would sooner put an arrow through my foot," said Raca, crossing her arms defiantly before her.

Zo caught a glimpse of Talon in the doorway. He'd removed his bow from his back and held his free hand near his ear, prepared to reach for an arrow. Poi and Ikatou stood behind him, equally prepared to prevent him from doing just that.

At Raca's declaration, Murtog finally lifted his head and turned to glare at her.

Zo couldn't help the gasp that escaped her lips.

Murtog the widower was young ... and handsome.

He kicked his stool out from under him and it crashed into several pieces against the back of the fireplace. "How *dare* you!" he growled, his voice filling the whole room, doubling over itself as it bounced off stone.

Zo took a cautious step toward the door, but Raca marched up to him, coming toe to toe with the man easily double her width and so tall she had to crane her neck to meet his eyes.

"We have an urgent message from the Allies and my father. You will either hear us or bring down the ire of the entire region upon your clan."

He blinked at her, struggling to comprehend the gall of such a tiny, fearsome creature. Finally, as though surprising even himself by the decision, he walked over to his bed, snatched a tunic that had been thrown there, pulled it over his head, and while fastening a leather belt around his waist called over Raca's head, "The cowards whimpering behind the door may enter." He looked over his shoulder as he made his way to one of the large chairs in the corner of the room. "But only if you possess a fraction of this girl's grit."

Talon pushed away the hands holding him back and entered with head held high. He gave Raca a furious look and stopped at her side. "Honored Chieftain." He offered Murtog a clipped bow. "I am Talon, son of Chief Naat." He cleared his throat, nodding to Raca. "My sister has had a long journey and *forgets herself.*" He grounded out the last two words.

Murtog nodded, acknowledging the introduction as Ikatou came forward and dropped before his chief on one knee, with head bowed in deep supplication. "My chief."

Muscles in Murtog's neck danced, his cheeks flexing and unflexing as he seemed to struggle to hold his rage.

He finally spoke through gritted teeth. "Rise. Your gesture is a lie."

Ikatou stood, but didn't lift his head. "I have never lied to you, my chief. Even before I left, I told you my plans. In your mercy, you didn't command me to stay."

"But you left, all the same."

Ikatou raised his head and his words took on a harder edge. "They were my family, Murtog. If *she* had been taken, you would have gone after her too."

A mighty roar erupted from Murtog. His fist flew through the air, connecting against Ikatou's cheek with enough force to knock the Kodiak onto his back. "Get out!" he commanded. "All of you!" He moved as though to strike Ikatou again, but Zo, out of a healer's instinct, leapt in front of him and, without thinking, thrust her hands against his chest.

"Stop!" Zo shouted. Then softer, she added, "If you care anything for your clan, you will hear what we've come to tell you." She pushed as much calm into him as she could muster. *Peace. Patience. Respite.*

Murtog's nostrils flared as he sucked air into his lungs. His stance relaxed. The angry lines cutting through his face softened. He lifted one of Zo's hands and examined the raised scars. Then he glanced down at Ikatou, who still lay on the ground with a hand pressed to his swelling cheek. "A blood oath?"

Ikatou nodded. He took his time climbing to his feet. Zo couldn't blame him. She'd check his pupils later to see if he'd concussed from the blunt attack.

"We have much to discuss," said Ikatou.

Chapter Sixteen

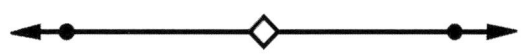

E<i>ighteen days.</i>
Gryphon stared at the ceiling of his tent, resenting Laden, Ikatou, and Ajax. All three were responsible for his misery. Days wasted without Zo here beside him. His arms literally ached with her absence.

Joshua and Sani sat in the corner of the tent, bickering as usual. They hadn't intended for their whispered argument to wake him, but he'd been up since they first started their latest contest.

"Ow!" Joshua complained, rubbing the back of his hand. "I wasn't ready that time."

Sani placed his hands out in front of him, palms up. Joshua placed his on top of Sani's, palms down. The person whose hands were on bottom was supposed to lift, flip, and smack the back of the hands of the person on top. It was a game of speed and reflexes many Ram children played. The object was to hit the person on top before they could pull their hands away. If they got a hit, their hands stayed on bottom. If the person on top pulled their hands away before getting struck, then the pair traded places.

Sani's hand flew through the air the moment they got back into position. Three *smacks* came in quick succession.

Gryphon bit into his hand to keep from laughing. Poor Joshua had only found one more thing Sani beat him at.

"How are you beating me?" he demanded. "I'm usually good at this game."

Sani, in his level voice, simply shrugged and said, "I'm faster than you."

Gryphon didn't have to see Joshua to know his cheeks and neck were likely as red as the flaming hair atop his head.

First, it had been a foot race. Then a game of riddles. Now, hand slapping. If the poor kid didn't win at something soon, Gryphon thought he might explode.

Smack, smack. A pause. *Smack, smack, smack.*

"Enough!" Joshua didn't even bother whispering anymore. "I have to be better than you at something!"

Gryphon rolled over, rubbing the sleep from his eyes as though he'd only just awoken. "Sani is a talented young man, Joshua. That doesn't mean you're not."

As expected, Joshua's face glowed almost as red as the backs of his hands.

"This coming from the man who taught me that 'if you're not the best, you're dead.'"

Had he really said that?

Probably.

"We're not on a battlefield, Joshua. Slapping hands is hardly a life-or-death skill."

Joshua jumped to his feet and launched himself at his pack. He produced a woolen sling and waved it over his head, victorious. "Your bow to my sling. First to kill a rabbit wins!"

Sani inhaled deeply, as though drawing in patience along with air. "Fine. But this is the last game, Joshua."

Wiggling his brows up and down, Joshua said, "What? Afraid

I'm going to win?" Joshua didn't wait for a response. He bounded out of the tent, red hands and all, prepared for battle.

Sani sighed again. "He's exhausting." He picked up his quiver and bow and followed Joshua out of the tent to hunt rabbits.

Gryphon dressed and followed them out to find breakfast. His guard wasn't waiting outside his door, nor had they followed him from the training fields last night after his talk with Laden. Gryphon could only assume they'd been ordered to watch him from a distance—probably Laden's way of thanking him for the information. The Commander knew as well as Gryphon that he had an entire army of Wolves milling about the camp who would have been more than happy to report any crime, real or imagined, that Gryphon committed—especially since half of them believed he was responsible for the sudden disappearance of those four guards.

That mystery still bothered him.

The person who had set fire to that tent was still somewhere among the people of the Allies. It had been too targeted an attack to leave any room for doubt. Whoever lit that fire had wanted Gryphon hanged for the deed. This unseen threat was smart, watchful, and patient. Definitely not an enemy to be taken lightly. They would have seen that Gryphon's guard hadn't been around him and chosen that moment to act. The plan would have worked, were it not for Laden's levelheaded leadership and Sani's testimony.

As he walked through the tents, he was met with either a sneer or a frown as Wolves stoked morning cook fires and went about their chores. Most probably didn't appreciate that a Ram had been granted the freedom to walk about camp, especially after the fire. In their hate-filled minds, he was guilty. A threat.

Gryphon ducked inside Laden's tent, surprised to find the Commander not there as usual to take his breakfast.

Millie must have read his surprise. "He's overseeing the team of men preparing the Kodiak sector for Murtog's arrival." She set down a bowl of porridge and a plate of sausage links.

"Are you trying to fatten me up?" Gryphon lifted a sausage to her in salute before taking a bite. He couldn't stifle a groan of pleasure as he chewed. "I'll never be satisfied with trail food again."

Millie did her best not to appear flattered, making her usual scowl pained. She used the folds of her dress to grab the kettle from over the fire so not to burn her hand.

"Tell me, Millie, do you honestly think Murtog and the rest of the Kodiak will come?"

Milled filled his cup with the steaming brown tea and returned the kettle to the hook above the fire. "With Zo, anything is possible."

Gryphon nodded his agreement. He didn't like the idea of Zo baiting the Kodiak here, but the girl could be persuasive. He snorted at the irony of him, a Ram, sipping tea in an enemy camp. Yes, Zo was a woman for whom men would change the order of the stars. Even the thought of their last kiss made his hand tremble as he reached for his cup.

"I didn't start that fire," Gryphon said, when Millie set a hot scone on his plate.

"If the Commander says you're innocent, that's good enough for me." She gave a decided nod, but then her certainty seemed to waver. "Two more men went missing last night, did you know?" she spoke in low tones, checking the entrance of the tent for listening ears.

Gryphon's whole body stiffened. He swallowed and shook his head.

Millie wiped her brow with the hem of her apron. "Something is happening inside this camp." She took a step toward the tent flaps. "Be careful, Ram. Someone seems determined to make you out to be our enemy." She turned and walked stiffly out—likely to the Healer's Tent to look after the burn victims.

Gryphon studied the wall of the tent. His mind raced at the implication of this new development. He could easily fathom someone trying to sabotage his reputation. But were these missing men deserters, or had something actually happened to them? A sense of foreboding filled his gut. The Allies couldn't afford to have enemies working against them within the camp.

He finished his meal, determined to speak to Commander Laden. Just as he stood to leave the tent, the soft sounds of sniffling reached his ears. Pushing up from the table, careful not to make noise with the wooden chair, he walked toward the whimpering. Only one creature in this camp could be the owner of such a high, heart-melting sound.

"Tess?" he gently called. Half of the Commander's tent housed his paper-scattered desk; the other half was separated by a cloth divider. He pulled back the cloth to find a bed and a wooden chest. At the foot of the bed, Tess sat hugging her legs to her chest.

She looked up at Gryphon and quickly rotated to show him her back before hurriedly wiping the tears from her cheeks.

"Tess?" Gryphon frowned. "Are you hurt?"

Her back still facing him, she shook her head. The movement sent her wild blond hair dancing along her narrow back. A comb sat abandoned at her side.

Gryphon had almost no experience with children, but instinct brought him to sit on the ground a few feet away. "Will you tell me why you're crying?" he asked.

She shook her head again.

Gryphon grimaced then looked down at the comb. He cleared his throat. "I can help you with that … if you like."

She glanced back to see him gesture to the comb. Her big eyes were rimmed in red. "Do you know how?" she asked, raising an eyebrow in challenge.

"I will if you teach me."

Tess pinched her lips together and after only a moment's indecision, picked up the comb and crawled the few feet separating them. "Start and the bottom, and then work your way up." She handed him the comb, and as an afterthought added, "Don't tug."

Gryphon lifted a snarled portion of Tess's hair and carefully worked the comb through the blond strands. After a few minutes

Tess said, "You can go faster."

"But you said not to tug."

The little girl released a long-suffering sigh. "I just wish … " Her voice took on a shaky quality. Another sniffle meant more tears.

"What is it, Tess?"

She didn't answer and Gryphon kept combing.

Finally, with forced sincerity she said, "Zo usually combs my hair. Millie hurts."

"Is that why you're hiding in here?"

Tess shrugged. "I don't know."

Gryphon picked up another section of hair. "You miss her, don't you?"

He was getting better at knowing when to be gentle and when to be firm with the comb.

Tess wiped another tear from her cheek. Her back stiffened. "I don't miss her. I hope she never comes back."

Gryphon's hands froze in her hair. "You don't mean that." He finished combing the final section and set the comb down.

Without warning, Tess turned and jumped into his lap, pressing her wet face into his shirt. The effort of crying shook her tiny frame. Gryphon gathered her to him and held her, shocked by the sudden change. "It's all right, Tess." He caught himself swaying back and forth, rocking her again on instinct. "Shh, it's all right."

He held her for several minutes without pestering her further about her tears.

She eventually picked up her comb and left him, without another word, sitting on the floor of Laden's tent.

The next two mornings, before Gryphon took his breakfast, Tess arrived at his tent with comb in hand. No words exchanged. No questions about how she was doing. Tess simply looked up at him and offered the comb. On the second day, Joshua even let her practice braiding his shaggy red locks, lying down with his head in her small lap as she worked.

Gryphon did his best not to let the child see how pleased he was when he accepted the comb on the third day.

I'm going to miss this …

"One more!" Gryphon shouted to his gasping men when they reached the bottom of the foothills. His order wasn't received with groans as it had been during yesterday's sprints. He'd rewarded *that* reaction with three more trips up and down the mountain. This time, the men simply put their heads down and sprinted back up the mountain.

Gryphon paused a moment at the bottom—keeping an eye out for the youngest boys in his ranks—before digging his feet into the rich valley soil and sprinting after them. He'd overtaken the leader before they reached the top. "The Ram train this hard every day, men," he called down to them. He wanted to taunt them. He wanted them to be angry with him, to use that anger to push themselves harder.

They all reached the top a little faster than they had the day before. He nodded his approval and said, "Use the jog down to catch your breath. Dismissed."

Gryphon walked behind his men, taking in the distant sight of new tents being erected on the eastern edge for the Kodiaks. Earlier that morning, the camp awoke to find over fifty newly made spears snapped in two and a pair of Allied soldiers impaled near the armory. Laden was in a lethal mood, and the general animosity toward Gryphon had spiked yet again. At least his forty seemed to trust him.

Down below, a drum beat out a rhythm. Gryphon wouldn't have thought anything special of the beat were it not accompanied by other sounds—noises he'd never heard before.

He picked up his pace and trotted down the mountain, following the curious melody through the training fields to a Wolf campfire.

Five men sat around the fire clutching strange objects that produced the most amazing sounds under their nimble fingers.

The song was both high and low pitched. One man put his lips over an elaborate stick while using his fingers to cover the holes to manipulate the pitch. Another held a wooden box under his chin and dragged a stick across a row of strings.

Gryphon couldn't help but tap his toe to the beat of the music. His jaw hung open as the syncopated sounds consumed him. Inside Ram's Gate, no one was allowed to sing. Gryphon had spent his childhood fighting the melodies that came to him as he carved. He'd always been embarrassed by the time he'd spent humming those tunes and then trying to match words to the melodies. Most of his songs were the product of his lonely childhood. Music was a friend to an outcast boy who never quite belonged, and something to be ashamed of. But this ... the way the different pitches mingled and blended to create something completely new ... it was nothing short of exhilarating!

"Are Wolf musicians that much better than Ram?"

Gryphon looked over to find Gabe leaning back, resting on a barrel. It wasn't common for Gryphon to let someone sneak up on him. But the music had cast a spell upon his mind, requiring every particle of his attention to fully appreciate.

Instead of the ten hateful remarks he'd rehearsed for Gabe after learning about his deception, Gryphon simply shrugged and said, "We only have drums inside the Gate."

"Ah, yes. The Ram's determined goal of never having any form of amusement outside of the prizefight ring." He rolled his eyes. "How could I forget?"

The two men watched the musicians, neither feeling the need to bridge the huge chasm Gabe's lie had created between them. Gryphon was surprised by how little resentment he held for the Wolf. Mostly because he couldn't imagine the pain Gabe must endure knowing the girl he'd loved most of his life had chosen someone else. If their situations were reversed, Gryphon would have been desperate to win her.

Gryphon didn't feel too badly for him. Unless a miracle happened, Gryphon would be out of the picture in only a few short weeks.

Less than three weeks, he mentally corrected himself. *Only eighteen days ...*

"She'll want to dance."

Gryphon shot another glance in Gabe's direction.

"Zo." Gabe gestured toward the musicians. "She'll want to dance at the *Ostara*."

Shaking his head, Gryphon said, "I don't know how." He barely knew what music was, let alone how to dance to it.

"There are four staple dances that are favorites among the Wolves. I think it would mean a lot to her if you surprised her by learning them before the *Ostara*."

"That's only a few days away."

Gabe swatted away Gryphon's concern. "I'll have the boys come to the meeting tent tomorrow night. Tess and Millie can help us."

"W—why?"

Gabe scoffed. "I'm certainly not going to dance with you."

Shaking his head, Gryphon finally found his tongue. "No, why would you do that for me?"

Gabe's jaw flexed as his attention turned back to the fire. "It's not for you, Ram." Seconds passed. Finally, Gabe swatted his shoulder and said, "Tomorrow night," before walking away from the light of the fire.

Zo, Ikatou, Talon, Raca, and Poi gathered around a long table with Murtog seated at the head. The upper body of a large Kodiak bear was mounted to the wall above his head. Deep blue gems gleamed from the dead creature's eye sockets and its arms extended as though it would love nothing more than to rip Zo's limbs from her body before devouring the rest of her whole.

Zo shivered, unable to pull her gaze from the morbid creature, its beautiful eyes refracting the torchlight of the private room.

The company had been given the chance to soak in the chief's private hot springs that morning. A large Kodiak woman had attended both Raca and Zo, slathering a black, silky mud onto their bodies and faces before allowing them to rinse in an equally warm, freshwater bath. They were given new clothing adorned with fine gems and expensive cloth while their own was washed. Everything they gave Zo was too large. When Raca's clothing fit to perfection, the woman shrugged and explained, "They were made for a child." Both Zo and Raca had laughed.

Now as the dishes from their morning meal were being cleared, Zo marveled at the positioning of those at the table. Raca sat at the chief's right and Zo sat at his left. The seating arrangement had been intentional and Zo couldn't help but notice the chief's attention to Raca. Though he spoke barley a word throughout the course of the meal, Zo caught him casting curious glances at the girl when she wasn't looking.

Murtog clasped his oversized hands on the table and in his rumbling voice said, "Tell me of this blood oath and why you've come."

Ikatou opened his mouth to speak, but with a simple raised hand, Murtog silenced him. "Not from you." He turned to Zo. "The healer will speak."

Where to begin? And why did she have to be the one to tell the story? Then an idea struck her. She'd never spoken about what happened the day her parents died, but standing in Murtog's room, feeling his grief and mourning, Zo knew *that* was the story Murtog needed to hear.

She took a deep breath. "The first time I heard the battle call of a Ram horn was at the age of twelve. We lived with a large and powerful pack on the outskirts of the Valley of Wolves. At the sound of the deadly horn, my mother insisted I climb inside a woven basket and handed me my sleeping little sister, making me promise to stay hidden no matter what I heard before closing the lid.

"The holes of the basket were large enough to peek through. I witnessed my father's murder at the door of our hut as he tried to defend us. I remember hugging my sleeping sister to my chest as my mother was beaten and dragged from the room." Zo's voice caught, but she knew she had Murtog's attention. The bear chief gripped the edge of the table with white, shaking hands.

She continued, "Commander Laden raised us as his own. Brought us to the Allied Camp. But I couldn't run away from my hatred of the Ram. Desperate for revenge, I begged to be used as an Allied spy inside the Gate. That's where I met Gryphon."

Zo went on to explain her time inside the Gate, their perilous escape, the Nameless march to meet the Allies, her run-in with the Clanless, and her promise to Ikatou that saved her life and earned her the scars of the blood oath.

Ikatou leaned forward and pressed his hands against the table. "The Kodiak people want those who were taken from us returned." He pointed at Zo and she tried not to flinch under the heavy burden of a simple finger. "This girl is the key to healing our clan. Laden sees her as a daughter and because her fate is connected to that of the Nameless slaves, Laden has agreed to help us take back what is ours." His voice rose, and he took several labored breaths to control himself before quietly adding, "But he will only agree if the Kodiak will join the fight."

Before Murtog could reply, Raca added, "My people have been forced from the Nest. My father and his warriors stand with Commander Laden in the fight against the Ram." Her voice carried such power and passion, Zo couldn't help but envy her. "If there was ever a time that the Ram might be defeated, it is now, with the full force of all three clans joined together."

Zo added, feeling desperate. "The Wolves and Raven along with a handful of Kodiak will attend an *Ostara* at the beginning of next week. All of the leaders of the region who have reason to fight the Ram will be in attendance. The Allies need you. Commander Laden asks that you leave your Cave and join the counsel that will determine the fate of so many." *Mine especially*, she thought.

Murtog grumbled. "Laden and I have spoken before."

"Please," said Raca. Her hand stretched out to rest on his forearm.

Murtog flinched and then stilled under Raca's touch. Slowly, he looked down at the small brown hand resting gently against his mighty arm. Raca met his gaze, her hand unmoving, her expression supplicant but unafraid of the volatile chieftain.

Murtog's chest rose and fell once.

Twice.

Then, in one painfully slow movement, he pulled his arm out from under Raca's, pushed back from the table, and left the room.

Raca stared at her hand, still resting on the table, in silent shock.

They slept that night on cots in the antechamber of the chief's rooms. They hadn't seen the chief for the rest of the day. Talon and Ikatou agreed that they would leave under the cover of night, a few hours after the clan settled to sleep, and after a quick nap in the cabin head back to the Allies.

Zo's stomach churned as she lay next to Raca. Neither pretended to sleep as the failure of their journey weighed heavily upon them. Like it or not, in a few hours they'd leave to report their failure to Commander Laden.

A muted but distinct roar filled the cave, then died, making Zo think it was only the product of too little sleep and too much worry. Then the roar sounded again. Louder than before.

"What was that?" Talon asked. He pushed himself up off his padded bed and walked over to the large wooden doors that sealed off the chief's wing of the Kodiak cave system.

"It could be an uprising," said Ikatou. "My people are hungry for vengeance. If word of our arrival and dismissal leaked to the clan, Murtog might finally taste the frustration of his people. Loyalty can only go so far."

Talon unlatched the door and pushed it open. "The guards are gone."

Zo and the others climbed to their feet just as another thundering roar filled the cave.

"An uprising?" asked Zo.

"What will they do to Murtog?" asked Raca.

Ikatou held up a hand, silencing the group. "Listen."

A deep voice, faint but distinct, interrupted by yet another roar.

"It can't be," muttered Ikatou.

Without warning, the Kodiak bolted through the door and down the moonstone tunnel. Raca strapped on her quiver and reached for her bow in one flowing movement. She nocked an arrow and approached the doors with caution.

"No," said Talon, already walking toward her.

"Try and stop me," was her only response before sprinting out the door and into the spiraling tunnel after Ikatou.

Talon growled and ran after her, leaving Zo to trail after him.

The noise ahead grew louder. Between the echoes of her footfalls, Murtog's voice seemed to fill every inch of the cave, bouncing off stone in riotous glory. She burst into the main cavern to find it filled to capacity with Kodiak adorned in fur and buckskin coverings. Every head towered above Zo's. Off to the side, Murtog stood with arms outstretched and an obvious sheen of tears trailing down his face. "The time for mourning has passed. Tomorrow, we march to avenge our loved ones, and soon, to bring them home."

The battle cry that followed forced Zo to clamp her hands over her ears. Murtog walked off the dais a true chief and passed Zo, Raca, and the others back down the moonstone tunnel to his chambers without a word.

Zo took Raca's hand in hers and squeezed. The Raven princess stared after the Kodiak chief, mouth hanging open and the beginnings of a smile lighting her beautiful eyes.

Ikatou carried no such self-discipline. He sprinted over to Zo, took her by the waist, and tossed her five feet in the air. "You did it!" He wrapped her in a giant bear hug that cut off both circulation and air. When he finally set her down, Zo looked back over to Raca and grinned. "I don't think *I* did anything."

Chapter Seventeen

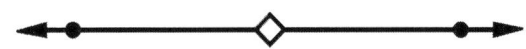

Gryphon couldn't bring himself to cheer with the rest of the Allies when the first wave of Kodiak emerged from the gap and made its way down into the narrow valley, exactly one week and a day following Zo's departure.

He was consumed with relief at Zo's return, at her success in coming closer to fulfilling the blood oath—at the chance he'd have to pull her into the protective cage of his embrace and hold her for just a moment. But another emotion flared hot within him.

His clan.

What would become of them? No matter how justified the Allies were in defending themselves and gaining back what was taken, Gryphon couldn't help but mourn the future of his people should these clans actually defeat the Ram.

The Wolves had arrived from the southern passage only yesterday, swelling the camp with fathers, sons, wives, and daughters old enough to attend the *Ostara*. Laden had explained that it was customary for Wolf fathers to show off their daughters at these gatherings. By day, the pretty girls dutifully looked after the family cart, and by night they danced and made merry with potential suitors.

When Gryphon voiced his concern about having women and children journeying to the camp with so much unsettled in the region, Laden had assured him that the southern passage was still safe to travel thanks to a rotating regime of Allied guards. "Besides," he'd said, "we need to remind these men what they're fighting for."

Gryphon impatiently scanned the crowd of Kodiak for Zo. She must have spotted him first, because she pushed her way between a wall of Kodiak and rushed toward him.

"Gryphon!"

His heart leapt into his throat as she jumped into him, wrapping her legs around his hips and burying her head into his neck. "I missed you!" she cried.

Gryphon laughed and spun her around in a full circle, pulling her to him with probably too much force. He set her down but didn't release her, planting a solid, delicious kiss on her forehead, his hands firm yet tender on her upper arms. "I missed you too, Zo." She hovered there, her full lips taunting him, especially the bottom one. He longed to pull her away from all of the planned festivities and taste them properly.

A hand on his shoulder killed the thought. He looked up into the terse face of Commander Laden and released his hold on Zo, taking a sheepish step back so Zo might greet the person closest she had to a father.

That's when he noticed the bear.

Gryphon wasn't used to looking up at anyone, but the Kodiak before him, outfitted with a long fur cape fastened in front by a single bear claw, stood a few inches taller than him. From massive shoulders hung thick arms covered in black ink. Black paint smeared beneath his eyes framed a wide nose with nostrils flaring as he studied Gryphon.

Murtog, chief of the Kodiak.

"Chief." Laden stepped between Gryphon and the beast of a man, offering a slight bow and then a hand of welcome. "Thank you for joining us. Allow me to personally see you to your tent. We have men on hand prepared to get you settled before tonight's celebration."

"This is the Ram I've heard so much about? Where are his chains?"

Gryphon gritted his teeth, but Laden robbed him of the chance to answer.

"He is a guest in my camp, Chief." Laden didn't feel the need to explain more, but lifted a hand to usher the chief and the long stream of men in his wake to the eastern portion of the valley, where Ikatou and the other Kodiak already camped. After briefly locking eyes with Gryphon, Murtog scowled and turned to follow Laden.

Zo snaked her arm through his and whispered into his ear, "I think he likes you."

Her eyes danced with mirth and such flirtatious relief it made his heart double its speed and his stomach turn flips. She squealed as he wrapped her up by the knees and tossed her over his shoulder like a sack of grain.

A few passing Kodiak eyed him with disdain, but he didn't care. He'd never seen her so carefree, so unaffected by the troubles surrounding her. Ikatou's bellowing laughter followed them as Gryphon ran her up the mountain, putting to shame any of the sprints he'd done that week. When he finally set her feet to the ground she grabbed two fistfuls of his shirt and pulled him against her until their lips met with the energy of a hundred battles.

She had the terrifying power to alter him from trained, self-composed soldier to animal with just a look … a touch. How could he survive without her? Moreover, how could he leave her to meet Ajax and Chief Barnabas knowing there was a very real chance he might never return?

"What's wrong?" Zo released his imprisoned lips. She had read his emotions a lot since they reunited in the wilderness. Her healing abilities went beyond pushing emotion and healing energy, as before. Now, she seemed to take the emotional temperature, sampling the energy around her as one might sample a tray of desserts.

"Is something troubling you?" Concern shown in the downward sloping lines of her face. Was it possible that she still doubted him? What would she think when she learned about the other mishaps of camp? Would she blame him for those too? The idea that she might not trust him hurt more than Ikatou's fists.

Her breath tickled his ear as her lips grazed the skin of his neck. "My blood oath is as good as fulfilled, Gryph. We're together. Joshua and Tess are safe. Everything is finally working out." A pause. "Isn't it?" More concern. More uncertainty.

"I missed you." It was all Gryphon could manage.

That earned him a tentative smile. *Such a beautiful smile.*

He leaned in and captured her lips once more before pulling her close and resting his chin on her head. For all of his physical and tactical prowess, he never felt as powerful as he did when she was in his arms. But the exhilaration was cheapened by the monumental lie still separating them. Every time he allowed himself to think of a future life with Zo, Barnabas's sneer pushed hope from his thoughts like a bird from its nest.

A cool thread of peace washed over him, dampening his anxieties about the uncertain future.

Zo again. Reading his fears. Healing him.

"Thank you," he said, kissing the top of her head once more.

"Don't thank me." The light tone of her voice seemed forced. "Every healer charges a fee for her work."

"Oh really? And what is my fee?"

"A dance at the festival."

Gryphon's anxiety flared again, and Zo allowed herself to really laugh. "Relax!" She patted his chest. "There's a first time for everything."

"Did you already comb your hair?" Zo asked. Tess's hair was so fine that it was usually a nightmare to work through. Today there wasn't a single tangle.

"Yep."

The girl was growing up so fast. It wouldn't be long before Tess wouldn't need her so much. She remembered looking forward to that day, once. But the lines between sister and mother blurred so much in their relationship, and Zo couldn't help the twinge of regret that time was passing so quickly.

"Two more braids, and I promise not to touch a hair on your head for a full week!" said Zo, as she wrestled her little sister back into the chair. Zo tied off the final braids with a strip of cloth and connected them in the middle to rest as a blond crown upon her head. As a finishing touch, Zo tucked a few sprigs of lavender she'd harvested from Millie's garden into the braid.

"There." She pushed the last stem through. "You're perfect."

Tess hopped up, ready to run from the tent, but Zo caught her arm before she could dash out. "You know that I'm done, don't you?"

Rather than come right out and ask, Tess simply froze, staring at the tent wall—wanting to hear, but not wanting to appear too eager.

Zo sighed. "Now that the Kodiak are here and Laden has the men he needs to fight this war, there's nothing else the Allies need from me other than my work as a healer."

"You'll find a reason to leave again," said Tess. "You always do."

Zo pulled Tess around to face her, hands clasping the girl's thin upper arms, eyes penetrating with promise. "I'm sorry for everything you've endured over the last few months, bug. But wasn't it worth it to bring Joshua and Gryphon into our lives?"

Tess blinked a few times and finally nodded, her gaze on the dirt floor.

"From now on, wherever I go, you will always be with me."

Tess glanced up. "Promise," she demanded. "Promise on the graves of our parents."

"Tess," Zo exclaimed. "Don't say such things."

The little girl folded her arms, causing the puffs of her sleeves to bunch and gather. "If you don't promise, you don't really mean it."

Insecure. Afraid. Uncertain. Agonizing need to feel comforted. Zo read her sister, and her heart broke.

"I promise you, Tess. We will stay together until the day some man steals your heart and sweeps you away from me."

Zo stepped out of her tent, smoothing down the front of her skirt, already feeling a blush warm her cheeks. She wore the most impractical pair of shoes, the soft fabric hugging her feet like gloves. She'd pulled both the shoes and the elaborately embroidered skirt from the chest of possessions that used to belong to her parents. Millie said her mother had worn the dress to the *Ostara* where she first met Zo's father, who had traded a whole cart of provisions for the right to court and marry her.

The skirt, with its swirling patterns of floral clusters, hugged her waist and flowed down her legs until the hem barely kissed the ground. She wore a white blouse with a fitted leather jerkin over the top. It was strange to wear her mother's clothing. In all of her memories, her mother was so much larger than her. To think that her mother was this size—her size—when she met and married her father amazed and even frightened Zo.

She closed her eyes, and for a brief, unguarded moment, allowed her hopes to get the better of her. What if Gryphon and Laden had come to some kind of arrangement while she was gone? They'd certainly seemed on better terms, and Laden *had* done away with Gryphon's guard. It was foolish to hope, but what if tonight—with her in the same dress that helped her mother secure her father—

Gryphon finally asked her to be his forever?

In the distance, a steady beating drum signaled to all the camp that the festivities were about to commence, as was tradition. Women and men filtered from their tents dressed in their best toward the training grounds, which had been turned into a proper meeting place for an *Ostara*. Carts lined the perimeter of the large open space, filled with foodstuffs and other wares. Oil lanterns hung from tall hooks staked into the ground before each cart and a massive bonfire roared in the center, leaving ample room for dancing. The carts would remain over the course of the next three days as goods were traded, supplies purchased, and young girls who'd come of age from all of the surrounding Wolf Packs were thoroughly admired and courted.

Zo looked around the field for a sight of Gryphon, Tess, or Joshua, and saw only a few familiar faces from the camp.

Commander Laden beckoned her from his position on a dais constructed from wood at the head of the camp. He was joined by all of the clan leaders, with the addition of Gabe, who sat in deep conversation with Chief Naat. Raca was also there, sitting on the edge of her seat on the other side of her father. Her hair was pulled up off her neck into a series of elaborate knots and braids atop her head. Her fitted buckskin dress left her defined shoulders bare. Around her neck hung at least ten beaded and feathered necklaces. In all their time together, it was the first time Raca ever really looked the part of a Raven princess.

Zo approached Raca first and offered her a small curtsy.

"Oh, please. We're beyond that." She reached out and took Zo's hand.

"Have you spoken with him yet?" Zo asked, tilting her head in Murtog's direction. The Kodiak chief sat on the opposite end of the dais with chin resting on fist as he surveyed the crowd. Raca had spent their entire journey from the Kodiak Caves avoiding the chief.

"Not yet. He's been busy, and I'm not sure he desires my company."

"Of course he does. The man left the Caves for you."

Raca swatted her arm. "Don't say such things. He came because it was the right thing to do for his people."

Zo shrugged. No doubt Murtog was here for his people, but Raca had been the arrow to wake him from his mourning. Zo was sure of it.

Without pomp or ceremony or speeches, the Wolf musicians began their music with a nod from the Wolf Alpha seated next to Laden. With the Wolves so spread out across the Valley of Wolves, the Alpha was more of a figurehead than an outright leader. The Wolves had long ago agreed to support the Allies, not on the Alpha's word, but by vote from each pack. Still, it was tradition for the Alpha to signal the commencement of every *Ostara*.

With that nod, lute, drum, pipe, and fiddle jumped into a melody that had Zo's foot tapping and hips swaying without her permission. Gabe turned from Chief Naat and stood before her with hand extended.

"Will you dance with me, Zo?" He fidgeted. "Someone must start things off." Then he added, "For old time's sake?"

From the corner of Zo's eye, Raca nodded encouragement, as if watching would bring her pleasure.

Zo placed her hand in Gabe's. "I'd love to, old friend. I only hope you can keep up."

They were joined by only a few other couples. Zo and Gabe bowed and curtsied to the guests of honor on the dais then turned and bowed to each other. A wicked glint shone in Gabe's eye as he gripped her waist and took her by the hand. The steady beat of the drum reached deep into her chest, past the plight of the Allies and the hunger of the region, past fear of losing loved ones and the worry of failure. All Zo heard was the steady rhythm of her heritage.

Her feet moved without any encouragement, the dance steps more instinct than practice. Laughter filled her chest and spilled from her mouth. She tipped her head back as Gabe spun her across the dance floor. Her skirts flew around her legs and the bonfire danced along in her blurred view. The crowd clapped out the life-giving beat and other couples joined the dance.

When the music stopped Zo's vision didn't, and she began to fall before Gabe caught her against his firm chest. He gave her a brotherly squeeze, then—once she had her feet—stepped away and offered a deep bow. Zo responded with a curtsy of her own, and the pair walked arm in arm out of the center of the clearing. Another tune picked up where the first left off but Zo needed a minute to catch her breath.

"You are a fine couple," Chief Naat said as they neared the dais.

Gabe squeezed her hand and said, "We're only dear friends, honored chief."

The chief looked over Zo's shoulder and frowned. "A pity."

Just then, Gryphon arrived with Joshua at his side. The boy's hair was combed and his clothing clean. "All this time, I thought your shirt was brown!" Zo exclaimed, wrapping the boy in a quick hug, his cheeks heating to match the flaming red of his hair.

"You should talk," said Joshua. "Is that a skirt?"

Gryphon ruffed the boy's hair, turning it back into the familiar mess Zo loved. "Never offend a man's dance partner," he said in his delicious, deep voice. Zo used to cringe whenever she heard his Ram accent. Now she associated it not with the Ram, but with the kind, gentle man she'd come to love.

"Dance partner?" she asked. As much as she wanted to dance with Gryphon, he didn't know the steps to the traditional dances of the Wolves. She accepted his hand just as the music shifted from a fast-paced jig to a slower melody.

In this dance, men were supposed to take their partner by the waist and let their free hand hang by their side. It was called the "Seeing Dance," the point being to allow the couple to really look at each other and talk as they moved through the complicated steps.

"If you want, I can teach you," Zo offered. "You're coordinated enough that I'm sure you'll learn it in no time."

Gryphon led her to a spot close to the fire and musicians. "I think I'll be fine, thank you."

He took her waist in his warm hand and, without missing a step, led her through the dance. Zo gawked at him. Though it was slower, this dance was not as simple as the one she'd had with Gabe.

"How did you—"

"Gabe."

Her mouth formed a round O as her gaze shifted to Gabe, who watched them from a spot near the dais where he danced with Raca. A tear of gratitude leaked from the corner of her eye. It was the perfect apology for his dishonesty and such a Gabe thing to do.

"He's not all bad," said Gryphon, echoing her own thoughts. His face turned distant and after a few moments he added, "If anything should happen to me in this war, you should—"

Zo's mirth quickly dissolved into something completely different. "Don't," she warned. "Don't even speak it!"

Gryphon sighed and pulled her close enough to plant a chaste kiss on her forehead. "I have no intention of giving you up, even to death. I just want you to know that your future happiness is everything to me and if it *had* to be someone else, I can't think of a better man."

He'd said it. Giving voice to the fear she'd ignored since they arrived in camp and he'd accepted a training position in Laden's army. Zo had lost so much since her parents' deaths. She'd endured the Gate, the Clanless, and the Caves. But losing Gryphon after everything they'd managed to survive would be the end of her. Of that she had no doubt.

"Hey," he took her chin between thumb and forefinger. "Forget I mentioned it. Tonight is supposed to be a celebration."

The song ended, and Laden called for the attention of the crowd, cutting off the Wolf musicians before they could start into another melody.

"Usually an *Ostara* brings together packs from across the Valley of Wolves to trade and discuss threats to the region. This historic event marks the first *Ostara* to officially include Wolf, Raven, and Kodiak. As such, we will break tradition and invite our brothers of the wing and claw to entertain us with some of their native songs and dances." He turned to Chief Naat, who didn't seem at all surprised by the announcement.

The elderly man stood and escorted his daughter down the dais to a crowd of clustering Raven positioned around the fire. A drum pounded a deep *boom*, and was soon joined by the clattering of wood blocks being scraped and clapped together in rhythmic variations with the drum. Four men with feathered headdresses and feathers fastened down their arms walked on either side of Raca, then stood motionless.

Gryphon led Zo to the side of the gathered crowd, near the musicians.

Raca stretched her arms out wide and, with the grace of a bird, began to dance. Zo's gaze shifted between Raca's beautiful movements and Murtog seated at the dais. The Kodiak barely blinked as he watched her fluid movements. The costumed Raven men chanted and spread their arms out wide, showing off their long black feathers, their voices rising and falling as they chanted a language Zo had never heard. No matter how elaborate the men's synchronized movements were, Raca was clearly the object of everyone's attention.

The end of the dance left Murtog sitting at the edge of his chair, his mouth agape and his ever-present scowl replaced with something resembling awe. His dark eyes tracked her all the way back to her seat and lingered there, unabashed even when she returned his stare.

Twenty Kodiak sporting war paint and mostly bare chests jogged out into the center of the circle. Murtog blinked away the spell Raca had cast over him and stood to face his men and the rest of the Allies gathered. He unclasped his fur cape and let it fall to the floor before stepping to the edge of the platform. Arching his back, with thick veins sprouting along his neck, he shouted, "It is death! It is life!" in the largest, most terrifying voice Zo had ever heard. She felt herself being partially tucked behind Gryphon's back, as if the war cry—though only meant to be a form of entertainment—warranted his protection.

She smiled and nudged him until she could move to stand in front of his large chest where, his arms wrapped around her waist. "Sorry. Call it instinct," he whispered in her ear.

Murtog jumped from the platform and landed in a crouch with one fist planted in the ground. In Kodiak form, the men shouted their war chant, smacking elbows to fists, pounding their thighs and chests like wild animals and occasionally sticking out their tongues.

"Why?" Zo asked.

"They're trying to intimidate. They think it's a frightening gesture."

Zo couldn't help but agree. Seeing these mountainous men and knowing they were fighting for the same cause brought new hope to her heart. With the Kodiak and the full might of the Raven, even the Ram might fall.

The war dance ended in one final "Ha!" from the Kodiak men and the Allies cheered, likely as encouraged as Zo.

"We're going to survive this war, Gryphon." She hugged the arms draped around her waist.

Gryphon didn't respond.

Chapter Eighteen

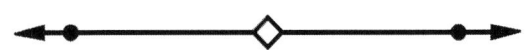

Gryphon received the summons to meet immediately after wishing Zo a good night at the door of her tent. He'd been caught staring like a fool at the closed tent flap while longing stabbed at his gut when Laden's messenger found him. Saying goodnight to Zo when he was used to spending his nights in the wilderness with her tucked close to his side was his least favorite part of staying in the Allied Camp.

He needed to marry her. Needed it more than he needed food or water, sleep, or even air. But how could he approach Laden for the right to have her with war looming around them? He couldn't do that to her, not while sitting at death's feet.

Approaching the heavily guarded door to Laden's tent, Gryphon tucked his feelings for Zo away. He relaxed his shoulders and rolled his head to loosen up the stiffness in his neck.

The guards stepped aside at his approach and Gryphon fought the urge to correct them for not searching him for weapons. Laden, of all people, should have instructed them in such things.

Inside the tent, amber light flickered from the torches surrounding Laden's long table. Laden waved him forward and gestured for him to sit at the one remaining chair at the foot of the table. Chief Naat sat with Talon at his side. On the opposite side of the table sat Murtog and Ikatou. Gabe was also there, seated beside the Wolf Alpha. With their fair complexions, the two Wolves could have passed for father and son. But where Gabe kept his face clean shaven, the Alpha grew his mustache so long it was braided on either side of his lips until it was lost in the matted hair of his yellow beard.

"We're all here," said Laden. "Every clan represented. Something, I would wager, that hasn't happened for more than two centuries."

Murtog didn't hide his distaste in sitting at the same table as Gryphon. He leaned forward and said, "Skip the introductions, Laden. Tell me how we're going to free my people."

"You said you had news," Chief Naat added with a nod.

"Gryphon?" Laden asked. "Why don't you do the honors?"

Gryphon had no way of controlling the scowl on his face. Forcing him to be the one to explain his people's weakness went a step beyond cruel. He hesitated, then finally said, "The Ram are moving south. Their food supplies are exhausted, and without the hope of obtaining the Raven grain stores they don't have another option except to migrate south to the fertile lands of the Valley of Wolves. Traveling with supplies, and accompanied by so many who aren't warriors, I imagine they're a day or two south of the Gate." He looked over at Ikatou. "I recommend trying to free your family when they are on the march. In fact," he cleared his throat, trying not to imagine the fall of an ax to his neck, "I know the perfect time to free them."

Chief Naat frowned, dragging the heavy lines of his face downward. "How could you know such a thing?" To Laden he added, "Have your scouts reported movement outside the Gate?"

Laden solemnly shook his head.

Gryphon stared at the dark gap between Chief Naat and Laden, not wishing to meet anyone's eye. "I'm meeting them where the river divides into two just north of the Valley of Wolves. I've promised the brothers of my mess I'd trade Barnabas my head if he will reinstate them back into the clan with a full pardon for failing him." His voice caught as he thought of Ajax and his little family. His old friend was the only reason Zo was still alive.

"What?" Gabe pushed away from the table, standing over Gryphon with fists balled as though he'd like nothing more than to tear him apart. "Does Zo know?"

"None of that now, Gabe."

"But, sir!"

"Later. We'll find a way around this, but right now we need to discuss our immediate actions."

Ikatou wiped fat tears from his eyes. Gryphon knew they weren't for him. He wept with joy at the chance to finally save his family. Instead of being offended that his impending death could bring joy to the Bear, Gryphon surprised himself by feeling happy for the man.

Murtog sat in stark contrast, shaking his head. "Lies," he muttered. He turned to Laden and spat. "How can you trust this Ram traitor? I will not commit my men to a mission that is clearly a trap."

Laden steepled his fingers, his elbows resting on the wooden table. "It is understandable that you would question Gryphon's story. He is a Ram and a stranger to you. I sent a scouting party to monitor the Gate two weeks ago. I agree that we should wait until official word comes, confirming Gryphon's story." He leaned forward and pressed a firm finger into the table and added, "But know this … " His gaze traveled to Gryphon. "He is an honorable man. I would trust him with my life."

Murtog turned to Gryphon. "Your mess brothers. Did they know you were headed for the Allies?"

Gryphon held his gaze. "My best friend is the only man I've spoken to. He knew of my plans to bring Joshua and Zo to the Allies. I honestly don't know how much information he would relay to Barnabas."

"We have to assume Barnabas will expect an attack," nodded Chief Naat.

"But he wants Gryphon's head, as a matter of honor," said Laden. "*And*, he'll want as many of his troops to witness the execution as possible. It is the Ram way."

Gryphon's gaze snapped to Laden. He was sure Zo didn't know about Laden's heritage and was willing to bet few in this room, if any, did. What would these clan leaders think if they discovered Gryphon wasn't the only Ram in this tent?

"Listen," said Gryphon. "I've told you what I know. I am going to meet Barnabas where the river splits in exactly two weeks' time. I've brought you this information not because I don't care for my clan—a part of me will always be a Ram, whether they claim me or not. But I can't stand by and watch the Valley of Wolves, with its women and children, be attacked. Not when I can do something about it." He pushed back from the table and stood. "If you choose not to act, let it be on your heads. Not mine."

He only made it three steps away from the table before Laden's voice froze him in place. "You are not excused, Ram."

Gryphon turned his head. He knew Laden's hostility was mostly just for show, but it didn't make him appreciate it any more.

"Sit," the older Ram ordered.

Gryphon hesitated only a moment before turning and taking his seat at the foot of the table. His nostrils flared at being spoken to as though he were a child prematurely leaving the dinner table.

"I have a plan," said Laden. "But without your help, we cannot succeed. What I'm about to ask of you is no small thing, Gryphon."

Tired.

It was the only feeling Gryphon could register. Whatever Laden's plan, Gryphon didn't want any part of it. For once, couldn't he just fulfill his simple purpose and let fate decide the rest? He wanted to walk away, but, ironically, the Ram blood inside him defied any such weakness. *For Zo,* he thought. *I will do this for her.* And if somehow, by some unforeseeable miracle, the fates preserved him and allowed them a chance at forever, it would all be worth it.

He met Laden's eye, and though it nearly killed him, said, "I am your man, Commander. What would you have me do?"

Stone hefted a rock the size of Zo's two fists and spun in a circle, releasing the stone at the perfect moment. It flew through the air as though buoyed up by the cheers of the Nameless as it sailed over the other contenders' rocks and landed four feet in the lead.

Eva put two fingers to her lips and whistled her praise. In the few short weeks she'd been with the Allies, her pregnant belly had finally grown to the point where her condition was obvious. Even though the Ram were no longer her clan, it must have been odd for her to sit among strangers set upon hating her heritage.

After the wedding ceremony tonight, she and Stone could make a new life. New traditions to pass down to their growing family and the people once known as the Nameless.

The Freeman, she had to remind herself again.

It was a small band of men and women. But if the Allies ever managed to free the rest of the Nameless inside the Gate, the Freeman numbers would swell. They'd need to find a place to settle and put down roots. There were laws to establish, farms to plant, and trade to build, but at least they had each other—something that had never been a possibility while inside the Gate.

Zo leaned over, and with hands hovering over Eva's swollen stomach asked, "May I?"

Eva nodded and Zo set her hands on her pregnant belly. She closed her eyes and gently pushed her love into the womb of the unborn child. A boy, if her reading of the baby's spirit could be relied upon. "You bear the child of a chief." Zo smiled, pulling away with some reluctance.

Eva beamed at her soon-to-be husband as Stone shook hands with the other men in the competition.

"I bear Stone's child. That is all I care about." She spoke softly, her hand still supporting her belly while staring longingly at the man she loved.

Throat tightening, envy gnawing away at her insides, Zo had to look away. Eva and Stone reminded Zo too clearly of what she didn't have. Of course she knew Gryphon cared for her, and when she approached Laden last night after Gryphon had seen her safely to her tent and demanded to know whether Gryphon had asked for her hand, Laden had been gentle in saying he hadn't.

How foolish she was! Her cheeks heated even at the thought of wearing her mother's dress to the *Ostara*. She'd let the romantic idea of Gryphon's proposal cloud the fact that, though Gryphon might care for her, he likely wasn't in any frame of mind to make his connection to her permanent. He'd been different since arriving in camp, so quick to criticize her people. And whenever he smiled there was always something restricting the emotion. Something holding him back.

Cheering from the crowd drew Zo out from her useless self-pity. Eva whistled her approval along with the rest. Her hair had grown a few inches since it was shaved inside Ram's Gate. Today she wore a wreath of wildflowers like a crown on her head. Combined with her dark eyes and high cheekbones, she looked nothing like the girl who'd knifed a Ram scout on their journey here.

The games lasted all day. Men sat in pairs on the ground, holding a small rope with their feet pressed against their opponent's. The object was to pull the other man off the ground. There was spear throwing. Shot-putting. Sword fighting with blunted, wooden blades. Even a contest at the pond to see which man could hold his opponent under the water the longest.

"I hope you don't believe the talk," said Eva, not taking her eyes from the games.

Zo frowned. "Talk?"

"About Gryphon. They're just rumors. People are fools when they're afraid. Whatever the Wolves believe, the Freemen are behind Gryph."

"Eva," Zo said, frustrated now, "I don't even know what you're talking about."

Eva hesitated, clearly regretting bringing it up in the first place. "It started with the fire the day before you left. Every few days something else happens. Men gone missing. The damn on the river breaking. A day's worth of newly crafted spears destroyed. Last night more than thirty men were up sick. Some think the food stores have been tampered with."

"And people believe Gryphon did all of these things?"

Eva frowned. "Not everyone. But the problem is, no one can prove that it *wasn't* him."

"That's ridiculous!" said Zo.

Could she really blame the Wolves for pointing their finger at Gryphon? He was the only Ram, aside from Joshua and Eva, in the camp. Laden's words the night of the fire rang again in her ears.

He has motive.

Zo shook her head, ashamed she'd even entertained the idea. This was Gryphon.

"Ridiculous," she said again, mostly to herself.

At Eva and Stone's insistence, the wedding was a simple affair. Eva's bleached wool dress kissed the floor, plain except for the green braided sash that sat above her rounded stomach. She'd traded her wildflower crown for one of wheat mixed with different textures and shades of leaves. The yellow wheat created something of a halo around her head.

"The wheat is a Ram symbol for abundance," Gryphon whispered to her.

Zo almost made a remark that food was all the Ram ever thought about, but refrained. There was nothing funny about hunger. Living in the Valley with her parents as a child, Zo had seldom experienced the pains of hunger. But inside the Gate, hunger was a constant companion. Especially among the Nameless.

Laden stood before Eva and Stone, facing the vast congregation of Allies who'd come to witness the event. The crowd quieted with expectation as Laden looked between the couple. Instead of launching into a long speech about the sacredness of the occasion, the Commander simply nodded to Stone and stepped back, as if to let the pair sort everything out on their own.

At the unspoken cue, Stone stretched out his hands toward Eva, palms up. Eva smiled at him, tears gathering in her eyes. She reached out to him and placed her hands down on his forearms. He gripped her forearms in return, and together they stared at one another for several long moments.

Zo drank in the adoration of Stone's expression as he whispered words to his bride. Words not shouted for the crowd. Whatever he said, it belonged to Eva alone. Zo leaned forward, her breath catching at the sweetness of the sacred moment.

The couple paused. More tears, but no words.

Gryphon must have sensed Zo's anticipation because he leaned down and with his breath tickling her ear said, "It is Ram custom for the bride not to accept his vow until she's taken the time to consider his promises. A way to keep him in suspense."

A shiver of longing rushed up Zo's spine as she and Gryphon locked eyes. One heartbeat. Two. She studied every inch of his face so close to hers. His thick black lashes and rich brown eyes. The masculine contours of his cheeks. The stubble along his jaw.

"I love you," she whispered, before she could stop herself.

Simple truth, and right as calling summer grass green, but she hadn't meant to speak the words aloud. A violent blush rushed to her cheeks and she had to look away. They sat close enough that, as she turned, her cheek brushed his and the usual smell of pine that clung to him made her shiver. When his breath caught at the connection, she sensed his longing mix with hers.

Longing and *hesitation.*

Because I am a Wolf? Because he has a guilty conscience?

It took every ounce of her will to turn back to the bride and groom on the dais. Gryphon put his arm around her back and dragged her closer to his side. "I will always love you, Zo," he spoke into her hair. "No matter what the future brings."

"Gryphon?" she said, breathless. Again, the words spilled unbidden and unwanted from her mouth. "You didn't start that fire, did you?"

In one question, all of the heat of their exchange turned to ice. Gryphon startled, angling his body away from her, and she instantly wished she could call the words back. His jaw clenched along with his fists and his eyes focused intently on the couple on the dais.

The crowd burst into applause and cheers. Zo glanced up to find Eva wrapped in Stone's determined embrace as they kissed, unabashed by the audience. Stone lifted Eva into his arms, lips still locked with his new bride as he walked her off the platform.

"No matter what you want to believe," said Gryphon, "a part of you will always see the Ram in me as someone you can't fully trust."

Zo batted away tears and Gryphon left her sitting alone on the bench, ashamed to admit he was right.

Chapter Nineteen

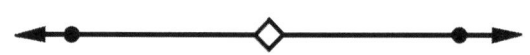

Gryphon sat up in his bed panting from the nightmare. His forehead dripped sweat. He looked around the dark tent, chest heaving to catch his breath. It took him a few moments to process that his dream really had been a dream. But when he closed his eyes again, he saw Zo's body lying at an odd angle covered in her own blood, a spear pinning her stomach to the ground. Her lifeless eyes stared up at him, seeming to beg the question, "*Why didn't you stay?*" and "*I thought you loved me.*"

Gryphon suddenly couldn't breathe. He yanked on his boots and stepped over Sani's body—his little Raven guard dog—to push away the tent flap.

"Where are you going?" Sani asked, still half-asleep. Joshua snored on the opposite side of the tent.

"Just need some air," Gryphon wheezed. "Go back to bed."

For once, Sani didn't protest or make a comment about Gryphon's safety being his concern. He simply nodded and let his head fall back down to the pillow.

Gryphon set out at a jog through the sleeping camp, trying not to think about Zo doubting his character. Hiding from the reality that she was right to doubt him.

He'd lied to her by not disclosing his plans to leave. His betrayal was every bit as cold as her mistrust. But pain was pain, whether a person deserved to feel it or not.

He tried to draw air into his lungs, but his windpipe was still too constricted by his own panic to allow it. He passed through the training field and up into the foothills where he'd spent time with Zo. When he finally reached the top, he dropped to his hands and knees and gasped and sputtered on the little air he could draw in. An angry, guttural sound escaped his lips. So weak. He hated himself for *feeling*.

He collapsed on the ground and felt his racing heartbeat against the rocky soil beneath him. Turning his head to one side, his cheek pressed against the dirt, Gryphon's breathing relaxed and he finally managed to slip into that numb place he'd known well from a childhood filled with beatings and systematic starvation.

He didn't know how long he lay there, shirtless and cold in the foothills, before the startled cry of a man ripped him from his semi-conscious state.

Pushing to his knees, Gryphon strained to listen. If he wasn't mistaken, he thought the sound came from the slot canyon at the north entrance of the valley.

Another shout. Maybe a hundred yards off. Definitely by the north entrance.

Gryphon shot to his feet and sprinted in that direction, cursing all the while that he didn't have any kind of weapon on him. He considered shouting to wake people from the camp below, but that would cost him the element of surprise, and he had no idea what enemy—if any—he'd face. He could only imagine it was the menace who started the fire and had been doing other damage to injure Gryphon's reputation.

Not again.

Gryphon slowed the closer he got to the north entrance. From somewhere in the slot canyon, a man cried out in pain, the sound echoing softly off the stone walls, too faint to be heard by the sleeping camp below. Another man—who Gryphon assumed to be an Allied soldier—sprinted out of the slot canyon, pressing a horn to his lips to signal for help. But the horn only sputtered. The man unable to draw a full breath as he ran.

Stop, you fool. Blow the horn.

Behind the Allied runner, silhouetted like a lithe demon, another man gave rapid pursuit, a spear held just above his shoulder and a shield strapped to his back.

Ram.

Before Gryphon had time to react, the Ram hitched up his front leg and launched the spear.

Gryphon bolted from his place in the brush and sprinted toward the Ram. Below them, the anticipated cry of the Allied soldier sounded right before Gryphon opened his arms wide and lunged at the spear-thrower.

Training took over thought. They landed hard. Hands clasped the sides of Gryphon's head, ready to break his neck with a single movement. But Gryphon anticipated the attack and in quick succession, thrust his palm upward into the Ram's nose, threw his arms out wide, braced the man's shoulders, and drove his knee up into his groin.

Only a cheap shot when life isn't on the line.

He grabbed a fistful of the Ram's hair, unsheathed the dagger Ram liked to carry at their calf, and pressed the blade to the Ram's neck.

"How many are you?"

The blade moved over the man's bobbing Adam's apple, but he didn't say a word.

A sharp whistle called out from the slot canyon. A distinct sound that brought back memories of Gryphon's training.

A whistle to check for status.

One whistle response: use caution. Two whistles: All clear.

Gryphon pressed his eyes together and whispered, "Forgive me," before dragging his knife across the man's throat, severing the windpipe.

He lifted the man's round shield from off the ground, and replied with two quick whistles.

Movement caught Gryphon's attention from the direction he had just traveled. Had an Allied soldier followed him from camp? Was it possible that the weak alert of the lookout had actually awoken someone?

Torn between warning the Allied soldier coming up the hill and giving away his identity to the Ram behind him, Gryphon stood frozen for a moment, surprised that there really wasn't a question that his primary goal was to protect the sorry fool who followed him from camp.

He'd have to play this out.

It was impossible to tell just how many men waited at the mouth of the slot canyon. Ram scouts usually traveled in pairs. But what if this wasn't a traditional scouting party? What if Barnabas had dispatched a full mess unit?

It might explain why Laden's scouts had yet to report movement at the Gate. Multiple scenarios raced through Gryphon's mind, his training so ingrained in him he barely hesitated before deciding on a course of action.

The round shield blocked his bare chest, and he made sure to pretend like he watched his back as he made his way back to the slot canyon. Whoever waited for him at the top would never question that their man had survived the attack. Gryphon's only chance depended now on Ram pride and the cover of night.

Blood dripped down onto the handle of the knife. Gryphon wiped his hand along his bare stomach and gripped the knife again, rolling it over and over in his hand. This little blade and round shield seemed too insignificant to face an unknown threat. But for the sake of the stranger at his back, he had to convince the Ram he was their brother.

As Gryphon moved closer to the slick-rock canyon entrance, a voice from within carried barely to his ears. "Two teams. Reconnaissance only. Stick to the perimeter of the valley and report in thirty, before the next watch."

The owner of the voice wasn't visible, still protected by the walls of the slot canyon.

Gryphon stood frozen, his shield and the cloak of night still hiding his identity. This was no scouting team. Those were the orders of a mess leader, which meant around twenty of the most lethal men in the region. And Gryphon was the only thing standing between them and Barnabas learning not only the location of the Allied Camp but their numbers.

For Zo, Joshua, and Tess's sake, he couldn't let that happen.

Two groups of men spilled from the slot canyon, each keeping to the outer rock wall. Gryphon ducked his head, holding up his shield-bearing arm to block his face as he darted into the canyon and took up position at the back of the smaller group.

His hands shook, his breathing spastic and too loud as he peered over his shield to make certain his ruse had actually worked.

No shouts of alarm. The Ram focused, as they were trained to do, on the potential threats ahead.

Gryphon left a good ten feet between himself and the last man, and after only following for a few feet, carefully retreated backward into the narrow slot canyon. He sprinted into the depths of the suffocating, five-foot wide slot canyon, jumping over the body of what appeared to be a Wolf soldier before reaching a thin gap that required him to turn sideways to squeeze through the towering, pinched walls of slick rock. These narrow walls that had once triggered his fear of tight spaces now might be his salvation.

He took a giant breath, and praying for some kind of miracle, yelled at the top of his lungs. "Ram!" He shouted the warning over and over again, hoping the fool walking up the hill after him might hear and sprint back to warn the Allies.

He prayed he could hold the mess unit off long enough for others to come.

The pounding of boots over stone echoed along the walls of the slot canyon. Gryphon peered over the shield through the two-foot-wide gap, crouched into a battle stance and gripping the small knife now tacky with Ram blood.

The tight canyon was so dark, Gryphon barely saw the first Ram rush toward the gap with spear held high above his head.

Gryphon hefted his shield upward to block the Ram's spear as it shot through the narrow gap. Thrusting his knife up and under the shield, Gryphon's blade sliced through flesh all the way to the hilt. The Ram cried out in pain. His spear clattered to the ground near Gryphon's feet.

Blindly reaching for the spear on the ground, Gryphon heard the gravelly sound of the Ram he'd stuck sliding down the rock, trapped by his brothers at his back, stone on each side, and Gryphon's shield in front.

Another spear lodged into Gryphon's shield. The mess hoisted a man—probably their Striker, up and over their dying brother, but Gryphon anticipated the attack and jabbed his newly acquired spear up at the elevated man now struggling to reach him.

Another kill. Another addition to the fast-forming wall of bodies.

With the way blocked by the dying, the Ram pulled their wounded brothers from the crevasse. Gryphon doubled his grip on the spear. Sweat rolled into his eyes and he blinked it away.

Silence. Heart pounding in his ears.

Armor scraped stone. A Ram soldier spidered up the wall above Gryphon, high enough that a jab from Gryphon's spear wouldn't reach him.

Gryphon could have thrown his spear, but couldn't risk losing his best weapon for survival.

Another Ram soldier slid through the gap on ground level, but also stayed just out of Gryphon's reach. The man above had made it through the gap at least twelve feet above his head. Gryphon held his shield aloft, while at the same time driving the spear through the gap toward the man at ground level, but he was still too far out of his reach.

Too many threats to Gryphon's one shield and spear.

Where are the Allies?

Another man shimmied through the pinched rock, using the shoulders of his brother on the ground as a stepping-stone.

Gryphon didn't have time. He'd have to take one of them out and expose himself to the others.

The decision was made for him when the highest climber pushed off the rock and fell through the air with spear cocked, ready to strike.

Gryphon crouched into a ball, raised the shield overhead and braced for impact.

It came like a boulder from the sky. The Ram connected with his shield and rolled to stand behind him. Gryphon thrust his spear upward and caught him in the thigh. Behind them two more Ram scurried through the narrow gap. Gryphon turned and threw his only knife into the gap, turning back to block the attack of the man behind him before even seeing his knife connect with its target.

Fire sliced his side from rib to navel as he spun out of reach from a blade. Trusting his strength more than his eyes, he tackled the man, earning him another gash—this time in the shoulder—as they went down together.

Gryphon hit his head against stone in the fall, but managed to roll on top of the Ram.

New shouts echoed off stone. Cries of pain. Cries of those inflicting pain.

The Allies. Finally!

Gryphon pinned down the Ram's arms as he sat on his chest, but the Ram wrapped his legs around Gryphon's torso and pulled him onto his back. The impact forced the air from Gryphon's lungs.

Movement caught his eye—a small figure climbing the rock high above. A child? His vision spun as he struggled with the man on top of him. The battle sounds swelled and died inside his head—heartbeats alternating between awake and unconscious.

Awake. The Ram searching the ground for a weapon.

Darkness.

Awake. The silver glint of a knife raised above his head.

Darkness.

Awake. The small, boyish figure perched above them. An arrow drawn.

Darkness.

Gryphon rolled onto his side, the violent sounds of battle replaced by whispers and oaths. Next to him, a Ram lay on the ground, an arrow sticking up out of his chest, his fingers clutching it as though he'd spent his final breaths trying to wrench it from his body.

Ever fighting. A Ram through and through.

"You died on your shield, brave one." Gryphon's voice came out raspy and nearly inaudible. He placed his hand on the Ram's shoulder, looked up in search of the boy, and then collapsed to the ground in exhaustion.

Zo's eyes flew open at the sound of booming drums and the staccato shouts coming from outside the tent.

"What's happening?" Tess cried.

Zo cursed the gray darkness of early morning and swung her legs around, jamming her feet into well-worn boots. Feeling her way through the dark tent, she hurried to Millie's cot. The older woman moaned and slowly sat upright.

"I think we're under attack," said Zo. "You and Tess prep the healing tent. I'll be right back."

"You can't leave!" shouted Tess. "You promised."

Zo took her sister by the hand, kissed her palm, and placed it firmly in Millie's. "We need to know what we're up against. I'm counting on you, bug. Help Millie. I'll be right back."

Zo didn't bother with a torch as she sprinted out of the tent. The sun was yet to rise over the cliffs of the valley, but dawn wasn't far off and the glow of morning filled the gray-blue sky. Lanterns had been lit around the camp and men raced past her wearing half-buttoned trousers with weapons slung across their backs.

She ran a short distance to Gryphon's tent and caught Joshua scrambling out the flap, blinking and distorted.

"Where's Gryphon?" she asked.

"Gone," said Joshua. "Sani too."

Zo's heart dropped into her stomach. "Where are you going?"

"After him, of course." Joshua took off at a full sprint in the direction of the men.

It seemed the entire Allied Camp had answered the drums as they headed like a syncopated pack north toward the slot canyon entrance to the valley. If the Ram were foolish enough to bring the battle to the Allies through that small canyon where they'd be forced to travel in single file, they had no prayer of survival.

It had to be something else. But what?

The ground sloped upward. The men of the camp jogged ahead. Some carried torches while most relied only on the moon for guidance.

"Hunt them down!" someone yelled.

After five minutes of trying to keep pace with Joshua, a stitch knotted Zo's side. The crowd of men thickened, but Joshua wouldn't be deterred as he shoved his way to the front of the group, leaving a trail for Zo to follow.

"Clear a path!" a familiar voice called.

Gabe. It had to be.

"Transport the injured. Three to a man. Get them to the Healer's Tent. Careful!"

Zo burst through an opening in the crowd of men to find three Allied soldiers lying lifeless on the ground at the mouth of the slot canyon. Others stirred in obvious pain.

She ran toward the wounded and something caught her arm. "You shouldn't be up here," said Gabe. "It's not safe."

Zo pushed his hand away. "They're hurt," was her only explanation as she ran past him to the first wounded man in her path.

Stab wound. Shoulder. "I need a shirt!" she yelled. The man nearest her pulled his shirt over his head and offered it. She bundled the fabric and pressed it against the wound, earning a sharp curse from the wounded. "Keep pressure on the wound and get him to the tent."

She hurried over to the second man and stopped short. The left side of the man's face was split completely open from hairline to chin. The torchlight cast harsh light over shadow and bone, flesh and fatty tissue in the cheek. Blood filled the eye socket, the eye itself splayed open in tatters.

Less blood. Non-fatal, as gruesome as it was.

Zo had seen many wounds, but they never ceased to cause her near physical pain. She knelt beside the man, forgetting the other soldiers looking down at her. She ran the tips of her fingers along the man's good cheek. "You're going to be all right," she whispered near his ear. He looked so young. Sixteen or seventeen at most.

Eyes closed, she offered a quick blessing to help numb the pain then nodded to the men around her to carry him down the hill to the Healer's Tent, where she could work on him properly.

Zo winced as a sharp pain shot across her own cheek.

Silence swept through the ranks in a wave that started at the mouth of the slot canyon and crashed over the men outside. Hair on the back of Zo's neck stood on end as four Raven emerged from the slot canyon, each carrying the corner of a blanket. Other Raven solemnly joined them, bearing up the sides so as to not jostle the small, lifeless boy inside.

"No." Zo took off at a run but Gabe leapt out and hooked her by the waist.

"He's gone," he whispered in her ear.

"You don't know that!" Zo shouted.

Gabe clamped his hand over her mouth, and she shoved it away, furious.

"Listen to me." He gave her a light shake. "The Raven see death differently than you and I. I'll explain later, but please, for their sakes, don't make a scene."

Gabe supported most of her weight as she watched, helpless, as the Raven walked Sani's body down the hill. She spotted Joshua standing alone, hugging his arms to his chest and shaking all over.

Zo collected herself enough to lean away from Gabe and close the few steps separating them. "I'm so sorry," she said, wrapping him up in a hug he didn't return. Tears collected in his eyes. He worked his lips from side to side, fighting emotion that begged to release.

Then Zo's own heart plummeted with dread.

"Gryphon," she said. She ran to the slot canyon and after taking only two or three steps in, halted.

Blood.

Sprayed on the walls. Soaking the ground.

Ram soldiers staring up at the sky with lifeless eyes, their shields discarded on the ground. Light finally peeked over the high canyon wall, casting the morbid scene in what should have been cheerful light.

"Zo?"

Zo startled, and said, "Go back, Joshua. You shouldn't see this."

"Where is he?"

Zo didn't know how to answer him. She didn't dare look into the faces of the men, too afraid that one of them would be Gryphon.

"I'll find him. You go back."

Joshua snorted his disgust at the idea and walked into the slot canyon ahead of Zo, stepping over the bodies of his clansmen as he tried to avoid touching the bloody rock walls. Voices up ahead had them doubling their time. They turned a corner to find Laden, covered in blood and dragging away the body of a Ram soldier from a narrow place in the slot canyon.

"Where's Gryphon?" she ran toward Laden.

"You shouldn't be in here," the Commander growled. "Neither of you."

Zo took a few steps back, nearly stumbling over a spear on the ground.

"I'm here, Zo." Gryphon, covered in blood, slid through the narrow crevasse and fell to his knees when he cleared the gap.

Relief hit Zo like a bucket of cool water. She and Joshua both rushed him, each kneeling on either side of him. "What happened?" she demanded. A long, deep gash ran along his side. He wore no shirt, and his chest, arms, and shoulders were covered with scratches.

Gryphon didn't have the chance to answer before Laden cut him off.

"Your boy just single-handedly stopped a full mess unit from taking our location back to Barnabas." Laden reached a hand out to Gryphon to help him stand. "He's a hero."

Chapter Twenty

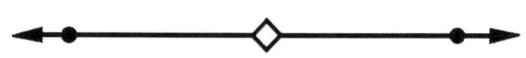

Gryphon never once took his eyes off Zo when they returned to the Healer's Tent as she administered fifty-seven stitches, four blessings, multiple ointments, and one fitted eye patch to the men injured in the attack. Zo leaned against the leg of a wooden worktable as she melted to the floor. Resting her chin on her knees, she stared out at the sleeping forms of the men—boys, really—whom she, Millie, and Tess had attended.

At some point, the sun had reached its highest place in the sky and fallen into the western horizon, casting warm light through the tent flaps and turning the fabric honey amber.

Tess gathered the remaining soiled bedclothes and took them out for cleaning. "You did well, kid," Zo said to Tess.

And the little girl had. Gryphon doubted she'd ever seen anything so gruesome as the men she helped Zo work on today. But with the coming battle, this was only the beginning.

Zo let her head fall back and her eyes close.

Gryphon couldn't stand watching her sleep in such discomfort and didn't want to think about the price she'd likely pay for healing those men. When they first entered the tent, he'd refused her help. He still shuddered over the memory of her striking blue eyes darting up to meet his in cold defiance. Her mouth had set into a firm line before she'd turned away without another word.

It had been Millie who sewed Gryphon back together. The older woman's healing strength was nothing compared to Zo's, but at least he wasn't heaping more pain upon Zo.

Taking his time to swing his feet out of the narrow bed, Gryphon stood and walked over to Zo's side. His stitches tugged as he bent to lift her from the ground, but he ignored the pain.

She turned her face to nuzzle into him. For a few moments, he savored the feel of cradling her in his arms before her eyes flew open. "Your stitches," she said, her voice a low whisper.

"I'm fine," he promised, walking her over to the bed next to his and lowering her down. "After all you've done today, I think you deserve a proper bed."

She barely seemed to register the light brush of his lips on hers and the woolen blankets being tucked around her. Stars, she was beautiful. Gryphon watched the steady rise and fall of Zo's chest, the soft planes of her face, the fluttering eyelashes that kissed her tanned cheeks.

He was a man completely and utterly smitten.

"I'm worried about Joshua," she said, eyes still forced closed by exhaustion. Was she paying for the healing already?

"This isn't the first battle scene the boy has witnessed. Probably not the last either."

"But he's never seen his best friend … " Zo's eyes fluttered open. She sat up on the bed, placing a hand on her cheek. "Oh, Gryphon. You don't know!"

She slid her feet from the cot, and took his hand in hers. "Sani followed you. They say he saved your life."

Gryphon didn't remember standing. "What?"

"Laden told me Sani was the one to raise the alarm, but when told to stay back, he followed anyway. Sani climbed the rock wall of the slot canyon and made his way over to where you were fighting. The men said that when they found you, there was a Ram lying next to you with an arrow through his heart."

Gryphon couldn't swallow. Couldn't breathe.

"Is … is he all right?"

Tears filled Zo's eyes. She shook her head. "He didn't make it, Gryphon. I … I'm sorry."

Gryphon stood, numb and broken, and left the tent. *Joshua.* He said the boy's name over and over in his mind. He needed to find the kid. But when he reached their tent it was empty. He hurried over to the Raven sector, knowing his presence wouldn't be welcome but not caring enough to stop walking.

What had Sani been thinking? Gryphon shook his head, and a surprised sob escaped him. He fought back his emotions, knowing the Raven didn't welcome any form of outward mourning. They believed that if the people wept over their dead, the spirits of their loved ones would linger instead of entering into the afterlife. There would be no funeral for Sani. No words spoken over his grave. No tears shed. The thought made Gryphon want to punch someone.

Gryphon came to Chief Naat's tent. Two Raven guards stood still as statues at the door, confirming the chief was inside.

"May I speak with him?" Gryphon cleared the emotion from his voice. "Will he see me?"

The two guards exchanged an uncertain look. One ducked inside the tent and was out in only a few moments. "The chief is grieving. He will see no one."

"Where are Raca and Talon?" Gryphon asked. He had to speak to someone. He had to apologize. To kneel at their feet with shame for letting this happen to their beloved little brother.

"Raca has taken the trail south out of the valley. She threatened a quick death to anyone who followed her."

"And Talon?"

"With his wife and children."

Gryphon swore under his breath. "Please tell the chief ... " He stopped, unsure how to find the words to make something this horrible right. Untying the string of Sani's beads around his wrist, Gryphon held them out to the guard. "Please give these to the chief. Tell him I'm sorry. Tell him I didn't know Sani followed me. Tell him I wish it was me."

Zo walked with tender, slow steps along the trail through the southern canyon and out of the valley. Her muscles ached and head pounded, and an invisible gash on her side flamed hot with pain whenever she twisted. She'd stitched a man in that exact spot yesterday. Millie had warned her not to bless the wounds, but with some of the more dire cases, she'd given a little of herself in a blessing anyway.

When she examined the spot that morning, the skin where she'd purged the man's infection and coaxed the skin to heal was red and irritated. A thin, angry line had formed. Was it possible that she'd taken the man's infection into her own body?

A shiver rolled over her skin as she pushed away the thought. There had to be some way around this. In the meantime, she'd have Millie or Tess look at her when she got back to camp.

She fingered the knife sheathed at her side. Though she preferred not to wear the ugly weapon, the Ram attack at the north canyon yesterday had put her on edge. Somehow the Ram mess unit, trapped on both sides in the slot canyon, had managed to kill not just Sani but fifteen others before the Allies could stop them. Sixteen dead. Many others wounded. And this wasn't even a fair fight out in the open. If so few men could do that kind of damage while cornered, she shivered to think of what an actual confrontation with the Ram might look like. Living in the Allied Camp with all their numbers made one forget just how deadly an enemy the Ram were.

Laden had teams scouting for miles in every direction, looking for any sign of the Ram. Early reports proved that no one was anywhere near the camp, but the Raven teams he'd sent to scout the lands nearer Ram's Gate wouldn't return for another day or two at best.

The southern entrance to the valley was all but forgotten. The only area south of here belonged to the Wolves who were friendly to their cause. Still, Zo clutched the knife at her side.

After three painful hours of hiking, Zo hadn't seen a single person on the trail. Not even the person she had hoped to find.

Poor Raca.

The feisty Raven princess already carried so many burdens without the added blow of losing her brother. Zo caught herself rubbing the space around her heart—massaging the ache that collected there when she thought of losing someone so close to her again. If it had been Tess, Zo couldn't imagine carrying on.

There wasn't much Zo could do in this battle other than try and save lives and offer a bit of compassion. And she intended to do just that, despite the grief she'd get for leaving camp without telling anyone.

The canyon opened up to a vast bench overlooking green rolling fields littered with pockets of dark trees. A blue stream cut through the valley and wispy, white clouds moved across the enormous blue sky. The view demanded appreciation. Zo settled against the trunk of a tree at the edge of the bench and leaned back, letting the view block out memories of empty eye sockets, torn flesh, and splattered blood.

She took a deep breath, inhaling the smell of cedar and clean air.

An arrow cut through the sky to her right and embedded into the branch of a tree not ten feet away.

"Leave me!" Raca's strong voice penetrated the foliage surrounding Zo. Though the girl was still not visible from Zo's current position, she could tell the arrow came from just below the bench.

Zo opened her mouth to apologize—she'd been warned Raca didn't want company—but stopped short when someone else beat her to it.

"You shouldn't be alone." A male voice. Less familiar, but so distinct it really could only belong to one person.

Zo winced at the pain in her side as she shifted onto her stomach and peered over the ledge. Two figures, opposites in every way, stood fifteen feet away from each other. If Zo didn't know them both better, she might have thought they'd met here to settle some old feud. Raca seemed perfectly ready to rip the bear's head off.

"I'm so tired of people telling me that I shouldn't be alone. That I'm not capable of taking care of myself. My brother is *dead!*" Her voice caught, thick with emotion. "Let me mourn him in my own way."

Murtog took a tentative step toward Raca. He wore his long dreads of hair unbound so they fell around his shoulders. His sleeveless tunic left his tattooed, muscular arms bare. Across from him, Raca clutched her bow at her side, her other hand balled into a fist, and her chest pumped as though the lid stoppering her control was ready to blow.

"I know a thing or two about loss," said Murtog. "I know what it's like to want to retreat into your pain and let it swallow you up. There is a time to be alone," he took another step toward her, "and there is a time to be comforted."

Then, in a smaller, gentler voice, he said, "Please. Let me comfort you." His hands shook at his sides. How someone could manage to look so small and vulnerable in such a large body was beyond Zo. Though his voice communicated one thing, his demeanor said something entirely different. *Let us comfort each other.*

Raca dropped her bow into the high green grass and pushed the pads of her hands into her eyes, as though literally forcing back her tears. Murtog closed the distance between them with a few careful steps. "Why do you fight the pain, Raca? You must let it out. Give it a voice or it can never leave you."

In barely a whisper, "I don't know how."

More steps. Murtog stopped so close if he reached out, he could easily touch her. "I can help you."

Raca lowered her hands and looked up into Murtog's handsome face.

Suddenly Zo regretted letting her presence go unannounced for so long. She lay frozen on the ledge, afraid to move and ashamed for not wanting to leave.

Raca brushed away a tear from her cheek. "I should not cry over him. I … I cannot. For Sani's sake."

"Then don't cry." Murtog closed the remaining distance between them and slowly raised his arm as an invitation. Raca didn't hesitate before stepping into his embrace, swallowed up in the safety of Murtog's massive arms, her cheek pressed against his chest.

"Shout your pain, princess. Let the gods know what they've taken from you."

When Raca didn't respond, he placed a hand to her ear, filled his chest with air and shouted at the sky with such force, Zo startled and inched backward. Again and again, he filled his chest with air and released it in the most agonizing lament Zo had ever witnessed. On the third yell, Raca joined him, throwing her head back and releasing a heart-wrenching cry of pain.

Afterward, she tightened her hold on Murtog and buried her face into his chest. Shoulders shaking in silent sobs, she practically collapsed into Murtog's embrace. He swept her legs out from under her and carried her like a child over to a boulder, where he sat and leaned back with her still swallowed up in his arms. Light reflected off the sheen of tears on his face.

Zo didn't know if they were tears for his lost wife, tears for Sani that Raca wasn't permitting herself to shed, or tears of something beautiful.

New hope and possibilities.

Perhaps it was all three.

Zo backed away from her spot on the ledge, careful not to make sound. She headed back through the canyon, satisfied with Raca's healing even though it wasn't by her own hands.

Chapter Twenty-One

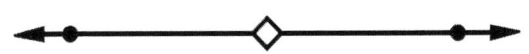

Ten days before Gryphon's planned meeting with Barnabas, the flap of the Healer's Tent flew open.

"We need to talk." Gabe stared down at Gryphon, accusation punctuating every line in his face and every taut muscle in his stance.

Gryphon pushed up to his feet and followed Gabe out past the sea of tents. They didn't stop until they reached the practice field on the northern edge of camp. He hadn't planned to come to this field today. His stitches were only two days old and he'd promised Millie that he'd rest for a few days.

Gabe wandered over to a barrel filled with wooden practice swords. He plucked two from the pile and threw one to Gryphon. The long sword was a preferred weapon of the Wolves. A weapon Gryphon despised, favoring the short swords of his people that allowed for closer combat.

Gabe and Gryphon circled one another twice before Gabe finally spoke his mind. "How could you do this to her?" He brought the blade down over Gryphon's head with more force than Gryphon anticipated, nearly causing him to drop his weapon into the dirt as he blocked.

Redoubling his grip, Gryphon winced at the eerie tug of his stitches. He blocked another strike and said, "What are you talking about?"

"I've been driving myself mad with guilt over my lie to you both," Gabe growled. He advanced again, with so much speed Gryphon struggled to keep his feet. "I've stepped away. Trusting you to protect and honor her."

A crowd gathered. A captain of the Wolves fighting the Ram outcast didn't happen every day.

Gryphon spun, ducking under one of Gabe's blows to land a solid hit on the man's back. "I've been trying to tell her. It's been hard the past few days, since the Ram attack." A lie. The truth of the matter was quite simple: There was a wedge growing between them, a divide he didn't know how to cross. And with so little time left, he didn't want to give her another reason to despise him. "I'll tell her."

Gabe brought down his weapon over Gryphon's head. He couldn't block in time. Couldn't move away fast enough. He leaned away at the last second and wood connected with his collarbone, splitting the sword in half.

White pain lanced across Gryphon's shoulders and neck. He straightened, each man panting as they surveyed the other. "You know what your problem is?" said Gabe, the broken practice sword still clutched in his hand. "You think you're invincible. You've escaped your clan twice now. You saved us all from the Gate." He took a few steadying breaths and dropped the broken sword in the dirt and leaned in to whisper so none of the men around them could hear. "But no man can expect to waltz into a Ram execution and live to see another day. Not even you."

Gryphon massaged the spot where Gabe had marked him. Already a large welt rose on the tender skin. "I don't plan to survive."

"You're going to break her heart." Gabe rubbed his cheek and let the hand smear down his face. "And it kills me to say this, but you were the one who put it back together after her parents were killed.

Losing you would destroy her all over again."

She doesn't trust me. "What are you saying?" said Gryphon.

"I'm saying that you need to either tell Zo your plans or take Zo and leave this place. Take it from me," he rested his hand on Gryphon's shoulder, directly over the rising welt, "lies only bring sorrow and regret."

The next morning, Zo found Gryphon sitting alone with his back to her on the bank of a small stream just outside camp. The water gurgled past, rolling over rocks and pebbles on its way. Sunlight reflected off the shiny silt below the surface, casting a spray of black dots in Zo's vision. She shielded her eyes and took another silent step forward.

"I want to be left alone," said Gryphon. He kept his back to her as he tossed a pebble into the stream.

Zo's stiffened at his cold tone. Empty. She'd heard that tone before. A long, long time ago. So long ago it might have been a dream. Her father sitting on the grass overlooking the valley while sharpening his weapons. He had wanted to be left alone too, the night before the Ram came.

Zo tried not to let disappointment creep into her voice. "If that's what you want."

Gryphon's head whipped up and he was almost instantly on his feet. "Zo!" He closed the distance between them in two strides and took her by the hand. "I thought you were one of Laden's guards asking me to join another meeting," he explained.

"No, it's all right." Zo pulled away. "I understand if you want some time to yourself." He'd been devastated by Sani's death. And he wasn't alone. The entire camp seemed to be swallowed up in mourning. Mourning for the loss of a Raven prince, and plagued by the reminder that even inside the Allied Camp, they weren't completely safe.

If Chief Naat's runners didn't return soon with news of the Gate, they'd be forced to send another team. If a full mess of Ram had found them, there was a chance even Barnabas knew their location. Whispers around camp said a battle was looming, but no one seemed to know specifics, and Laden hadn't given her so much as a hint of his plans when she'd cornered him on the subject.

"No." Gryphon took her hand again and this time held it with more intensity. "I want you to stay." He cleared his throat as though intending to speak but didn't. When had things turned so awkward between them? Gryphon was never unsure of himself.

He led her back to the bank of the stream and together they sat with their backs to a granite boulder as they listened to the gentle flow of the shallow water rolling over rocks.

"There's something I've been meaning to talk to you about. Something I've wanted to say for a while now," said Gryphon.

Zo shook her head. "I'm sorry I doubted you about the fire. I've been feeling so strange and insecure." She sighed at her rushed, jumbled admission. "I know you're unhappy here and—"

"Stop." He turned away and threaded his hands through his hair. "You're right not to trust me."

Zo shook her head. She'd been a fool to even think Gryphon could be anything but honorable. Reaching for his arm, she grabbed him and forced him to face her. "I love you, Gryphon. I trust you. I was wrong to question you before, and I will not make that mistake again."

Gryphon reached out and took her face in his hands. His thumb briefly grazed her cheek. Back and forth, feather soft. Gentle, as though he might break her if he wasn't careful.

She was stronger than he knew. Much stronger.

His hand trailed down her arm to her side and rested on the hilt of the dagger. "Why do you carry this?" His breath came quick, like he'd been running.

She wrinkled her nose, surprised by the change in subject. "For protection, why else?"

Gryphon shook his head. "You have no business carrying this weapon."

Zo sat back, shocked. "I think I've earned the right to carry a blade, Gryph! Women of your clan carry them everywhere."

Gryphon climbed to his feet and offered Zo his hands to help her up. She stared at them then used her own power to stand.

"Don't be offended. I'm not suggesting you're too weak to carry a knife."

Perhaps, but you're still dodging the question. Zo's hands shot to her hips and in that moment she knew she looked like Tess in one of her fits. "Then what *are* you suggesting?"

Gryphon folded his arms across his chest. His angular face studied Zo as he considered her.

"What?" Zo's voice rose.

"Say a man tries to attack you from behind." Gryphon slowly took hold of her waist and spun her around. The weight of his hands made her blush. She closed her eyes and fought the urge to lean against his strong frame as he stepped right behind her. Thigh to thigh. Back to chest. The heat of his body at her back acted as a tangible energy between them. "He goes to grab you." Gryphon wrapped his heavy arms around her. Pinning her arms to her side. "What do you do?"

Zo took her time to consider, soaking in the moment, resisting the urge to lull her head back onto his shoulder, to find the warm hollow of his neck with her lips. "I fight." Zo meant to speak with more volume, but only a whisper escaped her wanting lips.

"Exactly. And when the man realizes you're not worth the fight ... " Out of nowhere, a dagger pressed to her throat. Her dagger. He turned her around and tucked the knife back in its case.

"Men wear swords because they are strong enough to keep them.

Not because they have earned the right to carry them. You," he touched the tip of her nose in a playful gesture, "lack a man's strength and must make up for it in cunning. Ouch!"

Zo held her hidden knife to his stomach. They were pressed so close together that he hadn't seen her go for it. "That," he pushed the blade away from him, "is exactly what I mean."

Zo removed the large dagger from the belt at her waist. "I trust your judgment." She offered it to him with a shy smile. "Here, I doubt anyone will ever have the chance to take it from you."

For once she didn't weigh the ramifications of her actions. Before her mind caught up with her body, she stepped closer to him, threading her arms beneath his to wrap around his torso. Trying to squeeze despair from his frame like she might extract venom from a wound.

He kissed the top of her head then pulled back a little to find her cheek. Then he paused by her lips. "I shouldn't—there's something … " Then he groaned and gave into the demanding energy between them. Their lips met in a fury of need. His hands ran the length of her spine until they settled on her hips and pulled her even closer. His mouth moved with hers in earnest passion. A fire exploded in Zo's chest, and a sense of rightness consumed her being. Whatever demons Gryphon battled, they were no match for *this*.

After several long, yet entirely too short minutes, Gryphon pulled away, panting, though their foreheads still kissed. "I shouldn't be doing this."

"What shouldn't you be doing?"

He took a step back and gestured to the space between them. "Pretending like nothing is wrong."

A heavy weight dropped onto Zo's chest, pressing out all the wind in her lungs. "And what is wrong, Gryphon?"

Gryphon wrung his hands around the leather casing of Zo's dagger. "Nothing you or I can fix." He turned around and growled. "I can't do this!"

Zo took a step back. Surprised by just how painful four words could be. Her shaking fingers hovered over lips that only moments ago confessed her feelings for the man before her. The man who admitted that, whatever his feelings for her, they weren't enough.

Was living inside the Allied Camp so horrible? In time he might adjust. By wanting him to try, did she demand too much?

"Gryphon, I'm sorry you're unhappy." She wanted to reach out to him and close the disgusting space separating them. But this gap seemed much wider than just the few feet. "Once this blood oath is fulfilled, we can take Joshua and Tess and leave this place. Go wherever you want. We don't need to live among the Wolves." She blushed hearing the desperation in her own voice. "That is, if you still want me." How pathetic she sounded.

Gryphon's face turned to a mask of stone. "Where I am going, you cannot follow."

A horn sounded in the village. At the same time one of the Laden's runners broke through the trees, panting, with hands on knees. "The Commander needs you, Ram."

Zo and Gryphon glanced north to the gap in the mountain, where a thin line of men jogged down from the slot canyon to the foothills.

Gryphon wouldn't look at her. "The Raven scouts have returned. Commander Laden will be making an announcement soon. I should be with him when he does." He offered her a sad smile. "Can we talk about this later?"

"Why bother?" Zo battled back tears. "You're leaving."

He offered a slow nod. "Please," his voice broke, "forgive me." He took off at a sprint through the trees. Never looking back.

Zo watched the place where he disappeared, feeling cold with his absence. What kind of announcement would Commander Laden make that involved Gryphon's presence?

Too many questions. Too few answers. But one thought came to mind, louder and stronger than any horn.

I've lost him.

Instead of following Gryphon back to camp, Zo walked in the opposite direction along the stream. Rubbing a chill from her arms, Zo blinked back tears. Here the grass grew long, in some places as high as her knees. She kept her back to the energy buzzing around the camp and focused her attention on the persistent water rolling over and around rocks to get to its final destination at the small lake.

A breeze swept through the valley, forcing the tall grass to dance and shiver around her shins. With the breeze a rancid, stomach-churning smell drifted toward her, carried down the sloping foothill. The farther she walked away from camp the more pungent the scent became, until she was forced to cover her nose with both hands.

Zo walked faster. The hair along her forearms stood on end. The rank scent triggered a gag reflex, singeing the inside of her nose. The grass was so tall that she didn't see the bodies until almost stepping on an outstretched arm.

The bodies of the four men were lined next to each other on the ground in a morbidly perfect row. They lay bloated, their skin a reddish-gray hue. Blood clotted in deep lacerations across each of their necks. Again, symmetrical. Though the bodies had decomposed some, it wasn't hard to identify the four men who'd gone missing the night of the fire. The Commander's personal guard all wore the same notches in their belts. These were Gryphon's guards.

Zo gagged, hand still covering her mouth, as she took a step backward. The sun reflected a lone dagger staked into one of the dead men's chest. Tied to the hilt with a delicate red ribbon was a glass bottle with a cork stopper.

In the space between heartbeats, Zo recognized the bottle. Glass the same tinted brown. The height and narrow width.

Suddenly, the careful arrangement of the men, the ribbon, the exact type of bottle Zo stole time and again from the Ram Medica to send messages down river to the Allies—it all pointed to one person.

These men were meant to be found. This bottle … this bottle was for her.

Old fear, sharp as talons, gnawed at her insides as she inched closer to the bodies. Cold sweat broke out on her forehead. The ground seemed to shift from side to side in a dizzying sensation. With a shaking hand, Zo reached down and tugged at the tail of the perfect red bow.

The bottle dropped and rolled into the open neck of the dead guard, and Zo's fingers brushed his flesh as she snatched it up and stumbled away, emptying the contents of her stomach in the long grass.

The stench burned her throat and nostrils, and she crawled toward camp and away from the bodies. When she finally trusted her legs to carry her, she staggered to the stream and plunged her hands into the water, splashing it into her face. Cleansing the death from her body.

Still shaken, Zo sat back on the bank and concentrated on dragging air through her lungs to calm her racing heart. Only then did she uncork the bottle and slide the rolled paper free of its glass cage.

> *You and the traitor will never be free of me. My eyes see everything. My reach is limitless and my revenge will be sweet and terrible.*
> *-S*

Zo's head snapped up. She glanced around the thin trees and tall grass, suddenly wary. That woman. That demon could be watching her, even now. But how? Was Chief Barnabas's Seer so cunning? Were her spies inside the camp? Had they always been?

Memories of her interactions with the Seer inside Ram's Gate came flooding back. Her small dark eyes that weaseled into Zo's thoughts. The woman had an eerie way of knowing everything that happened inside the Gate and was known for her exquisitely brutal punishments for even the slightest infraction. She was the reason Joshua had nearly died in the prizefight and consequently, the reason she was broken as a healer.

Everything that had happened since they'd arrived—the fire, the sabotaged spears, the poisonings—it was all her. Taunting them. Wanting Zo and Gryphon to know they hadn't truly escaped her. That they never would.

Zo shattered the bottle against the rocks and sprinted back to camp, taking the smell of the Seer's victims with her.

Chapter Twenty-Two

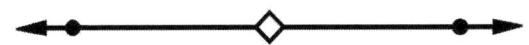

Ram never retreat.

It was a philosophy drilled into him as a child and reinforced in every training session since. In drills, he never slackened when his body wanted to surrender. In the few skirmishes he'd survived, even when outnumbered, he'd never backed down. When he finally made the decision to get Zo out of the Gate, he'd followed that dangerous course to the end and beyond.

Ram never retreat.

But now, running back to the Commander and away from Zo and the glaring omission that stood between them, the forbidden word *retreat* alternated with *coward* in his mind. Not only did his self-respect demand he turn around and face her, but the knowledge that Zo deserved his honesty screamed he return and explain everything.

He didn't turn around. The taste of her lips shamed him all the way to the Commander's tent.

By dusk, most of the camp was in chaos. Men barked orders, boys ran messages, and animals bellowed the occasional complaint as heavy packs were secured to their backs. Gryphon walked among the throng of confused soldiers who'd been given orders to pack. Families of both the Raven and the few Wolf women and children who'd lingered after the *Ostara* were given the same instructions. All questions would be answered in only a few short hours when Commander Laden addressed the Allies.

Gryphon had arrived at Laden's tent at the same time as the Raven scouts. Murtog, the Wolf Alpha, and Chief Naat were already in council with Laden. The scouts not only confirmed that the Ram had begun their march from Ram's Gate to the Valley of Wolves, but that a massive caravan of Nameless traveled with them.

Laden and the others agreed that it was time to evacuate the camp in the morning. No one would rest easy tonight after the announcement.

If it were Gryphon's decision, he would have waited until the morning to give orders. There was no sense letting his men lose valuable sleep when tomorrow they could march away that nervous energy. It was unreasonable to ask a man to wait till morning when his family's safety hung in the balance.

He certainly wouldn't have waited a night, not even an hour, before journeying to protect the people he loved. He winced under the weight of his own thoughts. He didn't want to think about Joshua or Zo or even Tess. Too painful.

As if the kid could sense his thoughts, Joshua stumbled out from behind one of the many tents scattered across the camp.

"Gryph!" He tripped over his feet and flopped into Gryphon's side.

Gryphon reached out to help him gain his balance. Like any half-grown pup, the kid's feet had always seemed too big for his body.

"Where have you been?" Joshua leaned into Gryphon. His breath reeked of yeast and barley.

"What have you been doing?" Gryphon shook his shoulders.

"Looking for you," he said, breathing a particularly foul mouthful of air onto Gryphon with that last *you*.

"Where, in the bottom of a mug?" Gryphon hooked Joshua's upper arm and hauled him through the camp. Men darted out of his path, likely seeing the crazed glint in his eyes. Joshua did his best to keep his feet beneath him as they moved.

Gryphon ripped open their tent and sat Joshua down on the cot. "I leave you alone for five hours and come back to find you drunk?" Of all the timing.

Joshua covered his ears. "Why are you yelling?" he moaned, and fell face first into his bedroll. Without Sani, the tent was too large for just two people. The thought made Gryphon ill.

"They didn't think I was brave enough to try it, Gryph," he spoke into his pillow. "I had no choice." After a few long, sleepy breaths he added, "I should have been the one to follow you that night." A few more breaths. "I'll never be great. Never prove myself." His chest rose and fell in sleep.

Gryphon sighed. Is this what would happen when he was gone? Who would be here to punish Joshua for being an idiot? Who would guide him into manhood and complete his training? Zo loved the boy, sure, but there were just some things a woman couldn't teach.

Joshua's snoring officially ended any lecture that Gryphon felt welling up inside of him. Words would have to wait until morning.

Gryphon thought of Zo as he walked to Laden's tent that evening. He hadn't seen her since their time by the stream. No matter how enticing Gabe's idea of taking Zo and fleeing the camp, he'd only ever had one option. He'd march with Laden in the morning and trust the fates to determine the rest. Strange that walking *away* from Zo could be so much harder than walking *to* Barnabas.

One night.

One night to make sure the people he loved were cared for. One night to tell Zo the truth. It would be hardest on Joshua. Left alone to learn this new life outside of the Gate. Zo would turn to Gabe. They would marry and have children. Gabe would take care of her and Tess. They would be happy.

Gryphon had to consciously force himself to relax his jaw.

One night to say goodbye.

"Ah, Gryphon," said Commander Laden. He clapped him on the back and led him over to stand with a group of his officers, each with five slashes on his belt. The Ram used a similar method of showing rank. Laden's Ram heritage was seeping throughout the camp and no one even knew it.

Gryphon shook his head, marveling at the thought.

Laden bounded to the training field platform before the gathered Allies awaiting his announcement. He moved with the agility of a young man, though he had to be nearly fifty. He cut an impressive figure with his dark eyes catching the final rays of sun. His cape billowed around him in the wind, but he stood as a boulder of strength, unyielding to man or weather.

The shifting feet and nervous whispers of the Allies died as Commander Laden's deep voice carried over the crowd. "Allies! Many of us have lived and trained in this valley for several years in anticipation for a chance to engage our enemy outside Ram's Gate. We've left our families and our homes to fight under the banner of the Allies. Tomorrow our sacrifices and training will be justified. The time for waiting has past."

A flurry of voices scattered around the field. Laden held up his hands, and they quieted again. "The Ram have abandoned the Gate to invade the Wolves." He paused for the shocked reactions of his men. "We knew this day would come and a plan is in place. At dawn we break camp to intercept them." A chorus of howls broke from the crowd. The volume was staggering, the pitch eerily soft and loud at the same time.

Laden's voice softened once the soldiers quieted. "The women and children of camp will take the southern canyon to the Valley of Wolves. A small contingent of men will accompany them to the Wolves' shelter bunker. It is the safest place for them now."

With that one statement, all of the Allies' vibrato drained, replaced by hard realities. Even though it seemed illogical to send the women and children to the very place the Ram planned to attack, everyone knew it was their only option. The survival of these men's wives and children now depended entirely on the army's ability to hold off the Ram at the narrow pass north of the Valley of Wolves.

"The rest of us—Kodiak, Wolf, and Raven—will march out to intercept our common enemy." More cheers. More worried glances between family members who would soon have to bid each other farewell. More shifting feet.

"Say your prayers tonight, boys, for tomorrow we march to meet Barnabas and his Ram."

As he spoke, Gryphon could almost hear a familiar cadence in his tone, reminding him strangely of home. But then again, maybe it was just the subject matter.

War belonged to the Ram.

Looking out at the sea of stunned men, many who had wives and children to protect, Gryphon couldn't help but feel sorry for them. Many of these soldiers would not live much longer than he. Training to fight for a cause was one thing. Marching out to look death in the face was quite another.

The troops were dismissed and chaos erupted as everyone spoke at once. Zo pushed past a few men to get to Gryphon's side. She clutched his arm until her knuckles turned white. After a few moments Gabe appeared, scooping up Zo's free hand.

There was no use trying to shout over the chorus of voices. "Come to my tent!" Gryphon said and gestured her to follow. Zo didn't let go of Gryphon's arm until he held open the flap for her to enter. Gabe met his eyes in challenge as he too stepped inside the tent under Gryphon's stern gaze.

Didn't the Wolf realize he'd already won the battle for Zo? There was no need for him to be territorial. Gryphon tied the tent shut and turned to find Zo crouching next to Joshua as he slept.

"What happened to him?" She shot Gryphon an accusing look.

Gryphon sighed. "I'm not sure, but it smelled like mead."

"You let him drink?"

"I found him like this when I came back from … the stream." Gryphon winced. The morning had been a disaster. He'd spent his time by the stream trying to find a way to say goodbye when she had come upon him. She'd looked the part of an angel as rays of sunlight reflected off her smooth skin. He'd kissed her—more like devoured her—and then unintentionally spit her out. And here she was again, beautiful and tempting in her simple dress. He wanted nothing more than to hold her and trace the smooth lines of her body, but knew that would only make leaving her even more unbearable.

She deserves better.

Zo dug through the little satchel strung across her shoulder. She was never very far from the oils and herbs of her trade.

"Don't," said Gryphon. "Let him face the morning headache. Maybe then he'll think twice before making a drinking bet with a stranger."

Zo hesitated, then nodded and closed the satchel.

Gabe seemed like he might burst. "Have you told her?"

"Told me what?" Zo asked.

Before Gabe could say anything, Gryphon said, "Commander Laden is dispatching a group of soldiers to escort all who will not be fighting to the Valley of Wolves. He expects you, Tess, and Joshua to join them." Gryphon had made sure of it.

Gabe's eyes narrowed, the tension in his stance tangible.

"But the blood oath," Zo protested.

"Laden does not need your help in this. There is a plan in place."

"Laden *needs* me at the front. I'm his best healer," Zo shot back.

"You're not well," Gryphon's voice was soft yet still somehow commanding. "And Tess is too young to be near the battle. He is taking Millie with him."

"One healer? And where will you go?" Zo felt her chin rise, daring him to admit his plans to leave her. He'd said as much before, but she wanted him to own it out loud.

"I'll travel with Laden and the men in my command," he cleared his throat, "and leave before the fighting starts."

Color drained from her beautiful face, making her seem more like a child than a fearless spy. "You're really leaving, then. Just like that." Her back went rigid as she gathered herself. She clamped her lips together and fought the emotion threatening to spill over in her eyes. She opened her mouth to say something, but closed it again. Finally, she managed, "And Joshua?"

"Zo."

"I fell in love with you as your *slave* inside Ram's Gate. But you," her neck and face flushed hot, "you claim you want me, but … " She pushed the back of her hand to her mouth, biting back a faint sob, and bolted from the tent.

"Wait, Zo!" This couldn't be the last time they spoke. He needed to make things right, somehow.

Gabe clamped his hand over Gryphon's shoulder before he could follow Zo into the encroaching night.

"Let go," said Gryphon.

"Not until you tell me why you refuse to tell her about Ajax." Gabe looked past him to where Zo had been. "Why let her believe you don't care for her? Why not explain you're offering yourself as a sacrifice to Barnabas for your mess brothers?"

"Do you honestly think that would have hurt her less, knowing I'm walking into my own execution? You know how stubborn she can be. She would have marched all the way to Barnabas if she knew the truth."

Gabe didn't speak for several minutes, then finally nodded. "Fine." Then, not a beat later he said, "But there's something I have to know—call it payment for my silence with Zo."

Gryphon stared at the Wolf. "What is it?"

"Why tell the Allies about your plan? Why not just go there alone? I know a part of you is still loyal to your clan."

Gryphon looked away and spoke through his clenched teeth, "Because I can't leave this world knowing I could have stopped a slaughter and didn't."

"So you alert both sides, and let fate decide if the Ram prevail or if the Wolves keep their home." He tilted his head to the side, trying to grasp the logic.

Gryphon didn't trust in fate. She was a fickle thing, and in no ways dependable.

"Now I need something from you, Gabe." He scratched the back of his head. "A favor."

"Anything within my power."

Gryphon filled his chest with air and slowly released it, as if the words would come easier if they had wind behind them. "I know you will take care of Zo and Tess. I just … " The full weight of Gryphon's situation finally hit him. His voice broke with pain. "Can you help Zo look after Joshua for me? See that he grows into a decent man." Gryphon didn't trust himself to breathe. "He's a good kid … he'll probably cause you loads of trouble." He managed a tortured smile that felt wrong.

Gabe frowned and nodded. "On my honor, I will take Joshua in as one of my family. I'll fill your role as his mentor and friend. He will have my sword wherever he goes."

They shook hands, and Gabe yanked him into a hug. "You're a good man, Gryphon."

"You're just glad you get Zo to yourself."

Gabe clapped him on the arm. "Maybe." His usual wicked grin was too forced, making the words sad despite his efforts to lighten the mood. He didn't want to win her like this.

"Please," Gryphon said soberly, "tell her the truth after I'm gone."

Chapter Twenty-Three

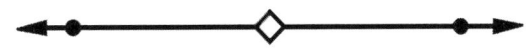

Gryphon led his band of forty to the slot canyon and allowed himself to look back over the camp one final time. His forty marched at the head of the Allied army. Behind him, a trail of Wolf and Raven followed in single file. They'd take up proper ranks once they left the slot canyon to begin the seven-day journey. The plan was to arrive early so the men would have fresh legs when they faced the Ram.

The tail of the caravan was comprised of mainly Kodiak and Stone's Freeman. While Gryphon, the Wolves, and the Raven marched directly toward the Valley of Wolves, following the river south once they exited the suffocating canyon, the rest would set up camp in some abandoned caves northeast of the place where the rivers intersected. Once the Ram army reached the rivers, the plan was to flank them from the rear, freeing the Nameless as well as any women and children who sought refuge from the battle.

The whole plan hinged upon the Ram army traveling faster than the Nameless and women and children of their clan. Laden suspected that the Ram would anticipate a fight and would not want their families caught in the attack.

Entering the slot canyon, Gryphon cringed as he approached the narrow gap where he'd blocked the Ram mess's escape. The place of Sani's death. Gryphon shrugged off his pack and held his round shield off to the side as he inched sideways between the two walls of rock. He swallowed the bile of guilt and wiped at the sweat of his brow as he reached the other side.

Shouldering his pack, he turned to continue out of the canyon only to find someone blocking the way.

"May I walk with you?" Chief Naat gestured that Gryphon should lead.

Gryphon hesitated a moment before taking to the trail again, the old chief only steps behind him. From the first moment Gryphon had stepped foot on the Nest, Chief Naat had hated him. And now, after Sani, Gryphon couldn't blame him. He half wondered if the old man would put an arrow through his back, walking behind him as he was.

"My son died an honorable death. He does not require your guilt or your shame."

The sweat on Gryphon's brow returned. He climbed over a waist-high boulder blocking the trail and thought to offer the old man help, but immediately buried the thought as Chief Naat nimbly scaled the rock on his own.

"Sani carried the spirit of my grandfather. Wise beyond his years. He understood that this mortal life was only the beginning … a period of probation." A pause. "I don't think he ever felt content in this world. His spirit belongs with our ancestors. He is home. My heart is heavy with loss, but I rejoice in knowing he lived an honest life."

Gryphon nodded and cleared the tension from his throat. "He was a mighty man trapped in a young body. I … I'm sorry."

A hand clamped Gryphon's shoulder, causing him to freeze in place. "No, Ram. I am the one who should apologize." He scrunched his wrinkled brown forehead and regarded him with eyes filled with wisdom and years. "I see you clearly now." Another long pause. He reached out and pushed his withered fist into the skin over Gryphon's heart. "Your heart is good." Slowly lowering his hand, he bowed his head to Gryphon. "When this battle is over, know that you will always have a place with the Raven." He pulled Sani's beads from a pocket in his sleeve and placed them reverently in Gryphon's hand.

"Wear them in battle so that my son's spirit can still fight to keep you safe."

Zo watched as the last of the men disappeared into the slot canyon, and for the third time since Joshua awoke repeated, "Yes, it was definitely alcohol poisoning."

Joshua kneaded his fingers into his scalp. "How could I have been poisoned? I wasn't the only one who drank from the vat."

"Yes, but you were the only one who drank a whole pitcher."

The embarrassment on his face matched the brightness of his hair. "I've made a mess of everything. I should be with Gryphon. He needs me."

Zo fought back a smile. The last thing Gryphon needed was Joshua at his heels, getting in harm's way. "He'll be fine, Ginger." She rolled the muslin bandages in tight cylinders as she spoke. Three more and then she'd have to find another task to keep her mind occupied. How would she survive not knowing if Gryphon was alive and well, or if he …

She cut the thread of that thought and tucked the roll of muslin tighter. He'd only been gone an hour and she was already crazy with irrational stress.

She hadn't confided in him about the Seer's message. Laden had said he'd put his leaders on alert, but the Seer wasn't the Allies' greatest threat … it was the massive army marching toward the Valley of Wolves.

"I'm worried about him, Zo." Joshua must have read her mind. "I had the strangest dream last night."

Zo was only halfway listening. Tess had coughed into her hand then gone back to touching the medical dressing. "Tess, you may as well throw that away. You know better."

Tess at least had the decency to look embarrassed.

Joshua walked over to the smoldering morning fire to dispose of the dressing for Tess. "Do you want to hear it?"

"Hear what?" Zo asked, counting the rolls of bandages in her mind.

"My dream."

More about Gryphon. She couldn't escape the thought of him for even a minute. "Tell me." She set down her work to give Joshua her undivided attention.

"I was resting on the cot. You, Gryphon, and Gabe were talking about Gryph leaving with the troops to intercept the Ram. Then it was just Gryphon and Gabe. The Wolf was mad about something. He wanted Gryph to tell you the truth. Something about meeting Barnabas. I don't really remember it all."

Joshua folded his fingers into his palms.

Zo leaned over to stop his anxious hands. "You're worried."

Joshua nodded. "It's just … I *know* it was a dream, because Gryph wouldn't do this without telling me. At least I don't think he would. But then, when I woke up I somehow knew that he was gone, and everything about the Ram moving south to the Wolves. How did I know that if … " He shook his head, as if doing so would clear the cobwebs from his thoughts to reveal the truth.

Zo picked up another strip of muslin. "You must have been partly awake when we came in to talk after Commander Laden's announcement last night."

Joshua slowly gathered his feet beneath him. Zo had never seen someone's skin pale before her eyes, but that is exactly what happened. Color leaked from him like blood from a head wound. He stared off into the distance in a state of paralyzed shock. "He wouldn't. He just wouldn't. Not without talking to me. Not without saying a proper goodbye. I'll kill him myself ... "

"Tess! Clear the cot. He needs to lie down," ordered Zo as she stood next to him to help him keep his balance.

"I will not lie down." Joshua's lips pinched tight, his brows knit together.

Zo tried not to panic, but she understood Joshua's look. It could only mean one thing: Gryphon's lie. He'd said he couldn't be trusted. Before she realized it, she was shaking him. "Tell me what you heard. Tell me!"

Joshua's voice sounded far away. "He's not coming back, Zo. Something about sacrificing himself for Ajax and the rest of the mess." He gasped for air and a pathetic sob escaped. "He's going to let Barnabas execute him."

"What?" It was a stupid thing to say. As if having Joshua repeat himself would change what she'd heard. Zo grabbed her neck, wishing there was some way to open her throat to allow more air to pass through. "How dare he?" she seethed. "I don't care if they are his brothers! How could he abandon us?"

But then it hit her. He hadn't abandoned her at all. He'd lied. Not about loving her, about leaving.

"Where I'm going you can't follow." Gryphon had said.

He was protecting her again; just like he had ever since the first moment he'd defied orders when he discovered she was a Wolf back in Ram's Gate.

Didn't he realize that their lives were connected now? That by offering up himself, he was also offering up any hope she'd ever had for happiness? Squashing it like a bug on the ground.

"That's why he was talking to Gabe," said Joshua. He'd managed to compose himself some, but his nose still ran and his eyes were swollen. "He wanted Gabe to take care of us."

"And Gabe didn't think we should know about this?"

Joshua shrugged. "Told Gryph he wouldn't say anything until … after."

Zo darted into the tent and yanked open the pack on the floor. She threw a change of clothes and a few shirts into the bag along with her kit.

"What are you doing?" asked Tess. Joshua was on her heels.

"I'm going after them." Zo tucked her thick wool blanket into a tight roll and fastened it to the pack.

Tess dropped to her bedroll next to her and quickly began tucking and rolling it into a lumpy ball. "No, Tess. Absolutely not!"

Tess moved on to gathering things for her pack, ignoring Zo's demand.

"It's too dangerous." Zo heard an unfamiliar growl in her voice but was too enraged with Gryphon to curb her anger.

"Joshua, get your things. I'll talk to Millie about rations."

Tess stomped her foot and propped her fists on her hips. "You *promised*, Zo. You promised on the graves of our parents that you wouldn't leave me again. If the redhead gets to go, then I should too. You need me!"

Zo stopped packing and pulled Tess to her chest. "Little lamb," she whispered into her soft, blond hair. "You are so brave, but this is just too dangerous for you. You are the last healer in camp. They need you to look after people here. Would you really leave them without a healer?"

"Nice try. They're headed to the Valley of Wolves. You told me yourself that there are more healers there than anywhere else in the region. Besides, they are walking *away* from the fight. You're walking right into it." She crossed her arms. "You need me." The tremor in her voice and the anguish in her round, glossy eyes said, *And I need you.*

Zo hesitated. Closed her eyes and sighed.

"We should take the extra bandages." Then under her breath added, "Gryphon's going to need some patching up when I'm through with him."

It took nearly an hour to gather the proper supplies for the journey. Zo, Tess, and Joshua set out over the crest of the hill with their packs secured on their backs and capes billowing in the wind sweeping through the valley. Gryphon would be furious, but Zo didn't care.

Just as they reached the mouth of the slot canyon, they spotted Raca walking along the western wall headed in their direction. She carried a heavy pack, with her usual bow and quiver fastened to her back.

"Going somewhere?" Zo asked when she joined them inside the slot canyon and out of sight from the valley below.

"My father will kill me, but this is my fight just as much as it is anyone's. Against a foe like the Ram, one man, or *woman*, might be the difference between victory and defeat."

Raca looked between Zo, Joshua, and Tess. "I'm in no position to judge, but—"

"This is a rescue mission," said Joshua.

Tess nodded sternly at his side. "We're going to save our family."

Zo sputtered, taken aback by her sister's definition of Gryphon. But the more she thought about it, there was such a sense of *rightness* to calling them all a family. If she was honest with herself, it was what she'd been fighting for all along.

A family.

Could something so wholesome be born from so much death and heartache?

Raca didn't question Tess's explanation for leaving. She simply nodded and hitched up her pack. "I can't think of a more noble goal." But then to Zo, she whispered, "Protect these children, Healer. Be the protector for your family that I couldn't be for mine."

Chapter Twenty-Four

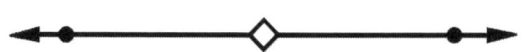

"Let's run through it again," Laden said to the chiefs in his small travel tent, two days after leaving the Allied Camp.

"No matter how many times you repeat the plan, it will not change the fact that the Wolves and Raven cannot stand alone against the Ram," Chief Naat said, massaging his fingers into his forehead. "By the time the Kodiak finish freeing the Nameless, we'll be in our graves."

Gryphon couldn't help but agree, but found it difficult to rouse hope for anything at the moment. Days. That was all he had left. But it felt as though the end had already come and gone when Zo ran out of his tent. Joshua hadn't even been awake to receive his goodbyes. It was probably for the best since the kid would have been clamoring to join him. But regret singed Gryphon's thoughts as he considered his life with the boy. Surprisingly, his biggest regrets were verbal omissions. He should have told the boy how proud he was of him. How much he loved him. Why hadn't they taken the time to laugh more often?

"What do you think, Gryphon?" Laden asked, waking him from his daydream.

Gryphon cleared his throat. "I think nothing can be decided until we get more information. I can't imagine the Ram traveling too far ahead of their families. They'd need the manpower to manage their slaves. But I also don't think they will bring their families to the river to meet us in battle." He rubbed the back of his neck. "If I were Barnabas I'd setup camp a few hours travel from the river. Close enough to rush back to, but far enough from the fight to keep their loved ones away from harm."

Laden said, "If the Kodiak and Freeman can get to their people right after the Ram leave to meet our armies, they have a good chance of getting to the river in time."

The Alpha leaned forward, all beard and scowl. "You honestly think we can hold them that long?" He shook his head. "Against the full force of the Ram, it will be a slaughter."

Gryphon frowned. "I just don't see another way."

Murtog said, "How many soldiers do you think Barnabas will leave to protect his people?"

"Depends." Gryphon shrugged. "Barnabas will have scouts canvassing the area. I think it wise to let them see our numbers, or at least part of them. If they feel the threat is great enough, they might pull all their mess units forward, making the Nameless an easy target."

Laden nodded. "We're forgetting that Barnabas plans to kill Gryphon at the river. He'll want *all* of his troops to witness the event."

The clan leaders shifted uncomfortably, shame at using Gryphon's death to their advantage causing them to avert their eyes.

"My men have the least experience in battle," Stone cut in. "But most of us still have family and friends among the Nameless. We can free our people without Murtog's help. The Kodiak can join with the Wolf and Raven."

"No," said Murtog. "My men will not fight until we secure our families." Both his tone and demeanor left little room for argument.

Laden sighed. "It's settled then. I'll have runners stationed in the area so we know what we're dealing with. The Kodiak and Freeman will hang back, keeping to the southern caves, letting the Ram pass. Once they free their people, they'll join us, flanking the Ram forces."

He leaned forward, massaging his forehead with fingertips. "Let's pray the Ram take the bait and come at us with everything they have." His faced turned to stone as he surveyed the men around him. "All that leaves is for us to stop the strongest fighters in the region from reaching the Valley of Wolves. Our wives and children depend upon it."

On the morning of the third day of their journey, the jittery Wolves under Gryphon's command ate a quick breakfast and broke camp. As soon as packs were secured Gryphon gave the order, "Link!"

Forty men scurried into their new formation. Gryphon counted a full six seconds before every man was in position with shield raised and spear ready.

"Today the Allies will cover fifteen miles. You will keep formation that entire time. Everything must be in unison. You will walk in formation, hike in formation, eat and even piss in formation. Is that understood?"

"Yes, sir!" they shouted.

One man in the front row looked slightly over his shoulder, probably considering the consequences of the last command.

Gryphon nodded to the new leader of the front line, an able soldier with ample experience. "They are yours. Lead on." Gryphon stepped aside as the orders to march were given. He spent most of his time jogging circles around the perimeter of the phalanx, instructing men to tighten gaps and step in sync. The rocky terrain made it difficult for them to stay as compact as they should. One line would hit an obstacle and speed up once they passed it, abandoning the men behind them.

"Talk to each other!" Gryphon growled. "Your families depend upon you staying in formation!"

By afternoon, Gryphon grew so frustrated that he propped his spear up on his shoulder and drew his sword. All four lines of the phalanx halted to watch Gryphon launch the spear over fifty yards until it sank deep into the trunk of an Elm tree. "Any Ram you encounter will see even the narrowest gap and make you bleed for it." Gryphon motioned for one of the younger boys in the company to retrieve the spear. The boy took off like a frightened rabbit. "Next time … " Gryphon scanned the faces of every man of his forty. "Next time *you* are my target."

The men whispered to each other, pointing at the spear with pale faces, some shaking their heads in worry. Many had never faced a single Ram, let alone an army of professional phalanx warriors. They were afraid. Gryphon could taste it. Fear was healthy. To be afraid, an entirely different beast. The difference subtle, yet distinct.

"Link!" Gryphon yelled.

The boy came running back with the spear, panting from his sprint. "You're not really going to attack us as we travel, are you, sir?"

Gryphon accepted the spear. He balanced the heavy shaft in his hand. Gryphon knew he had the attention of every man in his company. "If this phalanx can't defend itself against one Ram, how will it survive twenty?"

"But what if you hit one of us? What if someone is killed?" The boy had nerve to question his word. Inside the Gate he would have been whipped for such a cowardly remark.

"Defend your man and that won't happen." Gryphon walked away, letting his words sink in.

Gryphon threw his spear eight times that day. Eight times his phalanx blocked the attack. The men watched him wherever he went, walking in such tight formation that Gryphon scarcely saw their faces as they moved. Every other company of forty marched past; eyeing Gryphon with contempt as his own forty inched along. His men arrived at camp hours after everyone else. When Gryphon gave orders for them to disband, they practically collapsed from fatigue.

As they moved around the camp, Gryphon noted that most of the lines still walked together out of habit. They took meals in line, and even slept near the men whom they defended with their shields.

Pleased, Gryphon left them to seek out Commander Laden.

"We're traveling too slowly," said Joshua, casting a pointed glance in Tess's direction. Raca nodded her agreement.

As determined as Tess had been to keep pace, Zo couldn't deny that they were losing ground little by little every day.

They'd left the slot canyon and traveled the hilly terrain east until connecting with a main road. Mountains climbed on either side, making the pass the only way to easily travel southward through this section of the region. The Iiná River ran south along the side of the road, providing travelers plenty of fresh water and even some fish, especially during spawning season.

Zo kicked a rock and sent it splashing into the drink. If Gryphon really cared about her more than his pride, he would never have left.

She kicked another rock.

"We should run and take turns carrying Tess," said Zo, interrupting a long stretch of silence. "The Ram army will travel this road to get to the Valley of Wolves. They are marching somewhere behind us. And if we want to reach Gryphon before … " Zo hitched up her pack and looked away, unable to finish the morbid thought.

Joshua nodded. "What do you say, Tess? Should we assume the usual position?" The freckles on his face blended together as he scrunched up his nose in a forced attempt at humor.

Tess practically threw her pack at Zo before jumping up to sit on Joshua's shoulders.

They started at a slow jog and worked into a moderate run, just enough to stretch Zo's legs without overexerting. She guessed they had at least two days of travel before the Allies intercepted the Ram where the two rivers diverged. Two days of knowing the Ram marched at their backs.

That night the four huddled together for warmth on a shelf they'd found while exploring the steep cliffs off to the side of the road. Raca had insisted she couldn't sleep unless they were elevated, and the ledge offered a decent view of the road. She and Joshua had carefully covered their tracks while Zo helped Tess up the mountain. Without a fire, the threat of humans was minimal, but it left nothing to scare away other predators.

"Why did you let us come?" Joshua whispered into the night. It was Zo's watch, but he'd been restless for the better part of an hour before sitting up and leaning back against his palms. Tess had fallen asleep on his leg, pinning him in place. Raca curled up beside her.

Joshua stared up at the night sky. "You could have slipped away without us. Just like Gryphon."

Zo had certainly thought about doing that very thing. "Several reasons."

Yes, she'd promised Tess not to leave her again, but the whole truth ran deeper than an underground spring. Ice cold and completely filtered of all of her good intentions, the truth was she needed Joshua to help convince Gryphon to abandon his plan. Gryphon cared for Joshua more than anyone else in the whole world. Gryphon would do anything for the kid.

Joshua was quiet for a while. "He loves you." The words hung on the stale breeze like a bubble of promise that might pop at any moment.

He left me. Zo mentally corrected.

Just like her parents.

Chapter Twenty-Five

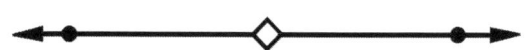

Out in the muddy plains of the valley, Gryphon didn't know whether he wanted to speed up or stop. Either option was a vile, cruel beast that ripped at the thin strings of his heart. There was no winning this battle. Not for him.

"Link!" Gryphon called when camp had broken. The sound of forty shields sliding into tight formation brought back a little piece of home. Gryphon had always loved that sound. It was the sound that preceded adrenaline. Adrenaline preceded victory.

Funny how something that once mattered more than anything else could be degraded to merely noise. Walking in stride with the men he'd grown to respect over the past few weeks, Gryphon thought of other noises.

Joshua's easy laughter. His endless questions about anything and everything. The sound of his clumsy feet as he stumbled through the brush. Tess's high-pitched voice that rang like bells and chimes even when she was vexed. The sweet sound of Zo's sigh as he kissed her by the stream.

Gryphon shook his head. It wouldn't serve him to focus on such things. Not when his men depended on him.

Such little time.

"This is where our paths split, young Ram."

Gryphon turned to find Ikatou with one foot planted in the soil and the other propped on a rock. The man had adopted a glow ever since learning the Allies would help free the Nameless. "I want you to know that, even though we don't technically have our families back yet, my brothers and I have deemed Zo's blood oath complete. We'll perform the ceremonial release with Zo when the conflict is over."

"That means a great deal to me, Bear. Thank you."

Ikatou pushed away from the rock and reached out to grasp Gryphon's forearm. Gryphon returned the gesture. "I will see you in the life after this one." He cleared his throat and looked away, but not before Gryphon caught sight of tears rolling down his cheeks. "None of this could have happened without you." He pulled out an ugly bear claw dagger and drew it across his palm, right next to the bright pink scar made when he'd promised Gryphon to protect Zo on their trip to the Caves. "I would call you my brother by blood."

"What kind of blood oath is this?" asked Gryphon, wearily.

"The kind that binds families." He offered Gryphon the hilt of the claw-blade. "I would be honored to call you my family and give you a place in my house. My posterity will be stronger with you in my line."

"Even in death?"

The Kodiak nodded. "Even in death."

Gryphon dragged the rudimentary blade across his palm and shook Ikatou's hand, grafting his blood to that of the Bear.

"We are family now." Ikatou offered him a clipped nod, and left to join the rest of the Kodiak and Freemen headed to a grouping of nearby caves. Their resting place until the Ram army passed by, assuming they'd covered their tracks properly.

Looking down at his bloodied hand, Gryphon noticed Sani's beads. For a man without a clan, he certainly felt connected.

Gryphon looked up to see Gabe jogging back from his own command of forty. Men nodded in respect as he worked his way down the train of Allies. Gryphon had hardly seen the Wolf since the night before they left the Allies' stronghold.

Gabe stepped in line with Gryphon. The two men walked side by side, neither bothering to offer a greeting. After a while Gabe finally said, "There is talk that your forty will lead us out to battle. Many other captains have adopted your … training methods. I have too."

Gryphon gave Gabe a knowing look. "I will not be leading anyone anywhere. You know that as well as I do." Gryphon grounded his knuckles into his side. "Besides, Commander Laden makes the decisions. Not I."

"Exactly." Gabe looked around to make sure they weren't overheard. "What if Laden orders you to stand down?"

"We have a deal," said Gryphon. "When the two forces are set to battle, I will join him on the field to meet Barnabas. The exchange will happen as planned. My brothers' lives depend upon it."

Gryphon trusted Laden enough to know that he would keep his word.

"Can't you convince your mess brothers to join us? I'm sure many of them look up to you as their Striker."

Gryphon frowned. "Perhaps they did at one time. Not now." He shook his head.

"I have to ask you something that's been bothering me for weeks."

Gabe took Gryphon's lack of objection as an invitation. "Inside the Gate, when I was to be executed and you let me fight, why didn't you just kill me?"

Gryphon didn't answer at first, but eventually the truth spilled out. "She loved you." He snorted. "I couldn't watch her suffer."

Gabe's eyes narrowed. "Yet you would let me watch her suffer?"

Zo awoke to the sound of skittering rocks and murmured voices. The sky outside was still mostly dark. She thought of the disturbance more as a nuisance than anything else until she propped up onto her elbow and glanced down.

Choking on her gasp, she crawled over to Raca and shook the Raven princess's arm. "Ram."

With that one word, Raca's eyes flew open. Together they slithered to the edge of the cliff and peered down at the formal procession of deadly men. The Ram marched in tight formation, five wide and in clusters four rows deep. A small gap in ranks divided each mess unit of twenty men. They wore their traditional fur-lined boots with boiled leather vests and wrist guards, their notorious round shields held like a mantra at their chests.

"Too soon." Raca breathed an unsteady breath. "No one expected them to come so far so fast."

Given the winding, curving nature of the canyon road, the ranks of Ram mess units seemed to go on forever. And since there was no other path south, waiting was the only option.

"Hopefully the Nameless are far enough behind so we can follow the Ram," said Zo. She had to find some way to overtake them. Some way to get to Gryphon before he … well, *before*. But with Tess in tow, she didn't see that happening.

I can't lose you too, Gryphon. I refuse to let you go.

"Murtog," Raca whispered under her breath. "I hope you've covered your tracks."

It took nearly two hours for the Ram to pass. Zo drew a line in the dirt for every Ram mess that marched by. One hundred and fifty-two lines in the dirt. Almost three thousand men—well more than the two thousand anticipated by Commander Laden. More than even Zo imagined, given her time inside Ram's Gate.

Where had they all come from? How could she have been so wrong? With a force this large, the Ram would barely be outnumbered two to one, and they had a history of defeating their enemies even when they were outnumbered ten to one.

The Allies were depending on their numbers to save them. Without that, what hope was there for victory? And if they failed, what would happen to the Valley of Wolves? To the Raven and Kodiak refugees? The Ram raid that took Zo's parents replayed over and over in her mind. Panic hijacked her breath. The Allies had no business fighting. They needed to retreat. Race to their loved ones, and leave this region all together.

"We wait an hour and then we leave," said Raca with a firm nod.

Zo couldn't disagree. "The pass opens up to forest soon. We'll have to run through the night and take our chances with the Ram." Zo swallowed, not daring to think what would happen if they were caught.

After hours of nerve-splitting walking in the Ram's fresh tracks and with—what they assumed were—a host of Ram who didn't make up the main fighting force at their backs, Zo, Tess, Joshua, and Raca crossed the Iiná river under the cover of night to the forest on the other side. If they'd continued walking east, they would have eventually run into the river Totoom. For now, they walked the land wedge that divided the two living bodies of water.

Undergrowth scratched and snagged at Zo's legs as they pounded through the trees. Pine branches whipped Zo's face, their woodsy scent lingering with the sting of the needles. Raca kept a steady pace, jumping and ducking through the foliage with animalistic agility. She rarely looked back to make sure the others were on her tail.

Zo welcomed the challenge—any pain was worth reaching Gryphon before the Ram—though it took most of her waking brain to concentrate on not falling with Tess strapped to her back. After a few hours of relentless running, Raca finally slowed to a halt.

Joshua nearly ran into her. The boy didn't even seem tired. "Why are we stopping?" he complained.

In contrast, Zo felt as though her legs were detached from her body, wobbly and numb. She didn't trust them to support her weight so she slumped down to the moist ground to stretch.

"Someone's been through here." Raca pointed to a series of bent branches and a few scattered footprints. If Zo hadn't been looking, she never would have noticed them.

"How could you see that while running?" she asked in unbelief. The veil of night cast a dark net over the forest, compounded by the rushing of the two rivers on either side of them. It wouldn't be long before the two bodies of water connected.

Raca didn't seem to hear her. "These tracks are fresh." She used her dark arms to wipe the sweat from her brow. "We passed the camped army hours ago. If it's a Ram scout, it means two things. First, we can't be more than a few miles ahead of the army. Maybe less. Second, they will see our tracks on their way back. Barnabas will send out a mess to track us down."

Joshua paced with adrenaline. "But we are so far ahead. We must have covered five miles of forest. They won't catch us before we reach the point where the waters meet."

Raca looked directly at Zo wrapping a blanket around Tess to help support her when carried on her back. "We're too slow."

Zo pushed up to her feet. Her knees complained and her vision spun, sending her off balance. "I can go faster," she said, even the thought made her want to vomit.

"Let's move." Raca hadn't even finished the word when an arrow cut through the air like a whistle and sank deep into the flesh of her left shoulder. She staggered a step then drew her bow and strung an arrow. "Run!" she called.

In half a second Tess wriggled off of Zo's back, hand firmly set in Zo's as Joshua drew his short sword.

"Go!" Raca growled.

The three immediately took off. All she could think about was how that arrow could have found a home in Joshua's chest. He could have died. It would have been her fault. "Faster, Joshua." The trees grew thicker, the unmarked path harder and harder to navigate. They took turns tripping and scrambling back to their feet.

Zo felt like her heart might explode, but she didn't dare stop. Raca twisted and let loose an arrow mid jump. The wound would catch up to her as soon as her adrenaline was spent. The rivers roared even louder with life on either side of them.

So close. Just a little farther.

They came to a felled tree blocking the trail. Joshua practically threw Tess over the four-foot-high log before careening over it himself. Zo helped Raca over when she crumbled on her first attempt. The Raven princess let out a ragged cry of pain when she landed hard on the other side, unable to support her weight any longer.

When Zo decided to offer herself as a spy inside the Gate, she'd had no intention of surviving. It was easy to be brave when you had nothing to lose. Looking back now, she could see that what she thought was bravery was merely selfish indifference. Now she wanted to live. She valued her life and the people in it. Bravery seemed impossible.

"Through here." Joshua beckoned, darting swiftly to the right. The trail became more rocky, the trees less dense. They would be harder to track but had little cover. Zo felt naked as they raced along. The rocky ground often moved beneath her feet, sending her painfully to her knees.

"Hurry, Zo," Joshua begged. The kid was thirteen years old and notoriously clumsy, but here, in the thick of danger, his focus was centered. Today Joshua was a Ram. Zo pushed to her feet and wrapped Raca's good arm around her shoulder, redoubling her efforts to put distance between them and the enemy.

All she could think of was how proud Gryphon would be of

Joshua. Of how badly she wanted to survive today so she might have the chance to tell Gryphon what a great job he'd done with the kid. For some reason that one desire seemed ridiculously important. A ferocious need.

But the shouts from their pursuers rang out close by, and no matter how brave, no matter how hard she tried, Zo knew she wouldn't have the chance.

Chapter Twenty-Six

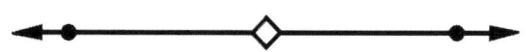

The Allies would reach the point where the two rivers converged by midday tomorrow. Gryphon's men marched in tight formation. The closer the men came to battle, the quieter they became. A common side effect. There was nothing like death to force a man to ponder the deeds of his life. The things left undone.

Gryphon drew his sword as they walked, turning the blade over and over in his hand, enjoying the feel of the hilt's comfortable grip. Like the handshake of an old friend.

He'd taken to calling out each of his men, one by one, to help them work with their sparring. He knew every one of their names now. They were, by nature, different from the Ram, but it didn't take long to see past their differences. They were good men. Humble, but strong. Willing to work hard. Less proud than the Ram. Driven to protect those they loved.

Their lives had value.

His entire life, Gryphon had been trained to think of everyone outside of the Gate as lesser. Human, yes, but only in the simplest, unimportant form. Zo had forced him to reconsider everything he'd ever believed to be true.

"Isaac," he called to the youngest member of his company. The boy rushed over, bouncing on the balls of his feet, his sword held aloft and a gleam in his eye. His enthusiasm reminded Gryphon of Joshua.

Gryphon swiftly knocked the sword out of his hand with a backward flip of his wrist. The young man turned around to pick up his weapon, and Gryphon pushed him face first into the dirt with his shield.

"Never turn your back on your enemy," said Gryphon.

A mud clot hung from Isaac's eyebrow when he rose from the ground. "Only a dishonorable coward would attack a man whose back is turned."

Gryphon nodded. "And only a fool would rely on his enemy's honor in the midst of battle." Gryphon crouched deeper into his stance, short sword raised. "Again."

The young Wolf had some basic skill with a blade, and he was light on his feet. He was almost as good as Joshua, meaning the kid had no chance against a Ram mess soldier. He didn't belong in this fight.

One of Commander Laden's runners sprinted up to Gryphon. "The Commander has called a war council. He needs you at his tent when we make camp for the night."

The last thing Gryphon wanted to do was sit through another meeting regarding a war he would not live to see. Laden had called for his opinion on several occasions, earning Gryphon the grudging regard of the other clan leaders and captains.

The runner didn't wait for a response. No one questioned Commander Laden. Gryphon had hoped to spend his last night with his men. He had explained to them several times that Commander Laden asked him to train them, not to fight alongside them. Every time the question arose a fleck of hope dimmed from their faces. They needed him. They would think he abandoned them when he left to confront his fate. Abandoned them like he abandoned Zo, Tess, and Joshua.

Why couldn't there ever just be one right answer? Gryphon was tired of feeling torn between two impossible choices. For once, he'd like to know that his actions would benefit everyone. That by protecting one thing he wasn't condemning another.

Gryphon didn't bother waiting to be announced when he reached the Commander's tent, much to the guard's distaste.

"Sorry, sir," said one of the guards as he trailed in after Gryphon.

"Leave us," said Laden.

"Yes, sir." The man eyed Gryphon with contempt before exiting.

"You needed me?" Gryphon's voice sounded as hollow as he felt.

"You're the first to arrive. Sit." Laden gestured to the open chair at his right.

"I'd rather not, sir." Gryphon folded his arms. He didn't want this to be a long visit.

"The men of the Allies have gone from hating your very existence to looking up to you. They are a superstitious lot. I'm told they hold your presence as a sign of victory."

Gryphon sighed. "No offense, sir. But if praise is your only reason for calling me to your tent, I'd like to be excused. I have no use for flattery. It will not bring my forty comfort tomorrow when I leave them to fight and die without me."

Commander Laden studied Gryphon for a long moment. The leader's hand cupped his own chin as he brushed the full beard now growing there. "Don't give yourself over to Barnabas. Stay and help me. Become a true leader of the Allies. Fight by my side." It wasn't a command but an earnest plea.

Gryphon couldn't seem to hold Laden's pained gaze. "I will honor the promise I made to my brothers." He cleared his throat and looked into the depths of Laden's wounded expression. "Will you honor your word, Commander?" All it would take was one nod from him and a swarm of guards could prevent Gryphon from fulfilling his duty.

Laden looked beyond Gryphon in a distant trance. "Fate is a cruel mistress, son. One day she kisses your cheek and the next she stabs you in the chest."

"Sir?" Gryphon pressed.

Laden stood and placed a heavy hand on Gryphon's shoulder. "You and I will leave camp before dawn. I'll see you to Barnabas myself when we meet on the battlefield in the morning."

Gryphon exhaled his relief. "Thank you, sir. But that isn't necessary."

Laden shook his head. "You're a good man, son of Troy. A little too good for my blood." He smiled, but the lines around his eyes didn't lift. "You make me proud."

One of Laden's guards ducked into the tent. "The others have arrived, Commander."

"Send them in."

The Raven Chief showed more feathers than skin. The shadows of candlelight exaggerated his crooked nose. He offered Laden a curt bow and stepped aside to make room for Murtog. A short train of lesser lieutenants followed. Gabe and the Wolf Alpha brought up the rear.

The tent flaps closed. As Gryphon scanned the powerful company, he couldn't help feeling like he didn't belong.

"I've called you all here to discuss tomorrow's strategy." Laden clapped Gryphon on the shoulder.

A few men nodded. The rest openly stared between Gryphon and Laden, intrigue scrawled across their faces. Laden launched into a detailed plan of attack that involved meeting the Ram head on in battle.

Gryphon offered his opinion when called upon but otherwise stayed relatively quiet. After a while, his eyes grew heavy and his mind clouded with thoughts of his own mortality. He didn't even try to mask his disinterest. It wasn't until the Raven Chief slammed his fist into the arm of his chair that Gryphon bothered to listen.

"I demand to meet Barnabas with you tomorrow. As Chief, it is my right," he said to Laden.

Gryphon leaned forward. "May I offer my opinion?"

Everyone in the circle seemed surprised by Gryphon's sudden entry to the conversation.

"I don't think anyone should go out to meet Barnabas tomorrow. It's not customary for Ram to treat war with formality. They don't acknowledge the other clans enough to bother. For them, this is just another raid."

Suddenly, a Raven warrior burst through the tent. "Chief Naat!" The short man panted to catch his breath. He wore his head shaven on either side of a four-inch mohawk. "Our scouts have Raca! She is injured. The healer is working on her, but suggests you come quickly." A pause. "The wound. It's deep."

Joshua felled a full-grown man with the slash of his short sword before realizing he was, in fact, Raven. The arrow had been a mistake. The shroud of night mingled with the fear of the Ram army so close had made the young warrior skittish with his bow. Help was called and Zo found herself in a makeshift Healer's Tent with Tess helping Millie grind herbs into a fine powder.

"Too much blood," said Zo for the tenth time. The human body wasn't meant to lose so much in such a little amount of time. The arrow sank deep into Raca's shoulder. The wound would have been manageable were it not for the sprint that followed. Her heart had literally pumped her blood out as she ran and now she lay white and ghostly, without so much as a cot to rest upon.

"I absolutely forbid you to give that girl a blessing, Zo." Millie used her forearm to wipe at the sweat beaded along her brow. Millie had been working on Raca for the last hour without much success. There was only so much the healing gift could do for a person. "Sometimes the body loses the will to fight." She nodded toward Raca. "It's up to her now."

"But I know I can help her beat this!" said Zo. With her new abilities, she could easily have Raca up and sipping broth by tomorrow.

"I forbid it." Millie set her jaw, closing discussion on the matter just as Laden stormed into the small tent.

"Zo," he growled. "Outside. Now."

Zo swept her hand down Raca's wounded shoulder and pushed *vitality* into the girl before standing to join Laden outside the tent. She stood too quickly and faltered just a bit before catching her stride.

Laden surprised her by pulling her into a tight hug the moment she exited the tent. "Dear girl." He gasped. "What are you doing here? You should be miles away with the other women and children."

Zo returned the embrace but ignored the question. "I counted the Ram as they passed us. One hundred and fifty mess units."

Laden's arms around her froze.

"That's three thousand men. A thousand more than I reported inside the Gate."

A heartbeat. Two. Three. "Who have you told?"

Zo faltered, "Nobody but Raca." Zo hadn't seen the wisdom in telling Joshua or Tess. They already had too much to fear.

"You need to evacuate these men," said Zo. "You're all going to die unless you run to the Valley of Wolves. Warn the people and leave the region. It's the only option."

"There isn't time, Zo," Laden whispered. "The Ram are already too far south. They could overtake an evacuation easily." He stared off into the night, unseeing. "We are the Wolves' only chance now." His eyes turned to steel. "And we will not abandon them. Not when we can fight."

The crush of gravel betrayed an approach. "How is she?" A deep voice. Familiar cadence whirled around her. A hurricane of thoughts and feelings and *moments* that summed up the man stepping out of the darkness.

Zo knew the moment he saw her. His fur-lined boots skidded against rock and he stood, eye-level, with Laden, blinking as though he didn't know what to do or say. Finally words did come, just not the ones Zo would have liked.

"What are *you* doing here?"

Laden touched Zo's arm and bent down to kiss her cheek. "I will be in my tent. Report in ten minutes to discuss your orders for the morning." A pause. "Twenty minutes."

Laden left her with Gryphon standing frozen five feet away.

"You shouldn't be here." Gryphon raked his hand through his hair, his eyes trained anywhere but at her. "I … I can't have you here."

Zo charged him.

Her fingers threaded beneath the leather weapon belt strung from shoulder to hip and she pulled him to her. His hands found their place around her waist and an explosive sense of rightness washed over her as his mouth met hers. Between kisses she said, "You're an idiot." He lifted her off the ground and her long legs locked at the ankles around his waist. He walked them away from the tents and deeper into the forest before setting her down on her own two feet again.

With all her self-control, Zo pulled away from him long enough to speak. She blinked away tears and pressed her head against his chest. "You left me to sacrifice yourself out of honor?" She gently pounded her fist into his chest. "How could you … how could you let me believe you didn't want me?"

Gryphon swept the hair from her face with his calloused hand, her cheek still pressed to his chest. His laugh came out as an ugly sort of sob that choked the back of his throat. "I didn't want you close to the fighting." Kissing the top of her head, he added, "I didn't know how to tell you I was choosing this instead of us."

"I thought you didn't love me. That you couldn't be happy with me because of my culture."

Gryphon pulled away and held her by the shoulders. "You are the other half of my soul, Zo." His solemn, deep voice caused chills to roll in violent waves up her spine. "There's nothing I wouldn't give for the right to court you and claim you properly. I would have devoted my life working to deserve your love and companionship. I would die for you, Zo."

A tear leaked down the corner of her eye, leaving a warm trail on her cheek. "But you won't live for me."

Gryphon's hands fell away from her shoulders and covered his face, roughly wiping away his own tears. "That's just it, Zo. It isn't my life to give. It belongs to someone else."

Zo shook her head. "No it doesn't." She pressed a hand directly over his heart. "Can't you feel it?" She looked up into his painfully handsome face, her body aching for him.

"It belongs to me."

Chapter Twenty-Seven

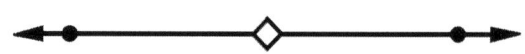

"Enter," came the rough voice of Commander Laden before Zo stepped into his tent. A single candle flickered on the square table, the only piece of furniture in the room besides his chair. "How are you holding up?" He rubbed the sleep from his eyes with the heels of his palms. Even in candlelight, Zo could tell they were bloodshot and swollen.

"Don't let him do this," said Zo. "You have the power to stop him. If you ever loved me or my parents, I *beg* you," her voice cracked, "please, force him not to go in the morning."

Laden frowned. "I've made the boy a promise, and on my honor, I will not keep him from meeting Barnabas."

"You two and your promises!"

Zo tried to take a step forward, but staggered and fell to the grass. A chill swept over her body. She assumed it was from the small blessing she'd pushed into Raca. Blood loss. Taking her infirmities as her own. Headache. Stiff, unresponsive fingers and toes. Dizzy spells.

Or perhaps it was just the knowledge that she couldn't convince Gryphon to give up his own honor.

Laden came over and helped her gain her feet. "You need to be in bed. This is all too much for you."

Zo clamped her hand around Laden's wrist, as much for balance as to get his attention. "You know so much about the Ram. You trained me and prepared me to enter the Gate. Please," she released his hand and took a deep breath to anchor her voice, "tell me what I should do for him. Some Ram custom that will help me say goodbye." She clutched her stomach as it rolled.

Laden frowned. "You really do love him, don't you?"

She couldn't admit or deny that she did. How could you properly describe the constant heat of the sun or the comfort found by the light of a fire on a cold night? It was her reality. No labels could do it justice.

"Before battle, women of the Ram stay up the night before their soldiers leaves to clean and polish their armor and weapons until they can see their own reflection in the metal. They consider it a small service compared to their husband's risk, but I know it means a great deal to them." He cleared his throat. "I meant to have one of my wards clean and polish a set of armor taken from the body of a Ram in the slot canyon … " His voice trailed off, and when he spoke again it was through thick emotion. "The shield is old, passed down from father to son in the Ram tradition. Ram see it as a mark of family and honor."

"May I take his armor to my tent tonight?" she swallowed. "May I clean it for him?"

Laden cupped her cheeks and bent down, pressing a fatherly kiss to her forehead. "Of course."

In her tent, Zo dipped a rag into an oil polish Millie had scavenged. She made slow work of cleaning the shield, moving the rag in methodic circles until the metal gleamed.

Zo was not Gryphon's wife, neither did she possess any claim to him, but she needed to do something. Some gesture to show her gratitude for all he'd done for her and Tess. Some way to demonstrate exactly how she felt about him.

Joshua hadn't come back from talking to Gryphon. Zo doubted she'd see him before morning. Tess sat on a blanket next to Raca, singing one of their mother's healing songs.

After an hour of work, all of the major marks and blemishes on the shield were gone, leaving behind a number of dents and grooves made by enemies who had failed to kill the shield's owner. Marks chronicling the life of a Ram.

The wax candle dripped low, becoming more fat than tall as time passed. Zo worked a whetstone along the edge of his sword. It made a chilling sound, a high song promising death. The skin on her arms turned to goose flesh. The vibration of the stone was felt from the tips of her fingers to the very center of her being.

The words of the blessing came unbidden. A song as high and sweet as the singing of the blade. She blessed sword and armor, shield and spear, pushing her love and strength into the metal and wood. And, surprising even her, the wood and metal accepted the gift. Fibers tightened. Metal fused and flexed into something … *more* than it was before.

Zo's eyes drooped. Her arms grew heavy. When the task was finally finished, Zo blew out the exhausted candle and didn't bother crawling over to blankets to sleep beside Tess. Instead, she lay down next to Gryphon's weapons and hefted the round shield over her body like a hard blanket. Looping her arm in the strap made it feel as though Gryphon was lying beside her, their arms locked.

Until sleep took her.

Gryphon couldn't sleep those final hours. But he did dream. He imagined Zo in his arms, the feel of her body. The honey sweet taste of her lips moving slowly against his. He let himself believe that they were companions for life. That they grew old together. They had a small farm with a vibrant garden filled with Zo's healing herbs. His shield hung on the wall as decoration more than a tool of war. He raised his children without beatings. Strong, like their mother. A happy life where he kept the people he loved safe from the struggle of the clans.

It wasn't real. Even in his dream, he knew it.

Chapter Twenty-Eight

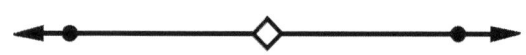

Zo had hardly gotten settled under Gryphon's shield when the sun woke her. She flipped over the shield and studied her pale complexion in its reflection. Her hair stuck out at odd angles and a line creased her cheek where the shield had pressed against it in the night. *Of all the times to want to be pretty,* she thought.

She released her night braid and let the long, dark strands flow where they desired. She straightened her billowing white shirt and scrubbed a streak of dirt from her jaw.

Satisfied, she turned the brilliant shield on its back and loaded Gryphon's weapons and armor on top. Zo lifted the shield with some difficultly, battling the weight as much as the balance of the load. Luckily, Gryphon's tent wasn't too far from hers. Most men were still in bed. The few that were up wandered among the tents, casting curious glances in her direction. Bacon grease and campfire smoke wafted through the air.

At Gryphon's tent she heard the faint rustling of movement from within. "Gryphon? Are you up?" She pushed open the tent flap just as he pulled up a pair of cotton trousers. His warrior chest leaped as he hurriedly tied the pants at his waist.

"I'm sorry," said Zo. "I ... " He was beautiful. All shoulders with thick ropes of muscle coiled around biceps and forearms, knotting in just the right places. "I shouldn't have barged in."

His eyes were red.

"I've brought you ... " She stopped, wishing she knew the proper way to do this. She wanted to do it right. "I'm not sure how this is done ... "

Gryphon wordlessly took the shield from her arms and set it on the ground. Zo could see his temples pulse as he clenched his jaw. He cleared his throat, never once taking his eyes off hers. "You didn't have to—"

"I wanted to." She swallowed hard. "Isn't there some sort of ceremony to this?" She gestured to the pile of armor resting on the ground next to him.

He nodded, speechless.

Zo bent down to pick up his shirt. She gathered the material around the collar and pushed up to her toes to drape it over his head. She lost balance and his warm hands took her waist, wrapping most of the way around her middle to support her. His touch made it impossible to think of anything beyond the warmth of his body. She wanted to drop the shirt to the ground and melt into him.

"Sorry." She cleared her throat. "You're too tall. Bend a bit."

A smile flirted with the corner of his mouth. He released her and obliged, bending at the waist in something of a bow so Zo could drape the shirt over his head. Zo grabbed a leather jerkin from the pile of armor as he threaded his arms into the sleeves of his white shirt.

She held up the jerkin vest and he slowly slipped his arms inside. The action turned him around. She let her hands slide along his waist as he moved back to face her. Zo's fingers fumbled over the buckles of his vest. Gryphon's chin found the top of her head. He exhaled deeply and lifted her thick midnight hair, pulling and twisting the thousands of dark strands until his fingertips knotted to her scalp at the base of her neck.

Zo's shaking fingers slipped on the buckle again. It took all her focus not to abandon the task. Properly appreciating Gryphon's touch required almost all her concentration.

She cupped the back of his knee for support as she fastened greaves to both shins. His hamstrings were pillars of rock, unmoving as she completed the task. His forearm braces came last. Zo fitted the braces into place then tightened the laces on the insides of his arms. She could feel his eyes boring into her, but didn't trust herself to meet his gaze.

The Ram horn would soon sound, calling him away. Gryphon had to be ready.

She brushed away the tears that managed to get past her defenses and stepped back to appreciate her handiwork. Mixed emotions coursed through her at the sight of Gryphon in Ram armor. Too similar to the armor worn by the men who killed her parents so many years ago. It inspired fear and pain. Hopelessness in its most acute form.

But when Zo looked past the boiled leather and metal, an entirely different feeling swept over her. Peace. Protection. Compassion. Gryphon was the embodiment of goodness.

The conflicting emotions were a tempestuous tide where hot and cold water collided to form a deadly current.

Zo belted on his sword, wrapping her arms around his middle. He bent down and pressed her body into his, freezing the task in a most delicious way. "How have we come to this, Gryph?" She spoke into his chest, "It seems impossible. Like a dream."

When she pulled back, his expression seemed heavy. "No matter what happens, Zo—"

"Stop." She didn't mean to raise her voice, but she didn't want to hear those words. They were the words her mother and father said to her as they prepared to defend their home. She hated those words.

She handed him his shield. "What is it your women say?"

Gryphon reached out to caress her cheek. "Come back with your shield, or on it."

Zo adamantly shook her head, grabbed his wrist, and kissed his palm. "That's a terrible saying."

Gryphon exhaled a painful sort of laugh. "It really is." He kissed the top of her head. "I love you, Zo."

Breathe. I have to keep breathing.

"I love you, too."

The deep grays and blues of early morning still shrouded the camp as the Allies came to life, preparing for battle. Clinking metal did little to distract him from his weighted thoughts. He received several sympathetic glances from his men making it clear that his fate was now public information. There was nothing like sympathy to help a man feel bad for himself.

Commander Laden materialized as an extra shadow among the trees. Gryphon soundlessly gathered his pack and rolled up his blanket before weaving through the men he'd grown to respect.

Gryphon hadn't slept the night before. After a few hours spent talking with Joshua, the boy had finally fallen asleep. Gryphon had left the tent and wandered the trail that led through the long pass to the Valley of Wolves. It had been dark, but the moon cast enough light on the Valley for him to see how vast and flat it was. Perfect for farming.

Runners confirmed the Ram army camped on the other side of the two rivers. The meeting for this morning was scheduled at dawn. Gryphon looked over his shoulder at the line of guards trailing them by twenty yards. The rest of the Allies wouldn't be far behind.

"Zo did a good job with that shield," said Laden matter-of-factly as they walked.

"How did you know?"

"She asked for your things." He looked over at Gryphon with pity, like he was already on the chopping block. "She loves you. It's a lot to give up."

Gryphon grumbled under his breath. He didn't want to talk to Laden about Zo. Even the thought of her made his legs turn liquid.

Laden went on, "She understands the tradition, Gryphon. With that one gesture she all but asked you to marry her."

"I know what it symbolizes," hissed Gryphon.

"And you're still ready to give her up?" Laden shook his head. "Sad."

A hot fire burned within Gryphon. His jaw clamped tightly, his teeth ground together. Every word that escaped was clipped with heat. "What kind of man would I be without my honor?" Gryphon rubbed his face in his hands to loosen the tension stored there. He wanted to rip out his hair. "She deserves better."

They walked along the bank of the river for another half mile. A thick fog had settled in the valley. Gryphon could hardly see more than twenty yards in front of him, making it easy to forget that the Allied army tailed them. Luckily they had the river for a guide.

Laden said, "What will become of the boy? I assume your death will make a difficult time for him."

Gryphon stopped walking. "My affairs are in order, Commander. Why the questions?"

Laden turned back to Gryphon with power in his stance. "I want you to change your mind. It's still not too late."

Gryphon stared at him. "I will not."

Laden sighed and shook his head, laying a heavy arm around his shoulders. "You can't blame me for trying. Come. Barnabas is as impatient as a lonely woman. Best not to keep him and your mess waiting."

With every heavy step, Gryphon thought of Ajax and the other men of his mess. He conjured their faces in his mind, cataloging details about each brother—his interests, his family, conversations had, and jokes shared. When he ran out of faces he started from the beginning again. Thoughts of Zo and Joshua and little Tess leaked through the crevasses, but Gryphon dutifully pushed them away every time.

He couldn't afford to think of what he would lose; only what he would save. Nature demanded a balance for his actions against his people. A payment for the lives lost and those spared. It was simply the way of the world. Gryphon's head was that payment.

Through the fog, the gentle sound of a second river met Gryphon's ears. The blurred shape of the sun crested the eastern mountain range. Gryphon hadn't realized he was cold until the filtered rays kissed his hands and cheeks.

By the time they arrived at the point where the two rivers formed into one, beams of sunlight had dissolved enough of the haze to make the images before him ethereal and dreamlike. The rugged form of Barnabas and a small band of guards appeared on the other side of the bank. Gryphon knew—lost in the mist behind them—sat a patient Ram army. Ahead, on Gryphon's side of the river, stood his mess brothers with Ajax at the lead.

"We agreed to meet at the peninsula between the two rivers." Laden never took his eyes away from Barnabas as he spoke. "Neutral territory."

"I don't need you to come with me, sir. It won't be safe."

"I'm coming," Laden said.

Following custom, Gryphon walked the traditional three steps behind Commander Laden as they waded through waist-high water to get to the stretch of land in the middle of the two rivers. The pull of the river combined with the unsure, rocky footing made Gryphon almost lose his balance. The water was cold and alive.

He scanned the faces of his former mess again. Ajax struggled to hold his gaze; his head bowed, it seemed, with guilt.

Barnabas waited for them in the center of the strip of land. He rested both hands on the edge of his round shield, making thick triceps jump beneath the healthy layer of fat stored there. "I thought I'd never see you again, Striker."

Gryphon opened his mouth to respond, but Commander Laden cut off his words. "That was the plan. The years haven't been kind to you, Barnabas."

Gryphon looked between the two men and frowned. *Striker?* Why had Laden never told him? Unimportant information. But Gryphon's nagging subconscious disagreed.

"Don't tell me *you're* Commander Laden." Barnabas belted a twisted laugh that turned the air sour. "Is that what you're calling yourself these days, Troy?"

Troy.

Gryphon took an involuntary step backward. He looked between Commander Laden and Barnabas. Their mouths moved, but all sound muffled. Dozens of memories from Gryphon's childhood carried a connection to that one name. Taunts from his peers growing up, the extra trainings from his instructors, the promise of more violent yearly beatings … all because of that one name. One terrible legacy from which he'd spent most of his life desperate to escape.

Gryphon looked to Laden to have the Allied Commander correct the mistake. Laden couldn't be his Striker father.

A mere coincidence.

Gryphon assumed his father had been captured. Killed.

Barnabas saw Gryphon's confusion and broke into a fit of laughter. "Are you serious, Troy? You honestly didn't tell the boy?" He sucked back his laughter. His face reddened. His cheeks shook and his voice turned deadly with hate. "Were you too ashamed to let him know who you really are, or too ashamed to claim him?" He gestured between them. "The son repeats the sins of the father. Not a new tragedy, I'm afraid."

Laden stepped forward, unwilling to return Gryphon's questioning glare. "My son has come to pay ransom for the lives of his mess. As his blood, I demand the right of substitution."

Barnabas shook his head. "You forfeited any right you once claimed the day you ran away like a coward with your deformed child. Your son is a traitor, Troy. I will have his head."

The Commander pushed his traveling cloak off his shoulders to show the Allied Crest embroidered to his chest. "Let me be clear. I am Troy Laden, Commander of the Allies, and I am offering you my life in exchange for my son's."

Barnabas, Laden, the two rivers, they all disappeared. Gryphon was back in the front room of his home inside the Gate. He was younger, maybe five or six. Old enough to have his first beating but young enough not to understand why. His mother was rolling out bread dough by the kitchen fire. Gryphon stared up at the spear and shield hanging on the wall, wondering why he never got to meet the man who once wielded the weaponry. Wishing he could believe that his father was an honorable man who hadn't been captured in battle.

Even at that age he understood the shame. His father wasn't buried with his shield. The giant metal circle had literally hung over Gryphon's head all his life. A symbol of weakness. For as long as he could remember, Gryphon had worked to restore the dignity of his family name. To belong to something greater than he was.

"You left me and mom." Gryphon didn't even know if anyone could hear the mumbled words. It didn't really matter if they could. He needed to process the shock. "You left us to save my ... my sister." He blinked to clear the fog from his eyes. "She died five years ago."

Laden looked like he'd swallowed a squirming frog. "I left you a sealed letter with Gabe back at camp. It explains everything. I'm sorry, son."

"Well, isn't this charming." Barnabas rolled his eyes. "I accept your offer. I don't blame you for abandoning your little band of Allies, Troy. Were I in your position, I'd likely do the same, but then I never would have left my clan in the first place." The slight curl at the corner of the chief's lips made Gryphon want to ram his fist against his fat nose. "Should I accept your surrender now?" said Barnabas.

"No," Gryphon and Laden said at the same time, in the same tone. Now that Gryphon knew the truth, the similarities between them were overwhelmingly obvious. True the heavy scarring distorted Laden's features. Even still, he should have seen past the angry lines to the thick shelf of dark eyebrows, the dimpled chin, the defined jaw, their identical build.

He'd been so blind.

"Good," said Barnabas casually. "My men have looked forward to this day with great anticipation. There is no honor gained in wiping out a clan without a decent fight." His smile dripped venom. "Who is your successor?" He pulled a long sword from his belt.

Gryphon couldn't look at his father. "He doesn't need one, because I don't accept his offer."

"Gryphon will lead the Allies," said Laden. Both Barnabas and Laden stared at each other like they hadn't even heard Gryphon.

"So be it." Barnabas slowly drew his sword and signaled the men from Gryphon's mess to meet them.

"No!" Gryphon shoved Barnabas in the chest then turned on Laden. His commander father caught his wrist and flipped him around, pinning his arms to his chest in one fluid motion.

"Let me go! I won't let you do this. I won't let you." Gryphon struggled out of his father's grasp and faced him, panting. "You haven't earned the right to die for me or my brothers. I won't live the rest of my life in your debt. Not when it was you who left and forgot me. You, who stripped me of honor from birth. I'm done mourning my father. I'm done!"

Gryphon balled his fists. He didn't have the right to be angry. Leaving Gryphon was selfless, brave, and ironically something he, Laden's son, had mimicked years later with Zo and Joshua.

But when was anger ever rational? Gryphon had to let his rage out or else he might drown.

"Son," Commander Laden said with his hands raised to rest on Gryphon's shoulders.

Gryphon batted them away. "Stop calling me that. I am not your son." The words echoed over the sound of the two rivers.

Pain manifested itself throughout the Commander's whole body. Across his face. Along the set of his shoulders. In the buckling of his knees. Laden's hand smeared down his face. "You're right." He looked away. "I'm sorry."

But Gryphon wasn't right. He was angry. There was a difference.

Zander and the rest of the mess reached Barnabas. Not one of his brothers would meet his eyes. Shame. Gryphon understood, because he felt it himself in so many ways and on so many levels. If only he could take back those bitter last words.

Barnabas shook Ajax's hand. "You and your men have done as I required. I remove your banishment and welcome you back into my good favor." Then he pointed toward Laden and Gryphon. "Seize your fallen brother and his traitor father so we can be done with this business."

"This isn't what we agreed upon!" shouted Laden as he worked frantically to fight off the swarm of men around him and Gryphon. "Let my son go!"

Gryphon plowed his way through the mess of bodies toward his father, but his brothers were too numerous. They grabbed him by his arms and legs and pinned him to the ground. "Release him! This is my debt. Release him!" Gryphon shouted until his voice went raw.

Harsh light gleamed off Barnabas's heavy blade as he bounced it between each hand. Delight played about his face, making him seem more like a child than the ruthless Chief of the Ram. Gryphon's brothers forced his father to his knees and pressed his head to a tree stump.

"Father! No, Father, please!"

"You're a good man, son," said Laden.

Barnabas raised the blade over his head.

"I'm so sorry, Father. I'm so—"

The blade whistled as it cut through the morning haze. All of the air compressed from Gryphon's lungs. He slumped deeper onto the ground, no longer fighting the men he once called family who rested on top of him. Mucus mixed with dirt and the sting of tears that would not fall.

Chapter Twenty-Nine

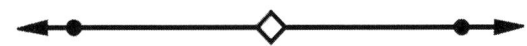

Zo had promised not to watch. She was supposed to be miles away by now with Tess, Millie, and Joshua, retreating to the narrow pass that led to the Valley of Wolves. But how could she relinquish the chance to see Gryphon through his final minutes? She knew he didn't want her there, but leaving him felt too much like a betrayal.

For once, Tess didn't put up a fight about leaving with Millie while Zo and Joshua stayed behind. Being forced to watch the prizefights inside Ram's Gate had cured her of wanting to be anywhere near the rivers for Gryphon's execution.

Zo held Joshua's hand as they waded through the icy river. Mist blanketed the morning, allowing them to get closer than they ever thought possible.

"This is enough," said Zo. She blew warmth into her shaking hands, but it did little to abate the relentless cold. Gray outlines of Gryphon and Laden wandered through mist ahead, so blurred it became impossible to tell them apart. It didn't matter. They didn't actually want to see the execution in detail—she really didn't want to see it at all—but needed to witness the moment his spirit passed from this life to the next. To soak in every last second of his mortality.

Joshua silently wept at her side, wiping tears and shaking every bit as much as she was as they climbed out of the river. Zo wrapped her arm around him as he crumpled into a ball and slumped to the ground with Zo to await the worst moment of their lives.

Blurred voices reached them, murmurs lost in the rushing river. The meeting must have begun.

Gryphon's shouts cut through the mist and had both Zo and Joshua back on their feet, clinging to one another. Without Joshua as an anchor, Zo might have been tempted to run ahead, but for the boy's sake, she stayed planted behind the tree.

"Father! No, Father, please!"

An unearthly wail rent the air.

And Zo was running …

Barnabas kicked aside Laden's bloodied form lying next to the red-stained tree stump. "Bring Gryphon." Barnabas gestured toward Gryphon, licking his lips, as though savoring the flavor of splattered blood.

The hands holding him froze in indecision, and Gryphon took advantage of the hesitation, rolling out of their grasp and jumping to his feet and sprinting ten yards away.

"Bring him here!" A purplish vein throbbed in Barnabas' forehead.

The brothers of Gryphon's mess looked to Ajax, their leader. "Sir, the debt. It's paid." Ajax's voice held a desperate edge.

Barnabas's face wrinkled in fury. "I said, bring him here!"

Gryphon slowed and turned to track their pursuit. He backed away toward the safety of the river where the Allies waited.

"Grab him! Now!"

Gryphon took a few more steps backward, his attention turned to Ajax, his battle brother and best friend. They stared at one another, communicating regret, sympathy, admiration. Ajax set his mouth in a firm line. His face twisted with rage as he gave Gryphon one final nod and turned back to Barnabas. "Did you plan to honor our agreement with the same cowardice as you did Laden's?" he scowled at his chief. "Where is your honor, Barnabas?"

Before Gryphon could cry out a warning, Barnabas flung the knife. It flew end over end through the air, its blade flashing in the low light until it sunk to the hilt in Ajax's neck.

A jolt of terror *zinged* through Gryphon's body.

A small hand wrapped around his, yanking him back. Barnabas shouted, "Stop them!" but the rest of the men in Gryphon's old mess stood frozen at the sight of the bloodied form of Ajax on the ground.

No.

Gryphon was running. He faintly registered the sun burning off some of the mist. Zo and Joshua pulled and pushed him away from Barnabas. They splashed through the river as Commander Laden's guard raced to their aid, swords out, bows drawn.

But no Ram followed them.

"Should we pursue those men, sir?" the head guard asked Gryphon, gesturing to the sullen men heading north, away from both Barnabas and the Allies. Gryphon watched his brothers jog away in tight formation. Ajax's place in the phalanx was painfully empty. "No, Captain. Let them go."

Barnabas reached the bank on the opposite side of the river Iiná. Holding a head by the hair in his raised hand. A full mess of Ram soldiers stood at his back. "I'll look for you on the field, Striker. You and your whore," he called over the soft sounds of the rivers.

Zo's hands tightened on Gryphon's arm. Joshua held fast to his other. Numb with shock, Gryphon barely recognized their presence in this whole nightmare. "You shouldn't be here. Either of you."

"Whose ... head?" Zo kissed his hand before threading her arms around his middle. With her touch his senses sharpened and the shock subsided, making way for raw pain.

Gryphon growled and gently pushed Zo and Joshua behind him. He yanked a spear from one of the Allied guards standing at his side and extended his arm back as he sprinted for momentum. In fury more animal than human, he hitched up his leg and launched the spear an impossible distance across both rivers. Barnabas caught the spear in his shield. The force nearly knocked him off his feet but even from this distance it was clear Barnabas's sickly smile didn't waver.

"I will kill that man," said Gryphon. "I swear it."

Gryphon's brothers, the only family he'd known since his youth, disappeared into the trees. Broken men without a clan.

Gryphon towed Zo and Joshua away from the river. Ahead of them, not four hundred yards away, the battle-ready line of Wolves appeared through the thinning mist. "Retrieve the Commander's body," Gryphon ordered the guards at his side.

"Y'sir!" came the reply.

"They are treating you like their leader," said Zo, tilting her head up to see his expression as they continued their brisk pace toward the wall of Wolf soldiers.

"I *am* their leader," he said.

Laden's guards cloaked the body and reverently hoisted it on Gryphon's oversized shield. "Take him somewhere safe until burial," said Gryphon.

As the men carrying the body passed, a bloodied hand slipped loose from the cloak. Commander Laden's ring reflected the faint morning light. Zo stopped walking. Her hand involuntarily went to cover her mouth.

Chapter Thirty

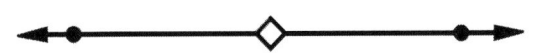

Zo walked in stunned silence. Laden, the closest thing she had to a parent ... gone.

Gryphon pulled Zo and Joshua closer to him as they continued to distance themselves from the rivers. "I couldn't stop him." He coughed out a sob. Emotion rolled off of him as he battled tears. "I couldn't save him."

Zo clung tighter to Gryphon's arm. "I saw the sword fall and thought it was you." She wiped her eyes with the heel of her hand, desperate to remove the image from her mind.

"Laden offered Barnabas his own head in my place. I didn't know ... " Gryphon swallowed. His voice dropped into a rasping moan. "He's my father, Zo. Barnabas confirmed it. They were mess brothers before Laden left to save his daughter ... my twin sister."

Zo shook her head. "I ... it can't be." It seemed like Commander Laden had always been a part of her clan. But then, the resemblance between them was obvious now that she knew it, and their characters were so similar. Was it possible? Could the man who had been such a big figure in her own life also belong to Gryphon?

"He knew he wouldn't survive the morning. He planned his death, just like one of his battle strategies. I saw it in his face last night." He swallowed. "I'm so sorry."

She could practically *taste* his guilt. When would he learn that he wasn't responsible for the choices of others?

"I don't think Laden was ever truly happy. There was always something gnawing away at his happiness." She tugged at his arm with dawning understanding, forcing him to stop walking. "I think it was you and your mom. I think he missed you both and that guilt was a chain he carried with him ever since leaving the Gate."

"What now?" she asked with rising dread that Gryphon would again have to leave. It seemed there would always be some reason for them to be apart, some jealous force in the universe that wouldn't allow their happiness.

Struggling to swallow, Gryphon pulled both her and Joshua into the circle of his arms and said, "I almost abandoned the most important people in my life." He set his jaw. "I will not make that mistake ever again."

"So we're not going to fight?" Joshua said, breaking his silence.

Gryphon smiled, a strange wave of peace seemed to wash over him. "We can't spend our whole lives running from Barnabas and the Ram." He ruffled Joshua's hair. "This ends today."

"Give me a job," said Joshua.

"Get Zo out of here. Help her and the healers with the wounded. Protect them while I'm gone." And to Zo, he added, "No blessings."

Zo nodded.

"Not good enough. I need to hear you swear it."

Zo cupped his cheek and lightly brushed her lips along his. "No blessings. I swear."

He kissed her again, with more force than before. A man who'd cheated death and needed to do it again.

"Gryphon?" Zo's stomach knotted. The invisible cord connecting them tugged at her gut. "Can you win?" Zo knew it wasn't fair to demand such an answer, but she needed to know if there was hope or if this was goodbye. Forever.

Gryphon leaned down and pressed his forehead against hers. "After Laden's sacrifice, and knowing you're waiting for me, I think I could do anything."

Zo nodded and wiped at the tears forming in her eyes. She placed a hand on either side of his face, his whiskers tickling her palms. "I believe you." She kissed his forehead. "Lead them, Gryphon. Lead them, and come back to me."

Gryphon walked the remaining distance to the waiting Allies, feeling a thief. He'd stolen his father's life, his mess brothers' clan, the Allies' leader, Gabe's woman, and Zo's heart. All in only a matter of weeks.

At twenty yards, Gryphon could just barely make out the restless shuffling of feet from the massive gathering of Allied soldiers. At ten, he could see the defeat in their stances as easily as he could spot a gap in an enemy's armor.

Chief Naat stood with Gabe before their men. The lines on their faces were stretched horizontal, drained of all color. When they turned and spotted Gryphon, neither seemed surprised to see him. Gabe placed a heavy hand on his shoulder. "I'm sorry for your loss ... Commander."

"You knew his plan to take my place," said Gryphon. Saying it aloud confirmed the truthfulness of the statement. "You knew, and still you let me ... " Gryphon swallowed. The image of Barnabas's sword slicing through the air replayed in his mind. "I wish you had told me."

In his gravelly voice, Chief Naat said, "We followed Laden's wishes." And that settled the matter. "Laden wanted you to lead these men." The old man pressed his hand to Gryphon's heart. "His spirit will linger with you to see the battle through." He said it not as a comforting platitude but as a fact.

Chief Naat folded his arms. "We don't have much time."

Gryphon swallowed and tore his eyes from the chief, casting his gaze out over the vast gathering of expectant, uncertain faces. Faces he would have marked as enemies not long ago.

Men his father wanted him to lead.

"Gryphon?" Gabe stepped closer. "Will you do this? Will you help us?"

Heat filled Gryphon's chest, burning outward through every limb until it completely consumed him. Could he do this? A sense of destiny nearly blocked the words from passing his lips.

He closed his eyes and nodded. "For my father's sake."

Chief Naat looked down to Sani's beads, still tied to Gryphon's wrist, and offered a sad sort of smile. "What are your orders, Ram?"

Gryphon's mind raced. *Two thousand inexperienced Wolves to Barnabas's three thousand Ram. Narrow field surrounded by thick pine and fir trees. Low visibility. A little over one thousand Raven archers.*

One-to-one odds until the Kodiak and Freeman arrive. If they arrive.

"Gryphon?" said Gabe. "Your orders?"

Other leaders had gathered. They looked at him like hungry children expecting to be fed. Gryphon glanced over their shoulders at the despondent soldiers whose fate he now carried.

"We cannot defeat the Ram in head-to-head combat," Gryphon finally said.

"Our scouts estimate we will outnumber them three to one once Murtog and Stone join us," said one of the lieutenants.

Gryphon crossed his arms. "Good odds by any Ram standard."

"Commander Laden thought—"

"Commander Laden isn't here!" Gabe and Chief Naat flinched at Gryphon's poor choice of words. "Listen." Gryphon massaged his temples. "Even if we outnumbered them five to one, we still couldn't beat them at their own game."

"If we surrender, the Ram will be merciless when they raid the Wolf clan," said Gabe. "Failure means death and starvation."

"I'm not suggesting surrender," said Gryphon. "I'm suggesting we exploit their greatest weakness."

Gabe twisted up his lips. "And what is that, brother?"

An evil smile stretched across Gryphon's face. "Pride."

Gryphon spent the following minutes explaining the plan of attack. As he spoke, the leaders grew quiet, eyes round with disbelief, but Gabe was nodding and shifting his weight in anticipation.

"It will never work," said a Raven.

"It's perfect!" said Gabe.

"It might be insane, but it's our only option unless we're willing to lose the majority of our men in battle, which I am not," said Gryphon, thinking of Isaac and the other young boys of his forty.

"How do you know Barnabas will fall into your trap?" asked Chief Naat.

It was true. The entire plan hinged on Barnabas's reaction. Gryphon thought back to his time spent with Barnabas, of his Ram arrogance and low opinion of anyone lacking Ram blood. "He'll take the bait."

The Raven folded his arms across his chest. "And if he doesn't?"

Gryphon looked him in the eye. "He will."

Chapter Thirty-One

The eerie sound came just after Gryphon sent half the Wolf and Raven soldiers away.

"Is that the wind?" asked Gabe. He and Gryphon stood like statues in the white mist that swept through the canyon. It shifted like a ghost, at times making it impossible to see more than a spear's throw ahead of them. A thousand Wolves formed twenty-five mess companies at Gryphon's back.

"It's not the wind." He listened to the ghostly Ram battle horn, muted by the dense fog. The eerie chorus broke off and was followed by pounding Ram shields that rolled like distant thunder.

Wolves shuffled their feet staring blindly out toward their enemies with bated breath.

"How far out?" asked Gabe.

Gryphon squinted through the mist, but it did him little good. "I'd say at least a half-mile. Maybe less. They're preparing to move."

Gryphon didn't have to turn around to sense the unease of his men. Their fear thickened the air, suffocating Gryphon's resolve. He'd staked their lives on an admittedly reckless plan. A plan that demanded unfathomable courage.

Have I asked too much of these men?

Gryphon shook his head. The time for doubt had long passed. He would not allow fear to cripple his mind. Instead, he thought of Zo. Her graceful movements as she sang her washing song under the light of the full moon. He thought of Joshua's unruly red hair and the hundreds of freckles that dotted his face. Then he thought of the countless Nameless who had suffered under Barnabas's reign, of the innocent Wolf women and children who would die tonight if Gryphon and his men couldn't stop this army.

Fear turned to anger. Anger to determination.

"The men are frightened, Gryph," said Gabe, echoing Gryphon's own thoughts. During his time with the Wolves, Gryphon had learned to respect their bravery. But even a lion cowers in the shadow of a mighty dragon.

Gryphon turned to face his troops. He walked through the thick fog down the line of men with shield and spear in hand, staring directly into the very souls of his soldiers. Their focus turned from the Ram army to Gryphon prowling the line of their defenses. The twenty-five mess units fit snugly into the narrow strip of bald earth framed by thick woods and sloping hills. Wild wheat grew around their ankles, helping to firm the soggy spring ground. The fate of all of the clans would be settled on this soil.

Gryphon walked the length of the troops, then returned to stand next to Gabe and drove his spear deep into the ground. "I am not one of you." He spoke boldly, projecting his voice to reach all of his men. "I cannot know the suffering you have faced because of the Ram."

Low voices rumbled throughout the troops. Gabe stepped over to Gryphon and said, "What are you doing?"

Gryphon looked over his shoulder. In the distance he heard the faint clattering of metal. The Ram were on the move.

"The men we fight today have more experience than you. They are stronger. They are masters of war and will take great pleasure in seeing you fall by their spears. They will show you no mercy.

"It has been said that defeating the Ram in open combat is impossible. But I say a man is capable of *anything* if he is defending his family. This day will be remembered as the day men looked directly into the eyes of the giant and slew him. Stand strong, men! Link tight! Hold your line, dig your feet in, and fight knowing your children depend upon your courage!"

The men yelled with weapons raised in the air, their chests heaving, fire glowing in their eyes.

Gryphon could hear the sound of splashing water as the Ram entered the river. *Two hundred yards, maybe less.* "Link!"

Shields scraped together. Metal glowed, reflecting the white mist. Gryphon took his place in the front weak side of his own forty. The men acknowledged him with determined nods. Gabe found his position with a different mess on the opposite side of the field.

The Ram army came to a halt, a fact Gryphon noted only by the absence of the sounds of metal and marching.

Deafening silence washed over his men as they stared out into the white abyss that blanketed their foe. A bird chirped in the trees at their backs.

Quiet.

The rivers rolled over rock in the distance. Someone vomited at the back of the mess. Gryphon looked over to see sixteen-year-old Isaac wet himself.

Quiet.

Gryphon filled his lungs with air and shouted with all his breath, "Forward!"

Zo practically dragged Joshua onward. They couldn't waste even a second in their retreat to the sanctuary in the Valley of Wolves. If they were followed, it could mean death for the women, children, and elderly Wolves who'd evacuated the city.

"You can let go of my wrist." Joshua tugged his hand free, but Zo snatched it right back.

"I know that look, Joshua. You want to go fight with Gryphon."

"I won't run off," he said. "I swear."

Zo hesitated then released her grasp. "Sorry. I just couldn't bear the thought of you both fighting today."

"I know." If it was possible to sulk while jogging, Joshua managed it. His head hung and he didn't seem to care whether he stepped on stick or stone along the trail.

"I'm sorry, Ginger. I know this is hard for you."

Joshua tripped and righted himself. He wiped his nose on his sleeve and trekked on. Zo pretended not to see him falter. Might as well let him keep what remained of his wounded pride.

It didn't take more than an hour to pass through the narrow canyon that acted as the entrance to her childhood home. Unlike Ram's Gate, the Valley of Wolves was mostly farmland divided among family groups called Packs. Low walls of cobblestones gathered from the fields marked the boundary lines dividing plots of wheat and barley. The soil looked dark and healthy, unlike the sandy tan soil of the Ram. The fields were well tended and appeared twice as lovely to Zo because she knew that they were tilled by hard-working farmers and their families, not slaves.

Joshua seemed to forget his troubles as he studied the land around him. "No wonder Barnabas wants this," he said, not taking his eyes from the brilliant valley before him. Beyond the farmland, the ground sloped upward. There, in the foothills of the great mountains, a high wall of carved granite protected the village proper. If the Alpha's orders were obeyed, the people of the Valley would have abandoned their homes and retreated to the safety of the village keep, known as the Den.

Zo looked longingly at the farms lying on the outer rim of the valley, knowing it was too dangerous to seek out her old family home. If the Ram army managed to defeat Gryphon and the Allies—something Zo didn't want to consider—they would come straight to this valley to claim their prize.

No. She would lead Joshua to the shelter to wait out the storm with the rest of the Wolves unfit for battle.

Zo pulled Joshua to her side and rested her head against his. He'd grown in the last few months. Soon her head would meet his shoulder. "Come on, Joshua. We shouldn't linger."

"No, you shouldn't."

Zo and Joshua whipped around to find a woman with dark hair pulled back into a harsh bun. She carried a task whip at her side and wore a boiled leather vest. Her familiar black eyes tracked Zo in a predatory way. "Wonderful to finally see you, my dear. I was beginning to wonder if you decided to stay and fight alongside the traitor."

The silver sound of a whetstone running against metal tickled Zo's ears. The Seer peered hungrily over the length of the blade then stroked it again.

"Where is the deserter Eva?" she asked conversationally. With a wave of her hand, three of the Seer's men stepped out of hiding, surrounding Zo and Joshua in a perfect ring. The Seer gulped up the victory, her black eyes dancing with mirth.

"I look forward to seeing how her pregnancy has progressed. I'd like to make sure the baby is well before I cut it out of her worthless body."

Joshua's hand rested on the hilt of his short sword, exposing a portion of the blade from its sheath around his waist.

Zo reached out and took his arm. *No, Joshua. Please don't.*

His whole body was a tightened spring, shaking with the need to release.

Chapter Thirty-Two

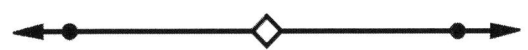

The line of Ram warriors broke through the mist at a sprint. Gryphon and his men only had a few seconds to prepare for the impact. Shields *boomed* together as the two armies collided. Gryphon roared as he pushed against his shield, using his spear to stab at the enemy through the thin gaps of the Ram phalanx. The force of the Ram kept Gryphon and his company on their heels, struggling to find purchase in the soft soil and hold ground.

So this is what it feels like to be on the other side of the Ram.

A single wave of Raven arrows cut through the mist. They shot from a long distance into the Ram troops. The arrows bounced off Ram shields—a nuisance more than a threat—causing little if any damage to the enemy. By now, the archers would have retreated back into the tree line, a few leaving their bows behind as evidence of their abandonment.

"Push!" Gryphon grunted.

A wide gap formed as Gryphon's shield mate fell back. A Ram spear shot through the gap and into a Wolf's thigh. He howled in pain as he struggled to push against his shield and keep his weight forward. The spear stuck out of his leg like a stick in messy red mud. With one slash of his short sword, Gryphon cut through the shaft of the enemy spear. The splintered remains made a sickly suction noise as he yanked it free of his mess brother's leg. Chunks of flesh clung to the spearhead. Blood drooled down the wounded man's leg, soaking his pants. To his credit, the Wolf didn't fall. Gryphon jabbed back at the enemy with even more vigor than before.

"Push!" Gryphon called into his shield so the sound would carry along the line. "Move them back!" He dug in and with the help of the three men at his rear, was able to gain several feet of ground. He stabbed again with his spear and this time connected with flesh. The enemy fell and Gryphon took advantage, advancing farther until the Ram soldier was trampled underfoot. Gryphon could feel the man's bones break beneath his feet. A wail of agony ended with a quick jab of his shield mate's spear.

Gryphon looked down and vaguely recognized the Ram, mangled as he was. Stomach rolling, he vowed not to look into the face of another Ram if he could help it.

Forgive me, brother.

Gryphon's side of the mess had made more progress than the other. The mess bowed into an L shape, folding around the enemy like the open mouth of a monster preparing to crush its prey. From the corner of his eye, Gryphon could tell his mess was having a great deal more success than others near him.

The noise was so loud he could hardly distinguish cries of pain from grunts of exertion. With a quick glance to his side, Gryphon saw the Wolves in the next mess over pushed back so far, bodies began to fall at the feet of the Ram.

He blocked an attack with his shield and jabbed his spear into the chest of a faceless Ram.

Gryphon pulled three Wolves behind him from their place in the phalanx and motioned to the battle raging next to them. "With me!" he beckoned, drawing his sword.

Having broken through the Ram line, Gryphon and those who remained of his forty approached the enemy from behind. The Ram were so focused on moving the Wolf phalanx backward that they didn't even notice Gryphon and his men until it was too late.

Gryphon slit a man's throat while stabbing another through the heart. He was onto his next man before the dead weight of his victims crumpled to the ground. Half of the Ram in the rear line lay dying or dead before the other five could defend themselves.

The Wolf mess gained ground as Gryphon and three other Wolves battled for their lives from behind. Gryphon made quick work of the men, determined not to look at their faces, knowing his resolve would waver if he recognized another victim.

I have no other choice. I have no other choice. He chanted the phrase over and over in his mind, timing his blows to the rhythm of the words. *I have no other choice. I have no other choice.* The Ram phalanx broke formation. Gryphon slashed and stabbed, wild in his hypnotic frenzy. By the time he finished, his hands and forearms were slick with blood.

Gryphon looked around the field for Barnabas, but there were too many bodies, too many men still locked in phalanx trying desperately to gain advantage.

Gryphon spotted Gabe across the field crossing swords with two Ram soldiers at the same time. He feinted right and slashed an enemy behind the knees. The man crumpled to the ground, the major tendons of his legs severed.

Around him Wolves fell on all sides. Limbs detached. Blood spilled. Cries for mercy ignored. Gryphon hoped he'd given the others enough time as he pulled the small horn from its place in his belt and blew.

Gabe finished off the second attacker, met eyes with Gryphon, and brought his own horn to his lips.

"Retreat!" Gryphon ordered, twisting away from a fatal slash aimed at his chest. He wasn't fast enough. The blade cut through his boiled leather armor, earning him a shallow cut along his side and back.

The horn won him unwelcome attention from the Ram around him. He blocked an attacker and tried to break free without engaging in an actual fight.

Cold fire ran the length of his side from the wound. Gryphon turned and barely had time to block a blow that would have taken off his head. He used his free hand to sink his dagger into the man's stomach.

"Retreat!" he yelled.

The Wolves obeyed as best they could. Many forgot to guard their own escape and took a spear to the back.

"Form up!" The order came from Barnabas, standing bloodied and bold fifty yards away.

Gryphon looked to the safety of the trees then back at Barnabas. He should stick to the original plan. There wasn't time to linger. Every moment was vital.

But the reminder of Barnabas's sick smile haunted him.

Rage won out.

He took off at a wild sprint toward his father's killer barely caring to knock away the few swords that stood between them. Barnabas would pay for the lives he took, for the crimes he'd committed against Laden and the countless Nameless in his possession.

When he was only twenty yards away, Gabe tackled him from behind. They tumbled to the earth and rolled several times before gaining their feet again. Gabe grabbed his arm and tried to tow him away. The chaos thinned as the Ram found formation and the remaining Wolves ran for the safety of the trees in retreat.

"We have to leave, now!" said Gabe.

"I have to kill him!" Gryphon yanked free his arm. Gabe, more than anyone, should know how desperately Gryphon needed his revenge.

Gabe grabbed him again. "There's no ti—"

A Ram dagger sank into Gabe's left shoulder. Gryphon picked up a spear from the ground and lodged it in the attacker. Gabe studied the hilt for a confused moment then yanked it free.

Gryphon looked longingly in Barnabas's direction then turned and pushed Gabe toward the trees. The Wolf staggered, but kept his feet. "I have your back. Now run!" Gryphon yelled, using his shield to deflect spears launch at him from behind as they raced toward the tree line.

"Don't let him escape!" Barnabas's voice bellowed behind them.

Gabe tripped and Gryphon stumbled head first over the Wolf's limp form. He jumped up and tried to tow Gabe along, but his friend lay unconscious on the ground.

Ten Ram soldiers charged them. Gryphon hoisted Gabe's body over his shoulder with a grunt and ran as fast as his burning legs would carry him. Arrows shot from the trees passed his head, aimed at his pursuers. Heavy Ram footfalls thundered at his back, quickly closing the distance. One by one the Ram hit the ground with a *thump.*

Bless those Birds!

Gryphon ran past the tree line, deeper and deeper into the thick forest, until all sight of the blood-soaked meadow and Ram army were lost to the trees. Men ran to his assistance as he crumpled to one knee.

"Take Gabe as far from here as you can." Gryphon took a few greedy breaths, not once peeling his eyes from the direction of his enemies. "Is everyone in place?" he panted.

"Yes, sir. Waiting for you, sir."

Gryphon nodded and climbed back to his feet. He could hear the traditional shouts from the Ram as they reveled in their victory. Barnabas would send teams to hunt Gryphon and the insignificant number of Wolves who escaped the field, but he would let the men celebrate first.

"Enjoy your victory, Chief. It will be your last." Adrenaline hammered in every vein of Gryphon's body as he sprinted deeper into the woods.

Chapter Thirty-Three

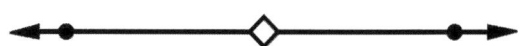

Gryphon bolted through the narrow ravine leading to the mouth of the canyon—the only entrance to the Valley of Wolves. The walls on either side of the path were sheer, angled at a steep grade; so steep it would take the use of two free hands to climb. Pine trees grew from the sidewalls, their trunks bending at right angles to reach the light of the sun. Raven nodded their allegiance as they perched like birds from the branches and behind rock jutting from the walls.

Gryphon hoped they could conceal themselves well enough to deceive Barnabas and his men. Small veins of water wove through collections of polished rock on the ravine floor. The path curved like a snake, creating blind corners that Gryphon hoped would work to their advantage.

As he reached the end of the ravine, the Wolf Alpha and Chief Naat greeted him. "Where is Gabe?" Chief Naat craned his neck to see past the bend of the trail.

"Injured but safe. I left him in the care of a pair of his men."

"You're alive. That's something, I suppose," grunted the Alpha as his fingers ran the length of this light beard. "Do you think they know our plan?"

Gryphon considered the battle. "They are celebrating victory even as we speak."

"You're certain?" asked the Raven.

Gryphon could still hear the shouts of victory in his mind, mocking the sacrifice of the Wolves lost in battle. "Even without the help of the other clans, the Wolves fought well." Gryphon looked away. "We were … convincing."

They heard the hurried footfalls of the scout before they saw him turn the corner. "Sir, the Ram. They're marching."

"How long?" Gryphon's eyes narrowed.

"Ten, maybe fifteen minutes, sir."

Where are Stone and Murtog?

Gryphon looked to the Raven warriors dotting the mountainsides and prayed their arrows would be enough. He placed a hand on the Raven Chief's shoulder. "Your men will wait for my signal?"

Chief Naat offered a sober nod.

Gryphon walked ahead with the Alpha, just outside the mouth of the narrow canyon where the other half of the Wolf forces stood. They were joined by the bloodied Wolf survivors. The Allies last line of defense.

"Whatever happens, do not let them past you. Work together or they'll cut through your defenses like clay." The adrenaline wafting off his men was almost tangible as they hid themselves on either side of the canyon exit. They needed to create the illusion that the way was clear. "Quiet down and wait for my order to strike!" Gryphon called as loud as he dared.

Satisfied there was nothing more he could do, Gryphon concealed himself behind a boulder, bouncing on his feet to keep his muscles warm. Sitting still, he might have had time to consider the consequences of failure.

Before Zo could stop him, Joshua charged the Seer, sword in hand.

"No!" Zo cried out. But it was too late. One of the Seer's men stepped in to parry the attack but Joshua's momentum carried him forward as man, boy, and Seer collided.

"Stupid, worthless boy!" The Seer shoved him off her chest. A red gash above her brow wept two distinct trails of blood down her face and into her eyes.

"You bring Gryphon and your clan shame." She wiped the blood from her eyes. "You always have." Joshua rolled backward to gain his feet but another soldier leapt forward and threw his fist into the boy's face.

Joshua's head whipped back. His body went limp and flew through the air before landing in a sloppy skid on the ground. Lifeless. Broken.

Hands clamped down on Zo's arms, binding her wrists behind her back. She screamed and bucked, gaze fixed on the motionless form of Joshua on the ground. He'd tried to defend her. He'd probably felt it was his duty.

"Bring the boy. The chief will enjoy this pair for our first prizefight in our new home."

"How?" Zo gasped, between sobs. "How did you get here?" The pass was blocked with Wolves. There was no way the Seer and her men could get past them this morning.

"There are two passes that lead to the Wolves, my dear."

Realization dawned. Impossible. "You came through the slot canyon and the Allied Camp. The southern pass."

The Seer laughed. "I've known about that camp for years."

"Commander Laden—"

"Is a fool to think he could keep something so large from the Seer." Her voice took on a hard edge.

If what she was saying was true, the Ram could have invaded the Allies long ago. "What stopped Barnabas from—"

"Barnabas didn't know about the Camp until recently. Men can be so fickle, you know. They let their pride override logic. I am the chief's eyes and I allow him to see only what is best for our clan."

If only Zo could get her hands free. She'd managed to pull energy from men in Gryphon's old mess when they'd held her captive in the wilderness. If she could just manage to break her bonds, she could do it again.

Glancing back, Zo saw a soldier carrying Joshua over his shoulder. The kid's gangly limbs flopped around, making the journey difficult.

Zo stumbled. The hands holding her biceps caught her but not before her knee jarred against the ground. "Where are you taking us?" she asked, tugging again on the ropes securing her wrists.

The Seer's smile spread like a slow blooming flower across her face. "The battle, of course." She moved right into Zo's path, forcing the entourage to halt as she leaned close to Zo. "I want you to witness every life you can't save, every son of the Wolves whose blood spills. To see what happens when animals contend with the only worthy clan in the region."

Chapter Thirty-Four

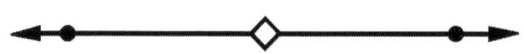

G ryphon's heart beat heavily in his ears, so strong that he hoped Barnabas and the surviving Ram troops couldn't hear. The sound of boots crunching against loose river rock carried through the canyon. It was hard to tell exactly how far away the Ram were from the mouth. One turn? Maybe two?

Gryphon looked up the sheer walls on either side of the ravine, where hundreds of Raven perched in hiding. Their arrows would be hungry for Ram blood. Hopefully they could marshal themselves until he gave the signal.

The sound of the approaching army grew louder, echoing off the walls of the ravine. Even though the Wolves managed to reduce their numbers some, the majority of the approaching Ram army was still intact. Gryphon's plan was like catching a tiger by the tail. One wrong move and they'd get the teeth.

"Steady," Gryphon whispered to the restless men around him.

Finally, when the echoing clatter of the Ram army seemed to surround them, the first wave of soldiers turned the corner. The path was so narrow that only ten men could travel abreast at one time.

Barnabas walked alone before the whole group. He carried his massive round shield on one arm but his sword remained sheathed at his hip. He studied the walls on either side of the ravine with such intensity that Gryphon feared the Raven would be spotted if so much as a toe were exposed. Gryphon pressed back against the rock, his chest rising and falling as he steeled his nerves.

Fifty yards between them. Barnabas led his troops forward without pause.

A little farther. A little farther.

Forty yards.

Thirty yards, and more Ram continued to turn the corner. There were so many. Many more than Gryphon had estimated. For his trap to work, they all had to fit into the straight stretch of ravine floor that arrowed out of the canyon.

Twenty yards. The army still turned. More Ram came.

Out of time. Out of room. *Please let this work!*

With only fifteen yards separating them, Gryphon stepped out of hiding with hands raised in surrender.

"You!" Barnabas nearly fell over in surprise.

"We need to talk," said Gryphon.

Barnabas's wicked laugh rose to a hysterical level. "It's like you *want* to die, boy!"

"I've come to offer the Ram a chance to turn around."

Barnabas's joy dissolved quickly into rage. "You are in no position to bargain."

"A chance to do the right thing," Gryphon continued, raising his voice so he could be heard by the entire Ram army. "The people whose homes you intend to steal do not have to be your enemy. You've seen plenty of fertile, unclaimed land for the Ram in your travels. You don't need to fight. There is no honor in killing the innocent!"

Barnabas's face turned three shades redder. His many chins wobbled and he literally shook with fury. "How dare you."

Then someone deep within the ranks of the Ram shouted, "Speak your proposal!"

Barnabas whipped around, searching the throng of soldiers to see who had spoken. Had word of Barnabas's mistreatment of Gryphon's mess reached to the other men?

"If you will walk away from this valley, forsake your chief, and release your Nameless, I offer you a life outside of war, free of beatings and hunger, where your families hold higher rank than your mess. More to the point, I offer you a chance to leave this canyon alive."

No one moved to retreat. Gryphon hadn't expected they would. Still, these were his people. He had to give them a chance. He cupped his hands to his mouth and shouted, "You are not fighting for the security of your families, Ram! You are fighting for bloodlust and pride. Put down your weapons and leave with your lives, knowing there is fertile land to be had outside the walls of Ram's Gate."

Silence descended over the large group of warriors. Metal clinked as men shifted their weight from one restless foot to the other. Murmuring broke out through the ranks. Arguments. Anger. Doubt.

Barnabas drew his sword. "You, the son of a dead traitor, threaten our lives? Offering mercy as if you were the captain of our fate. How will you enforce your righteous threat? You have no family. No clan. Your pathetic army has failed you. You're nothing!"

Gryphon cast his eyes to the ground. It was time to give the signal. His people had had their chance—something he had demanded from the Allied leaders when he first devised this plan. It was time to end this. But Gryphon didn't move.

He couldn't do it.

Barnabas growled and ran at Gryphon with sword raised. Gryphon deftly blocked the blow and grabbed the chief by the neck. His long fingers squeezed Barnabas's throat. "This is for my father," he whispered. He lifted his hand and saluted his old chief, touching two fingers to his brow—the signal his men had been waiting for.

Hundreds of Raven arrows cut through the concentrated mass of the Ram army. Waves of men fell, unprepared for the attack. Those without an arrow sticking from their chests tried to create a shield hedge for protection. Too many bodies lined the narrow trail that they couldn't form solid links.

Barnabas wrenched Gryphon's arm away from his neck and slammed him against the mountain. Gryphon stumbled and rolled away from Barnabas's desperate blade.

"You once told me the Ram would never fall," Gryphon yelled over the chaos surrounding them. He dodged an attack and almost lost his grip on the blade while blocking another.

Gryphon whistled his signal and a wave of Wolf warriors rushed past to join in the fight. "You were wrong, Chief."

Barnabas fumbled backward as Gryphon advanced, swinging his sword with all the anger in his heart. He sliced an arm, his chest, and then his back as the chief retreated to the side of the mountain.

Gryphon approached the panting leader slowly, as a cat stalks its prey.

Barnabas sank to his knees. His sword clattered to the rocky soil as he gulped air. "Mercy."

"Mercy?" Rage burned the edges of Gryphon's vision. Sweat ran into his eyes. "I'm surprised you know the meaning of the word."

Barnabas cowered lower, his pleading gaze fixed on Gryphon. "I can still call my men off," he said.

Gryphon looked at the ongoing battle. The mess units not inside the pass during the ambush were entering. Strong and certain. Spears flew. Shields locked. The Ram were … regrouping. The advantage shifted. Blood spilled as the Ram pushed farther and farther though the canyon.

No! Gryphon wanted to cry out.

Then he heard it. A new kind of thunder filled the pass, so loud and terrifying that it seeped into Gryphon's bones and rattled his heart.

"Impossible," said Barnabas.

Beyond the battle, flooding into the canyon like a sea of giant devils, the Kodiak army charged into the fray. Murtog, easy to spot at the head, wielded a large staff with ruthless precision. Others fought with axes and some charged forward with only their bare hands. The Wolf lines rallied as the Kodiak advanced, sandwiching the remains of the Ram army.

Barnabas shifted and Gryphon turned back to him, pressing the tip of his blade into the chieftain's chest. "Spare their lives," he panted. "Call surrender." There was no sense in killing these Ram. The Allies had won. The conflict was over.

"Surrender!" Gryphon growled. The wails of dying men punctured Gryphon's very soul. He'd go mad if he had to watch more.

"I ... surrender." Barnabas dropped his head and fell to his knees. The horn that usually hung at the chief's side was only a few feet away on the ground. Gryphon bent down and reached for the familiar horn. The Ram horns were sacred to his people. A symbol of power.

Gryphon pressed the horn to his lips and blew three times—maybe the first time a Ram horn was used to call surrender. It took a few minutes for the fighting to die down. Some Ram simply refused to throw down their weapons. Others knelt on the ground, raising their hands above their heads.

It was a huge victory that felt more like a rough stone lodged in the pit of Gryphon's stomach.

Gryphon sheathed his sword and turned back to the white-faced Ram Chief. "Go join your men until I decide what to do with you." He turned his back and marched toward the Valley of the Wolves. He had his dagger ready, anticipating an attack, even before Barnabas charged him from behind.

In one swift movement, Gryphon spun and dragged the blade across Barnabas's throat. The chief's eyes doubled in shock, his mouth agape, as he slid down the wall. Butter melting in a hot pan.

Gryphon didn't want to celebrate with his men. He took almost no joy from the victory. Lost and numb, he walked toward the Valley of Wolves with no idea where to find Zo and Joshua.

He took three unbalanced steps out of the pass—out of view from his men—then fell to his knees and wept.

Chapter Thirty-Five

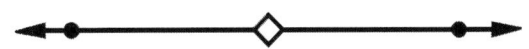

At the mouth of the canyon, Zo watched the Seer's face turn reddish purple when Gryphon pulled the Ram horn to his lips and blew the Ram's call of surrender. The Seer pulled her men back into a small niche tucked against the mountain wall.

Joshua lay face down in the dirt with hands bound behind his back, his cheek pressed to the ground. Both she and the boy were gagged; the foul smell of cloth in her mouth stirred her stomach in violent waves.

At least the boy was conscious and alive. For now.

Gryphon staggered out of the pass with hands bloody and chest rising and falling rapidly—hyperventilating, if Zo wasn't mistaken.

Zo tried calling out to him, trying to use her tongue to force the cloth from her mouth.

Her voice didn't carry through the gag, and a soldier's hand clamped over her mouth, further blocking her efforts.

Move, Gryphon. Run.

But he didn't run. Bent over as he was, he didn't even see the Seer slip out of the niche behind him.

Zo bucked and fought, but her strength was nothing to the Ram holding her. *Please, no. Please, no. Please, no.* She tried pulling energy from the man holding her, but with hands bound, she barely grazed his skin with one fingertip. His skin under her finger went cold, the hands holding her shook, but Zo's little weapon wouldn't be enough.

The Seer pulled a dagger from her belt, the sound of her whisper-soft steps lost in the commotion from the pass.

Slamming down on the foot of her captor, Zo threw her head back in a wild rush of adrenaline. The Ram's hand slipped from her mouth. She screamed Gryphon's name just as the Seer sprang forward, driving her Ram blade into Gryphon's back.

Gryphon collapsed face first into the ground, the hilt of the blade erect.

The Ram soldier firmed his grip on her again, but when Stone and a small band of Freeman bolted out of the canyon, he released his hold and ran.

"Don't lose him," Stone ordered.

The Seer cried out as Stone tackled her to the ground.

Zo sprinted with hands still bound behind her back toward Gryphon.

"Help!" she screamed. "Someone, help!" *No. Please. Please, no.* She dropped next to Gryphon in a slide. "Talk to me, Gryphon."

A groan was all he managed. He lay on his stomach with eyes pinched shut in pain. Zo wormed up onto her knees, tugging at the ropes binding her wrists in panic.

"Hold still," Chief Naat's smooth voice sounded at her back. He cut the bindings on her wrists and Zo hissed as circulation flowed back into her arms.

"Gryphon," she sobbed. She carefully pulled out the knife and pressed her palm over the wound while trying to listen to his heartbeat through his back. "Please. Please."

Blood oozed from the wound, pooling around her palm and through the gaps of her fingers. Without hesitation, she pushed her healing energy into him, holding nothing back. One of her mother's blessings flowed from her lips, helping the energy along to the beat of her chant.

Loving Gryphon was as natural and right as breathing, and the energy poured through her with abandon. Her hand heated from the contact, but the rest of her began to cool as the life force drained from her body.

Suddenly, a hand lifted one of hers from off of Gryphon's wound. A gentle, brown hand lined with age and calloused from hardship.

"Chief Naat?" Zo found she could barely lift her head. Her body crumpled on top of Gryphon's with one healing hand still pushing energy into Gryphon's wound.

"Use me, child."

"But—"

"My days are numbered. The creator beckons me. My ancestors are waiting. It is meant to be."

Zo was drowning. Slipping under the surface of consciousness to a place beyond awakening.

"How do you know I can … " A broken question, but all Zo could manage.

"Our shaman can help you. He can help build up the dam of your energy again."

"How—"

"There's no time. Use me to heal him, child." The chief held her hand over his heart. The pulse of life beckoned her. Willing. Ready. "Sani would want this."

With the little energy she had left, Zo pulled from the chief, filling her soul with warm *life* and transferring it to Gryphon. Little by little, her energy restored, filling the white places of her body with colorful heat, until she was conscious enough to recognize Gryphon moving beneath her hand. She quickly pulled away from the chief, mortified to see him lying on the ground beside her.

Still. Gone.

"Zo?" Gryphon said. He gingerly rolled to sit with legs crossed in front of him, his cheeks a healthy color and the wound at his back sealed over, much like Joshua's had under the fir tree outside Ram's Gate.

Zo crawled into his lap and closed her eyes as his arms settled around her. When she opened her eyes she looked up to find a crowd of soldiers, including Talon, Stone, and Murtog standing around them. Blood covered their hands and clothes, weapons hanging limply in their hands. Talon dropped to his knees by his father and bent his head in prayer.

Gryphon tugged her closer to him and placed a kiss on top of her head. Though he likely meant to reassure her, Zo could only feel a sense of peace in knowing the sacrifice had been the *right* thing.

"When I lost consciousness I dreamed you died," he said. "That I couldn't reach you." He paused, collecting himself. "I saw my father. I saw him for who he really is."

One by one, their audience left them.

"He loved you," said Gryphon as he kissed the top of her head again. "I only wish he could have seen us together." Gryphon paused again, running his hand up and down her arm. "He wanted that for us."

Lacing her hands through Gryphon's, Zo let her head sink onto his shoulder and together they sat looking over the Valley of Wolves. "He loved you, too, Gryphon." She leaned up and kissed his cheek. "And so do I."

Gryphon and Joshua picked their way through the carnage of the canyon while men helped the wounded to a healing site that had been erected just inside the Valley of Wolves. Zo and Tess were assisting the other Wolf healers who'd been summoned to tend to the injured, be they Ram, Wolf, Kodiak, Raven, or Freeman.

Most of the fallen Gryphon encountered on his way back to

the joining of the two rivers were strangers. But every so often, the familiar face of a Ram caused him to pause and drop to the ground in a moment of silent prayer—pleading for mercy from the great creator to ensure the man's soul made its proper place of rest.

Joshua didn't stray more than a few feet from Gryphon's side the entire way. His left eye was swollen and purple.

"What will happen to the rest of us?" the boy asked. "Will the Wolves enslave the Ram?"

Gryphon looked up from where he knelt on the ground. "No, Joshua." He stood and put an arm around Joshua's shoulder, surprised by how much the boy had grown over the last year. "But it's going to be a painful recovery."

A drop of rain hit Gryphon's face. Another, his arm.

They reached the other end of the narrow pass with heavier steps than they had entering it. Turning the final corner to where the land opened up and the rivers converged, Gryphon halted with jaw hanging open.

"Who are they?" Joshua asked.

Women and children gathered around their Kodiak fathers and spouses. Other children with both light and dark skin danced along the banks of the river, kicking up water and laughing. The rain fell harder, washing away the stain of war.

"It's the Nameless, kid."

Lines of confusion blended the freckles of his face. "They look … different."

Gryphon cuffed Joshua's shoulder. "I don't think *they've* changed, Joshua. You and I just see them differently now."

A giant roar sounded from the far side of the field. Ikatou's hearty laughter filled all of the hollow places of Gryphon's heart as the Bear gathered his daughters and wife into his massive embrace.

More jubilant shouts of reunion. More tears mixed with rain, healing both ground and heart.

I wish my father could see this.

Murtog threw open the flap of the hastily erected Healer's Tent. Rain dripped down his face and hair and onto his already sopping tunic. He scanned the injured men lying on ground until his eyes locked upon Talon sitting beside the small, still form of his sister.

Zo stepped between Murtog and his goal before the Kodiak could make a scene. The large man's nostrils flared and the corners of his mouth sank as fury mingled with the pain on his face.

"She sleeps, Murtog." Zo set a hand on his arm to send him a dose of *serenity*. "She took an arrow to the shoulder, but the wound is healing. She's out of danger."

Without peeling his eyes from Raca, Murtog nodded before sidestepping Zo.

Talon rose to greet him. "Murtog." Talon offered a subtle bow of the head.

"Greetings, Raven Chief. I'm sorry to hear about your father," said Murtog. Again, he didn't bother pulling his gaze from Raca. It was as though the rest of the room, the rest of the world, didn't matter.

"We're taking him back to the Nest for burial," said Talon. "My sister will not be strong enough to make the journey."

"Talon?" Raca's eyes fluttered open and Murtog dropped to his knees by her side. As gently as he might pluck a wildflower, he lifted Raca's hand as he pressed it to his lips.

Raca's other hand reached out to him, her fingers trailing the length of his brown jaw. "I was so worried for you," her voice a whisper.

"I'm here, little bird." He cleared his throat, the muscles in his jaw flexing. "When I heard you followed us," he coughed back emotion, "that you were injured … " He kissed her hand again, unable to finish.

Talon glanced at Zo and smiled before walking out of the tent.

Zo backed away as well, far enough to hear the faint, deep rumblings of Murtog without understanding his words. She turned to find Gabe standing behind her, his left arm bound in a sling. His hair was wet from the rain, turning it a light brown instead of its usual blond. The handsome smile she'd come to expect from him didn't quite reach his eyes as he navigated the bedrolls on the ground.

So many wounded. So much loss. But there was something tangible in the air. A mist of collective *hope* radiating from the injured that made it easier to see happiness in the midst of so much suffering.

"What is that for?" Zo gestured to the pack slung over Gabe's good shoulder when he finally reached her.

"I'm leaving right after the Commander's burial and wanted to say goodbye. The Alpha is sending me to lead a group of Wolves back to the Allied Camp location. The surviving Ram—mostly women and children—need men to help erect homes. The crops are already planted and will be enough to give them a decent beginning."

"You've done so much already. Can't he send someone else?"

Gabe cleared his throat, and looked away. "I actually volunteered."

Zo didn't know what to say.

"Gryphon's a good man, Zo," he said. "You and Tess will be well cared for. I really am happy for you." He smiled again, this time a hint of his usual mirth filling his features.

"Thank you, my friend," said Zo.

Gabe bent down and kissed Zo's cheek. "You are the waxing moon, Zo. None of this could have happened without you."

"Without *us*," she corrected.

Gabe offered a nod and tapped the end of her nose with his fingertip before leaving her to stare after him.

Suddenly her hand filled with Tess's. She smiled up at Zo, looking more like their mother every day, as a subtle stream of *peace* emanated from the little hand.

"Thank you, bug."

Chapter Thirty-Six

*D*ear Gryphon,
    If you are reading this then you have led the Allies to victory. I would have given anything to see you face down such a mighty force.

By now you know that I was the man who left you and your mother all those years ago. I can only imagine the shame you felt for having such a father.

I want you to know that leaving you and your mother was the hardest thing I've ever done. But I won't apologize for my actions, just like you shouldn't apologize for the circumstances that took you from the Gate.

There are so many things that reside outside of a man's control, son. True courage is not measured in battles won. It is in finding the right course of action and following it, no matter the repercussions. You are a leader. It is your destiny. I formed the Allies to protect those who could not protect themselves. Don't let these people down. Be their advocate, Gryphon. They will need you.

All my love and respect,
Your Father

Gryphon carefully folded the letter after rereading it for the fifth time.

"They're ready to start, Gryph." Zo stood by the door of the tent wearing a long white gown that fell gently over her curves. Half of her midnight hair was braided in a crown atop her head. The rest cascaded freely down her back. Tess stood by her side wearing the same striking white. Each protected the young flame of a candlestick from the evening breeze.

Gryphon rose from his father's pine desk that had been brought over from the Allied Camp and tucked the letter into his shirt. He accepted his own candle from Zo. Her warm lips brushed his ear as she whispered, "You look very handsome, Commander."

Gryphon let his candle feed off Zo's light then together they stepped into the starry night. Gryphon swallowed a gasp as at least a thousand candles lit a path to the resting place of his father.

Joshua held Laden's giant shield with reverence to his chest. The same shield that used to hang above Gryphon's family hearth. Tess walked over and took Joshua's free hand, her tiny tears dancing in the light's reflection.

"Let's go," said Gryphon.

Zo threaded her arm through his and together they followed Joshua and Tess down the lighted path that led to Laden's final resting place. As they passed, Raven, Wolf, Kodiak, and Freemen all knelt in respect, the lights of their candles held high to illuminate the pathway to heaven for their fallen leader.

A Ram custom.

Among them, Sara stood with baby Jax in arms, her sister, Eva, and new brother-in-law, Stone, at her side.

At the bottom of the hill, Murtog nodded to Gryphon and used his torch to light two giant pyres on either side of the grave. Once the blaze caught, he stepped back in line with Raca, his newly betrothed. The casket sat before the cavity of earth, ready to find peace beneath the soil of Gryphon's new homeland. Women offered flowers to Zo and Tess, who each tore petals from the stems and muttered words lost to the night's breeze as they sprinkled them over the casket.

Zo's eyes sparkled beautifully with tears as she and Tess stepped aside so Joshua could place the shield over Laden's remains.

Gryphon went last. He dropped to one knee and bowed until his forehead grazed his father's shield.

"I'm proud to be your son."

Epilogue

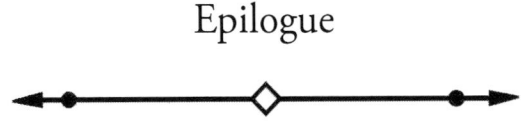

Three years later

Zo knelt in rich soil, thinning a row of new carrots from the kitchen garden on the side of a simple log home. Faint smoke curled out of the chimney and spring flowers lined the walkway to a covered porch.

The wheat fields were just showing their color and the high mountains in the distance boasted a blanket of green. A tall, dark-haired man cut through the fields toward her, carrying a spade while balancing a two-year-old boy on his shoulders. He wore a light woven shirt. No boiled leather. No weapons.

"Mama!" the little boy squirmed down this father's broad shoulders and ran in a precarious line toward Zo with arms outstretched.

Zo dusted the dirt from her hands just in time to snatch the little boy up. "Hello, Troy. Did you help your father in the fields?"

The boy nodded obediently and Zo kissed his full cheeks before setting him back on his own two legs. He instantly wrapped his little arms around his father's calf.

"You shouldn't be working out here. Joshua and I can tend the garden," Gryphon said.

"Ram in my garden?" She raised an eyebrow at him. "You'll mistake my lettuce for weeds."

Gryphon rolled his eyes. "Will you never let me live that down?" He smiled, offering his hand to help Zo stand. She leaned into him, resting her head against his chest, fitting perfectly under the wing of his embrace.

The new life growing inside her kicked in response. "She likes when you're near."

Zo positioned Gryphon's hand over her growing stomach just in time to feel the unborn babe kick again. Zo didn't know how to explain that she knew their child was a girl. Just as she *sensed* the moods around her—a skill that had dampened some with the help of the Raven shaman—the growing child gave off a feminine aura.

Gryphon lifted Zo's chin with a finger. His soft brown eyes studied her face, his attention so absolute her cheeks warmed. Ever so slowly, he bent and touched his lips to hers for one brief, delicious moment. "You are happiness, Zo."

She smiled up at her husband. "You are home."

THE END

Acknowledgements

This final book of the NAMELESS trilogy marks the end of an incredible journey through a world in which I have come to love writing. This book—this trilogy—could not have been possible without the support and professional expertise of some very dear friends and family.

Thank you to my parents—all four of you—for supporting me in this wild adventure, to Whitnee and Matt for the child swapping that has made much of my book travel possible, to Casey, Libby, and Boss for making my life rich and meaningful.

Tahsha, Jo, Lois, Margie, and James, your friendship and love mean the world. Brad, my never failing beta ninja, thanks for keeping me honest. The rest of the game night crew, you are the definition of friendship and loyalty and have been such a huge support over the last three years. Thank you for putting up with me.

I have amazing critique partners who helped me discover the potential of this final book. Lois, Amy, and Nichole, thank you for being brave enough to tell me to rewrite … again and again. Wendy Buhler and Melanie Fillmore, thank you for being some of my first cheerleaders.

To Georgia McBride and the team at Month9Books: thank you for the edits, cover design, promotion, and faith in this series. It's been a fulfilling journey and I'm grateful for the opportunity to get to know and work with you all. Jaime Arnold, you will be missed!

Amy Jameson, my agent and friend, "thank you" doesn't seem adequate. I look forward to chasing a few more dreams together.

Clint, your belief in me is the greatest gift I've ever received. With you I am fearless. You are everything.

JENNIFER JENKINS

With her degree in History and Secondary Education, Jennifer had every intention of teaching teens to love George Washington and appreciate the finer points of ancient battle stratagem. (Seriously, she's obsessed with ancient warfare.) However, life had different plans in store when the writing began. As a proud member of Writers Cubed, and a co-founder of the Teen Author Boot Camp, she feels blessed to be able to fulfill both her ambition to work with teens as well as write Young Adult fiction.

Jennifer has three children who are experts at naming her characters, one loving, supportive husband, a dog with little-man syndrome, and three chickens (of whom she is secretly afraid). Visit her online at www.jajenkins.com.

OTHER MONTH9BOOKS TITLES YOU MIGHT LIKE

NAMELESS

CLANLESS

Find more books like this at http://www.Month9Books.com

Connect with Month9Books online:
Facebook: www.Facebook.com/Month9Books
Twitter: https://twitter.com/Month9Books
YouTube: www.youtube.com/user/Month9Books
Tumblr: http://month9books.tumblr.com/
Instagram: https://instagram.com/month9books

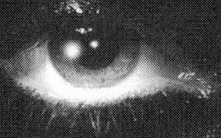

"Jenkins brings edge-of-your-seat adventure to this
intriguing new world. I can't wait to read more!"
- Jessica Day George
New York Times bestselling author of
SILVER IN THE BLOOD

NAMELESS

JENNIFER JENKINS

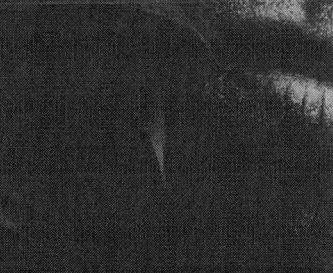

JENNIFER JENKINS

CLANLESS

Printed in Great Britain
by Amazon